Dark Eagle

The Wraith

by

K. M. Ashman

Copyright K. M. Ashman, January 2025

All rights are reserved. No part of this publication may be reproduced, stored, or transmitted in any form or by any means without prior written permission of the copyright owner. All characters depicted within this publication are fictitious, and any resemblance to any real person, living or dead, is entirely coincidental.

To Subscribe go to:

K. M. Ashman.com

Also By K. M. Ashman

The Exploratores
Dark Eagle
The Hidden
Veteranus
Scarab
The Wraith
Silures
Panthera

The Brotherhood
Templar Steel
Templar Stone
Templar Blood
Templar Fury
Templar Glory
Templar Legacy
Templar Loyalty

Seeds of Empire
Seeds of Empire
Rise of the Eagle
Fields of Glory

The India Summers Mysteries
The Vestal Conspiracies
The Treasures of Suleiman
The Mummies of the Reich
The Tomb Builders

The Roman Chronicles
The Fall of Britannia
The Rise of Caratacus

The Wrath of Boudicca

The Medieval Sagas
Blood of the Cross
In Shadows of Kings
Sword of Liberty
Ring of Steel

The Blood of Kings
A Land Divided
A Wounded Realm
Rebellion's Forge
The Warrior Princess
The Blade Bearer

The Road to Hastings
The Challenges of a King
The Promises of a King
The Fate of a King

The Otherworld Series
The Legacy Protocol
The Seventh God
The Last Citadel
Savage Eden
Vampire

Character Names

The Occultum

- **Seneca** - Roman Tribune and leader
- **Marcus** - Former Centurion
- **Falco** - Former gladiator
- **Sica** - Syrian assassin
- **Decimus** - Occultum veteran
- **Cassius** - Member of the Occultum
- **Lepidus** - Roman Senator and patron/supervisor of the Occultum

Roman Military & Leadership

- **Aulus Plautius** - General commanding Rome's Britannic expedition
- **Vespasian** - Commander of the Second Legion (Legio II Augusta)
- **Emperor Claudius** - Emperor of Rome
- **Lucius Gabinius** - Legion's quartermaster
- **Cassius Longinus** - Intelligence officer for the legion
- **Quintus** - Dockmaster at Rutupiae (undercover Occultum contact)

Former Occultum

- **Veteranus** - Former Occultum member, now allied with Mordred
- **Raven** - Former Occultum scout and traitor working with the druids

Other Romans

- **Tribune Atticus** - Roman officer who disappeared with his patrol

- **Lucius Faber** - Decurion of the Batavian Auxiliaries rescued by Lepidus

Britannic/Celtic Characters

- **Mordred** - Powerful druid leader on Isla Mona

- **Talorcan** - Belgic scout working for Rome

- **Kendra** - Warrior-priestess on Isla Mona, shows interest in Veteranus

Historical Figures

- **Togodumnus** - Britannic king who fell in battle against Rome

- **Caratacus** - Brother of Togodumnus who escaped and continues resistance

Map

Britannia

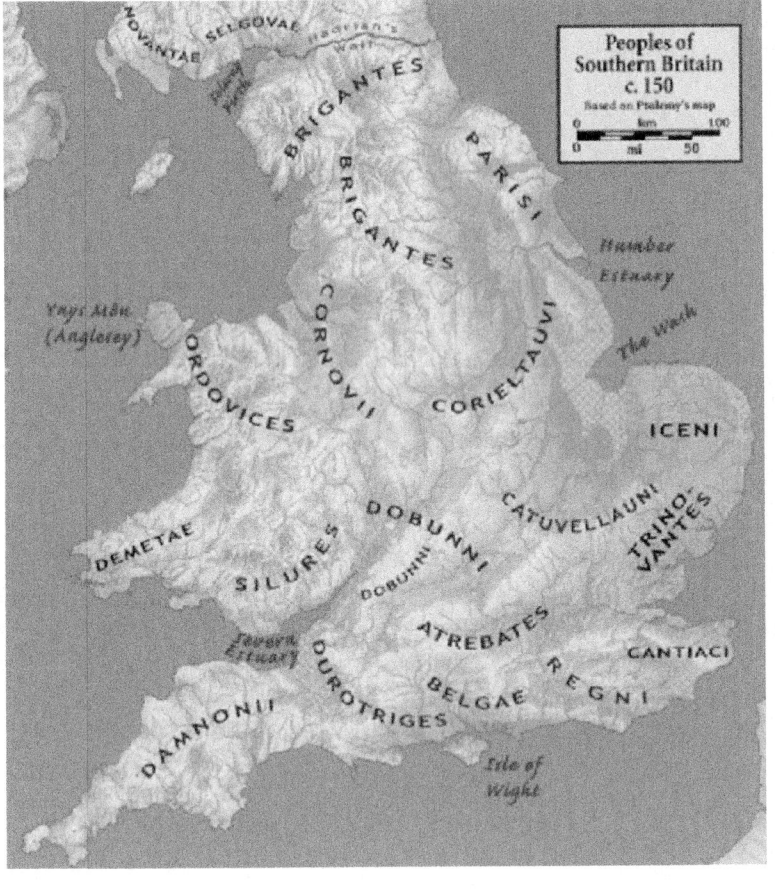

Prologue

The stench of death rose from the valley floor like incense in a temple, thick and cloying. Aulus Plautius stood motionless on the hilltop, his weathered hands clasped behind his back as he surveyed the aftermath of battle. Beneath him lay the muddy banks of the Tamesis, now carpeted with the fallen. The afternoon sun gleamed dully off Roman armour and Celtic torcs alike, making no distinction between victor and vanquished in death.

'A victory,' said Plautius, 'but at what cost?'

His voice carried to the small group of officers who stood respectfully behind him. None responded immediately. The question needed no answer when the evidence lay sprawled across the marshy ground before them, thousands of bodies, Roman and Briton, their blood soaking into the foreign soil.

The wind shifted, bringing with it the distinct metallic scent of blood mingled with the brackish river water. The crows had already begun their feast, dark specks moving amongst the sea of corpses. Here and there, burial parties moved methodically, separating Roman dead from the celts. The legionaries would receive proper rites; the barbarians would remain where they fell.

Vespasian stepped forward to stand beside his commander, his face etched with exhaustion. Two days of brutal fighting had left even the most hardened officers drained, their usual military precision giving way to a grim acknowledgment of survival.

'The crossing was costly,' said Vespasian, gesturing towards the river where armoured bodies still floated, caught in the reeds. 'They contested every span of water.'

'As we would have done,' replied Plautius quietly.

Below them, the broad, glistening snake of the Tamesis wound through the landscape, its waters running faintly pink where they passed the heaviest fighting. The Celts had transformed the river into a death trap, and the legions had been forced to prove, once again, that Rome's might could overcome any obstacle, though not without sacrifice.

'Togodumnus fell in the fighting,' said Geta, the Legate who had led his men through the thickest of the battle. Blood still crusted along his temple where a Trinovantes sword had nearly ended his military career. 'His body was identified among their dead.'

Plautius nodded.

'And Caratacus?'

'Escaped,' said Geta. 'Our scouts report he withdrew westward with a substantial force. The defeat has not broken him.'

The silence stretched between the men as they contemplated what this meant. One Britannic king dead, but his brother, perhaps the more dangerous of the two, still at large, still capable of rallying resistance.

'Camulodunum lies ahead,' said Plautius eventually, turning his gaze northward where the tribal capital waited. 'Their strongest settlement and seat of power. We must take it quickly, before Caratacus can reorganise his forces.'

'The men need rest, Domine,' said Sabinus, the youngest of the officers. His armour bore the dents and scrapes of recent combat, and dark circles shadowed his eyes. 'We've fought without pause for days.'

'Rest?' Vespasian interjected, giving a short, humourless laugh. 'In war, the only rest comes with victory or death. Caratacus will not be resting.'

'Neither shall we,' said Plautius firmly. 'We advance on Camulodunum at first light. The Emperor expects results, not excuses.'

The mention of Emperor Claudius brought a subtle shift in the officers' posture. Their commander had been explicit from the beginning, this campaign was as much about politics in Rome as it was about conquest in Britannia. Claudius needed a military triumph to secure his precarious position, and they would deliver it, regardless of cost.

8

'How many did we lose?' Plautius finally asked the question that had been weighing on them all.

'Nearly a thousand,' said Geta solemnly, but Celts' losses are at least ten times that number.'

'And yet they fight on,' mused Vespasian. 'Their homes invaded, their warriors decimated, and still they resist.'

From the distance came the sounds of the forward Roman camp being established, the rhythmic hammering of tent pegs, the clatter of armour being repaired, the low murmur of men sharing memories of fallen comrades. The machine of war continued its relentless forward motion, even as the day's dead were gathered.

Plautius turned from the battlefield at last, his grey eyes meeting those of his officers. There was neither triumph nor despair in his gaze, only the calculating assessment of a man who had seen enough campaigns to know that initial victories often heralded the bloodiest fighting yet to come.

'Gentlemen,' he said, 'what we have won here is not Britannia, but merely a foothold. The true conquest is still to come. Caratacus is probably regathering his forces as we speak, and the druids will fan the flames of resistance in every village and settlement across the island.'

The men nodded grimly. They understood the weight of what lay ahead, months, perhaps years of campaigning in hostile territory, against an enemy who knew the land intimately and had nothing left to lose.

'The worst may still be to come,' continued Plautius, 'but Rome has never faltered in the face of barbarian resistance. We will secure this island, tribe by tribe, river by river, until the name of Rome is spoken with both fear and reverence from coast to coast.'

As the sun began its descent towards the western horizon, towards the unconquered territories where Caratacus rallied his forces, Plautius cast one final glance at the battlefield below. Tomorrow would bring new challenges, new battles, new deaths. But that was the price of empire, measured out in blood and iron on foreign soil.

Behind him, a lone eagle circled high above the carnage, its piercing cry cutting through the heavy air. Like Rome itself, it surveyed the land below, patient and predatory, knowing that in time, all would submit to its rule.

Chapter One

The Mare Nostrum

The Mare Nostrum gleamed like burnished bronze beneath the setting sun, its surface rippling gently against the hull of the Roman trireme. Salt spray kissed the air, mingling with the scent of pine tar and the ever-present odour of too many men confined to too small a space. The vessel cut through the waves with practised precision, its destination the turbulent shores of Britannia.

Seneca leaned against the ship's rail, his dark eyes fixed on the horizon. The gentle rocking of the deck beneath his feet had become familiar over the past few days, almost comforting in its rhythm. Behind him, the boisterous laughter of his men carried across the sea breeze, a sound that brought a slight curve to his otherwise serious mouth.

'I swear by Jupiter's cock,' bellowed Falco, his voice carrying easily over the steady splash of oars, 'she was as tall as a Germanic spear and twice as deadly!'

'And yet somehow you survived,' said Sica, his Syrian accent giving the Latin a melodic quality despite the deadpan delivery. The small, bald man sat cross-legged on a crate, methodically sharpening a knife that seemed to materialise from nowhere. 'Truly, the gods favour the foolish.'

A chorus of laughter erupted from the gathered men. Marcus, straight-backed even in relaxation, shook his head with poorly disguised amusement.

'Favour me?' Falco spread his massive arms wide, nearly striking a passing sailor who ducked with practised ease. 'She was the one who missed her chance at perfection! I offered her marriage, comrades. Marriage!'

'The poor woman,' murmured Cassius, glancing up from the wax tablet he'd been studying. 'Imagine waking to that face every morning.'

Fresh peals of laughter rang out, drawing curious glances from the ship's regular crew who had learned to give the strange unit a wide berth. The Occultum were known by reputation only, and most men
preferred to keep it that way.

'You offered marriage to every dancer from Rome to Alexandria and back again,' said Marcus. 'One might question your sincerity.'

Falco clutched his chest in mock offence.

'I was sincere every time! But this one...' His voice softened unexpectedly, and something genuine flickered across his scarred features. 'This one I would have given up the Occultum for. Left it all behind in a heartbeat.'

A brief silence fell over the group, the admission striking a chord too true to mock. Each man there had contemplated, in quiet moments between battles, what it might be like to leave behind the blood and death, to build something that lasted longer than the next mission.

From his position at the rail, Seneca exchanged a knowing glance with Decimus. The older man sat apart from the others, his grizzled features impassive as he observed the younger men with the patience of a veteran who had heard it all before.

'And what would you have done?' asked Decimus finally, his weathered voice cutting through the sudden quiet. 'Settled down? Grown olives? Raised fat children?'

Falco's boisterous energy dimmed slightly.

'Perhaps. Is that so strange?'

'For you?' said Sica, testing his blade's edge against his thumb. 'Yes. The day you settle down is the day I become Emperor.'

The tension broke again, laughter resuming as Falco launched into an even more outlandish tale of his exploits in a particular bathhouse in Rome. Seneca watched them, these men who had become more than comrades through blood and shared peril. Their faces were relaxed now, bronzed by weeks in the

Mediterranean sun, temporarily unburdened by the weight of their duty. He knew it wouldn't last.

Decimus moved to join him at the rail, his movements slower now with the stiffness that came from old wounds and advancing years.

'They need this,' said the older man quietly, nodding towards the group. 'The stories, the laughter. It helps them forget what waits in Britannia.'

Behind them, Cassius was recounting his own leave, the story considerably tamer than Falco's wild tales. Stories of peaceful days by the Tiber, fishing and swimming, as if storing up tranquillity to counter the violence to come.

'I spent three days teaching my nephew to ride,' he said, a rare softness in his typically stoic demeanour. 'The boy has a natural seat. He'll make a fine cavalryman someday.'

'Gods willing, he'll never need to be,' said Marcus quietly and turned to the Syrian. 'And what of you, Sica? How did you spend your leave? I don't recall seeing much of you in Rome.'

The Syrian's face remained impassive.

'I had business.'

'Business?' Falco laughed uproariously. 'Is that what you call it? What poor soul did you send to the underworld during our rest?'

Sica's dark eyes flickered up, meeting Falco's gaze without emotion.

'No one who will be missed.'

The statement hung in the air, neither joke nor confession, but something in between. It was a reminder of what they were, men chosen not just for their fighting prowess but for their ability to do the necessary, regardless of its nature.

Decimus turned to Seneca, their conversation private beneath the renewed banter.

'So, what do you make of our orders?'

Seneca gave a deep sigh.

'Vague, as always,' he said. 'I know there is a man to be killed, but Lepidus was reluctant to share the name. Apparently Plautius will brief us fully when we get there.'

Decimus nodded, thoughts turning to their patron in Rome. Senator Lepidus had been the Occultum's shield within the political arena for years, protecting them from those who would use them as pawns in Senate games. If he had sent them to Britannia with such urgency, the situation must be dire indeed.

'We should arrive within the week, weather permitting,' said Seneca. 'And then we'll see what awaits us.'

'Cold, wet, and hostile, if past experience is anything to go by,' said Decimus with grim humour.

The sun had nearly disappeared now, casting long shadows across the deck. The laughter of the men had taken on a different quality, slightly forced, as if they too sensed the approaching end of their respite. Each day would bring them closer to Britannia's shores, closer to whatever blood-soaked mission awaited them. For now, though, they had the ship, the sea, and each other's company. Seneca allowed himself a moment to appreciate it, knowing such moments were rare in times of war.

'I think I'll join them,' said Decimus suddenly, straightening with a grunt of effort. 'Falco's stories grow more outlandish when fuelled by wine. And I intend to give him exactly that.'

Seneca nodded, a small smile touching his lips.

'Go. I'll be there shortly.'

As Decimus moved away, Seneca remained at the rail, watching darkness settle over the waters. Behind him, Falco had launched into yet another tale, this one involving three Nubian dancers and a very angry camel. The absurdity of it brought genuine laughter from the men, a sound that carried across the water like an offering to whatever gods might be listening.

Seneca allowed himself one final moment of peace, one deep breath of salty air, before turning to join his men. The Occultum would face whatever waited in Britannia as they had faced everything else, together, with steel in their hands and resolve in their hearts.

But that was tomorrow's concern.

Chapter Two

Britannia

The command tent stood at the heart of Legio Augusta's encampment, its weathered canvas still bearing the scars of previous campaigns. Inside, oil lamps cast flickering shadows across the military council gathered around a makeshift table of planks laid over empty supply barrels. A large map of the surrounding territories was spread across it, its edges weighted with daggers and bronze cups.

Vespasian stood with his hands planted firmly on the table, his gaze sweeping across the faces of his senior officers. At forty, he carried himself with the confidence of a man who had risen through the ranks on merit rather than merely family connections. Though not tall, his compact frame radiated authority, and the hardened veterans around him gave him their complete attention.

'The situation, gentlemen,' said Vespasian, his voice cutting through the low murmur of conversation. 'Let us have it plainly.'

Antonius Macro, the Primus Pilus of the legion, stepped forward, his weathered face grave in the lamplight. Twenty-five years of service had left their mark on the veteran Centurion, his body a map of scars from a dozen campaigns.

'The Second has performed admirably, commander. Our casualties at the Tamesis crossing were fewer than the other legions.'

'Facts, Macro,' said Vespasian. 'Not flattery.'

Macro straightened, chastened but not offended. 'Three hundred and forty-two dead. Six hundred and seventeen wounded, though nearly half of those should be fit to return to duty within a month. The men's spirits remain high after the victory.'

'And supplies?' Vespasian asked, turning to Lucius Gabinius, the legion's quartermaster.

'We've sufficient grain for three weeks at full rations,' said Gabinius, consulting his wax tablets. 'Longer if we supplement with local resources, but we are expecting a supply column within days.

16

Medical supplies are strained, particularly linen for bandages and honey for wound dressing.'

'The Britons use a moss that grows on the oaks here,' interjected Macro. 'Our medicus says it works nearly as well as honey for preventing rot in wounds.'

Vespasian nodded.

'Good. See that it's gathered and distributed.'

'The engineers have already established two pontoon bridges across the Tamesis,' Gabinius continued. 'The recent rains have made the approaches difficult, but we've laid timber trackways to prevent the wagons becoming mired.'

Vespasian traced his finger along the river on the map, his gaze drifting to the north-eastern quadrant where Camulodunum awaited.

'Intelligence,' he said sharply, turning to Cassius Longinus, a shrewd-eyed Greek freedman who served as his chief of reconnaissance.

'Our scouts report Britannic forces regrouping to the west and north,' said Longinus, moving forward. 'Smaller bands harass our supply lines from the south, but nothing our auxiliary cavalry cannot handle.'

'And Caratacus?'

'Elusive. We've had three reported sightings in the past two days, each in different locations. He moves constantly, gathering supporters from the outlying tribes. Our best intelligence suggests he intends to avoid direct confrontation for now, preferring to bleed us through skirmishes and ambushes while building his strength.'

'A sound strategy,' muttered Vespasian, 'for a barbarian.'

'They may lack our discipline,' said Macro, 'but they're not fools. They've seen what happened at the Medway and Tamesis. They won't face us in open battle again unless forced.'

Vespasian's eyes narrowed as he studied the map.

'The terrain favours them. Forests, marshes, hills, perfect for ambush and swift retreat. Whereas we excel on open ground with

room for manoeuvre, where our discipline can be brought to bear.'
His gaze moved methodically around the circle, mentally checking off
his key personnel.

'Where is Tribune Atticus?' he asked suddenly, his brow
furrowing.

The officers exchanged glances, the absence suddenly
conspicuous.

'I know he led a patrol yesterday morning, commander,' said
Longinus carefully. 'Towards the northwest.'

'And?'

'I do not think they have returned yet.'

Vespasian's expression darkened.

'A patrol led by a Tribune of Rome is missing for an entire
day, and I am only hearing of this now?'

'The patrol was due back by nightfall,' said Longinus,
maintaining his composure in the face of Vespasian's growing anger.
'I dispatched riders along their intended route when they failed to
return, but they found nothing, no signs of battle, no bodies, no
tracks beyond the halfway point.'

'How many men were with him?'

'Two contubernium of auxiliaries. Sixteen men, all mounted.
Batavians from the Ala Primae.'

Vespasian cursed under his breath. Twenty-four hours
missing with no sign of engagement meant either they were lost, had
been captured or had been killed.

'What was their assigned route?' he demanded.

Longinus indicated a northwestern path on the map,
following a track that ended abruptly at the edge of the recently
conquered territory. 'They were to reconnoitre as far as this river
crossing, then return. A straightforward mission, twelve miles out and
back.'

Macro cleared his throat.

'Commander, there may be more to it. One of my men was
on guard duty at the eastern gate yesterday morning. He reported

18

that Tribune Atticus appeared... eager.'

'Eager?' repeated Vespasian, 'What is that supposed to mean?'

'The Tribune questioned my man about a report of some Celtic horsemen sighted beyond our perimeter. Heavily armed warriors, possibly a chieftain's bodyguard. When told they had moved beyond his patrol route, he seemed overly interested and demanded more information about the terrain.'

'Do you think he decided to pursue?' asked Vespasian.

'I know not, Domine, but it is a possibility.'

Vespasian's face hardened.

'That fool. Chasing after glory when we need information. If he's alive, I'll have him flogged before the entire legion.' He stared at the map, considering the options. 'If they have been captured, the information they may divulge under torture could cause us problems.'

'Atticus would die before betraying Rome,' said Longinus firmly.

'Every man believes that until the hot irons come out,' replied Macro grimly. 'And the Druids have methods that make our torturers seem as gentle as nursemaids.'

'We need to know what happened,' said Vespasian, turning back to the map. 'Longinus, show me where your search parties found the last trace of the patrol.'

The intelligence officer indicated a point on the map, well short of the river they had been assigned to reconnoitre.

'Here, Domine. The tracks led further northwest from this point, towards a densely forested area beyond our current reconnaissance range.'

'Options?' said Vespasian, looking around the circle.

'We could dispatch a full cohort,' suggested Longinus. 'Sweep the area completely.'

'No, too slow, too noisy,' said Macro.

'A century of picked men then?' suggested Longinus. 'Light

19

marching order, minimal equipment?'

'Still too many,' said Macro. 'In that terrain, stealth is paramount. We need trackers, scouts, men who can move unseen.'

'I agree,' said Vespasian firmly. 'This requires special skills.' His gaze settled on Longinus. 'Is the Belgic scout still with the legion? The one who served with the Occultum in Germania?'

Longinus nodded slowly.

'Talorcan? Yes, he's been serving with our reconnaissance elements since Medway.'

Vespasian turned to a waiting orderly.

'Bring me the Belgic scout. Immediately.'

The orderly saluted and departed swiftly, leaving the command group in thoughtful silence.

Less than half an hour later, the flap of the tent opened, admitting a gust of damp night air.

'Domine, the Belgic scout is here,' said the orderly.

'Good, send him in.'

Talorcan entered, tall and lean, with long black hair and a pointed beard in the style of his people. His leather and wool attire was a mix of Roman military issue and native craftsmanship, practical rather than regulation.

His eyes, startlingly pale against his weather-darkened skin, scanned the gathering of officers before settling on Vespasian. He offered a nod that acknowledged rank without quite reaching deference.

'You sent for me, Domine' he said, his Latin accented but fluent.

'One of my Tribunes is missing,' said Vespasian without preamble. 'Along with sixteen auxiliary cavalry. They were last seen heading northwest, beyond our secured territory. I need them found.'

Talorcan's expression remained impassive.

'When did they leave?'

'Yesterday morning. They should have returned by nightfall.'

Talorcan nodded, absorbing the information. It had rained since then so the ground would still hold tracks.

'Our search parties found their trail leading here,' said Vespasian, indicating the position on the map. 'It continued northwest, towards this forested area.'

Talorcan studied the map, his eyes tracing the contours of the terrain.

'The Nervii Forest,' he said quietly, almost to himself. 'It's bad ground with dense woods, broken by bogs and ravines. Good for hunting, even better if you wanted to set an ambush.'

'You know it?' asked Longinus with surprise.

'I have family there,' he said. 'Or at least I did before all this...' He left the sentence unfinished.

'I heard that ground was sacred to the Trinovantes?' said Vespasian. 'Tell me about it.'

'All grounds are sacred to Celts,' replied Talorcan. 'But those hills in particular contain burial grounds, shrines, places where the veil between worlds is thin. The druids use it for their blood ceremonies, especially at the dark of the moon.'

Vespasian's eyes narrowed.

'Which is in seven days' time.'

A chill settled over the gathering. The druids' hatred for Rome was legendary, as was their influence over the Britannic tribes. If Atticus and his men had been captured and taken to the forest ahead of a druidic ceremony...

'Can you find them?' asked Vespasian, breaking the silence.

Talorcan met his gaze.

'If they still live, probably. If they're dead...' He shrugged, not needing to explain the alternative.

'Then you'll leave at first light,' said Vespasian. 'I want them found, or at least confirmation of their deaths before I commit any further forces.'

'No,' replied Talorcan, drawing shocked looks from the Roman officers. Before anyone could rebuke him for insubordination, he continued. 'I will leave tonight. The rain has stopped, and there's half a moon. Enough light for tracking, not enough to be easily seen. By dawn, I can be where your search parties lost the trail.'

Vespasian studied the scout's face, searching for any sign of deception or overconfidence. Finding none, he nodded.

'Very well. Tonight. How many men will you need?'

'None,' said Talorcan.

'Unacceptable,' broke in Macro. 'We don't send men alone into hostile territory.'

'One man can move faster and quieter than many,' interrupted Talorcan, addressing Vespasian rather than the protesting Centurion. 'I'm not going to fight, only to find. If I locate your Tribune, I'll return with the information. Then you can send your cohorts.'

Vespasian considered the option, weighing military doctrine against practical reality.

'And if you're captured or killed, we'll have lost our best scout with nothing gained.'

The ghost of a smile touched Talorcan's lips.

'I won't be captured.'

'Your confidence is admirable, but I'm not risking another Roman asset on a solo mission,' said Vespasian firmly. 'You'll take at least one man with you.'

Talorcan's expression cooled.

'Not one of your legionaries. They move like pregnant cattle in the forest.'

Macro bristled at the insult, but Vespasian held up a hand to forestall his objection. 'Longinus, who among your reconnaissance section would be suitable?'

'Rufus Cato,' replied the intelligence officer eventually. 'A former hunter from the Alpine provinces. He's accompanied Talorcan before.'

Talorcan gave a reluctant nod.

'The mountain man will do. He's quiet enough, and his eyes are sharp in the dark.'

'Then it's settled,' said Vespasian. 'You and Cato will depart tonight. Your mission is to locate Tribune Atticus and his patrol, assess their situation and report back. Do not engage the enemy unless absolutely necessary for your survival. Better to bring back information that can save the next patrol than die in a futile gesture. May Fortune favour your hunt.'

Talorcan nodded once, a gesture of acceptance rather than deference, and turned to leave the tent, the weight of the mission settling across his shoulders like a familiar cloak.

As the tent flap closed behind the Belgic scout, Vespasian turned back to his officers.

'The rest of us have a campaign to plan, gentlemen. Tribune Atticus's situation, while concerning, cannot delay our advance on Camulodunum. The Emperor expects results, not excuses.'

Chapter Three

Rutupiae

The wooden hull of the trireme groaned as it nudged against the wharf at Rutupiae, sailors scrambling to secure mooring lines to freshly installed bollards. Gulls wheeled overhead, their raucous cries mingling with the shouts of soldiers, sailors, and dock workers that filled the air. The natural harbour was crowded with vessels of all sizes, from military transports to merchant ships and fishing boats, all creating a floating forest of masts and rigging that spoke of Rome's determination to secure its newest conquest.

Seneca stood at the ship's rail, watching as a fresh century of legionaries disembarked from a larger vessel nearby, their armour gleaming in the weak Britannic sunlight. Despite having only just arrived after a long voyage, the soldiers formed up in disciplined rows on the dock, Centurions barking orders as they prepared to march to their assigned postings.

'Eager lads,' said Decimus, coming to stand beside him. 'Not yet acquainted with Britannia's particular charms.'

'They'll learn soon enough,' replied Seneca, his eyes taking in the organised chaos of the port. 'The mud and rain will dull that shine within a week.'

Behind them, the rest of the Occultum gathered their gear, the relaxed atmosphere of the voyage evaporating as they prepared to step onto Britannic soil. Each man moved with practised efficiency, checking weapons and securing equipment with the silent focus that came from years of dangerous missions.

'Look at them,' said Falco, nodding toward the fresh troops. 'So pretty and clean. Like girls dressed for a festival.' He hoisted his massive frame from the deck where he'd been lounging, stretching until his joints popped audibly. 'I don't recall being that young.'

'You were never young,' said Sica, securing an extra dagger in his boot. 'You were born old and ugly.'

24

'And you were born a viper,' retorted Falco with a grin. The banter was familiar, comfortable, but tinged now with the awareness of
what awaited them.

'I'm more concerned with what we're walking into,' said Marcus, joining them. 'Plautius isn't summoning us for a victory parade.'

'Precisely why we should have enjoyed ourselves a bit longer in Rome,' grumbled Falco. 'That dancer...'

'Enough about the dancer,' interrupted Marcus. 'You'd think she was Venus incarnate the way you drone on.'

'She was,' muttered Falco, though the usual force was absent from his complaint.

'Time to move,' said Seneca, noting that their ship was now securely moored. 'Gather your gear.'

The men shouldered their packs and followed Seneca down the gangplank. The wooden planks of the dock creaked beneath their feet as they stepped onto Britannia, the smell of saltwater mingling with the earthy scent of the nearby marshes and the less pleasant odours of a military port.

'Pleasant,' remarked Cassius, wrinkling his nose. 'Reminds me of Alexandria's less reputable districts.'

'You would know,' said Falco with a snort.

They moved aside as a line of mules laden with supplies clattered past, drivers cursing as they urged the stubborn animals further inland. Nearby, a Centurion berated a group of legionaries struggling with a heavy ballista, his creative profanity drawing appreciative nods from Falco.

'That man has a gift,' the ex-gladiator observed. 'I've not heard someone called the ill-conceived offspring of a three-legged goat and a syphilitic Parthian before.'

'Expand your reading,' suggested Cassius dryly.

Seneca paid them little mind, his attention focused on navigating through the crowded dockyard.

'The dockmaster's office,' he said at last, gesturing toward a squat stone building that stood apart from the wooden warehouses lining the waterfront. 'We're to receive updated instructions there.'

They made their way across the dock, avoiding the organised chaos that surrounded them.

'This place has grown quickly,' observed Seneca. 'When we left
it was little more than a muddy beach with a few hastily constructed piers.'

'Rome builds quickly,' said Cassius, looking around with the practiced assessment of a former merchant. 'Today's camp becomes tomorrow's fortress, next year's town.'

As they approached the dockmaster's office, the door swung open, and a weather worn official emerged, clutching a wax tablet and shouting orders to a subordinate. He froze momentarily at the sight of the Occultum, something in their demeanour causing him to reassess whatever he had been about to do. His eyes darted over them cautiously, judging the way they walked, the way they held themselves, their appearance.

'My name is...' started Seneca but the dockmaster cut him short.

'I know who you are, you're expected. Come inside.'

Seneca nodded to his men and stepped through the doorway into the building. The dockmaster followed him inside and firmly closed the door behind them, shutting out the clamour of the busy port. The interior was unexpectedly orderly with shelves of neatly arranged records lining the walls, and a large table dominating the centre of the room, covered with maps and manifests.

The dockmaster turned and fixed Seneca with an appraising stare, his eyes sharp beneath bushy grey brows.

Seneca met his gaze evenly, then reached beneath his cloak.

'I assume you need some form of identification?'

'No,' said the man, his voice surprisingly cultured for one who managed the rough business of a military port. 'I know exactly

26

who you are and why you're here. Lepidus sends his regards.'

'Lepidus,' said Seneca. 'I should have known. The Senator's reach extends farther than I thought.'

'Indeed,' said the dockmaster and moved to a side table to pour two cups of wine from an earthenware jug.

'In that case,' said Seneca, accepting the offered cup, 'perhaps you can direct us to General Plautius. We need to collect our orders and move quickly.'

The dockmaster's expression hardened suddenly. He set down his own cup untouched and leaned forward, both hands planted on the table between them.

'You're going nowhere, Tribune. Sit down, we need to talk.'

Seneca remained standing, studying the man with renewed attention. The weathered face spoke of years at sea, but the eyes were not a dockmaster's eyes. They held the calculating assessment of a man accustomed to measuring threats, to weighing lives in the balance of greater concerns.

'Who are you?' asked Seneca.

The dockmaster smiled thinly.

'Someone who once served alongside Lepidus before I managed manifests instead of agents.' He gestured again to the chair. 'Please, Seneca. What I have to tell you is for your ears alone, and I'd rather not shout it.'

Seneca hesitated, then took the seat, positioning himself to maintain clear access to his blade.

'Do you have a name?'

'Many,' replied the man with a thin smile. 'But Quintus will suffice for now.' He leaned forward, lowering his voice. 'Lepidus feared his written communications might be intercepted. That's why your orders were vague.'

'And now you'll clarify them?'

Quintus nodded, his expression grave.

27

'I believe you were told there's a man to be killed.'

'I was,' said Seneca, 'but not his identity or location. Just let me know who and where, and my men will handle the rest.'

Quintus set his cup down deliberately, eyes fixed on Seneca's face.

'The man you seek is a traitor to Rome,' said Quintus. 'He has already caused us a lot of problems and needs silencing before he does any more damage. I also believe he is known to you. His name is Raven.'

Seneca went still, staring in shock as the information sunk in.

'Impossible,' he said finally. 'Raven is dead. I saw Mordred cut his throat myself. I watched his body fall to the floor, I saw his head float down the river as blood continued to pump from the severed neck. I am
not mistaken.'

'A substitute,' said Quintus flatly. 'A condemned prisoner with similar build, drugged insensate. The head you saw was his, not Raven's. The druids have perfected such deceptions over centuries, swapping one man for another in the dim light, controlling what you witnessed.'

He reached beneath the table and produced a small leather pouch. From it, he withdrew a bronze medallion and placed it on the table between them. Seneca recognised it immediately.

'This was found near the body of a Roman courier three weeks ago,' said Quintus. 'The man's throat was cut but it looked like he put up a fight.'

'Anyone could have taken this from Raven's body,' Seneca argued, looking up. 'It means nothing.'

'Perhaps,' conceded Quintus. 'But there's more.' He produced a document and handed it over. 'This message was intercepted from a Celtic runner trying to cross our lines before our advance on the Tamesis.

Seneca took the parchment, studying the Latin text inscribed upon it. The handwriting was unmistakable, the distinctive, precise

28

script of a man who had learned his letters later in life than most Romans, who formed each character with the same methodical care he applied to his scouting maps. Raven's hand.

'The northern approach remains weakly defended,' Seneca read aloud, the familiar handwriting making the words all the more damning. 'Cavalry patrols follow predictable patterns at dawn and dusk. Plautius expects reinforcements by the Kalends but is vulnerable until then.' He set the tablet down, a cold fury building within him.

'Again, this proves nothing. Handwriting can be forged.'

'And this?' Quintus reached into his tunic and withdrew a small object, placing it carefully on the table.

It was a carving, no larger than a man's thumb, a small wooden eagle meticulously detailed. Seneca had watched Raven work on dozens of such carvings during long campaigns, his nimble fingers constantly busy in the quiet hours of camp, transforming scraps of wood into tiny birds with remarkable skill.

'Found in the same courier's belongings,' said Quintus softly. 'A calling card, perhaps. Or a message for someone specific.'

Seneca picked up the carving, turning it in his fingers. The craftsmanship was unmistakable, down to the distinctive way the wings folded against the body. He had one almost identical in his own pack, a gift from years past.

'All this time,' said Seneca, his voice barely audible, 'and he was working against us.'

'Perhaps not always,' said Quintus with a sigh, 'but regardless of when or why, he now serves as Mordred's advisor. We've identified three supply convoys he's helped ambush, and at least two scouting parties found with their throats cut, Roman fashion, not Celtic.'

Seneca's fist closed around the wooden raven, knuckles white with tension.

'Where is he now?'

29

'That's the problem. We believe he moves between tribal settlements, gathering intelligence, but returns frequently to Mordred's sanctuary on Isla Mona.'

'Mona,' repeated Seneca, the name familiar from intelligence reports. 'The druid stronghold.'

Quintus nodded grimly.

'Their holiest place, protected by dangerous tides and hundreds of fanatical warriors. As far as I am aware, no Roman has ever set foot there and lived to tell of it.'

'And Lepidus wants us to go there to kill him,' said Seneca.

'He does but the final decision is yours. This isn't a simple assassination, Tribune. This is a mission deep into enemy territory, to a place considered impenetrable, to kill a man who knows all your methods and tactics intimately.'

'He was my brother in arms,' said Seneca, his voice hardening with resolve. 'My responsibility. His betrayal ends by my hand.'

'Your loyalty is commendable,' said Quintus, 'but your oath is to Rome, not personal vengeance.'

'They are the same in this case,' said Seneca rising from his chair. 'What aid can you offer?'

Quintus studied him for a long moment, then nodded.

'Very well. I have maps, reports on tides and coastal approaches
to Mona. I also have some intelligence on Mordred's compound, though much of it is years old. I'll have the documents sent over. It also goes without saying that any coin you may need, just let me know. Lepidus has authorised unlimited aid.'

'Provide everything you have,' said Seneca, all hesitation now gone, replaced by cold determination. 'We'll find our own way in.'

'And if Raven sees you coming?' asked Quintus. 'He knows how you think, how you move.'

Seneca's expression darkened.

'Leave that to us,' he said, 'I'll be in touch.' With that, he

30

turned away and left the building. Outside, his men waited, their faces showing varying degrees of curiosity and concern.

'Seneca?' said Marcus, 'what's happened?'

Seneca looked at them, these men who had fought beside him through countless dangers, who had bled with him, killed with him, suffered with him. Men he trusted with his life. Men like Raven.

'We have our mission,' he said, his voice controlled despite the rage burning within him. 'And our target.'

'Who?' asked Falco, straightening to his full, imposing height.

Seneca met each of their gazes in turn, ensuring they understood the gravity of what he was about to say.

'Raven.'

The name fell like a stone into still water, sending ripples of shock through the group.

'Impossible,' said Marcus, echoing Seneca's own first response. 'Raven is dead.'

'No,' said Seneca. 'He lives. And he has betrayed everything we stand for, everything we've fought for.'

The men exchanged glances, disbelief warring with the growing realization that their Tribune was deadly serious.

'Where?' asked Sica, practical as always, already mentally preparing for the hunt.

'Isla Mona,' said Seneca, 'on the west coast. They want us to go there, find Raven and eliminate him.'

A heavy silence followed, each man calculating the immense danger such a mission would entail. Penetrating the druids' most sacred
sanctuary was tantamount to suicide.

'When do we leave?' asked Decimus, his weathered face showing neither fear nor hesitation.

'We'll take some time to plan properly first,' said Seneca. 'This cannot be rushed.'

'I still can't believe it,' said Falco. 'We all had our suspicions, but this is... *unbelievable.*'

'There is no mistake,' said Seneca. 'I've seen the evidence myself. He still lives, and apparently, he kills Romans. And for that, he dies, by my hand.' He started walking away, his men falling in behind him automatically and as they moved through the bustling port to find their assigned quarters, Seneca's mind raced with memories of the man he had called friend. Raven's quiet competence, his unmatched skill as a scout, the lives he had saved through his warning of ambushes and hidden dangers, all of it now cast in shadow by the revelation of his betrayal.

By the time they found their assigned tent, his path was clear. Whatever bond had existed between them was severed forever. Raven was no longer a brother, no longer a comrade, he was simply a target. And the Occultum never failed to eliminate their targets.

Chapter Four

Isla Mona

Veteranus sat upon a weathered log, his calloused fingers absently tracing the grooves in the ancient wood as he watched the sun begin its descent over the western valley. The fiery orb hung suspended between earth and sky, bathing the landscape in hues of amber and crimson that seemed to set the world ablaze. From his vantage point high on the ridge, he could see the patchwork of Mona's sacred groves and clearings stretching toward the distant sea, the shadows between them deepening with each passing moment.

He had forgotten how long he had been on this sacred island, each day bleeding into the next like blood spilled in a stream. The chains that had once bound him physically were gone now, removed weeks earlier after Mordred had deemed him sufficiently 'prepared' for greater understanding. Yet Veteranus knew the invisible bonds that held him here remained stronger than any iron.

His hand drifted to the scarab tattoo on his shoulder, the mark that had supposedly bound him to Mordred's bloodline. He still refused to accept it as truth, yet doubt gnawed at him with each passing day.

'Lies,' he muttered to himself, the word carried away by the evening breeze. 'Elaborate lies.'

But the memories of what he had witnessed a weeks earlier returned unbidden, sending an involuntary shudder through his frame.

Veteranus closed his eyes, but the images remained, burned into his mind with horrific clarity. The child's screams still echoed in Veteranus's dreams, rising to an impossible pitch before being abruptly silenced as the creature, for there was no other way of describing it, descended upon him.

Later, Mordred had approached him, his expression serene, untouched by the horrors Veteranus had witnessed.

'You see only death,' the druid had said. 'But we see rebirth. The child is blessed, chosen to carry our message to the gods themselves.'

'Murder,' Veteranus had spat. 'Savagery disguised as piety.'

Mordred had merely smiled, the expression never reaching his cold eyes.

'You still view the world through Roman eyes, kinsman. In time, you will understand.'

Kinsman. The word burned like poison in Veteranus's thoughts. He refused to accept it, refused to believe he shared blood with these people. Yet the doubt remained, a shadow lurking at the edges of his mind.

Mordred had reminded him he was free to leave whenever he wanted, but Veteranus was not convinced, suspecting it was a ruse. The following day, he had walked straight to the edge of the settlement, past the watchful eyes of the druids and warriors, waiting for the moment they would block his path. None had. He had continued down to the shore, where boats lay pulled up on the sand unguarded. No one had followed. No one had called him back.

And yet, he had not left.

Day after day, he had told himself he would leave on the morrow. That he would take a boat and return to the mainland, find his way back to Roman territory, and report everything he had seen. But each day, he had remained, driven by a need to understand what was happening on this island, what role he was meant to play in Mordred's grand design.

'World-changing,' Mordred had called it, on the rare occasions he spoke of the future. 'The restoration of true order to a corrupt empire.'

The sun's lower edge now touched the distant hills, casting long shadows across the valley. Somewhere behind him, in the grove, the evening rituals would be beginning. The druids with their white robes and golden sickles, the warriors with their blue-painted bodies and ancient chants. He had observed them from a distance, keeping himself apart from their ceremonies. But each night, the pull grew stronger.

He was no fool. He recognized manipulation when he saw it. The carefully measured revelations, the slow acclimatization to their ways, the subtle reminders of his supposed connection to their bloodline, all designed to draw him in, to make him receptive to their cause. And yet, he could not deny that something within him responded to their words, their rituals, their certainty. It frightened him more than any battlefield he had ever faced.

A soft footfall behind him broke his reverie. He did not turn, knowing without looking who approached. Her step was distinctive, deliberate yet light, like a predator accustomed to moving silently through forests.

'Mordred sends for you,' she said gently, her voice carrying the lilting cadence of the island's people.

Veteranus exhaled slowly, his gaze still fixed on the setting sun.

'Does he expect me to come running when called, like some loyal hound?'

'He expects nothing,' she replied. 'He offers.'

He turned, regarding the woman who stood a few paces behind him. Kendra, they called her. A warrior and priestess both, if such a thing were possible. Her dark hair was braided tightly against her scalp, intricate patterns that spoke of rank and heritage. Blue whorls adorned her face and arms, not the crude warpaint of common warriors, but the permanent marks of one initiated into deeper mysteries.

'And what does he offer this time?' Veteranus asked, unable to keep the bitterness from his voice. 'Another display of barbarity? Another 'revelation' to convince me of my heritage?'

Kendra's expression did not change, but something flickered in her eyes, disapproval, perhaps, or disappointment.

'He offers explanation,' she said, 'and warmth and brotherhood.'

35

Veteranus scoffed.

'Brotherhood? With the man who orchestrated that butchery three nights past?'

'There is more to Mordred than you have seen,' Kendra replied. 'Come. Join him at his hearth this night. If you truly seek understanding, you will find no better place to begin.'

Veteranus hesitated. Every instinct warned him to refuse, to maintain the distance he had carefully kept these past weeks. Yet the need to comprehend these people, to make sense of the madness he had witnessed, drove him forward. If he was to escape this place, truly escape it, not just in body but in mind, he needed to understand.

'Very well,' he conceded at last. 'Lead on.'

Kendra turned without another word, setting a brisk pace down the hillside and the settlement welcomed them back with the warm glow of hearth fires and the rich scent of cooking meat. Children darted between the roundhouses, their laughter carrying on the evening air, while women tended to cooking pots and men gathered in small groups, sharing tales of the day's hunting or fishing.

It was disturbingly normal. These people, whom Veteranus had witnessed partake in ritual sacrifice, now moved about their evening tasks with the mundane ease of any village across the empire. The contrast made his skin crawl.

Kendra led him to the largest structure in the settlement, Mordred's longhouse. It stood at the centre of the village, its thatched roof rising high above the surrounding buildings, its timbers carved with intricate symbols that seemed to shift in the fading light. Two warriors flanked the entrance, their spears crossed before them. They parted without a word as Kendra approached, granting them passage.

The interior was warm and surprisingly bright. Rushlights burned in iron holders along the walls, and a great hearth dominated the centre of the space, its flames casting a golden light throughout the hall. Woven tapestries hung from the rafters, depicting scenes of battle, ritual, and what appeared to be genealogies, intricate webs of

36

symbols connecting generations.

At the far end of the hall sat Mordred, not on a throne as Veteranus might have expected, but on a simple wooden bench. Around him gathered a small group: a woman with silver-streaked hair whose bearing marked her as his wife; two younger women who shared Mordred's sharp features; a broad-shouldered man whose arm was draped protectively around one of the women; and three children who played quietly at their feet.

It was a family gathering, utterly at odds with the image of the cold, calculating druid that Veteranus had constructed in his mind.

Mordred looked up as they entered, his stern features softening into something that might almost be called a smile.

'Veteranus,' he said, rising to his feet. 'You honour us with your presence.'

Veteranus did not reply immediately, his gaze sweeping the assembled group. These were not the wild-eyed fanatics of the sacred grove. They were a family, gathered in comfort and apparent affection.

'I was told you wished to speak with me,' he said at last, his tone carefully neutral.

'Indeed,' Mordred replied. 'But first, share our meal. Sit, eat, drink. There will be time enough for words when our bellies are full.'

He gestured to an empty space on a bench near the table. Veteranus hesitated, then moved forward and took the offered seat. A horn cup was pressed into his hand, filled with honey-sweet mead, while a wooden platter bearing roasted meat, bread, and early summer berries was placed before him.

'Eat,' urged the silver-haired woman. 'You've grown thin in our care, Roman.'

Veteranus glanced at her sharply, searching for mockery in her words, but found only sincere concern. He took a cautious sip of the mead, the warm sweetness spreading through him. The food followed, and despite his wariness, he found himself eating with appetite.

The meal progressed with surprising ease and Kendra joined them, settling beside one of the younger women. The conversation flowed around him, domestic matters, tales of hunting and fishing, discussions of the coming harvest, gentle teasing between family members.

Veteranus ate in silence, observing. This was Mordred as he had never seen him, a father, a husband, a grandfather. His stern features relaxed in the company of his kin, his normally piercing gaze softened by firelight and family. It was like watching a different man entirely.

As the meal drew to a close and the mead continued to flow, Mordred turned his attention to Veteranus.

'I see you have questions,' he said simply. 'Ask them.'

Veteranus set down his horn cup, his eyes meeting Mordred's across the hearth.

'I have seen you in two guises now,' he said. 'The cold-eyed druid who speaks of bloodlines and destiny, and now this, a man at his hearth, surrounded by family. Which is the truth?'

Mordred considered him for a long moment before answering.

'Both are true,' he said. 'Just as a warrior and man both exist within you. We are all many things at once, Veteranus, the face we show to the world depends on the circumstance.'

'And which face ordered the sacrifice of a child?' Veteranus asked, his voice hardening.

The room fell silent. The women exchanged glances, and the children were quietly ushered from the hall by one of the younger women. Mordred's expression did not change, but something in his eyes shifted, a shadow passing behind them.

'That is why you are here tonight,' he said. 'To understand what you witnessed.'

Chapter Five

Isla Mona

Talorcan and Cato rode their mounts quietly along the narrow forest path, the faint light of the moon filtering through the canopy leaves above.

'Hold,' whispered Talorcan, raising his hand and Cato drew his mount to a stop, the animal snorting softly in the cool night air. Ahead, the path narrowed between two ancient oak trees, their gnarled trunks creating a natural gateway into denser woodland. Talorcan dismounted in a fluid motion, his boots making no sound as they met the earth.

'The tracks continue through there,' said Talorcan, crouching to examine the ground. His fingertips hovered over the impression of a horseshoe. 'They passed this way perhaps two days ago.'

Cato nodded, his weathered face revealing nothing as he surveyed the forest ahead.

'They made no effort to conceal their passage,' he observed. 'Either overconfident or in haste.'

'Or both,' replied Talorcan, rising to his feet. 'Some young officers are too ambitious and fail to see danger when it is staring them in the face.'

The veteran scout's face hardened at this, the moonlight accentuating the severe planes of his features. The pursuit of individual glory at the expense of mission objectives was a familiar Roman failing, one that had cost many lives over the years.

They led their horses forward, the woodland growing denser with each passing hour. Sometimes they rode but where the undergrowth became too thick, they dismounted and guided their animals through the narrower passages, keeping to the trail left by Atticus and his auxiliaries.

The night deepened around them, the forest air growing cold

39

and damp, carrying the earthy scent of decay and new growth in equal measure.

'These are old lands,' murmured Talorcan, pausing to orient himself as the trail began to climb up steeper terrain, 'and have been sacred to the Trinovantes for generations.'

Cato grunted, a sound that might have been acknowledgement or dismissal. The Alpine huntsman had little reverence for local superstitions, but enough wisdom to respect the dangers they represented. Sacred ground meant druids, and druids meant a particularly unpleasant death for captured Romans.

The terrain grew increasingly challenging as they followed the trail upwards. The forest thinned in places only to become nearly impenetrable in others. Talorcan led them unerringly, reading signs imperceptible to less experienced eyes, a broken twig, disturbed moss, the subtle displacement of stones on a deer trail.

'They were following someone,' said Talorcan suddenly, crouching beside a small clearing where the evidence was clearer. 'See here, their formation changed. No longer a standard column. They spread out, moving faster.'

Cato knelt beside him, squinting at the ground.

'How many were they tracking?'

'A small group. Perhaps five or six riders, judging by the hoofprints. Their horses are unshod.'

The implications hung between them, unspoken but understood. As suspected, Tribune Atticus had abandoned his reconnaissance mission to pursue a band of Celtic warriors into increasingly hostile territory.

'Dawn approaches,' said Talorcan, glancing eastward where the faintest lightening of the sky had begun. 'We should find shelter before full light.'

Cato nodded. Daylight would expose them in territory where every tree might conceal an enemy scout, every ridge a potential ambush.

They continued up the slope until Talorcan identified a

40

suitable location, a thicket of dense holly and bramble nestled against an outcropping of weathered granite. The natural formation provided shelter on three sides while offering a clear view of the approaches from the fourth.

They secured their horses and moved to the forward slope of the hill. The position afforded them a commanding view of the valley below while keeping them concealed among the rocks and scrub. The first grey light of dawn revealed the vastness of the landscape spread before them, rolling hills cloaked in ancient forest, cut through with silver ribbons of streams feeding into the distant Tamesis.

'Beyond this point is unknown to me,' said Talorcan, his pale eyes scanning the horizon. 'The untamed heart of Britannia.'

Cato settled beside him, checking his weapons.

'Rest while you can,' said Talorcan, settling into a position that gave him clear sightlines across the valley. 'I'll take first watch. We'll move again at dusk.'

Cato nodded and retreated to a sheltered position among the rocks, arranging his cloak to ward off the morning chill. Within moments, his breathing had settled into the measured rhythm of a soldier accustomed to snatching sleep whenever circumstances allowed.

Talorcan remained motionless, his gaze sweeping methodically across the landscape below. Somewhere amongst those distant hills lay the answers they sought, the fate of Tribune Atticus and his auxiliaries. Whatever they discovered when darkness fell again would determine whether a rescue force would be dispatched or funeral rites performed in absentia.

The day passed in measured intervals of vigilance. They took turns at watch, one man scanning the landscape while the other rested in the shelter of the rocks or seeing to their horses. From their elevated position, the breadth of Britannia's heartland spread before them like a living map.

A road wound westward through the valley below, not the

41

meticulously engineered highways of Roman creation with their
precisely laid stone and careful drainage, but a well-trodden path
carved through generations of Britannic commerce and conflict and
despite the recent battle at the Tamesis crossing, people flowed
steadily along its length. Talorcan observed them with a hunter's
detachment, noting their numbers, their pace, the patterns of their
movement.

'The civilians flee,' observed Cato when he took his watch,
voice low as though the refugees might hear him across the vast
distance. 'They know what follows Roman victory.'

'They'll seek sanctuary with tribes further inland,' said
Talorcan. 'Places the eagle has not yet reached.'

In the middle distance, several settlements dotted the
landscape, clusters of thatched roundhouses surrounded by earthen
banks and wooden palisades. Columns of pale smoke rose from
central hearths, suggesting normal occupation despite the proximity
of Roman forces. Many Britons were not abandoning their homes
without cause... not yet.

Of greater significance were the war parties traversing the
road in both directions. Their numbers were concerning, thirty, forty,
sometimes fifty warriors, their spear points catching the light like stars
fallen to earth.

'Vespasian will want to know of this,' muttered Cato. 'Those
are not the movements of defeated men.'

Talorcan nodded.

'Their defeat at Tamesis was costly, but these tribes have
fought among themselves for generations. They know how to absorb
losses and continue.'

They marked the patterns of movement, committing to
memory details that would prove valuable for the Roman command,
the directions of travel, the apparent discipline of the war bands, the
equipment visible even from this distance. Such intelligence would be
worth as much as finding the missing Tribune.

As evening approached, they consumed a sparse meal of

dried meat and buccellatum but just before the sun set, Talorcan tensed suddenly, his attention fixed on a distant point.

'There,' he said, pointing toward a narrow peak rising from the forested hills. 'Smoke where there was none before.'

Cato followed his gesture, squinting against the dying light.

'A signal fire?'

'Perhaps.' Talorcan studied the thin column of smoke with narrowed eyes. 'It's too high for a settlement. That ridge would support no village, no crops, no grazing.'

The implication hung between them, unspoken but understood. Signal fires meant coordination. Coordination meant organised resistance.

'Worth investigating?' asked Cato, already knowing the answer.

'I think so,' said Talorcan. 'The Tribune's trail leads in that general direction so two purposes may be served by one journey.'

They prepared methodically, checking weapons, securing equipment that might make any unwanted noise. When night finally claimed the land, they checked their horses and leaving them behind with the last of the fodder, descended the forward slope.

Chapter Six

Rome

The Senate House stood as a monument to Rome's enduring power, its marble columns rising into the cloud-flecked sky like the spears of some ancient formation. Inside, sunlight filtered through high windows, casting elongated rectangles of brilliance across the mosaic floor where the men who helped govern an empire debated matters of state with varying degrees of passion and competence.

Senator Lepidus shifted on his cushioned bench, conscious of the subtle ache developing in his lower back. The session had dragged on interminably, the current speaker, a portly Senator from Sicily, expounding at exhaustive length on proposed tax adjustments for grain shipments from North Africa. His droning voice had begun to blend with the ambient sounds of shuffling feet, discreet coughs, and the occasional murmur of side conversations.

'Furthermore,' he said, consulting his notes with a self-important flourish. 'it must be understood that the tax revenue from Egyptian grain supplies has fallen by nearly twelve percent since the implementation of the last adjustment.'

Lepidus stifled a sigh. The bread supply for Rome was undeniably critical, but the minutiae of taxation rates hardly warranted such prolonged oratory. His thoughts drifted to more pressing concerns, specifically, the Occultum unit he had dispatched to Britannia. By now, Seneca and his men should have reached the invasion force, and he wondered if the dockmaster had delivered his message about Raven.

The heavy cedar door at the side of the chamber swung open, drawing Lepidus from his reverie. A young man in the formal toga of a quaestor entered and scanned the assembled Senators until his gaze settled on Lepidus.

The speaker faltered momentarily at the interruption before recovering his rhetorical momentum.

'As I was saying, the projected yield from the Alexandrian fields suggests that...'

The quaestor approached with disciplined steps, conscious of the dignity of the Senate chamber, yet undeterred by the ongoing proceedings. He bowed slightly to Lepidus and extended a sealed tablet.

'Senator,' he said, voice pitched low to minimise disturbance. 'This requires your immediate attention.'

Lepidus accepted the tablet with a nod of acknowledgment, noting the imperial seal pressed into the wax, not the larger seal of formal state business, but the smaller, more discreet one used for the Emperor's personal correspondence. A flutter of unease stirred in his chest as he broke the seal with his thumb.

The message was brief, inscribed in the precise hand of Claudius's chief secretary:

Your presence is requested without delay at the Imperial Palace. The Emperor awaits you in his private study.'

Lepidus read the words twice, their implications expanding like ripples in a pond. The speaker's voice faded to a distant drone as his mind raced through possibilities. For Claudius to summon him personally, outside the established protocols of Senatorial business was certainly out of the ordinary.

He became aware that the chamber had fallen silent. The Sicilian Senator had stopped speaking and was staring at him with poorly concealed irritation, as were many others in the assembly.

'Please forgive the interruption, colleagues,' said Lepidus, rising from his seat with deliberate dignity. 'I find myself summoned to attend the Emperor on a matter of some urgency. I beg your indulgence.'

The Consul presiding over the day's proceedings nodded with resignation. He was accustomed to the higher priorities of imperial demands.

45

'The Senate recognises the precedence of the Emperor's call. You are excused, Senator Lepidus.'

A murmur swept through the chamber, speculation, irritation, perhaps even relief at the momentary disruption of tedium. Lepidus gathered his writing implements and papers, securing them in his satchel before making his way toward the exit, conscious of the eyes following his departure.

The quaestor fell in step beside him as they passed through the cedar doors into the relative coolness of the colonnaded walkway beyond.

'A litter awaits you, Senator,' the young man said. 'The Emperor emphasized the matter's urgency.'

The litter's bearers, four sturdy men in imperial livery, straightened as Lepidus approached. The conveyance itself bore the subtle markings of the imperial household, enough to clear their path through Rome's congested streets without broadcasting the passenger's business to every curious onlooker.

Lepidus settled onto the cushioned seat, drawing the light curtain partially closed against the afternoon sun and prying eyes and as the bearers lifted their burden with practiced ease, falling into the smooth gait that distinguished skilled litter carriers from common slaves, he turned his attention towards what might await him.

It was certainly unusual for the Emperor to summon him directly and the implications were troubling. Had Plautius sent word of some disaster in Britannia? Had the Occultum's cover been compromised? Or was there some political manoeuvre at play, some court intrigue seeking to expose the shadows in which Lepidus operated?

The litter began its final approach to the imperial palace, passing through the outer security checkpoints with minimal delay, another sign of the summons's gravity. Guards in the distinctive uniforms of the Praetorian cohort stood at rigid attention, their eyes tracking the litter's passage with professional assessment.

The Forum receded behind them, the great marketplace of

Rome, both for goods and ideas, giving way to the more rarefied atmosphere of the Palatine Hill. Here, amid the homes of Rome's most powerful families and the expanding complex of imperial residences, the air seemed different. Thinner, perhaps, or simply charged with the unmistakable current of power.

Upon arrival he was met by a palace official, a Greek freedman by the name of Ionys who led the way past the many guards on duty at the gates. The imperial palace was a warren of different spaces, grand reception halls for state functions, intimate gardens for contemplation, and administrative chambers where the machinery of empire churned ceaselessly. Lepidus knew these spaces well, having traversed them countless times both during the short time of Claudius's reign, and that of the previous Emperor, though he had been a mere Legate at the time.

Ionys guided him through a series of corridors that grew progressively quieter, the marble floors giving way to mosaic designs of increasing sophistication. The decoration here spoke not of ostentation but of refined taste, fresco panels depicting scenes from Rome's mythic past alternated with landscapes rendered with remarkable skill. These were the private spaces of the imperial residence, where Claudius retreated from the performance of rulership to the often-solitary work of imperial governance.

They stopped before a plain cedar door, guarded by two Germani, massive men from beyond the Rhine whose loyalty to the Emperor personally rather than to Rome made them ideal protectors against the ever-present threat of conspiracy.

'The Emperor awaits within,' said Ionys. 'He is alone, save for Pallas.'

The mention of Claudius's chief secretary, Marcus Antonius Pallas, was significant. If Pallas attended, the meeting concerned matters of state rather than imperial whim.

The guard opened the door without announcement, and Lepidus stepped into Claudius's private study. The room

immediately challenged preconceptions of imperial luxury, its walls
bearing no gilded ornaments or exotic marbles, only well-stocked
shelves of scrolls and codices, evidence of the Emperor's lifelong
scholarly pursuits. Several oil lamps cast a warm glow over the scene,
supplementing the natural light from narrow windows set high in the
eastern wall.

Claudius sat behind a table, his posture betraying the
physical afflictions that had marked him from birth. Yet his eyes,
keen and alert, fixed on Lepidus with unnerving intensity for though
his body might falter, his mind remained formidable. Beside him
stood Pallas, a slender man whose unassuming appearance belied his
status as one of the most powerful individuals in Rome.

'Senator Lepidus,' said Claudius, his voice stronger in private
than the hesitant delivery he often affected in public settings. 'Your
promptness is appreciated.'

Lepidus bowed with precise deference.

'Imperator, you honour me with your summons.'

Claudius gestured to a chair positioned before the table.

'Sit. The matter before us requires neither ceremony nor
wasted time.'

As Lepidus settled onto the offered seat, he noted how the
Emperor's hands rested upon a scroll bearing the seal of the Britannic
campaign, correspondence from Plautius, almost certainly. The
observation heightened his wariness.

'I have received the latest dispatches from Britannia,'
Claudius began, tapping the scroll with a finger that bore the
imperial signet, 'and Plautius reports considerable success. The
crossing of the Tamesis proved costly but decisive. Plautius also
reports that Togodumnus fell in battle, and while Caratacus escaped,
his forces are scattered.'

'Favourable news indeed, Imperator,' replied Lepidus.

'More than favourable,' Claudius continued, a note of
genuine enthusiasm entering his voice. 'Plautius believes the tribal
capital at Camulodunum will fall within weeks. He says the back of

organized resistance has been broken, and the remaining tribal leaders have begun approaching our lines under truce banners, seeking terms.'

'A remarkable achievement in so short a campaign,' said Lepidus. 'Though the subjugation of the entire island will require years of sustained effort.'

Claudius leaned forward slightly, his gaze sharpening.

'You sound less convinced than my general, Senator. Do your own sources paint a different picture?'

'My sources largely align with the general's assessment,' replied Lepidus carefully. 'The initial phase of the conquest proceeds according to expectations. The tribes are divided, their coordination limited, and Camulodunum will likely fall as predicted.' He paused, weighing his next words. 'However, conquest and pacification are different challenges. The interior remains largely unmapped, its tribes numerous and fiercely independent. What looks like submission today may become organised resistance tomorrow.'

Claudius absorbed this assessment with a slow nod, exchanging a brief glance with Pallas before returning his attention to Lepidus.

'Your caution is noted, Senator. Yet it is precisely the current momentum that presents us with a singular opportunity.' He rose from his seat, moving with the laboured gait that had drawn mockery throughout his earlier life and approached a large map of Britannia mounted on the wall, a speculative rendering based on merchant accounts and military reconnaissance, with vast sections marked only with vague indications or left blank entirely.

'For four generations,' said Claudius, tracing the coastline with his finger, 'Rome has regarded this island with ambition yet hesitation. Julius Caesar himself landed, claimed victory, and departed. Augustus considered conquest, then deferred and both Tiberius and Caligula made proclamations but took no action.'

He turned back to face Lepidus, his expression hardening with resolve.

49

'I will not be remembered as the fifth Emperor to delay. This victory will be sealed properly, with the appropriate ceremony and authority.'

A cold understanding began to form in Lepidus's mind, though he dared not voice it.

'I intend to travel to Britannia,' Claudius declared, confirming Lepidus's suspicion. 'I will personally accept the surrender of the Britannic kings, consecrate the founding of our newest province, and return to Rome for a triumph that even the most cynical Senators cannot deny me.'

Silence hung in the study for several heartbeats.

'A bold decision, Imperator,' said Lepidus finally. 'Without precedent in living memory.'

'Precisely why it must be done,' replied Claudius. 'The people have seen no conquering Emperor since Augustus in his youth. They have endured Tiberius's reclusion, Caligula's excesses, and now they have an Emperor they did not choose. They require visible proof of divine favour, the conquest of an island that defeated even the divine Julius.'

The political benefit was clear. Claudius, who had come to power through the Praetorians rather than Senatorial acclamation, needed military prestige to secure his rule. A personal appearance in Britannia during its subjugation would provide precisely that.

'The logistical challenges will be considerable,' Lepidus observed, his mind already cataloguing the security risks such an expedition would entail.

'Already being addressed,' interjected Pallas, speaking for the first time. 'The imperial fleet has begun preparations and selected cohorts from the Praetorian Guard will provide security. The journey can be accomplished within weeks if conditions favour us.'

Lepidus nodded slowly, his expression revealing nothing of his inner turmoil. An Emperor in a war zone, in barely pacified territory, surrounded by hostile tribes with generations of grievances against Rome, it was a security nightmare beyond reckoning.

'You wonder why I have summoned you specifically,' said Claudius, returning to his seat with Pallas's assistance.

'I have served Rome in various capacities, Imperator,' replied Lepidus carefully. 'Some more visible than others. I assume I have something to offer?'

Claudius's mouth quirked in a ghost of a smile.

'Let us dispense with pretence, Senator. The Occultum operates under your direction and has done so since before my ascension.'

He reached into a drawer and withdrew a thin leather portfolio. From it, he extracted several documents bearing the imperial seal, authorization for expenditures, cryptic logistics requests, vouchers for specialized equipment, the paper trail of the Occultum's operations, laid bare. He spread the documents across the table between them.

'They cost the treasury a small fortune,' continued the Emperor, 'yet I have made no move to disband them. Indeed, their recent exploits in Egypt under Governor Postumus went a long way to remedying our little problem there and I have personally approved every requisition, every mission, every disbursement connected to your unit. However, more recently, I have taken a more detailed approach to determine whether the Occultum serves Rome or merely the ambitions of individual Senators and whether their results justified their expense and their unusual autonomy.'

The Emperor gathered the documents, returning them to the portfolio with methodical care as Lepidus looked on, worried that Claudius about to withdraw support from his unit.

'To be honest,' he continued, 'I am somewhat impressed with what I found. It seems your personal project have often delivered results that have advanced Roman interests without the messy complications of official military action. Particularly in handling matters too... shall we say… *delicate*... for traditional chains of command.'

Relief washed through Lepidus, immediately followed by

51

renewed wariness. Imperial approval was double-edged, it offered protection but demanded reciprocity.

'Which brings us to the present circumstance,' continued Claudius. 'As I have invested considerable state resources in maintaining your specialized unit, I think it is time for that investment to yield direct benefit to the imperial throne.'

He leaned forward, his gaze unwavering.

'I want the Occultum to infiltrate the tribal territories ahead of my arrival. They will identify and immediately eliminate any threat that might disrupt the proposed ceremony of submission. Any tribal leaders harbouring thoughts of resistance, any druids planning some fanatical disruption, any former Roman assets providing aid to the enemy, all must be immediately eliminated. My victory celebration must proceed without incident.'

'The unit you reference is presently engaged in addressing a specific threat in Britannia,' said Lepidus carefully. 'A matter with direct bearing on Roman security.'

'Then re-purpose them,' said Claudius. 'The narrative of Roman triumph must remain unblemished. The symbolism is too important to risk.'

'The timing may prove challenging,' Lepidus ventured, searching for diplomatic ground between refusal and acquiescence. 'The unit operates with minimal personnel and their current mission requires their full attention.'

'Then they will complete it before my arrival,' replied Claudius with the simple certainty of a man accustomed to reality conforming to his commands. 'Send word to your operatives, Senator. When I set foot on Britannia's shores, I expect them to be safe for Imperial feet with all
threats or risks eliminated. Cost is not an issue.'

The implication was clear, this was not a negotiation but a directive from Rome's supreme authority and Lepidus recognized the futility of further resistance.

'As the Emperor commands,' he said, inclining his head in

acceptance. 'I will communicate your instructions without delay.'

'Good,' said Claudius, the matter settled in his mind. 'Pallas will provide you with the details of our schedule. Ensure your men receive whatever they require to fulfil their duty.'

As Pallas presented him with a sealed document containing the expedition details, Lepidus's thoughts turned to Seneca and his men. They had been dispatched to eliminate a rogue operative; now they would be tasked with guarding an Emperor in the same hostile territory. The complication was immense, the timeline punishing.

'Is there anything else you require of me, Imperator?' Lepidus asked as he accepted the document.

Claudius studied him for a moment.

'Only your discretion, Senator, which I understand to be considerable. This expedition must appear spontaneous, a confident Emperor seizing the moment of victory. The reality of its detailed planning should remain between us.'

'Of course, Imperator,' said Lepidus but as he rose and prepared to take his leave, Claudius added a final observation that chilled him to the bone.

'Your Occultum has served Rome well in the shadows, Senator. Soon they will serve in a different capacity, still unseen, perhaps, but protecting the visible embodiment of Rome itself. I look forward to the results of their efforts, both current and future.'

The statement carried the unmistakable weight of imperial attention, something the Occultum had carefully avoided since its inception. As Lepidus bowed and withdrew from the study, he understood that regardless of how events unfolded in Britannia, nothing would be quite the same for Seneca and his men again. The Emperor's gaze had fallen upon them, and such attention, once given, was rarely withdrawn without cost.

Chapter Seven

Rutupiae

The port of Rutupiae had transformed in the months since they had seen it last. Where once there had been only hasty fortifications and temporary structures, now stood the beginnings of permanent Roman occupation. Stone foundations now replaced timber, and organized streets emerged from what had been mud tracks, the familiar grid pattern imposed upon Britannic soil with the inexorable certainty of Roman planning.

Seneca stood in the doorway of the ten-man tent that served as the Occultum's temporary headquarters, watching the methodical chaos of the military port. Supply wagons lumbered past, laden with grain, timber, and iron. Legionaries moved in disciplined formations toward the training grounds beyond the settlement's edge while merchants argued with quartermasters over prices and quantities, the commerce of conquest proceeding alongside its military aspects.

Behind him, Marcus loomed over the maps spread across a trestle table, his brow furrowed in concentration. The maps told different stories, depending on who had created them and for what purpose. Some showed detailed topography and settlements along the Roman march inland. Others depicted tribal territories with careful notations of allegiances and hostilities. A few, the ones that had captured Seneca's particular interest, were largely blank beyond the coastal regions, their empty spaces marked only with speculative notations: Terra Incognita or simply Hostile Territory.

'The eastern approaches to Mona are better documented than I expected,' said Marcus, tracing his finger along a river path marked on one of the more detailed maps. 'This appears to be a viable route, assuming the scouts' reports are accurate.'

Seneca turned from his observation of the port activities.

'And how many scouts have returned from those regions to confirm their accuracy?' he asked, though he knew the answer

54

already.

Marcus's expression tightened.

'Few?'

'None,' corrected Seneca. 'These markings are based on interrogations of captured tribesmen, each with their own reasons to mislead their captors.' He moved to the table and rested his palms on its rough surface, studying the maps with the careful attention of a man whose life would soon depend on their accuracy.

'These blank areas,' he said, tapping one of the featureless regions with a blunt fingertip, 'worry me the most. They acknowledge the fact that we just don't know what's out there.'

A commotion outside drew his attention and through the open flap, he watched as Falco and Sica returned from their procurement expedition into the port's growing commercial quarter. The massive ex-gladiator carried a bulging sack over one shoulder, while the smaller Syrian balanced two carefully wrapped parcels in his arms. Their contrasting figures, Falco towering and broad, Sica compact and wiry, drawing amused glances from passing soldiers.

'Our hunters return,' observed Marcus dryly. 'Let us hope their success matches their confidence.'

Falco ducked through the doorway, his bulk momentarily blocking the light.

'The provisions in this miserable outpost are worse than a siege camp in Parthia,' he announced by way of greeting, dropping his burden onto a bench with a heavy thud. 'The merchants here would sell rat meat to their own mothers and call it venison.'

Sica followed, setting his packages down with considerably more care.

'You exaggerate,' he said, his voice carrying the musical cadence of his Syrian homeland. 'The dried meat is adequate.'

'Adequate,' scoffed Falco. 'Is that what you call that salted leather they're passing off as beef?'

Sica didn't answer, instead he unwrapped a cloth to reveal several blades of varying lengths, their surfaces gleaming with a dull

55

sheen in the afternoon light. With methodical precision, he laid them out for inspection.

'Celtic iron,' he said. 'Better than our own in some respects. The local smiths have certain techniques worth studying.'

Seneca picked up one of the knives, testing its balance

'And the other supplies?' he asked.

'All acquired as ordered,' said Falco. 'Buccellatum, dried fruit, oats, salt. Enough for three weeks if we're careful.'

'Medical supplies?' asked Seneca.

'Limited,' admitted Falco. 'Some honey for wounds, willow bark for fever. The legion's medicus was reluctant to part with more without official requisition.'

Seneca nodded, unsurprised. Resources were always stretched thin in frontier posts, and their unofficial status complicated access to military supplies.

'The local herbs are effective,' said Sica unexpectedly. 'I spoke with a camp follower who has knowledge of such things. She provided these.'

He unwrapped his second package to reveal several bundles of dried plants, their faded colours and distinct aromas filling the room.

'This one stops bleeding,' he continued, indicating a withered yellow flower. 'This slows infection. This induces sleep when brewed.'

Marcus raised an eyebrow.

'Since when are you interested in healing, Sica?'

'Since I realized death is not always the most efficient solution,' replied the Syrian without emotion.

Falco laughed, the sound booming in the confined space.

'There's hope for you yet, my friend!'

More movement outside the doorway announced the arrival of Decimus and Cassius, returning from their own assignments. The older man entered first, his weathered face drawn with fatigue but his eyes alert as ever.

'We've managed to locate some horses,' he said. 'Not the best

56

stock, but sound enough for our purposes.'

A silence fell over the group as the reality of their mission began to sink in.

Falco broke the silence, his voice uncharacteristically subdued.

'This mission,' he said, looking at Seneca. 'Pursuing Raven to Mona... it's not like hunting some Parthian spy or Germanic chieftain. The druids have powers beyond...'

'They have knowledge, not powers,' interrupted Marcus firmly.

'Tricks and poisons and the manipulation of fear. Nothing more.'

'You believe what comforts you, old friend,' replied Falco. 'I believe what I've seen.'

The tension in the room thickened. Seneca observed the unease spreading through his men, hardened operatives who had faced death in a dozen provinces, yet who now shifted uncomfortably at the prospect of returning to Britannia's shadowed interior.

'The last time we ventured inland,' said Cassius carefully, 'we lost good men, and that was merely to extract information, not to penetrate the druids' stronghold.'

'This mission is different,' said Seneca. 'Then, we faced unknown threats. Now, we hunt a specific target, a man whose methods we understand intimately.'

'A man who also understands ours,' countered Decimus. 'Raven trained with us, fought beside us. He knows how we think, how we move.'

Seneca nodded, acknowledging the truth of this assessment.

'Which is why we will do what he does not expect,' he said. 'But first, we need better intelligence. Our maps are incomplete, our knowledge of tribal movements outdated.'

He paced the length of the room, his mind working through the tactical problems that confronted them.

'We need a scout,' he said finally. 'Someone who knows the western territories, who can move among the tribes without drawing attention. Someone who understands both Roman methods and local customs.'

'Talorcan would be the natural choice,' suggested Marcus. 'I thought he was supposed to be here waiting for our return.'

Seneca shook his head.

'Talorcan is unavailable. He's engaged in a mission for Vespasian.'

'What manner of mission?' asked Marcus.

'I don't know,' admitted Seneca. 'The details are closely held. Something concerning a missing Tribune and his patrol. Whatever the purpose, Vespasian has claimed priority.'

The revelation brought a fresh wave of unease. Military resources were always stretched thin in frontier provinces, but losing access to their most reliable scout represented a significant disadvantage.

'Then we require an alternative,' said Decimus, practical as always. 'Perhaps among the auxiliary forces? The Batavian cavalry includes men familiar with this country, Germania has traded with Britannia for centuries.'

'Too conspicuous,' replied Seneca. 'A Batavian might pass unnoticed among the northern tribes, but farther west, among the Dobunni or Ordovices? Impossible.'

'Then what do you propose?' asked Marcus. 'Without reliable reconnaissance, we risk blundering into ambush after ambush.'

Seneca moved back to the table, his eyes tracing the coastline on the map to the western extremity, where Mona lay separated from the mainland by a narrow strait. The island's outline was marked with a single notation in red ink: Druidarum Refugium, Refuge of the Druids.

'I have a plan,' he said after a moment of contemplative silence. 'One that Raven would never anticipate, precisely because it defies conventional wisdom.'

The men gathered closer, their scepticism momentarily

suspended by the conviction in Seneca's voice, and as dusk settled over Rutupiae, casting long shadows through the open doorway, the Tribune began to outline an approach that would carry them beyond the boundaries of Roman conquest, into territories where ancient powers still held sway, and where a former brother-in-arms awaited with unknown intentions.

Chapter Eight

Isla Mona

The hearth fire cast dancing shadows across the longhouse's timber walls, the flames creating an illusion of movement among the carved figures that adorned the wooden beams. Within this flickering light, three men sat in contemplative silence, each nursing a horn of mead, each measuring the others with practiced wariness.

Veteranus studied Mordred across the diminishing flames. In the firelight, the druid's visage transformed, one moment the benevolent patriarch who had presided over the evening meal, surrounded by family and followers; the next, something older and harder, a face that had witnessed blood sacrifices and commanded men to war. Despite the domestic setting and the absence of ceremonial robes, Mordred's eyes betrayed his true nature, calculating, cold, assessing everything with the detachment of a man who viewed individuals as pieces in a greater design.

Beside him sat Raven, more relaxed in posture yet no less vigilant. The former Roman scout wore Britannic garments now, woollen trousers, a belted tunic, a cloak of local weave. His fingers, once deft with mapping tools and Roman writing implements, now absently traced the intricate knotwork carvings on his drinking horn.

The women of the household had retired some time ago, taking the children with them to the sleeping quarters beyond the main hall. Kendra had departed last, her gaze lingering on Veteranus with an intensity that communicated more than casual interest. He had felt her eyes on him throughout the evening meal, watching his reactions, gauging his responses to Mordred's carefully crafted familial display.

'She finds you intriguing,' said Raven after she had left. 'And Kendra is not easily impressed.'

Veteranus took a measured sip of mead before responding, unwilling to be drawn into casual conversation about matters of attraction when more significant questions burned within him.

'A natural response to novelty,' he replied. 'I am, after all, something unfamiliar in her world.'

'Perhaps,' said Mordred. 'Though Kendra has encountered many Romans before. Albeit at the point of her spear.'

The implied threat hung in the air, delivered with such casual precision that it momentarily masked its deadly intent. Veteranus had grown accustomed to these conversational feints during his time on the island, statements that seemed innocuous until examined closely.

The fire crackled as a log shifted, sending a shower of sparks upward toward the smoke hole in the roof. Veteranus watched, a momentary distraction from the tension that had been building within him since his arrival. Tonight, with the household now asleep and only these two men as witness, he would ask what he had come to ask.

'So, why am I really here?' he said finally, setting his drinking horn on the stone hearth edge. 'And do not talk of bloodlines and heritage and destiny. Why have you truly brought me to this island?'

Mordred leaned forward with a sigh, the firelight accentuating the deep lines of his face.

'We have known of you for many years, Veteranus,' he said. 'Your childhood in the Subura of Rome, your catastrophic attempt at a military career in the legions, even your eventual recruitment into the Exploratores, where your talents for observation and survival in hostile territory were finally recognized.'

Veteranus maintained an impassive expression despite the unsettling precision of the druid's knowledge. These were not facts easily gathered, particularly his early military disappointments, which had been deliberately obscured in official records through the intervention of a sympathetic Tribune.

'I'll admit your time with the Occultum remains somewhat obscure,' continued Mordred, 'which is understandable in the circumstances. But we have pieced together enough to understand

61

that you left in disgrace and have been living out of sight ever since you escaped execution.

The casual mention of the Occultum, a name known to so few that even some high-ranking military officials remained ignorant of its existence, settled like cold iron in Veteranus's stomach. His gaze shifted to Raven, the implication clear.

'Yes,' confirmed Mordred, noting the direction of his attention.

'Raven has been most informative about certain aspects of Roman military organization. Though his knowledge of you specifically was limited to reputation rather than direct acquaintance.'

'We never served together,' said Raven, speaking for the first time since the conversation had taken its serious turn. 'But those who operate in shadows eventually learn of others who walk similar paths. Your name was mentioned with respect.'

'So why does my past life justify my captivity here,' said Veteranus. 'I fail to see what advantage you gain. Nobody even knows I am here and even if they did, nobody would pay a single denarius for my life.'

'You were never a prisoner,' said Mordred. 'Merely... a guest whose departure would have been inconvenient before certain truths could be presented.'

'And these *'truths'* include claims of shared bloodline?' Veteranus could not keep the scepticism from his tone. 'Convenient mythology to justify my presence here.'

'Not mythology,' replied Mordred. 'But we need not revisit that particular discussion tonight.' The druid took a slow drink from his horn, his gaze never leaving Veteranus's face.

'When we learned you had been deployed to Britannia,' he continued, 'we recognized an opportunity that might not come again. An asset with your skills, operating so close to our shores... it would have been negligent to ignore the potential.'

'Potential for what?' demanded Veteranus, 'to change my perspective as you changed his?' he nodded towards Raven. 'To convince me that my loyalty to Rome was misplaced and my place was here, using the coincidence of a badly drawn tattoo as evidence? I am disappointed, Mordred. I thought there would be a grander design.'

Mordred smiled, a subtle expression that never reached his eyes.

'We sought to present you with information and allow you to reach your own conclusions,' he said. 'Men of your intelligence and experience rarely respond well to direct persuasion. They require evidence, demonstration, time for reflection.'

'Hence the weeks of limited freedom,' said Veteranus. 'The gradual exposure to your community. The careful display of domestic tranquillity interspersed with glimpses of your more... primitive practices.'

'You make it sound manipulative,' said Mordred, seeming almost amused by the characterization.

'Because it is,' replied Veteranus flatly. 'Skilfully so, I acknowledge. But manipulation nonetheless.'

The druid inclined his head, conceding the point without apology.

'Effective strategies often appear manipulative to those who recognize their mechanics. It changes nothing about their validity or purpose.'

The fire had diminished to glowing embers, casting the longhouse in deepening shadow. A servant might have been summoned to rebuild it, but Mordred seemed content to let the darkness grow, as if it might encourage greater candour.

'You still have not answered my original question,' said Veteranus. 'Why me specifically? There are other Roman officers, other Exploratores you might have targeted. Why expend such effort on one man?'

Mordred studied him in the fading firelight, his expression becoming grave.

'Because you are unique, Veteranus. Your skills, your

background, your position within Roman military intelligence, these alone would make you valuable. But there is more.'

Veteranus leaned back, the scepticism plain in his weathered features.

'You speak as if your knowledge extends beyond what any intelligence network could reasonably gather,' he said. 'Not even Rome's vast web of spies and informants reaches so far or sees so clearly.'

A sound escaped Mordred that might have been mistaken for laughter, though it carried too much contempt to deserve the name. The druid's eyes reflected the dying embers with unsettling intensity.

'And there lies Rome's fundamental weakness,' he said. 'You believe yourselves to be the centre around which the world turns. You imagine your roads, your legions, your marble monuments represent the pinnacle of human achievement.' He leaned forward, shadows deepening the lines of his face, transforming his features into something more ancient, more elemental. 'While Rome was nothing but seven hills populated by goatherds and outcasts, great civilizations already stood in the east,' he continued. 'Cities that dwarfed your Rome in size and splendour. Nations with their own networks of intelligence, their own systems of governance, their own understanding of the world that extends back thousands of years.'

Raven nodded in silent agreement, his expression suggesting he had heard these arguments before and found them persuasive.

'You need look no further than Greece,' pressed Mordred, warming to his subject. 'The very culture Rome so eagerly plunders for its art, its philosophy, its understanding of the world. Even your most educated men study Greek, speak Greek, aspire to Greek ideals while simultaneously claiming superiority.'

Veteranus maintained his composure despite the unexpected direction of Mordred's argument. He had anticipated appeals to Celtic pride, to tribal loyalty, to the injustice of conquest, but this broader perspective, this positioning of Rome as merely one power among many, represented a more sophisticated challenge to Roman supremacy than he had expected.

'And what of Alexander?' continued Mordred. 'A single man who conquered territories that Rome, with all its legions and generals, has yet to subdue. Who united peoples from Macedonia to India under one rule. Who founded cities that still thrive while maintaining respect for local traditions and beliefs. Rome claims to emulate his example while understanding nothing of his methods.'

'Alexander died young,' observed Veteranus calmly. 'His empire fractured within years of his death. Hardly a model of sustainable governance.'

'Because his vision exceeded his time,' countered Mordred. 'But the principle remains. There exist other paradigms of power than Rome's endless legions and systematic destruction of native cultures.'

The calculated precision of Mordred's argument revealed depths of knowledge that unsettled Veteranus more than any display of druidic ritual. This was not the reasoning of a provincial priest concerned only with local traditions. This was strategic thinking on a global scale, informed by historical understanding and clear-eyed assessment of imperial vulnerabilities.

Veteranus found himself reassessing the man before him. In his mind, the druids had existed as creatures of shadow and blood, mystics who ruled through fear and superstition, their power derived from ignorance rather than wisdom. Yet here sat a man whose understanding of imperial politics and historical precedent would not have seemed out of place in a Roman governor's council chamber.

'An impressive perspective from a man whose people have no written language,' said Veteranus finally. 'No system of roads connecting your settlements. No aqueducts bringing water to your communities. No legal system beyond tribal custom and druidic decree.'

Mordred's expression did not change, but Raven shifted slightly, a minute tension entering his posture.

'Underestimate us at your peril,' said Mordred, his voice

carrying a subtle edge despite its measured tone. 'Rome makes this error consistently. You see absence of Roman methods as absence of civilization. You mistake different for inferior. Your empire builds roads to move armies; we maintain sacred paths that have guided travellers for millennia. You write on parchment and tablets; we preserve our knowledge through disciplined memory, unsulliable by fire or flood and you impose laws by force while we maintain order through tradition and shared understanding.'

The argument was delivered with such conviction that Veteranus found himself considering its premises before dismissing them. The mark of a skilled rhetorician, to present perspective as truth, to frame cultural differences as equivalences rather than deficiencies.

'If your civilization stands equal to Rome's,' he said, 'if your ways represent wisdom rather than savagery, then explain to me why I witnessed the murder of a child. Explain how ritual sacrifice serves any purpose beyond terror and control.'

Raven's expression had closed completely, his eyes fixed on the dying fire rather than meeting Veteranus's gaze. Whether this represented shame, discomfort, or something else entirely remained impossible to discern.

Mordred leaned forward again, the shadows playing across his
features like living things. When he spoke, his voice carried neither defensiveness nor apology, but rather the calm certainty of a man who had reconciled himself to difficult truths long ago.

'You speak of murder,' he said softly, 'yet serve an empire built on systematic slaughter. Tell me, Veteranus, how does Rome punish those who defy its will? Does it not nail men to wooden crosses and leave them to die over days? Does it not throw prisoners to wild beasts for the entertainment of crowds? Does it not burn alive those who commit certain offenses?'

The questions hung between them, uncomfortable in their accuracy. Veteranus knew all about the history of the Roman justice system in all its calculated brutality, the crosses that lined the Appian Way after Spartacus's rebellion, the arenas where condemned men died for public spectacle, the pyres where traitors burned, yet still he was compelled to defend her traditions, no matter how brutal.

'Rome executes criminals,' he countered, though his voice lacked the conviction he had intended. 'Those who have violated established law. Not innocents selected for sacrifice.'

'And who establishes these laws?' pressed Mordred. 'Who determines which gods may be worshipped, which traditions honoured, which lives valued? When Rome declares a native tradition illegal, does that not simply legitimise cultural destruction?'

Veteranus searched for the crushing counter-argument, the decisive point that would collapse Mordred's moral equivalency. Yet the words eluded him. Not because Mordred was entirely correct, Veteranus still recognized the fundamental difference between judicial punishment and ritual sacrifice, but because the comparison exposed uncomfortable similarities in outcome, if not intent.

'You kill to appease your gods,' he said finally. 'Rome kills to maintain order.'

'Both kill for perceived necessity,' replied Mordred. 'Both believe their purpose justifies their methods. The distinction seems less significant from beneath the blade.'

The truth of this observation settled heavily upon Veteranus. He had spent his life serving Rome's interests without deeply questioning the foundations upon which those interests were built. His loyalty had been tactical rather than philosophical, focused on effectiveness rather than underlying justification.

'You still haven't answered my question,' said Veteranus, deliberately shifting away from the moral quagmire. 'Why am I here? What do you want from me?'

Mordred studied him for a long moment, as if weighing some final decision. When he spoke again, the academic detachment had vanished from his voice, replaced by something more direct, more personal.

67

'As I have said from the beginning, you may leave whenever you wish,' he said. 'There are boats available and no-one will prevent your departure.' He paused, his gaze never leaving Veteranus's face. 'But I have seen something in you, Veteranus. Something beyond your skills, beyond your experience. A deeper search for meaning, for the assurance that your life has served some purpose beyond merely advancing Rome's borders. A hunger to build rather than destroy, to create lasting change rather than temporary advantage.'

The words struck with uncomfortable precision, identifying doubts that Veteranus had acknowledged only in his most private thoughts. The question of purpose had indeed haunted him through recent years, the growing suspicion that his service, no matter how skilled, merely perpetuated a cycle of conquest without deeper significance.

'I offer you this,' continued Mordred, his voice dropping further, becoming almost intimate despite the gravity of his words. 'A chance to change the course of history. To alter the balance of power not merely between Rome and Britannia, but throughout the known world. Your life, perhaps your death, in service to something that will echo through generations to come.'

'Grand promises,' said Veteranus, though something in Mordred's tone had captured his attention despite his scepticism. 'Yet still without substance.'

'Then allow me to provide substance,' replied Mordred.

For the next hour, as the fire died completely, Mordred outlined his plan. He spoke methodically, detailing a strategy so audacious in scope, so meticulously conceived, that Veteranus found his practiced composure gradually failing him, and, as the scope of the plan became clear, Veteranus felt his breath catch. The implications were staggering, a fundamental realignment of power that would shake Rome to its foundations without requiring its complete destruction. A transformation rather than mere resistance.

'This is impossible,' he said finally, shaking his head in reflexive denial. 'The coordination alone would require years of preparation, and the plan would require someone with intimate knowledge of Roman military deployment, someone with access to command structures, someone…'

He stopped abruptly as understanding dawned.

'Someone like you,' confirmed Mordred. 'You would administer the critical component of our strategy. Your position, your knowledge, your contacts, your abilities make you uniquely suited to the task. The future of the known world could be in your hands, Veteranus, all you need to is to say yes.

Chapter Nine

The Lands of the Trinovantes

The forest exhaled mist with each step Talorcan and Cato took across the valley floor, their progress measured by heartbeats rather than distance. The vast wooded expanse that separated them from their objective seemed alive with hidden watchers, though whether this sensation arose from tactical awareness or the primitive dread that ancient forests inspired remained unclear. It would have been faster with the horses, but the risk of discovery was just too big.

Talorcan led, his footfalls disturbing neither leaf nor twig as he advanced, each sense attuned to the subtle language of the wilderness. Behind him, Cato followed with commendable skill, his Roman training supplemented by the hard-earned wisdom of Alpine hunting grounds.

They had sighted no fewer than three encampments since leaving their observation post, one substantial enough to suggest a war band, the others smaller gatherings that might be hunting parties or family groups displaced by the Roman advance. Each required careful circumnavigation, adding hours to their journey but preserving the secrecy upon which their survival depended.

'The hill lies beyond that ridge,' whispered Talorcan during a brief pause, indicating a dark mass silhouetted against the pre-dawn sky. 'Where we saw the smoke.'

Cato nodded, conserving breath. The Roman's face remained composed, but the tightness around his eyes betrayed the strain of moving through territory where discovery meant certain death. Unlike regular legionaries who faced enemy soldiers on ordered battlefields, scouts understood the particular horror of capture, the prolonged suffering that awaited those who operated beyond the protection of Roman formations.

They reached the base of the hill as the eastern horizon began to lighten, the first tentative suggestion of approaching dawn.

'We should wait until nightfall,' suggested Cato. 'Go to ground while we still can.'

'We should,' said Talorcan, 'but we do not have the time. Whatever purpose that smoke served, those who made it may return. We need to check it out and get out of here as soon as we can.'

Cato acquiesced with a nod, checking his weapons with a final, methodical inspection. A scout's first instinct was to observe and retreat with information, but circumstances sometimes demanded more direct intervention.

Their ascent began, the hill steeper than it had appeared from a distance. Ancient oaks and twisted yews cloaked its slopes, their roots creating natural staircases in the damp earth. Neither man spoke as they climbed, communication reduced to hand signals and the occasional meaningful glance.

Halfway up the incline, the forest character changed dramatically. The trees thinned out, revealing a broad clearing that struck both men into momentary stillness. Within the open space stood carefully erected standing stones, dozens, perhaps hundreds of them. Some reached taller than a man, others barely knee-height, their surfaces weathered by centuries of Britannic rain and wind.

'A sacred place,' breathed Talorcan, the words barely audible even in the pre-dawn silence.

Cato made the sign against evil, a reflexive gesture that seemed to embarrass him even as he completed it.

'Druidic?'

'Older,' replied Talorcan. 'The druids came later, but they recognized power in these places. They added their own stones, their own rituals, but they did not create this.'

The stones bore strange inscriptions, though time had erased much of their clarity. What remained was fragmentary, spirals, interconnected circles, angular symbols that might have been language or might have been something else entirely. Vines embraced many of the memorials, thorny tendrils wrapping the ancient carvings as if nature sought to reclaim what human hands had shaped.

Talorcan moved forward into the ancient place, his focus constrained by sudden reluctance. Cato followed after a few moments' hesitation, his Roman pragmatism warring with instinctive caution. The air hung heavy around them, thick with unseen presence. Here, the boundary between the mundane world and something less definable seemed to thin, like a veil worn nearly to transparency.

'They honour their dead here,' said Talorcan, indicating markings on one weathered stone pillar. 'But also commune with them. These are doorways.'

'Doorways to what?' asked Cato, his voice tight with suppressed disquiet.

Talorcan did not answer immediately. His eyes tracked the arrangement of stones, reading purpose in their placement that remained invisible to his companion.

'To whatever lies beyond death,' he said finally. 'The Britons believe the dead do not depart entirely. They remain... *accessible* to those with proper knowledge.'

'Superstition,' muttered Cato, but the dismissal lacked conviction.

They crossed the stone field with increasing unease, both men sensing they traversed ground not meant for casual passage. The stones surrounded them, silent sentinels to rituals beyond Roman understanding. In the half-light, certain angles and shadows created the unsettling impression of movement at the periphery of vision, though when regarded directly, all remained still.

The upper slope resumed beyond the ancient burial ground, the forest closing around them once more. Their pace quickened, driven by unacknowledged relief at leaving the ancient site behind.

The growing light allowed better assessment of their surroundings, and they reached the hilltop with unexpected suddenness, the dense undergrowth yielding to an abrupt clearing. Both men halted at the boundary where vegetation had been deliberately removed, creating a perfect circle of bare earth surrounded by the forest's edge. The absence of natural transition from woodland to clearing struck both scouts with its wrongness.

Talorcan surveyed the open space with narrowed eyes, reading the ground with a tracker's precision.

'Multiple footprints,' he whispered. 'Perhaps twenty individuals. They formed a circle here. Look how the prints align, facing inward. They surrounded something, or someone.'

He moved forward with extreme caution, entering the circle while disturbing as little as possible. Cato remained at the perimeter, maintaining vigilance while his companion investigated. The clearing offered no immediate evidence of its purpose, no blood-soaked altar, no sacrificial pit, no ceremonial artifacts, only the trampled earth and the unnatural perfection of the clearing itself marked it as significant.

Talorcan completed his circuit, frustration evident in the set of his shoulders. Whatever had transpired here had been carefully cleansed of obvious evidence. He turned back toward Cato, preparing to signal their withdrawal, when his peripheral vision caught something his focused search had missed. Between two massive oak trees at the clearing's edge, barely visible in the strengthening pre-dawn light, stood a wooden post with something hanging from it.

Talorcan approached with growing caution, each step measured as the scene revealed itself with greater clarity and suddenly, he stopped, transfixed by the horror before him.

What remained could barely be identified as human. The body, male, judging by size and proportion, had been torn apart with savage violence. Great rents had opened the chest cavity, exposing ribs broken outward as if something had reached inside with terrible strength to reach the heart. Flesh hung in ragged strips, vast portions missing entirely, consumed by whatever had attacked. One arm remained connected to the torso by mere sinews, while the other was simply gone. The lower extremities were exposed with the genitals torn away and chunks of flesh missing from the thighs, the torn flesh evidence of bites taken directly from the body.

The face was partially intact, though the throat had been torn open to the spine, and the head lolling backward at an impossible angle contained no eyes. What remained of the features were contorted in a rictus of terror, capturing the final moments of a man who had witnessed something beyond comprehension bearing down upon him.

Most disturbing was the sheer ferocity evident in the attack, not the calculated violence of human enemies but the overwhelming brutality of a predator beyond natural scale. The ground surrounding the post bore scattered fragments of bone and gristle, evidence that the creature had fed extensively, yet left significant portions uneaten, as if

interrupted or driven by something beyond mere hunger.

'Talorcan?' Cato's voice, though quiet, startled the Belgic scout from his horrified assessment.

'Stay back,' he replied, though the warning came too late as Cato joined him before the grisly display.

The Roman's face drained of colour. 'By all the gods...'

'This was no ordinary execution,' said Talorcan, forcing clinical detachment into his voice to master his own revulsion. 'This was druidic work.'

Something caught his attention on the ground, and he crouched down to retrieve a piece of fabric protruding from beneath fallen leaves.

The cloth had once been vibrant crimson wool, quality material dyed with expensive pigment. Now it was stiffened with dried blood, the original colour barely discernible beneath the dark staining. Talorcan turned it in his hands, finding the distinctive, purple-bordered edge that marked it as part of a military cloak, not the standard issue of common legionaries, but the distinctive garment of a Roman officer. A Tribune's cloak.

He looked from the fabric to the mutilated corpse, understanding crystallizing with terrible clarity.

74

'Atticus,' he said, the name emerging as barely more than breath.

The implication hung between them, unspoken but undeniable. If this was indeed Tribune Atticus, then his entire patrol, sixteen auxiliary cavalrymen, had likely met similar fates. Seventeen Romans, subjected to druidic rituals whose purpose extended beyond mere execution into realms of sacrificial significance that neither scout wished to contemplate.

'We must return to Vespasian,' said Cato. 'Report what we've found.'

Talorcan nodded, but his attention remained fixed on the body. Something about the arrangement nagged at his understanding, the naked body, the terrible mutilation. This was too brutal, too rabid.

'The druids believe certain deaths open doorways,' he said softly. 'They believe suffering of specific kinds create openings between worlds. But this... I have never seen anything like this.'

'We have confirmation of Atticus's fate,' said Cato. That was our mission. Now let's get out of here.'

Talorcan nodded and the two scouts withdrew from the clearing, each man processing the implications according to his own understanding. For Cato, it represented an atrocity to be reported and avenged through Roman military might. For Talorcan, it signified something more ominous, something that he didn't understand yet, but whatever it was, it did not bode well for the planned occupation.

Chapter Ten

Rutupiae

Silence claimed the tent as Seneca concluded the outline of his plan. The men of the Occultum remained motionless, their faces caught between disbelief and calculation in the wavering lamplight. The crude maps spread across the upturned barrel-top commanded their attention, hand-drawn recreations of Julius Caesar's original charts, with their speculative coastlines and tentative notations of tribal territories. Falco broke the stillness first, his massive frame straightening as if physically rejecting what he had heard.

'A sea journey,' he said, the words falling flat in the enclosed space. 'You propose to reach Mona by circumnavigating the entire island?'

The question hung between them, its inherent challenge unmistakable. Seneca met his gaze without defensiveness, the decision having crystallized in his mind over days of consideration.

'I do,' he confirmed. 'It offers advantages no land route can provide.'

'Advantages?' Falco's incredulity broke through his usual deference to Seneca's authority. 'As far as I know, no Roman vessel has completed such a journey. The western waters are uncharted, the currents unknown, the coastal tribes universally hostile.'

Marcus stepped closer to the maps, his military mind already assessing the strategic implications rather than dwelling on the risk. His fingers traced the speculative western coastline, lingering on the blank spaces where certainty yielded to supposition.

'The distance alone presents significant challenges,' he observed, 'provisions, weather contingencies, navigational reliability, each represents a substantial unknown. And Caesar's charts are decades old,' he noted, indicating areas where the parchment showed attempts at correction by later hands. 'Made during brief exploratory sailings rather than comprehensive coastal surveys.'

'All true,' said Seneca. 'And precisely why Raven and Mordred will never anticipate this route of attack. Consider our alternatives. A land approach through the western territories requires traversing hundreds of miles of hostile terrain. Every village a potential trap, every forest a perfect setting for ambush. Mordred's influence extends throughout all these regions and his network of informants could track our progress from the moment we left Roman-controlled territory. Mordred is no fool. He will have surrounded himself with warriors fanatically loyal to the druids and not even a dog could get anywhere near without being detected.'

'And you believe a sea approach resolves these obstacles?' asked Marcus.

'Isla Mona is small,' replied Seneca, indicating the island's dimensions on the map. 'Once ashore on its eastern coast, we would be mere miles from any settlement it contains. We arrive rested, and at full strength, rather than exhausted from weeks of overland travel. We complete our mission and depart within hours.'

'It is a good plan,' said Sica, the quiet assertion drawing all eyes to his unassuming figure.

Falco turned toward him with exaggerated disbelief.

'A good plan? We're discussing sailing into completely unknown waters, guided by maps made before any of us were born, to land on shores that have never felt Roman boots to face probably hundreds of the fiercest warriors we have ever encountered. And you call this good?'

'I call it unexpected,' replied Sica, unmoved by the larger man's vehemence. 'The best approach is the one enemies cannot conceive. They may watch the roads and forests, I doubt they will watch the western sea.'

The simple logic of this observation shifted the atmosphere in the tent. The men exchanged glances, reassessing the proposal not as a desperate gamble but as a calculated risk, the sort of mission they thrived in.'

Marcus returned his attention to the maps, his tactical mind now engaged with solving problems rather than cataloguing obstacles.

'There is merit in the approach,' he admitted. 'But the practical challenges remain substantial. Securing a suitable vessel with crew willing to undertake such a journey will be hard enough, especially one with knowledge enough to approach a hostile shore without accurate knowledge of reefs or tidal conditions.'

'All significant concerns,' acknowledged Seneca. 'Yet each can be addressed through proper preparation. Caesar navigated these waters with vessels far less seaworthy than those available to us now and local fishermen possess knowledge of currents and coastal features not recorded in any Roman charts.'

Silence fell as the men contemplated the implications. Despite Seneca being the leader, the special nature of the group meant that everyone had a say, and all points of view considered.

As the sun began its descent toward the western horizon, Seneca surveyed his men, reading in their postures and expressions the transformation from scepticism to cautious commitment. Even Falco had shifted from outright rejection to grudging acceptance, his tactical mind engaging with how rather than whether. Finally, Seneca broke the silence.

'Our window of opportunity narrows with each passing day,' he said, 'so one way or the other, we need to make a decision. Are there any voices who would prefer the overland route?'

'Then we proceed,' said Seneca eventually, 'but the operation remains classified at the highest level, no one beyond this circle learns of our destination or approach.'

The men nodded in acknowledgment, the discipline of secrecy ingrained through years of covert operations. What had begun as a seemingly impossible proposal had transformed through collective expertise into a viable mission plan, though one still fraught with significant unknowns.

'All we need now is a boat,' said Falco.

'And Neptune's favour,' added Cassius, invoking the sea god

with only partial humour.

As darkness claimed the port settlement of Rutupiae, the men of the Occultum continued refining their approach to the seemingly impossible task before them, a journey that would test not merely their personal skills but their resourcefulness against the elemental forces of sea and storm.

Chapter Eleven

North of the Tamesis

The Roman fort rose dramatically from the conquered soil, nothing less than a declaration of lethal intent. It was a statement in timber and earth that proclaimed authority over lands held by other peoples since time immemorial and where ancient Britannic oaks had once crowded the hillside, ordered emptiness now extended outward to the precise distance a scorpion bolt might travel. No cover for approaching enemies, no concealment for gathering forces, no shadow in which surprise might lurk.

Construction continued without pause. Centuries of legionaries laboured in rotating shifts, their rhythm as precise as their formations in battle. The ditch deepened, the ramparts rose, the timber palisade extended its protective circuit.

Within the perimeter, barracks and headquarters and granaries took shape according to the template Rome imposed upon every territory it claimed, a military architecture that made soldiers from Hispania to Syria feel equally at home, equally certain of their position within the grand machinery of empire.

Outside this hive of disciplined activity, the Legio II Augusta stood in formal array. Five thousand men formed into a precise semicircle, their armour gleaming in the autumn sunlight, standards raised above each cohort. The polished eagle of the legion held the place of honour at the centre, its wings outstretched as if ready to take flight from its silver thunderbolt perch, and beneath its raptor gaze, the men stood motionless in dress uniform, their helmets reflecting the day's light with metallic brilliance.

The display represented significant investment of resources at a critical juncture in the campaign, thousands of fighting men temporarily removed from construction or patrol duties to stand in ceremonial formation, a commitment of assets indicating the gravity with which the Roman command regarded the occasion.

At the heart of the formation, the Aquilifer stood motionless, the golden eagle atop his staff rising a full head above the assembled officers, a gleaming symbol of dominion that commanded the attention of all present.

Flanking the standard-bearer, Plautius and Vespasian maintained the precise distance dictated by military ceremony, their positions creating a visual trinity of power, imperial authority manifested through eagle, general, and legion commander.

Aulus Plautius stared across the open ground towards the distant trees. At sixty, he carried the weight of his responsibility with practiced ease, his military career having spanned four decades of Rome's expansion. The silver threading his close-cropped hair and beard testified to campaigns fought from Germania to Illyricum, experience earned through wounds and victories alike.

Beside him stood Flavius Vespasian, a decade younger than his superior, and Legate of the Second Augusta. His gaze swept around the assembled legion, these were his men, trained under his discipline, their accomplishments a reflection of his command.

No unnecessary conversation passed between the men, no fidgeting disturbed their composed stance, only a field of silence disturbed only by the subtle creak of leather and the occasional call of birds returning to the distant forest edge.

The stillness broke with calculated ceremony, a horn sounding from the front rank, its clear note rolling across the cleared ground and into the distant trees. All eyes turned toward the forest margin where the road from the north disappeared into shadow.

Moments passed with no visible response, until two riders emerged from the forest.

The first rode slightly ahead and carried himself with the rigid dignity of the Catuvellauni, his iron torc, symbol of rank among his people, gleaming against the blue woad patterns that marked his throat and jawline. His companion, a weathered warrior of the Trinovantes, wore amber beads woven into his beard, the mark of a tribal council

81

speaker trusted to carry words with the weight of binding oath.

When they reached the midpoint between forest and formation, two Centurions stepped forward to intercept them. The riders dismounted and surrendered their weapons without protest, ritual daggers and ceremonial short swords that served now as symbols of authority rather than practical implements of war.

After being searched for hidden weapons, the two representatives advanced on foot, stopping just before the waiting commanders.

For a several moments, all four men stared at each other without flinching, each knowing that to look away implied weakness. No one spoke, but when the moment had stretched to breaking, Plautius stepped forward and gave a single command.

'Kneel.'

Chapter Twelve

Off the Coast of Britannia

The imperial liburnian cut through the Narrow Sea with practiced ease, its twin banks of oars rising and falling in disciplined synchronicity. Unlike the preceding days of turbulent weather, this morning had brought unexpected calm. The surface lay flat, mirroring the pale sky above, broken only by the vessel's wake as it drew a straight line from Gaul to Britannia.

At the prow, Senator Quintus Lepidus stood alone, his weathered hands gripping the polished rail, gaze fixed on the horizon where his destination would soon emerge from the morning mist.

He had dismissed his Praetorian escort to the stern, preferring solitude with his thoughts. The calm passage offered rare opportunity for uninterrupted reflection, a luxury Lepidus had permitted himself too rarely in recent years.

The Senate, with its perpetual intrigues and shifting alliances, allowed little time for solitary contemplation. Yet now, suspended between Rome's established provinces and its newest conquest, Lepidus found himself examining the path that had led him to this moment, and the instrument he had created for Rome's service.

Four decades earlier, a younger Lepidus had joined the legions with the entitled confidence of aristocratic youth. His family connections had secured him officer rank from the outset, bypassing the years of harsh discipline that common legionaries endured. Yet unlike many of his privileged peers who viewed military service merely as a necessary prelude to political advancement, Lepidus had discovered genuine fascination for the art of warfare. For years he learned from seasoned soldiers who had fought in many campaigns, taking on board both their successes and failures, and gradually, as he was given more and more command, he started applying the lessons in the field.

The pivotal mission had come during his service along the

83

Germanic frontier. Assigned to lead a detachment of Exploratores beyond Roman lines, Lepidus had been tasked with gathering intelligence on tribal movements before the legion's advance. The assignment carried significant risk with minimal recognition, success would be acknowledged privately; failure would be remembered publicly.

Over three weeks, his small unit had penetrated deep into Germanic territory. They identified enemy concentrations, eliminated key tribal sentries, sowed disinformation among hostile leaders, and mapped previously unknown terrain features that altered the legion's planned approach. When the main force finally advanced, they encountered enemies divided and disoriented, their defensive preparations compromised before the first javelin flew.

Lepidus slowly recognized the potential that a specialized unit might achieve when liberated from conventional military constraints and he presented his assessment to his Legatus, arguing for establishment of a permanent special unit focused on these unconventional approaches. The response had proved tepid and though occasional missions received approval, systematic implementation remained elusive.

A salt-laden breeze stirred Lepidus from his recollection. He shifted his stance, easing the persistent ache in his left knee, legacy of an ambush in Illyricum fifteen years earlier. The horizon remained empty, Britannia's coast still beyond visual range, though the captain had assured him they would sight land before midday.

His thoughts to return to the past, to the critical juncture when his advancement to Legatus provided the opportunity for him implement his vision, and he assembled a select group of operatives whose skills transcended the traditional boundaries of military service.

Each member was chosen with surgical precision, men, not only drawn from the Exploratores, but also from the fringes of Roman society, united by capabilities that were too dark for official sanction. They were not bound by conventional military hierarchies, but by a singular purpose that demanded absolute loyalty and unquestioning execution of their mission.

Their initial deployments validated Lepidus's concept beyond even his expectations. Missions deemed impossible through conventional approaches succeeded with minimal resource allocation. Threats to Roman interests disappeared without trace, and information beyond the reach of traditional sources flowed into command decisions, transforming strategic planning from approximation to precision.

The shadowed nature of their operations created perfect deniability for Rome's leadership and the unit existed in bureaucratic limbo, unauthorized yet tolerated.

Lepidus's eventual elevation to the Senate completed the arrangement, creating a direct channel between imperial will and operational execution. His military experience, political standing, and intimate knowledge of covert methodologies made him the ideal intermediary, able to translate Claudius's strategic objectives into specific missions while insulating the Emperor from operational details that might prove politically problematic if revealed.

But now, the Occultum had become a victim of their own success and Claudius's planned expedition to Britannia was far bigger than anything they had undertaken so far. The Emperor would arrive expecting a secure environment, his triumph over Britannia's tribes carefully choreographed to enhance his political position in Rome. Any disruption, particularly one orchestrated by a former Roman operative gone rogue, would transform triumph into embarrassment or worse.

The overwhelming task before him had driven Lepidus to abandon the comfort and security of Rome, to undertake this journey personally rather than trust to intermediaries or written communication. The Occultum had been tasked with assassinating Raven, and he hoped desperately that he would arrive before their mission started.

'Land sighted,' called the lookout from his perch, the words

85

pulling Lepidus from his reflections.

The vessel maintained its steady progress, the oarsmen's rhythm unchanged despite the approaching destination, and less than an hour later, the ship bumped against the freshly constructed dock.

The wooden gangplank groaned under the weight of the disembarking passengers, its damp surface slick with sea spray and as Senator Lepidus stepped onto Britannic soil, he surveyed the bustling port of Rutupiae. It had grown dramatically since his last visit, but he had no time for observation, he was here for one purpose.

Pulling the hood of his cloak further over his head, he strode forward, his coarse travelling garb giving him the appearance of an ordinary man, not one of the most powerful men in Rome. His destination was clear, the dockmaster's office, a timber structure near the heart of the port and as he ducked inside, he immediately saw a stocky, grey-bearded man bent over a wax tablet, muttering to himself as he scrawled something with a stylus.

Lepidus cleared his throat.

The dockmaster looked up, his eyes narrowing first in irritation, then widening in disbelief.

'Jupiter's stones…' Quintus exhaled, straightening as if he had been struck. His weathered face creased with something between surprise and unease. 'Lepidus? By the gods, I never expected to see you here.'

'Necessity makes strange paths for us all, Quintus,' he said with a guarded smile. 'It's good to see you again.' He stepped closer and held out his arm in a gesture of friendship.

Quintus took his arm and gestured towards a table.

'Wine?'

'Not at the moment,' said Lepidus, 'I'm here to find the Occultum. Are they still in Rutupiae?'

'No,' said Quintus, 'You just missed them. They left yesterday.'

Lepidus cursed loudly.

'If they only left yesterday,' he said, 'perhaps I can still catch them. I need a horse and a guide, someone who knows the roads. Where can I find one?'

'It won't do you any good,' said Quintus, 'they left by boat.'

Lepidus's breath stilled for a moment as the revelation sank into his stomach like a stone. The Occultum were not men to take to the sea unless absolutely necessary. Their missions were ones of stealth and land-based subterfuge, not open water, and worse still, there was no easy way to follow.

'Lepidus,' said Quintus. 'Whatever business you have with them, you may want to reconsider. No Roman has ever landed on Mona and lived to tell of it.'

'I have no other option, Quintus,' he said, 'one way or the other I need to find my men. And I need to find them fast.

Chapter Thirteen

Castra Victrix

Talorcan and Cato approached the eastern gate of the fort as the afternoon sun cast long shadows across the rutted ground. Three days of hard travel had left both men exhausted, their clothing mud-spattered and their faces drawn with fatigue. The horses they had borrowed moved with the sluggish gait of animals pushed to their limits, heads hanging low as they approached the palisade.

The sentries straightened as the scouts drew near, one raising a hand in challenge while the other peered at them with suspicious scrutiny.

'Halt and identify yourselves,' called the guard, his hand resting on the pommel of his gladius.

'You know who I am,' sighed Talorcan, 'just let us in. We have urgent information for Legate Vespasian.' There was a pause as the guard considered his response before Talorcan started to turn his horse away.

87

'Stop,' called the sentry. 'Where are you going?

'I'm too tired for this,' said Talorcan. 'If you are not going to let us in, I'm going to get some sleep. Just tell him we were here.'

Fear and realisation crept onto the guard's face, and he gestured them forward with a nod.

'Pass through.'

The interior of the fort bustled with disciplined activity despite the late hour. Construction continued on several interior structures, the rhythmic sound of hammers punctuating the ambient noise of a military camp in transition from temporary outpost to permanent garrison. They dismounted stiffly at the stables, surrendering their horses to a waiting groom.

'These need proper care,' Talorcan instructed, running a hand along his mount's sweat-streaked neck. 'They've served well.'

The groom nodded, assessing the animals with a practiced eye.

'I'll see to it.'

Cato stretched, wincing as his stiff muscles protested the movement.

'Let's make our report and find some hot food. I'm famished.'

Talorcan grunted in agreement, though food was the least of his concerns. The image of the mutilated body they had discovered remained burned into his mind, its horrific implications demanding attention regardless of physical discomfort.

They crossed the central parade ground toward the Principia, the administrative heart of any Roman fort. Unlike many of the still-incomplete structures, the headquarters building had been given priority, its timber frame already enclosed, and its entryway flanked by guards in full armour despite the relative security of the fort's interior.

'We need to see the Legate,' Cato informed the guards. 'We have a report from the northern reconnaissance.'

One of the guards nodded with recognition.

'Wait here,' he said and disappeared inside, leaving them standing under the gaze of his companion.

They waited in silence, each man lost in private reflection of what they had witnessed and what it might mean for the Roman occupation. Minutes later, the guard reappeared.

'The Legate will see you now. Follow me.'

The Principia's interior was spartan but functional, its walls of fresh-cut timber still exuding the scent of resin. Maps covered every available surface, charting the conquered territories with Roman precision while marking the vast unknown regions beyond with tentative lines and notations.

Vespasian stood at the central table, his weathered face illuminated by oil lamps that cast flickering shadows across the room. Beside him, his chief of intelligence, studied a document with narrowed eyes. Both men looked up as the scouts entered, their expressions instantly shifting as they registered the gravity in the scouts' demeanour.

'Leave us,' Vespasian ordered the guard, who saluted and withdrew, closing the door behind him.

Silence claimed the room for a moment as Vespasian studied the two men, reading in their stance and expressions that the news they brought was unwelcome. He lowered himself onto a chair, a gesture of
preparation for whatever grim tidings awaited.

'Report,' he said.

Talorcan stepped forward, meeting Vespasian's gaze directly.

'We located Tribune Atticus, Domine,' he said, 'or what remained of him.'

'Start at the beginning,' said Vespasian with a huge sigh. 'Leave nothing out.'

Talorcan outlined their journey in precise, economical terms, their tracking of the patrol's path, the discovery of the signal fire, and finally, the clearing where Atticus's mutilated body had been

89

displayed.

Throughout the report, Vespasian remained stone-faced, though tensing visibly when Talorcan described the condition of the body. Longinus made occasional notes on a wax tablet, his stylus scratching softly against the background of Talorcan's clinical report.

'And the rest of the patrol?' asked Vespasian, when Talorcan had finished. 'Any sign of them?'

'No bodies, Domine,' Talorcan replied. 'But many tracks leading westward from the site. In my assessment...' He hesitated, searching for diplomatic phrasing.

'Speak plainly,' Vespasian commanded.

'In my assessment, they are already dead men. If not physically, then in every way that matters. The druids will not have kept them alive without purpose, and their purposes offer no mercy.'

Vespasian struck the table with a closed fist, the sudden violence of the gesture startling in the quiet room.

'Damn that fool! He was given explicit orders, reconnaissance only. No pursuit, no engagement. Sixteen good men lost because one Tribune couldn't contain his ambition.'

'The torn cloak we found confirms it was him,' added Cato. 'There's no doubt.'

Vespasian said nothing for a few moments, absorbing the information in silence.

'You've both performed admirably under difficult circumstances,' he said eventually. 'Go get some hot food and proper rest. We'll discuss the implications of your findings tomorrow, once you've recovered.'

Cato saluted and turned to leave, but Talorcan remained where he stood, his eyes fixed on Vespasian with undiminished intensity. Vespasian looked up, recognizing that something remained unsaid.

'You have more to report, Talorcan?'

Talorcan waited until the door closed behind Cato before speaking. He stood rigid, clearly uncomfortable with what he needed to say.

'Domine, there is something else about the Tribune's death that... troubles me.'

'Speak freely,' said Vespasian. 'What concerns you?'

'The manner of his death,' said Talorcan. 'I've seen men killed by animals, by other men, by exposure to the elements.' He paused, searching for the right words. 'This was different.'

'Different how?' said Vespasian.

'The body wasn't just killed, Domine. It was... torn apart.' Talorcan's normally impassive expression faltered. 'I've never seen injuries like it. The chest was ripped open, the flesh taken in great chunks, not cut but... wrenched away. It was almost as if whatever it was that did this was desperate to get to the heart.'

Vespasian frowned, leaning back in his chair.

'A bear, perhaps? Or wolves? The forests here teem with predators.'

Talorcan shook his head firmly.

'No, Domine. I know bear attacks. I know wolf kills. This was nothing like that.' His voice lowered. 'The ferocity was beyond any natural predator I've encountered. And there's something else, bears and wolves kill for food or defence. This...' He hesitated again. 'This had purpose. A deliberate savagery.'

Longinus, who had been listening silently, stepped forward.

'The druids are known to use animals in their rituals. Perhaps they set trained beasts upon him?'

'No animal did this,' Talorcan insisted. 'At least, no animal I know.'

Vespasian's eyes narrowed with irritation.

'What are you suggesting, Talorcan? Some supernatural agent? I expected better from a man of your experience.'

'I suggest nothing, Domine. I report only what I observed.' Talorcan stood his ground, though his discomfort was evident. 'The body was positioned deliberately, bound to a pole. Whatever killed

91

the Tribune was permitted, perhaps encouraged, to feed upon him, probably while he was still alive.'

Vespasian exhaled sharply, frustration evident in his features.

'So, you bring me questions without answers, fears without substance.' He rose abruptly, pacing the small confines of the room. 'I need facts, Talorcan. Intelligence I can use to secure this province, not vague forebodings about unknown predators.'

'I understand, Domine.' Talorcan's face settled back into its stoic mask. 'I merely thought you should know everything I observed.'

The Legate stopped his pacing, studying Talorcan for a long moment. Finally, his expression softened slightly.

'Your thoroughness is commendable, even if your conclusions are... uncertain.' He sighed heavily. 'We're soldiers, not philosophers, Talorcan. We deal in what can be seen, measured, fought. Get some food and rest, 'we'll speak again tomorrow. Perhaps with clearer heads, we can make better sense of what you found.'

Talorcan nodded and turned to leave, but Vespasian called after him.

'Talorcan, one more thing.'

Talorcan paused at the doorway, looking back.

'Keep these... observations... between us for now. The men have enough to fear without tales of imagined unstoppable beasts in the forest.'

'As you command, Domine,' said Talorcan and left the room, leaving Vespasian and Longinus alone with the troubling implications of his report.

Chapter Fourteen

The Southern Coast of Britannia

The fishing vessel pitched and rolled across the southern waters of Britannia, its wooden hull creaking with each swell of the restless sea. Unlike the imperial trireme that had carried them to the province, this humble craft offered no shelter from the elements, no comfortable quarters in which to escape the constant spray of salt water and the persistent chill of the ocean wind.

Four local fishermen manned the vessel, weathered men with skin tanned to leather by years of exposure, their hands calloused from hauling nets and working rope. They moved about the boat with the easy confidence of those born to the sea, adjusting sails and reading currents with instinctive skill. They had accepted the Romans' silver with the caution of men who understood the value of silence, asking few questions beyond those necessary to navigate the perilous journey ahead.

The promised fortune, a small chest of imperial silver, rested beneath Falco's watchful gaze. The payment had been secured with one of Lepidus's promissory notes before they departed Rutupiae, a requisition that would raise eyebrows when eventually processed by imperial accountants, but by then, their mission would be long complete, one way or another.

The members of the Occultum sat along the edges of the boat, maintaining their balance with varying degrees of success. Marcus braced himself against the gunwale, his knuckles white with tension as he fixed his gaze on the distant horizon, a sailor's trick to combat nausea that seemed to offer him little relief. Beside him, Sica remained cross-legged and motionless, his expressionless face betraying nothing of his physical discomfort, while Cassius had long since surrendered to his body's rebellion, leaning periodically over the side, emptying what little remained in his stomach into the uncaring sea.

Only Seneca and Decimus appeared genuinely comfortable, seated near the vessel's stern where they could speak with some privacy, their heads bent close together, voices kept low beneath the persistent sounds of wind and water.

'The western coast offers few natural harbours,' Decimus observed, tracing a line on the crude map spread between them, a charcoal sketch based on their captain's knowledge rather than official Roman charts. 'The tides there are treacherous, according to our fishermen. We'll need to time our approach carefully.'

Seneca nodded, his weathered face creased in concentration.

'We'll land at night, under cover of darkness. A small cove or beach, anything that allows us quick access to the interior without being spotted from watchtowers or settlements.'

'And once ashore?' asked Decimus.

'You'll remain with the boat,' Seneca replied. 'Keep the crew ready for immediate departure.'

Decimus nodded, accepting the assignment without protest though his expression suggested he would have preferred to join the inland mission. At his age, however, his greatest value lay in ensuring their escape route remained secure.

'The rest of us will move inland,' Seneca continued, 'using forest cover where available. Our primary objective is locating the druids' settlement. Intelligence suggests it's near the centre of the island, possibly built around one of their sacred groves.'

'And Raven?' Decimus asked quietly.

'Once we identify his location, we eliminate him. Quickly and quietly, with no witnesses if possible. Then we withdraw before the druids realize what's happened.'

Both men recognized the optimism inherent in such a straightforward plan. Reality would almost certainly prove more complicated, especially in territory entirely controlled by such a fanatical enemy.

'Beyond the initial infiltration, detailed planning becomes problematic,' Seneca admitted. 'We'll need to adapt once we have better intelligence.'

'The Occultum's specialty,' Decimus observed with grim humour. 'Improvisation in hostile territory.'

Seneca allowed himself a small smile. Despite the uncertainty that awaited them on Mona, he maintained absolute confidence in his unit's abilities. They had infiltrated enemy strongholds from Parthia to Germania and extracted information and targets from situations deemed impossible by conventional military assessment. This mission, while uniquely challenging, would call upon the same skills that had made them the empire's most effective covert instrument.

The day dragged on, each hour marked only by the sun's gradual progress across the cloud-scattered sky. The coastline of Britannia remained visible to their north, a distant smudge of green and brown that represented lands not yet claimed by Rome. Occasionally, they glimpsed small fishing villages or hilltop farmsteads, the smoke from cooking fires rising in thin columns before being dispersed by the persistent wind.

Eventually, Seneca rose from his position, stretching muscles stiffened by hours of inactivity and made his way forward to where the captain stood at the vessel's prow.

'That land,' said Seneca, gesturing toward the distant shoreline visible far to their right, 'what can you tell me about it?'

The captain, a grizzled man named Brennos with eyes perpetually narrowed against the glare of sun on water, followed his gaze.

'Terra Silurum,' he replied, the Latin words sounding odd in his heavily accented speech. 'Land of the Silures. Though there are other tribes as well, the Ordovices to the north, the Demetae in the western peninsulas.'

'What manner of people are they?' asked Seneca, studying the distant coastline's rugged profile.

The captain spat over the side before answering.

95

'Fierce. Territorial. The kind of men who ask questions with spear points rather than words.' He adjusted the sail slightly as the wind shifted. 'The Ordovices keep mostly to themselves, hunters and herders in the high valleys. The Demetae trade occasionally with merchants brave enough to visit their shores.'

'And the Silures?' prompted Seneca when the captain fell silent.

The captain's expression darkened.

'The worst of them all. They're Britannic, yes, but different somehow. Some say they have Iberian blood in their veins, you can see it in their dark hair, their swarthy skin. They're secretive, suspicious of outsiders. Few traders risk their harbours, and fewer still return to attempt it twice.'

'What about the land itself?' he asked.

'As unwelcoming as its people,' Brennos replied with a gesture toward the coastline. 'Mountains that rise like fortress walls from the sea. Valleys so deep and narrow that sunlight touches their floors for only a few hours each day and dense forests where men have vanished without trace.'

'You seem familiar with it,' observed Seneca.

'I've sailed past it many times. Never landed there though.' A shadow passed across the captain's weathered features. 'Twenty years ago, a storm drove my father's boat onto their shores. The Silures found them before they could make repairs.'

He fell silent, and Seneca didn't press for details. The captain's tone had made the outcome clear enough.

'Your Emperor may conquer the eastern tribes,' Brennos continued after a moment, 'but the Silures? They'll retreat into their mountains and forests, and make your legions pay in blood for every step they take.'

Seneca's expression remained neutral, though he noted the captain's use of 'your Emperor' rather than 'our Emperor', a subtle but significant indication of where the man's true loyalties lay, despite his willingness to transport Romans for sufficient silver.

'And beyond Terra Silurum?' asked Seneca, gesturing farther west. 'What lies between there and Mona?'

Bran's eyes narrowed further. 'More of the same. Harsher coastlines, stronger currents. Then Mona itself.' He turned to face Seneca directly. 'I've kept my questions few, Roman, as our arrangement requires. But I must know, are you certain about this? Mona is not merely another island. It is the heart of the druids' power, their most sacred refuge. No Roman has set foot there and lived.'

'You need not concern yourself with our business there,' replied Seneca, 'only with delivering us safely and waiting for our return.'

The captain held his gaze for a moment, then shook his head and turned his attention back to the sea ahead.

'As you wish. But I won't set foot on Mona's shores myself. I'll put you ashore in a small boat, then anchor offshore until your return.'

'That was our arrangement,' Seneca agreed, before adding, 'How long before we round the southern headlands?'

'If the wind holds, late tomorrow,' Brennos replied. 'Then three more days to reach Mona, assuming the weather remains favourable.'

Seneca nodded and turned away, gazing thoughtfully at the distant shoreline of Terra Silurum. Somewhere beyond those forbidding mountains and forests lay their destination, and their target. Even if Raven suspected they would come for him, he would expect them to come by land, through the territories Brennos had just described. The sea route, while perilous in its own way, might yet provide the element of surprise they needed.

Chapter Fifteen

Rutupiae

Lepidus rode westward along the temporary but rapidly expanding Roman road that cut through the conquered territories of eastern Britannia. Four Praetorian guardsmen flanked him, their polished armour and crimson cloaks marking them as elite soldiers from the imperial household. Though they wore the trappings of ceremonial guards, each man was a veteran of multiple campaigns, handpicked for their combat experience as well as their loyalty to the imperial throne.

Their small party had been attached to a cavalry unit destined for Vespasian's legion on the front lines, the arrangement providing both security and administrative convenience and though part of him still burned with frustration at having missed the Occultum, Lepidus had adjusted his plans. There remained critical matters to discuss with Plautius, chief among them the impending visit of Emperor Claudius, a development that would transform the military campaign into a political spectacle with far-reaching implications.

The Britannic landscape rolled past as they rode. The process of transforming Britannia from hostile foreign territory to integrated provincial land had already begun, though the island's interior remained untamed and defiant.

They spent the first night at a transition camp, established along the supply route to support the legions' westward advance and the Praefectus Castrorum, seeing Lepidus's Senatorial insignia and imperial documentation, had immediately surrendered his own quarters to the distinguished visitor. Lepidus had accepted the courtesy with practiced grace, though he slept poorly. His mind was occupied with calculations of distance and time, how far to Plautius's

98

headquarters, how many days until Claudius's arrival, and how long until the Occultum's mission either succeeded or failed.

Two days after leaving Rutupiae, near midday, they crested a ridge and saw their destination spread before them. The fortress dominated the landscape, and as they approached the eastern gate, a sentry's horn sounded, announcing the arrival of persons of significance. By the time they reached the entrance, a small reception party had formed, junior officers hurriedly assembled to greet whatever dignitary travelled with a Praetorian escort.

'Domine,' the young Tribune bowed deeply, 'we had no word of your arrival. Please, follow me.'

Lepidus dismounted and handed the reins of his horse to a waiting groom. His Praetorian guards remained alert, eyes scanning the bustling fort interior with professional assessment.

'Your men will be accommodated in the officers' quarters,' the Tribune continued, gesturing toward a row of neat wooden structures. 'Your personal effects will be brought shortly.'

The fort's interior hummed with disciplined activity. Engineers oversaw construction of permanent buildings to replace the remaining tents and temporary structures. Legionaries drilled in formation on the parade ground, the rhythmic clash of their training swords creating a familiar backdrop to military life and messengers moved swiftly between command buildings, the administrative heartbeat of Rome's newest conquest.

Lepidus followed the Tribune through the organized chaos, noting with approval the orderly layout and efficient operation. Vespasian ran a tight command, the evidence visible in every corner of the fort.

They reached a modest building near the centre of the encampment. Inside, the Tribune showed him to a small but functional room containing a narrow bed, a writing table, and a single stool.

'It's not much,' the Tribune apologized, 'but it's clean. I'll send word of your arrival to the Legatus immediately.'

99

Lepidus nodded, dismissing the young officer with a wave. As the door closed behind him, he sank onto the bed, allowing himself a moment of private exhaustion. The journey had taken more from him than he cared to admit.

Within the hour, the same Tribune returned, his posture even more deferential than before.

'Senator, I apologize for the initial arrangements,' he said quickly. 'The Legatus sends his respects and has allocated more suitable quarters for a man of your standing. Clean garments will be provided, along with a hot bath. Additionally, you are invited to dine with him and General Plautius this evening after last light.'

Lepidus suppressed a smile. Word of his Senatorial rank, and perhaps his imperial connection, had clearly reached the right ears.

'Lead on, Tribune,' he said, gathering his meagre travel bag.

The new accommodation proved considerably more appropriate to his status. Located in the heart of the fort, the room was nearly three times larger than the first, with a proper bed, a writing desk with chair, and even a small brazier to ward off the perpetual Britannic chill.

Lepidus had barely finished inspecting the quarters when two servants arrived, carrying steaming buckets of water. They filled a copper tub positioned near the brazier, and placed folded linen cloths nearby, along with a flask of scented oil. Once done, they withdrew in silence and closed the door behind them.

Lepidus shed his travel-stained clothing and sank into the hot water with a sigh of relief, and as the heat seemed to penetrate deep into his bones, the familiar aches of age and hard travel began to dissolve, his muscles relaxing for the first time in weeks.

He closed his eyes, allowing himself this brief luxury before the more demanding tasks ahead. Claudius's planned visit represented both opportunity and danger, a chance to secure the new province firmly under Roman control, but also a thousand possibilities for disaster if the security situation deteriorated.

And beyond these immediate concerns lay the Occultum's mission to Isla Mona. Though he could no longer influence their approach, their success or failure could have profound implications for Rome's hold on Britannia. Raven's long service in the Occultum meant he knew far too much about Rome's secrets and he had to be eliminated before he did too much damage.

Eventually, as the water began to cool, Lepidus rose from the bath and dried himself thoroughly with the provided linen, appreciating the simple luxury of cleanliness after days in the saddle. The clean clothing laid out for him was plain but well-made, a simple tunic and toga suitable for a dignified Roman official rather than the elaborate Senatorial garb he typically wore in Rome.

Dressed and refreshed, he settled into the bed to wait, his mind reviewing the complex web of military and political considerations that would frame their coming conversation.

A few hours later, a sharp knock at the door drew him from his unbidden slumber, announcing his escort's arrival.

'Senator Lepidus,' said the same Tribune who had met him earlier, 'General Plautius sends his compliments and asks me to conduct you to the officers' dining quarters.'

Lepidus nodded and followed the Tribune through the fort's central thoroughfare. The day's activities were winding down as twilight settled over the encampment. Soldiers walked toward the mess halls, torch bearers made their rounds lighting the way posts that would illuminate the camp through the night, and the changing of the guard proceeded with practiced efficiency at key checkpoints.

The officers' dining quarters occupied a sturdy timber structure near the Principia.
Inside, oil lamps cast a warm glow over a room dominated by a single long table and three men rose to greet Lepidus as he entered.

He recognized Aulus Plautius immediately, the campaign's overall commander stood with the straight-backed posture that years of military service had ingrained into his bearing. Though in his

101

sixties, Plautius maintained the physical presence of a much younger man, his weathered face conveying both authority and the weary wisdom of a general who had seen too many campaigns to harbour illusions about the glory of war.

Beside him stood Flavius Vespasian, commander of the Second Augusta and nearly two decades Plautius's junior. Where the older general carried himself with the assured gravity of established authority, Vespasian projected focused intensity, a commander still building his reputation, still hungry for accomplishment. His calculating gaze assessed Lepidus with undisguised curiosity.

The third man, slightly apart from the generals, was the Praefectus Castrorum, the camp prefect responsible for the fort's logistical operations. A career soldier with the practical bearing of a man who understood that armies marched on supplies as much as courage, he nodded respectfully to the visiting Senator.

'Senator Lepidus,' Plautius stepped forward with an extended hand. 'Your arrival is unexpected but most welcome.'

Lepidus clasped the offered forearm in the traditional warrior's greeting.

'General Plautius. Forgive the lack of formal announcement. Events in Rome necessitated swift travel.'

'No forgiveness needed,' Plautius replied, gesturing toward the table. 'I value direct communication over protocol. You know Vespasian, I believe?'

Lepidus nodded to the younger commander.

'We've met briefly during state functions in Rome. Your reputation has grown considerably since then, Commander.'

Vespasian's mouth quirked in what might have been a suppressed smile.

'Success in the field tends to have that effect, Senator.'

'And this is Quintus Albinus,' Plautius continued, indicating the Praefectus Castrorum, 'the backbone of our operation here.'

The introductions complete, they took their places at the table. Servants appeared silently, bearing platters of food, roasted venison, freshly baked bread, and steamed vegetables, a hearty meal rather than elaborate.

As wine was poured, the conversation began with safe, neutral topics, the progress of construction within the fort, the condition of the roads between Rutupiae and their current position, and the unusually mild weather they had experienced since the Tamesis crossing.

But gradually, as they finished the main course and moved to sweetened fruits and nuts, the discussion shifted to the campaign itself.

'The campaign has cost us nearly a thousand men,' Plautius said, his voice betraying no emotion as he recounted the losses, 'but it broke the back of organized resistance around the two rivers. The tribal confederation Togodumnus and his brother had assembled no longer exists and several chiefs have already approached us with peace offerings.'

'The Trinovantes and Catuvellauni are effectively neutralized,' added Vespasian, 'though small bands continue harassment tactics against our supply lines. Nothing our auxiliaries can't handle.'

'And Caratacus himself?' Lepidus asked, sipping his wine.

'Escaped westward,' replied Plautius. 'Likely seeking support among the western tribes, the Silures, the Ordovices, perhaps even as far as the Deceangli.'

'So, what is your assessment of the overall situation?' Lepidus directed the question equally to both commanders.

'From a military perspective,' said Vespasian, 'the situation is favourable. We've secured territory from the coast to the Tamesis and established forward positions further northward. The Second Augusta now stands ready to advance on Camulodunum once final preparations are complete.'

'The campaign proceeds according to projection,' Plautius added, his tone more measured than his subordinate's. 'Though I would caution against overconfidence. Britannia is still an unknown quantity and needs to be approached accordingly.'

The conversation turned to politics in Rome, Senate reactions to the initial reports of victory, the positioning of various factions seeking advantage from the campaign's success and the allocation of resources for the continued occupation. Lepidus provided a succinct analysis of the political landscape, noting which Senators supported the Britannic campaign and which questioned its cost and strategic value. Finally, as the hour grew later and servants cleared away the remains of their meal, Plautius leaned forward slightly.

'And now, Senator, perhaps you might share the real purpose of your journey? I doubt you travelled all this way merely to update us on Senatorial gossip.'

Lepidus met the general's direct gaze with equal frankness.

'I assume you've received word of the Emperor's intentions?' he asked.

Plautius nodded, his expression revealing nothing of his personal thoughts on the matter.

'Ten days ago. A fast messenger arrived from Rome with sealed orders.' He paused, selecting his words with care. 'The Emperor plans to join us for the final subjugation ceremony at Camulodunum. A significant honour for the campaign.'

The diplomatic understatement hung between them. Both men understood the political calculation behind Claudius's decision, an Emperor with a tenuous claim to legitimacy seeking military prestige to solidify his position in Rome.

'And what preparations have you made thus far?' asked Lepidus.

'The usual,' replied Plautius. 'We are also adding additional fortifications along the approach routes. There will be vastly increased patrols and obviously appropriate accommodations constructed for the imperial party.' He took another sip of wine. 'There is, of course, the small matter of actually taking Camulodunum first, but I suspect you haven't travelled all this way merely to oversee arrangements I am perfectly capable of making myself.'

A hint of pride, perhaps even mild offense, coloured his words. Plautius was, after all, Rome's most senior military commander in Britannia, not some junior officer requiring supervision.

Lepidus set down his cup, meeting his old comrade's gaze directly.

'You're correct, of course. I'm not here to oversee your preparations, which I have no doubt are thorough and appropriate.' He leaned forward slightly. 'I'm here because the Emperor has specific concerns regarding potential threats to his person, concerns that go beyond conventional military security.'

'Assassination attempts?' said Plautius.

'Precisely,' said Lepidus. 'As you know, Claudius survived three such attempts in his first year alone and just wants to make sure things go as smoothly as they can.'

'And what does the Emperor propose as a solution to these concerns?'

'He has directed me to employ the Occultum to ensure his personal safety.'

Plautius paused and stared at Lepidus. The name was rarely spoken aloud, even among those aware of the unit's existence.

'I see,' he said eventually. 'A reasonable precaution, given the stakes. I assume they've already been dispatched?'

'Therein lies the problem,' said Lepidus. 'They were already on a mission when the Emperor's directive reached me. A mission concerning a former operative gone rogue.'

'Raven?' said Plautius.

Lepidus raised an eyebrow in surprise.

'You're well-informed.'

'Certain information crosses my desk as a matter of course,' replied Plautius. 'A former Roman scout providing intelligence to the druids represents a significant military threat, not merely a matter of internal discipline.'

'Indeed. And the threat has grown. Intelligence suggests Raven has been working closely with Mordred for a long time, coordinating resistance across tribal lines.' Lepidus took another drink before continuing. 'The Occultum was tasked with eliminating him before he could further compromise our operations, but now also we have the potential of the Emperor arriving in what is still dangerous territory, the risk is even greater. They departed a few days ago so we can only hope their mission is successful.'

'How much time do we have before Claudius arrives?' asked Plautius.

'Who knows,' said Lepidus. 'I suppose it all depends on how long it takes for you to subdue Camulodunum. Is there likely to be much resistance?'

'I wouldn't have thought so,' interjected Vespasian. 'We have already accepted the surrender of the Trinovantes and Catuvellauni, albeit from tribal elders and not Caratacus himself.'

'Well, whenever it is,' said Lepidus, 'Claudius intends to arrive with suitable drama, the conquering Emperor stepping onto foreign soil at the perfect moment to accept surrender from barbarian kings.'

'There is another matter,' said Vespasian, refilling the cups. 'One that may bear directly on your concerns.'

Lepidus raised an eyebrow in question.

'One of my reconnaissance units disappeared recently. Tribune Atticus and sixteen auxiliaries. I dispatched our best scout, a man named Talorcan to discover their fate. He returned yesterday with troubling news. The Tribune was found ritually sacrificed at a druidic site north of the Tamesis.'

Lepidus's expression darkened.

'Mordred's work?'

'Almost certainly,' confirmed Vespasian. 'But Talorcan reported unusual aspects to the killings, something he had never seen before. The bodies were not merely executed but torn apart with a savagery that exceeded even druidic norms. Something about the arrangement suggested a ritual beyond simple sacrifice.'

'A warning to other Romans who might venture too far?' suggested Lepidus.

Vespasian shrugged.

'Possibly, but Talorcan believes it was something more specific, a preparation of some kind. He thinks perhaps the druids are planning something significant, something that required blood sacrifice on an unusual scale. I initially thought it could be a preamble to another battle, but this discussion suggests it may be something else.'

'If the druids are preparing some grand gesture against Rome,' said Lepidus after a thoughtful pause, 'the Emperor presents an irresistible target.'

'Precisely my concern,' agreed Vespasian. 'Which is why I've ordered increased surveillance of known druidic sites within our territory and deep reconnaissance patrols along the western approaches.'

Lepidus nodded, his mind already calculating the next steps.

'Well, the hour is late,' said Vespasian, 'we should meet again tomorrow, and I'll have my intelligence officers prepare their latest reports on druidic activities. Perhaps together we can identify specific threats before they materialize.'

'Agreed,' said Lepidus, rising from his seat. He said his goodbyes to Plautius and both he and Vespasian walked toward the entrance.

'This scout of yours,' said Lepidus, 'Talorcan. Is he still here in the fort?'

Vespasian nodded.

'He is on a patrol at the moment but due back imminently.'

'I'd like to speak with him,' said Lepidus. 'His perspective on the druidic rituals might prove valuable.'

'Of course,' replied Vespasian.

Walking back to his assigned quarters through the torch-lit compound, Lepidus felt the first stirring of optimism since his arrival. Talorcan's presence was an unexpected advantage, at least one man he could trust and rely on in this increasingly complex situation.

Chapter Sixteen

Terra Silurum

The small vessel pitched gently as it cut through the waters off Britannia's western coast. Three days at sea had settled the Occultum into the rhythm of shipboard life, the constant motion, the confined quarters, the perpetual moisture that seemed to permeate everything and despite the relative calm of their journey thus far, the tension remained palpable among the men. They were sailing into hostile waters on a mission with no room for error.

Seneca stood at the stern, watching the coastline's undulating silhouette slide past. The weather had been unexpectedly favourable, with calm seas and steady winds driving them northward at a pace that exceeded even the captain's optimistic predictions. If conditions held, they would reach Mona ahead of schedule, affording precious extra time for reconnaissance before executing their mission.

Marcus approached, his steady gait adapting unconsciously to the vessel's movement. He joined Seneca at the rail, his gaze settling on the distant shore.

'The weather holds, at least,' he observed quietly.

Seneca nodded.

'For now. But Brennos tells me these waters are known for sudden changes.'

Forward on the deck, Falco sat cross-legged beside Cassius, both men engaged in a game involving knucklebones and small wooden tokens. Nearby, Sica methodically sharpened one of his many blades with practiced precision, the rhythmic scrape of whetstone against metal mingling with the constant sounds of water against hull.

Their contemplation was interrupted by the approaching figure of the Captain. His expression carried the distinct look of a man bearing unwelcome news, his weathered brow furrowed beneath salt-crusted hair.

109

'Tribune,' he said without preamble. 'We have a problem. Our water barrel is empty, we found a crack along the bottom seam. It must have been damaged during loading.'

Seneca's expression hardened, the news representing a significant complication. Fresh water was the most crucial resource for any sea journey, even one relatively close to shore.

'How bad is the damage?' he asked. 'Can it be repaired?'

'My men are already on it,' replied Brennos, 'but that doesn't solve our immediate need. We're have no more drinking water, and without rain we are unlikely to last until we reach Mona.'

Falco abandoned his game and approached, having overheard the conversation.

'How far to Mona from our current position?' he asked.

'A day and a night with this wind,' replied Brennos. 'Maybe less if the gods favour us.'

'Then why stop?' asked Falco, his logic seemingly straightforward. 'We have enough water in our waterskins. Better to press on than delay for repairs.'

Brennos shook his head, he was a man who had survived decades at sea precisely by avoiding such gambles.

'Not possible,' he said firmly. 'The return journey will take longer, we'll be fighting currents and likely headwinds. Without water, we'd never make it back. And we will be unlikely to fresh water on Mona, not without venturing further inland.'

'What do you propose?' asked Seneca.

Brennos moved to the port side, gesturing toward the coastline.

'If my charts are accurate, there's a substantial natural bay ahead.' His weathered finger traced the shape in the air. 'Along its northern curve, a river empties over the cliff edge, creating a waterfall directly onto the rocks below. It's well-known to any who trade in these waters. Well-sheltered from prevailing winds, with enough depth to bring the vessel close to shore. We can anchor safely and go ashore to refill our water supply.'

110

'And the local tribes?' pressed Seneca. 'What reception might we expect?'

Brennos's expression grew more guarded.

'The lands belong to the Ordovices, but there is treaty in place to allow all tribes to use the water supply during times of peace. But you are obviously not Celts so caution would be wise nonetheless.'

Seneca exchanged glances with Marcus, then looked toward the rest of his men, who had gathered around during the discussion. Frustration registered on their faces, the unexpected delay threatening their carefully planned timetable.

'How long will it take?' he asked.

'Half a day to get there and fill the barrel, said Brennos. 'Another half a day to get back on course.'

'Very well,' said Seneca finally. 'Get the barrel fixed as soon as you can. We approach after nightfall. I want to be back at sea before dawn.'

'As you wish,' said Brennos, turning to issue orders to his small crew.

As the vessel's heading shifted slightly eastward toward the coast, Seneca returned to the stern rail. The unplanned diversion represented more than mere inconvenience, it introduced an element of uncertainty into an operation where every detail had been meticulously calculated. Decimus joined him, the veteran's expression revealing he shared these concerns.

'An unfortunate development,' the older man said quietly.

'Indeed,' replied Seneca. 'We'll need to establish a security perimeter while Brennus's men take the barrel to the waterfall.'

'Leave it to me,' said Decimus. 'The less time we spend on that shore, the better.'

As darkness began to settle over the water, the outline of the bay emerged more clearly on the horizon. Seneca observed his men preparing for the night's work, checking weapons, securing any equipment that might make unwanted noise, reviewing their roles in

111

hushed conversations. The easy camaraderie of earlier had vanished, replaced by the focused tension that preceded dangerous operations. If fortune favoured them, they would be back at sea by dawn, resuming their journey to Mona with no one the wiser to their presence. If not... Seneca pushed the thought aside. In their line of work, dwelling on potential failure served no purpose. Better to focus on ensuring success through meticulous execution.

Night finally descended, wrapping the sea and shore in darkness
broken only by faint starlight. The waning moon remained hidden behind clouds, a fortunate circumstance that the men of the Occultum silently acknowledged as they prepared for their unplanned shore excursion.

Captain Brennos guided the fishing vessel with expert precision, keeping his voice low as he issued directions to his small crew. The sound of waves breaking against the shore grew steadily louder as they approached the sheltered bay, navigating by the black silhouette of the coastline against the marginally lighter sky.

'There,' Brennos whispered, pointing toward a luminescence splashing against a rocky shore in the darkness. 'The waterfall. The beach is just to the south.'

Seneca stood at the rail, his eyes straining to pierce the gloom. The absence of visible fires or torchlight along the shore was promising, suggesting no immediate human presence. Still, experience had taught him that absence of evidence was not evidence of absence, particularly in hostile territory.

The crew guided the vessel towards the sandy beach, far enough from shore to avoid grounding but close enough for their purpose. Two sailors lowered a small rowing boat over the side with minimal splashing, before returning to get the repaired barrel. Seneca turned to his men, who had gathered silently at his side.

'Marcus, Decimus, Sica, with me,' he said, his voice barely audible above the lapping water. 'We will go ashore to establish a secure perimeter. No one approaches the water source until we confirm it's clear.'

'What if you encounter resistance?' asked Cassius, adjusting the dagger at his belt.

'We won't engage unless absolutely necessary,' replied Seneca. 'If we're not back or don't signal within half an hour, assume the worst and make your own decisions.'

Falco nodded grimly.

'We'll be watching.'

Without further discussion, Seneca slipped over the side of the vessel, descending into the small boat. The others followed, each movement controlled to minimize noise. Two of Brennos's sailors joined
them, taking their positions at the oars.

Moments later, the small boat pulled away from the fishing vessel, the sailors at the oars using minimal strokes to guide them quietly toward the dark line of the beach. As they neared the shallows, the gentle sound of breaking waves grew more distinct, joined now by the distant rush of the waterfall, a steady roar that would help mask their movements but might also cover the approach of enemies. When the boat could go no further, Seneca turned to the sailors.

'Wait here,' he whispered, 'we'll return when it's secure.' With that, he slipped over the side into waist-deep water, the sudden cold sending a shock through his system. The others followed, moving slowly to avoid unnecessary splashing.

The four Occultum members advanced toward the shore, water resistance giving way to the drag of wet sand beneath their feet. They paused at the water's edge, crouching low as they scanned the darkness before them. The beach formed a narrow crescent, bordered by rocky outcroppings to the north and south. Beyond the sand, deeper shadows suggested vegetation, potential concealment for watchers.

Seneca signalled with his hand, and the men separated. Sica

113

moved like a ghost toward the southern rocks, his slight frame melting into the darkness with unnerving ease. Marcus took the northern approach, Decimus remained centrally positioned, ready to provide support where needed, while Seneca advanced directly inland, probing the boundary where beach met wilder terrain.

The sound of the waterfall grew louder as they moved, its constant roar to their left where the small river cascaded down the cliff face onto the rocks below.

Minutes stretched as each man carefully expanded their secure zone, moving with the caution of hunters in unknown territory. Seneca's eyes had fully adjusted to the darkness now, allowing him to discern subtle variations in the landscape, the outline of scattered boulders, the movement of shoreline vegetation in the gentle breeze, the darker patches where the ground dipped or rose.

No fires glimmered in the distance, no voices carried on the night air, and no footprints marked the damp sand save their own. The stillness was complete, broken only by natural sounds, water against rock, the occasional call of a night bird, the whisper of wind through grasses.

After completing his sweep, Seneca returned to their initial position, where Decimus awaited. Moments later, Sica and Marcus rejoined them, moving with the same silent precision that had marked their departure.

'Clear to the south,' reported Sica, his voice barely audible. 'No signs of recent passage.'

'Northern approach is secure,' added Marcus. 'Old tracks further up, perhaps a hunting party from days ago, but nothing fresh.'

Seneca nodded, weighing the information.

'The waterfall?'

'The path is visible but unused for some time,' said Marcus. 'It's overgrown in sections but passable.'

The absence of immediate threat was promising, but Seneca knew better than to assume complete safety. Tribal hunters moved with skill that rivalled their own, and druidic scouts were known to conceal themselves for days when necessary.

'We'll establish a perimeter,' he decided. 'Sica, take the high ground to the south. Decimus, position yourself where you can watch both the inland approach and the waterfall path, but at the first sign of company, we withdraw immediately. The mission takes priority over water, we can ration if necessary. Marcus, tell the sailors to bring the barrel.'

With the security plan established, Marcus moved back to the waterline, raising his arm in a deliberate signal toward the waiting boat, expecting to see immediate movement toward the shore, but instead, what he witnessed sent a chill through his body.

The small boat was already moving, but away from the shore, not toward it, abandoning their position without explanation. Marcus's brow furrowed in confusion, his mind racing through possibilities. Had they misinterpreted the signal? Had they spotted danger unseen by the shore party?

'Seneca,' he called in a harsh whisper, pointing toward the retreating boat. 'Something's wrong.'

The implications struck both men simultaneously, this was not a misunderstanding. Something deliberate was happening on the fishing vessel, and they were now cut off from both their transportation and their companions.

'Get the others,' Seneca ordered, already moving. 'Something is wrong.'

Chapter Seventeen

The Western Coast

On the fishing vessel, Falco leaned against the rail, his eyes fixed on the distant shore. The darkness rendered the landscape into varying shades of black, but his trained vision had caught Marcus's signal, the raised arm indicating the beach was secure.

'They've cleared the shore,' he said over his shoulder to Cassius, standing beside him. 'They can take the barrel in.' He turned his gaze to the rowing boat but frowned as he saw it was coming towards them instead of towards the shore.

'What's going on?' he muttered, leaning further over the rail to catch their attention. He made a sharp, urgent gesture to return to the shore, but the boat kept coming.

'Something's wrong,' he said quietly, a cold suspicion forming in his mind. He turned from the rail, intending to find Captain Brennos and demand an explanation, only to freeze at the scene before him.

Brennos stood directly behind Cassius, one hand gripping the Roman's hair while the other held a curved knife pressed against his throat. The captain's weathered face, previously open and honest, now wore an expression of cold determination.

'Don't move,' said Brennos in heavily accented Latin. 'His blood will flow before you take a single step.'

Falco's hands instinctively reached for his weapons, but he stopped as the blade pressed harder against Cassius's throat, drawing a thin line of blood that gleamed black in the starlight.

The fourth sailor had emerged from the shadows of the opposite rail, holding a long barbed spike, a fishing gaff designed to hook and drag large catches aboard. Its lethal point was aimed squarely at Falco's chest, the distance between them close enough that the sailor could drive it home before Falco could fully draw his sword.

Rage surged through the ex-gladiator, a familiar battle fury that had served him well in the arena. But the calculating part of his mind, the part that had kept him alive through countless deadly situations, recognized the futility of immediate action. Any move would mean
Cassius's death, certain and swift.

'What is this?' he demanded, his voice a low growl that barely contained his fury.

Brennos smiled thinly.

'Just a simple adjustment to our arrangement,' he replied. 'The chest of silver. Slide it across the deck. *Now.*'

The realization struck Falco with the force of a physical blow. The water barrel's damage had been no accident, it was a deliberate sabotage to force this unplanned stop, to separate the Occultum and leave those remaining aboard vulnerable.

His eyes locked with Cassius's. The other man's expression remained controlled, but a silent communication passed between them, a shared recognition of their predicament and the limited options available.

'The chest,' repeated Brennos, pressing the blade harder. Another drop of blood trickled down Cassius's neck. 'My patience is limited.'

The two sailors from the rowboat had begun climbing back aboard, eliminating any chance Falco had of trying to fight back. His mind raced through their options, searching for any advantage. The shore party was too far away to witness what was happening, much less intervene and by the time they realized something was wrong, it would be too late.

With deliberate slowness, Falco moved toward the small sea chest secured near the mast.

'You won't survive this,' said Falco, his voice deceptively calm as he reached the chest. 'When Seneca discovers your treachery...'

'He won't,' interrupted Brennos. 'By the time your friends

117

realize what's happened, we'll be long gone.'

Falco's hands closed around the wooden chest. It wasn't heavy, perhaps fifteen pounds of silver in total, but represented the lifeline that would have sustained their mission. With barely controlled rage, he slid it across the deck toward Brennos. One of the sailors from the rowboat intercepted it, checking the contents with a quick glance before securing the lid.

'That's all you wanted?' asked Cassius, his voice steady despite
the knife at his throat. 'Silver?'

'It's a fair price,' replied Brennos. 'Your lives for this chest. More generous than most would offer.'

Falco's eyes narrowed.

'So, what happens now?'

The captain's expression hardened.

'Now?' he said, nodding to the water. 'Now you jump.'

'Jump?' Falco repeated.

'Into the sea,' clarified Brennos. 'Both of you. Whether you reach shore alive is no longer my concern.'

Falco stared as the full scope of the betrayal became clear. Not merely theft, but abandonment in hostile territory, leaving six men stranded on enemy shores, hundreds of miles from the nearest Roman outpost.

'Do you think this ends here?' said Falco, his voice a dangerous whisper. 'That we just simply vanish? Rome has a long reach, Brennos, and an even longer memory.'

'I'll take that risk,' said Brennos. 'Enough talk now get into the water or the next sound you hear will be the sound of your friend's blood spattering the deck.'

Falco stared back for a moment longer, burning the captain's face into his memory, but knowing they had been outmanoeuvred, finally turned away and jumped into the sea.

On the shore, Marcus and the others stared out at the barely visible outline of the fishing vessel, its dark silhouette nearly indistinguishable against the night sky.

'They're raising sail,' said Seneca, disbelief evident in his voice as they could make out the shadowy movement of figures on deck.

'We've been betrayed,' said Marcus. 'We should never have trusted them.'

'What about the others?' asked Decimus beside him. 'Have they taken them with them?'

Marcus didn't answer, his attention suddenly fixed on new movement in the water. Two dark forms had appeared in the gap between ship and shore, moving steadily toward the beach with laboured
strokes.

They watched as the figures drew closer, occasionally disappearing beneath the small waves before resurfacing. The unmistakable sound of cursing, creative, fluent, and distinctly military in its vocabulary, reached them as the swimmers neared the shallows.

'Falco,' said Seneca, recognizing both the voice and its colourful content.

Without further discussion, the men waded out into the surf to drag their comrades from the freezing water.

'By all the gods in Rome's temples,' growled Falco as he staggered to his feet in the waist-deep water, his massive frame shaking with cold and fury. 'I'll hunt that treacherous Celt to the ends of the earth and feed him his own entrails!'

Cassius emerged beside him, his movements more controlled but his expression equally grim. A thin line of blood was visible on his throat, gleaming black in the starlight.

'What happened?' demanded Seneca as they reached the beach.

'The bastard betrayed us,' said Falco, his voice shaking with rage. 'The diversion, the cracked water barrel, all a deception to

119

separate us.'

'He had a knife to my throat before we realized what was happening,' added Cassius, one hand touching the shallow cut at his neck. 'They took the silver chest.'

The four men turned to watch as the fishing vessel's silhouette grew smaller against the horizon, its course already taking it well away from the bay and back toward the open sea.

The six men stood in silence as the full implications settled upon them. Stranded deep in hostile territory, hundreds of miles from the nearest Roman outpost, with limited supplies and no means of completing their mission to Mona. The betrayal was not merely theft, it was potentially a death sentence.

'He must have planned this from the beginning,' said Cassius, wringing water from his cloak. 'Watching us, assessing the value of what we carried, identifying the perfect moment to strike.'

'And the perfect location to abandon us,' added Marcus, gesturing to the dark landscape surrounding them. 'Ordovices territory.
Miles from any Roman patrol.'

Seneca turned away from the disappearing vessel, his mind already shifting from shock to strategic assessment.

'Kit check,' he ordered. 'What do we have?'

The men began methodically checking their equipment. Each carried weapons, basic survival tools, and limited rations in their sarcinae, standard procedure for Occultum operatives who never knew when they might be separated from their main supplies, but Falco and Cassius's sarcinae were still on the ship.

'Six gladii, eight daggers, two hunting bows with twenty arrows,' said Marcus as the inventory progressed. 'Flint and steel, medical supplies sufficient for minor injuries, four waterskins, all empty.' He paused. 'Food for perhaps three days if strictly rationed.'

'Maps?' asked Seneca.

'I have the coastal chart,' replied Decimus, producing a waxed leather case from his pack. 'Minimal detail for the interior, but

120

enough to establish our position relative to Roman territory.'

Seneca processed the information.

'We need to move,' he decided eventually. 'Find higher ground before dawn. We'll assess our position in daylight and then decide what to do but before we do anything else, we need water. Let's fill our waterskins, then find somewhere to rest and plan. Sica, take point, Decimus, rear guard.'

As the men gathered their equipment and prepared to move out, Seneca took a final look at the now-empty horizon where their ship had disappeared. The betrayal had cost them dearly, but in his mind, it only reinforced the necessity of their mission. If Brennos had so easily turned against them, how much greater was the threat posed by Raven, who knew not just their resources but their methods, their tactics, their very way of thinking?

With grim determination, he turned away from the sea and followed his men toward the dark, unknown interior of enemy territory. Whatever happened now, he was confident they would deal with it. After all, they were the Occultum…and this was what they did.

Chapter Eighteen

Castra Victrix

The fort at Castra Victrix bustled with activity as Lepidus made his way through the organized chaos toward the stables. A patrol had just returned, their mounts lathered with sweat, equipment caked with the distinctive reddish mud of the northern approaches. Men dismounted with the weary movements of soldiers who had pushed both themselves and their horses hard and grooms rushed forward to take the reins, while officers gathered to receive preliminary reports from the returning scouts.

Lepidus moved among them, his eyes searching for one man in particular. He had never actually met Talorcan but had heard enough about the Belgic scout from Seneca to form a mental image, tall, lean, with the distinctive braided hair of his people and eyes that missed nothing.

Several of the auxiliary scouts gathered near the water troughs, their mixed heritage evident in their appearance and equipment, a blend of Roman military issue and tribal influences. Lepidus studied each face, looking for the one that matched Talorcan's description.

At the far end of the stable yard, somewhat removed from the main group, stood a solitary figure attending to a dappled grey horse. The man worked methodically, checking the animal's hooves with practiced movements, speaking occasional words in a language that was neither Latin nor Britannic. His lean frame and the self-contained manner in which he operated marked him as someone who preferred his own company to that of the boisterous legionaries.

Lepidus approached, noting the details that suggested this might be his target, the intricate knife sheath of Belgic design at his belt, the mixture of Roman and tribal clothing, and most tellingly, the calculating assessment in his eyes as he registered Lepidus's approach without appearing to look up from his task.

'Talorcan?' Lepidus asked, stopping at a respectful distance.

The man straightened. He stood slightly taller than Lepidus, his weathered face bearing the faint blue traces of ritual markings long since faded but never fully gone.

'I am,' he replied, his Latin accented but fluent.

Lepidus extended his arm in the traditional Roman greeting, noting how the scout hesitated fractionally before accepting it, a man who operated in both worlds but belonged fully to neither.

'I am Lepidus,' he introduced himself. 'I believe you've done work for some associates of mine in the past.'

Understanding flickered in Talorcan's eyes.

'You're a long way from Rome, Senator.'

'Indeed,' agreed Lepidus. 'And with good reason. I'd like to discuss certain matters with you, but perhaps somewhere less... public.'

Talorcan glanced around the busy stable yard, where curious eyes had already noted the unusual sight of a senior officer conversing with an auxiliary scout.

'I need to tend my horse and make my report to the Tribune,' he said, 'but after that I will be at my tent preparing food. Behind the eastern stable block.'

Lepidus nodded.

'Until then.'

He turned and walked away, aware of the calculating gaze following him. Men like Talorcan did not trust easily, especially those who moved in the political circles of Rome. Trust would need to be earned through honesty and shared purpose.

Evening settled over the fort, bringing with it the relative quiet that followed the day's labours. Torches flickered along the ramparts where sentries maintained their vigilant watch, and from the central square came the distant sounds of off-duty legionaries dicing or sharing tales of home over watered wine.

Lepidus made his way past the eastern stable block, a small amphora of decent wine tucked beneath his arm. Beyond the main structures, in a small clearing sheltered by the fort's eastern wall, a solitary fire burned. Talorcan sat beside it, methodically turning a small spit on which a plucked duck roasted, its skin crisping in the flames.

The scout looked up as Lepidus approached, gesturing to a simple wooden stool across the fire. No others were present, Lepidus had learned that Talorcan did not share a tent with anyone else, preferring isolation to companionship, a choice that raised eyebrows among Romans who valued communal living but made perfect sense for a man who straddled two worlds.

'Senator,' he acknowledged as Lepidus sat.

'Your directions were adequate,' replied Lepidus, offering the wine. 'From the commander's private stock. Better than the sour vintage the legionaries endure.'

Talorcan accepted the amphora with a nod of thanks, setting it beside the fire before returning his attention to the duck. The bird had been expertly prepared, and the aroma of roasting meat filled the small clearing.

'Duck?' asked Lepidus. Nodding to the spit.

Talorcan nodded.

'Shot at dawn,' he said, 'my arrow took it clean through the neck as it rose from the marsh. Clean death makes for better eating.'

'A huntsman's wisdom,' observed Lepidus.

They sat in companionable silence as the duck finished cooking. Talorcan eventually removed it from the spit, dividing it with practiced efficiency and offering half to Lepidus on a simple wooden platter. The meat was tender and flavourful, seasoned with herbs Lepidus didn't recognize but appreciated nonetheless.

'I understand you recently found a missing Tribune,' said Lepidus eventually.

'What was left of him,' corrected Talorcan. 'Not a death I would wish on my enemies, let alone allies.'

'Plautius mentioned the unusual nature of the killing.'

'Unusual,' echoed Talorcan with a humourless laugh. 'A mild word for such savagery. He was not merely killed, Senator, He was torn apart by something I cannot explain.'

Lepidus leaned forward slightly.

'Something? Not someone?'

Talorcan's pale eyes reflected the firelight as he considered his response.

'I have tracked predators across half the known world, Senator.

I know what bear kills look like, what wolves leave behind. This was... different. The wounds suggested something different to any beast I've encountered.' He paused. 'And yet, the arrangement was deliberate. No animal dismembers its kills in such a manner.'

'Druidic work, then?'

'Possibly, but a ritual beyond what I've witnessed before. And I've seen much of their darker practices.' Talorcan took a careful sip of wine. 'Why does this interest a Roman Senator enough to bring him to this gods-forsaken frontier?'

Lepidus recognized the direct question as a test. Evasion would shut this man down completely; only honesty had any chance of establishing the trust he needed.

'The Occultum have been deployed to find Raven,' he said without preamble.

Talorcan froze, cup halfway to his lips.

'The Occultum are here? In Britannia? I thought they were in Egypt.' His surprise seemed genuine. 'I had no word of their return.'

'Few did,' replied Lepidus. 'And I assume they did not have the time. I understand they set out on a fishing vessel to take them to Isla Mona.'

'By sea?' Talorcan's brow furrowed in thought. 'When did they sail?'

'A few days past, from Rutupiae,' answered Lepidus, 'on a

125

local fishing vessel.'

'So why are you here?' asked Talorcan.

'I have a problem,' said Lepidus, getting straight to the point. 'The Emperor himself will be arriving in Britannia, possibly within weeks. He plans to personally accept the surrender of the tribal kings at Camulodunum, a public spectacle to enhance his political position in Rome. He has tasked me with making sure that the situation is as safe as it can be by using the Occultum to gather intelligence on some of the local tribes. Unfortunately, by the time I got here, they had already deployed.'

'And they cannot be recalled?' asked Talorcan.

'No,' confirmed Lepidus. 'And therein lies my dilemma. I cannot just sit back and do nothing in the hope they return sometime soon. I have to do something.'

'So, you seek alternatives.'

'I need intelligence,' said Lepidus directly. 'Information on druidic movements, on tribal gatherings, on any unusual activity that might signal preparation for an attack or disruption during the Emperor's visit.'

'If you are asking if I can go out there and seek that information,' said Talorcan, 'the answer is yes. But one man with so little time is limited to what he can do. By the time I have earned any trust, the Emperor will already be here.'

'I understand that,' said Lepidus, 'but I am more interested in what we discussed earlier, the remains of the Tribune you found out there on that hill. Even to a man as experienced as you, it seemed particularly brutal and far removed from anything we have seen before. And, being so close to here means it raises questions… questions that I need answered.'

'I have no answers,' said Talorcan. 'I told Vespasian everything I know.'

'You may not have any answers yet,' said Lepidus. 'But is there a chance that whoever or whatever killed him left a trail?'

'I saw some signs,' said Talorcan, thinking back, 'but they led west, deeper inland. Any group of men following would probably not return alive.'

'Ordinary men,' said Lepidus, 'but perhaps men like you and me would have a better chance.'

'You?' asked Talorcan, looking up.

'I may not be quite what I seem,' said Lepidus with a faint smile. 'But assuming we went back out there, do you think we could find out where they went?'

Talorcan set down his cup, his expression becoming more severe.

'What I saw in that clearing,' he said, 'disturbs the natural order. The druids have always walked a line between wisdom and darkness. Under Mordred's leadership, it seems they have finally crossed that line.' He paused, selecting his next words carefully. 'I have no love for Rome's expansion, Senator, but neither can I stand idle while such powers are invoked.' He paused, staring at the powerful man who had travelled halfway around the known world just to ensure the safety of the Emperor. 'So,' he continued at last, 'to answer your question, yes, I believe I can still track them.'

Lepidus nodded, his mind already working through the possibilities this presented. One man could not replace the Occultum, but a scout of Talorcan's calibre might provide the critical intelligence they needed to protect Claudius.

'I need to speak with Vespasian,' he said finally, coming to a decision.

'Vespasian is a soldier's commander,' acknowledged Talorcan with something approaching respect. 'He understands the value of good intelligence, even when it comes through... unconventional channels.'

Lepidus rose from his seat, mentally preparing for the discussion ahead.

'I'll speak with him at first light,' he promised. 'In the meantime, consider what you might need for such an undertaking.'

Talorcan nodded, remaining seated by his fire as Lepidus prepared to depart.

'Senator,' he called softly as Lepidus reached the edge of the firelight. 'One thing more.'

Lepidus paused, turning back.

'If the Occultum did indeed sail for Mona, and if they reach it, they will probably find more than just Raven waiting for them. Mordred has been gathering his forces for months so whatever he plans, it comes soon.'

'All the more reason to move quickly,' replied Lepidus. 'Rest well, Talorcan. Tomorrow brings new purpose.'

As he walked back through the darkened fort toward his quarters, Lepidus felt the first stirrings of hope since arriving in Britannia. The situation remained dire, the odds against them substantial, but in Talorcan he had found a potential ally whose unique skills might yet salvage their increasingly precarious position.

Chapter Nineteen

The West Coast

Nestled deep within the forest's embrace, the men of the Occultum formed a tight circle, their bodies pressed against the damp earth. Each man lay on his belly, heads inward toward the centre, shoulders touching in the confined space. Above them, the single tent they carried on their journey had been carefully unfurled, not for shelter against the elements, but as a shield to prevent prying eyes seeing the candlelight beneath. The worn canvas draped over their hunched forms like a protective skin, creating a cramped sanctuary where six hardened operatives now conferred in hushed tones.

In the centre, a single candle's flame danced precariously, casting trembling shadows across their weathered faces. The light was barely sufficient, but they dared not risk anything brighter. Seneca traced his finger along the crude map spread between them, the yellowed parchment crinkling softly under his touch.

'It looks like there is a ridge to the east,' he said. 'That suggests unfarmed land which in turn means denser forests. We'll move there before first light, go to ground and assess our options more thoroughly come nightfall.'

'And the mission?' asked Decimus, giving voice to the question hanging unspoken between them.

A heavy silence fell over the group. The betrayal had not merely stranded them, it had potentially derailed their primary objective, the elimination of Raven. Isla Mona lay many miles to the north on the far side of the bay, and even if they could reach the coastal approach, crossing the strait without a vessel would create a problem. Seneca looked down at the map.

'We are here,' he said, his voice barely audible above the gentle rustling of leaves in the night breeze. 'Based on the coastline and the river configuration, we've landed in territory controlled by the western Ordovices.'

129

The men studied the map intently, committing its features to memory. In their line of work, a man's survival often depended on his ability to navigate without written guidance, which could be lost or damaged at critical moments.

'Isla Mona lies here,' continued Seneca, his finger moving northward to indicate the island that represented their original objective. 'Between us and it stands this bay and then a mountain range.' He traced the craggy line that bisected the western peninsula. 'Difficult terrain under ideal circumstances. Potentially deadly given our current resources.'

'And beyond the mountains?' asked Marcus.

'A strait of water separates the mainland from Mona,' replied Seneca. 'it's not a great distance though the currents are said to be treacherous.'

Decimus leaned closer, his weathered face creased with concentration.

'And our own forces? Where would they be now?'

Seneca's finger moved eastward across the map, traversing a considerable distance before stopping at a river marking.

'The Tamesis crossing was around here. By now, they've likely advanced toward Camulodunum.' His hand shifted slightly northward. 'If they've maintained their pace, the Second and Twentieth would be somewhere in this region, establishing forward camps as they go.'

The map told a stark story, the vast distance between their current position eliminating any hope of Roman support.

'So,' said Seneca, 'we now face a choice. We can maintain our original mission, proceed overland to Mona, and attempt to eliminate Raven as ordered.' He paused, allowing the implications to sink in. 'Or we can cancel the mission, make our way eastward back to friendly territory, reorganize properly, and develop a new approach.'

'We do not have the supplies for either option,' said Cassius.

'We do not,' admitted Seneca. 'But we can forage and steal

what we need, but that would be easier if we go east. We'd be moving through areas more heavily populated, but also areas where Roman patrols might extend, at least in their outer ranges. It is by far the safer option. No one knows we are here and with care, we could reach Roman lines without engagement.'

'And the northern route to Mona?' asked Falco.

'Shorter in distance but significantly more challenging,' replied Seneca. 'The mountains are formidable, the tribes beyond them particularly hostile to Rome. And even if we reach the strait, we will still need to find a way across to the island itself. Even if we reach the island undetected, even if we somehow locate Raven and eliminate him, the moment the druids know he is dead, they will know we are here and we would be hunted from Mona to the Tamesis with no extraction plan.'

The gravity of this assessment settled over the group. The Occultum were no strangers to dangerous missions, but they typically operated with meticulous planning, with contingencies for extraction, with the reassurance of potential support if things went catastrophically wrong. Their current situation offered none of these safeguards.

'Questions?' asked Seneca, looking around the circle.

Decimus shifted slightly, his veteran's instincts prompting him to voice what younger men might hesitate to say.

'The mission parameters have changed dramatically,' he observed. 'No reasonable commander would expect us to maintain the original objective under these circumstances.'

'True,' acknowledged Seneca. 'Yet Raven's threat to Roman operations remains unchanged. Each day he lives, he provides intelligence to Mordred, intelligence that costs Roman lives.'

'What about a compromise?' suggested Cassius. 'We make for the Roman lines, but along a route that gathers intelligence on druidic movements. We may not eliminate Raven directly, but we could undermine his effectiveness by uncovering the druids' intentions.'

'There's another factor,' added Marcus quietly. 'Time. If we choose the eastern route, we might reach Roman forces within two weeks, assuming no major obstacles. The northern route to Mona, including the mountain crossing and finding passage across the strait... that could take significantly longer.'

'With correspondingly diminished supplies,' noted Falco.

Silence fell as each man contemplated the options before them. The decision would not be made lightly, lives depended on it, possibly including those of Romans who might die from intelligence Raven provided while they made their way back to safety.

'I won't command this,' said Seneca finally. 'Each of us must decide for himself. We've served together too long for me to simply order men to their potential deaths without allowing them voice in the matter.'

This departure from strict military hierarchy was characteristic of the Occultum's unique operational structure, a unit that functioned on mutual respect and shared commitment rather than blind obedience. In extreme circumstances, Seneca had always sought consensus rather than imposing his will, recognizing that men who chose their path fought more effectively than those merely following orders.

'I say we maintain the mission,' said Falco unexpectedly. The massive ex-gladiator had seemed the most affected by their betrayal, yet now his voice carried firm resolve. 'We were sent to kill a traitor. Nothing has changed except the method of our approach.'

'The risk is substantial,' cautioned Marcus, ever the tactical thinker. 'But the need remains urgent. I support continuing to Mona.'

'As do I,' said Cassius.

'What about you, Sica,' said Falco. 'You have remained silent throughout this. What are your thoughts?'

'The north is the hardest option,' he said quietly. 'That way lies danger and probable death. The east is easier and far safer.' He paused. 'I have made my decision.'

'Which is?' said Falco.

'Since when have we chosen the easier route?' said Sica eventually. 'I say go north.'

All eyes turned to Decimus, the oldest among them, whose experience often provided the final, decisive perspective. The veteran considered for a long moment before speaking.

'In my time with this unit,' he said carefully, 'and with others like this, I've seen missions abandoned for less compelling reasons than our current predicament. Yet I've also seen this group accomplish objectives that seemed utterly impossible.' He paused, looking directly at Seneca. 'I will follow whatever course you set, Seneca. My sword remains yours, as it has been since the beginning.'

Seneca absorbed their input, the weight of the decision settling across his shoulders. Six men, deep in hostile territory, choosing a path that might lead to all their deaths, yet unified in their determination to complete their assigned task despite circumstances that would have
broken lesser units.

'Then we proceed to Mona,' he said finally. 'We cross the mountains, find passage across the strait, locate Raven, and eliminate him as ordered.' His voice took on an edge of steel. 'And then, by whatever means necessary, we return to Roman territory.'

The decision made, the men's focus shifted immediately to practical considerations, the route they would take, the resources they needed to acquire, the methods they would employ to move unseen through lands where every Roman was an enemy to be killed on sight.

As they bent over the map again, tracing potential paths through the forbidding terrain ahead, each man silently acknowledged the gravity of their choice. They had chosen the harder path, the more dangerous mission, the objective that most directly served Rome's interests rather than their own survival, but in doing so, they had once again proven why they had joined the Occultum. To reach the inaccessible targets where others dare not go, to accomplish what most others dare not attempt, and to serve with a dedication that transcended normal bonds of loyalty or duty. Whether that dedication would lead to success or death remained to be seen but for now, they focused solely on the next step of a journey that would test every skill, every resource, and every ounce of determination they possessed.

Chapter Twenty

Isla Mona

The small dwelling assigned to Veteranus on Isla Mona kept out the persistent coastal wind, but did nothing to silence the turmoil raging within his mind. He sat on the edge of the simple pallet that served as his bed, staring at the embers of the dying fire without truly seeing them. Sleep had eluded him for days now, his thoughts consumed by the extraordinary revelation Mordred had shared.

The obvious answer had been an immediate, unequivocal refusal. To betray Rome, to align himself with her enemies, such actions would have once been unthinkable. For years he had been a weapon of the empire, honed and deployed against those who threatened Roman interests. Yet as the days passed, doubt had begun to creep in, subtle at first, then with increasing insistence. What loyalty did he truly owe to Rome? He had served her without question, carried out the empire's secret violence with ruthless efficiency. He had waded through blood in Rome's name, silenced voices that needed silencing, and eliminated threats both real and merely perceived.

And how had Rome repaid such service? With rejection and abandonment. His own brothers in the Occultum had turned their backs when he needed them most and those who had once relied upon him to murder Rome's enemies had ultimately discarded him, sentencing him to death as though his years of sacrifice meant nothing.

Now Mordred, a man whose existence he had been completely unaware of until his capture, offered something unprecedented: not merely an opportunity for revenge, but a chance to change the course of history itself. The plan the druid had outlined was audacious to the point of madness, yet possessed a terrible logic that Veteranus, with his extensive knowledge of Roman vulnerabilities, recognized as potentially viable.

He rose from the pallet and paced the small confines of his dwelling. Through the single window, he could see the village stretching toward the sea, fires glowing in hearths, people moving about their evening routines. These were not the barbarians Rome's propaganda depicted, mindless savages bent on violence and destruction. They were families, craftsmen, hunters, farmers. People defending their way of life against an empire that tolerated no alternatives to its vision of civilization.

For weeks, Veteranus had immersed himself in their daily life, observing their councils, their rituals, their methods of resolving disputes. He had witnessed tenderness between parents and children, fierce debates where reason prevailed over strength, and kindnesses extended to the weak or elderly that would have surprised many Romans who believed these 'barbarians' simply exposed their infirm to die.

And yes, he had also seen their darker aspects, blood sacrifices that Rome would condemn while ignoring the rivers of blood that flowed in its own arenas. Violence in defence of honour that Rome would label barbaric while conveniently forgetting the brutal suppression of those who dared resist its own expansion. The complexity of it all had chipped away at certainties he had once held immutable.

'Rome brings order,' he murmured to himself, repeating the justification that had sustained him through decades of service. 'Civilization. Law.'

But at what cost? The question haunted him now. Rome's peace was built on broken bodies, its civilization erected over the ruins of older cultures, its laws imposed without consultation or consent.

His thoughts turned to the tattoo on his shoulder. The scarab, symbol of rebirth, of transformation, of emerging into new life. The very mark Mordred claimed linked him to druidic bloodlines.

He had dismissed it initially as manipulation, a convenient

fiction to justify his capture and attempted conversion. Yet the evidence Mordred had presented, genealogies preserved through oral tradition, the distinctive shape of the scarab itself with markings specific to a particular family group, had begun to erode his scepticism.

What if it were true? What if his connection to this land and these people ran deeper than he had ever suspected? What if his entire life in service to Rome had been the true betrayal, a betrayal of his own heritage? The question was maddening in its implications, and he had spent many sleepless nights turning over what path to take, weighing options, calculating consequences, searching for certainty in a situation
where none existed.

In the end, the decision crystallized not around abstract loyalties or historical grudges, but around a simple truth: Rome had discarded him. Whatever he chose now would be for himself alone.

With sudden resolution, Veteranus reached for his cloak, his decision made. He left the hut and moved through the village, past the sacred oak where druids gathered for council, beyond the smithy where weapons were forged for the coming conflict and toward the longhouse, its high thatched roof visible above all other structures. Torchlight flickered from within, casting elongated shadows through the doorway where two warriors stood guard. They straightened as he approached, their expressions neutral but eyes alert.

'I would speak with Mordred,' said Veteranus.

The guards exchanged glances, then stepped aside to allow him passage. The timing of his arrival was clearly expected, perhaps even anticipated.

The interior of the longhouse felt cavernous after the confines of his dwelling, its high ceiling lost in shadow above the central hearth. At the far end of the hall, Mordred stood in conversation with Raven, their heads bent over what appeared to be maps spread across a large oak table. Both men looked up as Veteranus entered, their discussion falling silent. For a moment, the only sound was the crackling of the fire and the distant sound of a mournful owl.

In this moment of transition, poised between rejection and acceptance of Mordred's offer, Veteranus felt strangely calm. The turmoil that had plagued him for weeks had resolved into clarity. Whatever came next, he had chosen his path.

When Veteranus reached the table, Mordred finally broke the silence.

'Well,' he said, 'have you made your choice?'

Veteranus met his gaze steadily, no longer searching for deception or manipulation in those ancient eyes. He nodded once, decisively, and spoke just two words that would irrevocably alter his path forward:

'Teach me.'

The following night, Veteranus followed Mordred and Raven along a narrow path that wound through ancient oaks. Torches flickered at intervals, casting grotesque shadows that seemed to reach for him with elongated fingers. His mind was focused, his senses heightened by the knowledge that tonight, Mordred would reveal the secret that lay at the heart of his plans for Britannia.

They walked in silence, the only sounds their footfalls on the forest floor and the occasional night bird calling from the darkness above. Veteranus recognized the path, they were heading back to the clearing where he had witnessed the boy's sacrifice, a memory that still visited him in dreams, filling him with horror and doubt about the path he had chosen.

As they crested a small rise, the clearing came into view. It appeared transformed from his previous visit. The pit where the child had died so terribly, was now ringed with four wooden crates positioned at equal intervals around its circumference. A circular stone slab, perhaps three feet across, stood at the centre where before there had been only bare earth.

Torches surrounded the clearing, their flames unnaturally steady against the raised earthen bank surrounding the pit.

Mordred halted at the edge, turning to face Veteranus directly.

'Tonight, you join us truly,' said the druid, his lined face solemn in the flickering light. 'But first, you must prove both your trust and your courage.'

Veteranus nodded, though uncertainty flickered within him. He had made his choice to align with Mordred, yet something in the druid's tone sent a chill through him that had nothing to do with the night air.

'What must I do?' he asked.

Mordred gestured toward the stone slab at the centre of the pit. 'You will stand upon the stone,' he said. 'And no matter what happens, no matter what you see or hear or feel, you must not move from it. Not even a single step. To do so means immediate death.' His eyes held Veteranus's with unflinching intensity. 'Do you understand?'

'I understand,' replied Veteranus.

'Then proceed,' said Mordred, stepping back to allow him passage.

Veteranus approached the pit's edge, peering down into the darkness below. A crude ladder of wooden rungs had been set against the earthen wall. He descended carefully, the smell of damp soil and something more primal, a musky animal scent, growing stronger with each step.

When his feet touched the ground, he turned toward the stone slab. It seemed smaller now that he stood before it, its surface rough-hewn and stained with substances he preferred not to identify. With deliberate control, he stepped onto it, feeling the cold stone through the thin soles of his boots.

From this vantage point, he could see the four crates more clearly. Each was approximately four feet high, constructed of heavy timber bound with iron. Between the rough-cut slats, he glimpsed movement, shifting shadows that suggested something alive waited within.

Above, Mordred and Raven had retreated from the pit's edge. Their place was taken by a gathering crowd, warriors and druids forming a human circle around the excavation, their faces expressionless as they looked down upon him. Their numbers grew steadily until it seemed the entire settlement had assembled to witness whatever was to come.

The soft beating of drums began somewhere in the distance, a rhythmic pulsation that seemed to match the quickening of his heart. Low chanting joined the percussion, words in a language older than any Veteranus recognized, rising and falling like the tide against Mona's rocky shores.

Standing on the stone, suddenly very aware of its limited dimensions, Veteranus felt doubt creep into his mind. He had faced death many times in service to Rome, on battlefields, in dark alleys, during covert missions behind enemy lines. He had killed without hesitation when duty demanded it. Yet this was different, a ritual whose purpose remained obscure, whose outcome he could not predict or control.

The sounds from the crates grew more insistent, scratching, shifting, an occasional thump as something substantial moved within the wooden confines. The chanting above increased in volume and tempo, the drums beating faster, the participants swaying slightly as they gazed down at him. The torchlight caught the gleam of their eyes, reflecting back an anticipation that was neither kind nor merciful.

Suddenly, the noise stopped and the absolute silence that followed was more terrifying than the sounds had been, a vacuum of expectation that pressed against his ears like physical pressure. In that silence, Mordred's voice rang out, a single word that sliced through the night air with dreadful finality.

'Begin.'

The word had barely faded when the front of the first crate crashed open.

Chapter Twenty-One

Castra Victrix

The room fell silent as Lepidus finished outlining his plan. The oil lamps cast flickering shadows across the detailed maps spread over the central table, where three of Rome's most senior men in Britannia stood in a tense triangle. General Plautius maintained his characteristic composure, his weathered features revealing little. Vespasian, however, made no attempt to hide his shock and disapproval.

'Absolutely not,' Vespasian said firmly, breaking the silence. 'I cannot, will not, authorize a plan that puts a Senator of Rome directly in harm's way. Not without a heavily armed guard, at minimum.'

Lepidus shook his head, having anticipated this reaction.

'A heavily armed guard defeats the entire purpose. This requires stealth, not force.'

'Then send Talorcan alone,' countered Vespasian. 'He's our most experienced scout, perfectly capable of gathering the intelligence you seek without risking a patrician life.'

'Talorcan is skilled, but this mission requires more than simple reconnaissance,' replied Lepidus. 'It demands someone who can interpret what they find in the context of Roman security, someone who understands the political implications, someone who can make immediate decisions without referring back to command.'

Vespasian stepped back from the table in frustration.

'Let me understand exactly what you're proposing,' he said, his tone making clear he found the plan absurd. 'You, a Roman Senator, accompanied only by Talorcan, intend to return to the site where that horrific sacrifice was discovered, then follow whatever trail you find into gods-know-what territory, controlled by tribes who would consider your head the greatest trophy imaginable.'

'Precisely,' confirmed Lepidus calmly.

'All this on the mere hope that you might discover something useful about druidic intentions before the Emperor arrives,' continued Vespasian. 'Meanwhile, we're supposed to sit here and wait for the Occultum to magically reappear, having somehow completed their mission to Mona and returned across hundreds of miles of hostile territory.'

'We cannot afford to simply wait and hope,' said Lepidus. 'The Emperor's fleet is getting ready as we speak. If there is a threat being prepared, we must identify it now, while there's still time to counter it.'

Vespasian turned to Plautius, appealing to the senior commander's authority.

'General, surely you see the madness in this proposal. Even if we allow that a Senator might venture beyond our lines, which I strongly oppose, he wouldn't last a day in those territories, not even with his background as a Legatus.'

Plautius remained silent, his gaze moving between the two men with the measured assessment of a commander weighing difficult options.

Lepidus sighed deeply.

'A century of mounted auxiliaries would only draw attention. We need to move quietly, observe without being observed.' He looked directly at Plautius. 'I believe we should tell him.'

Vespasian's eyes narrowed.

'Tell me what?'

Plautius nodded almost imperceptibly, giving permission for something clearly discussed beforehand.

'Before I entered the Senate,' began Lepidus, his voice taking on a different quality, 'I was indeed a Legatus, as you know. But before that, I served for nearly fifteen years as an officer in the Exploratores in Germania.'

'The frontier scouts?' Vespasian's surprise was evident.

'Not just any scouts,' continued Lepidus. 'I specialized in deep penetration missions behind enemy lines. My unit operated independently, sometimes for months without contact, gathering intelligence on tribal movements, eliminating specific threats, disrupting enemy preparations.'

Vespasian stared at him with new eyes, reassessing the man who stood before him. The refined Senator had suddenly transformed in his perception, revealing unexpected dimensions beneath the political exterior.

'It was my experience in those operations,' Lepidus continued, 'that eventually led to the formation of the Occultum. I recognized the need for a permanent unit capable of undertaking missions beyond the capabilities of conventional forces, beyond even what the regular Exploratores could accomplish.'

'You created the Occultum?' asked Vespasian, disbelief colouring his voice.

'I conceived it, argued for its establishment, and initially trained its first members,' confirmed Lepidus. 'And although I eventually moved on to more... conventional roles in service to Rome, they remained under my control. '

Vespasian turned away, pacing the length of the room as he processed this revelation. 'So, you're not merely a Senator playing at soldier. You actually have experience in this type of operation.'

'Extensive experience,' said Lepidus. 'I know what I'm getting into. I've operated in similar circumstances before, though admittedly, some years have passed since I was last in the field.'

'Why not simply tell me this from the beginning?' demanded Vespasian.

'The Occultum's origins remain classified at the highest levels,' replied Lepidus. 'Few know of my personal connection to the unit. It's a detail I reveal only when absolutely necessary, and only to those with direct need to know.'

Vespasian continued his pacing, his tactical mind now engaged with the practicalities rather than the propriety of the Senator's proposal.

'Even with your experience, the risk remains significant. If you were captured...'

'I would not be taken alive,' interrupted Lepidus with calm certainty. 'That was always our operating principle, and it remains sound.'

The three men fell silent, the weight of the decision hanging in the air between them. The mission Lepidus proposed carried extraordinary risk, even for a man with his background. Yet the alternative, waiting passively while unknown threats developed, carried its own dangers. Finally, Plautius spoke, his voice carrying the decisive authority that had made him Rome's most trusted general in Britannia.

'If this is what you believe must be done, Senator, then so be it.' He turned to Vespasian. 'The decision is made. Our role now is to provide whatever support Lepidus requires to maximize his chances of success.'

Vespasian did not protest further. His military discipline prevailed over personal reservations.

'What do you need from us?' he asked eventually, turning back to Lepidus.

'Supplies for two men,' replied Lepidus. 'Local clothing, weapons typical of border merchants, dried provisions that can be consumed without cooking. And most importantly, detailed maps of the territories beyond our current lines, whatever intelligence you've gathered on paths, waterways, settlements.'

Plautius nodded.

'When do you intend to depart?'

'Tomorrow, before dawn,' said Lepidus. 'Talorcan knows the route to the sacrifice site. From there, we follow whatever trail presents itself.'

'And if you find nothing?' asked Vespasian.

'Then we continue north and west, toward areas of known druidic activity,' answered Lepidus. 'Somewhere in those territories, preparations are being made, for what, exactly, we don't yet know. But we must discover it before the Emperor arrives.'

'How will you report back?' asked Plautius, ever focused on practical considerations.

'We won't, unless we discover something of immediate significance,' said Lepidus. 'Any attempt to maintain communication increases our risk of discovery. We'll return when we have actionable intelligence or when time constraints demand it.'

Vespasian shook his head, still struggling with the unprecedented nature of the mission.

'A Roman Senator operating as a covert scout in enemy territory. The Senate would have apoplexy if they knew.'

'Then we must ensure they never know,' replied Plautius firmly. He turned back to Lepidus. 'I'll have the quartermaster prepare your supplies immediately. They'll be delivered to your quarters tonight. Is
there anything else you require?'

'Nothing,' said Lepidus.

'May Fortune favour your endeavour, Senator,' replied Plautius, 'Rome has few men of your... diverse capabilities.'

As the meeting concluded and Lepidus departed to make his final preparations, Vespasian remained behind with Plautius. The two commanders stood in silence for a moment, contemplating the extraordinary turn of events.

'Did you know?' asked Vespasian finally. 'About his background with the Exploratores?'

'Rumours only, until recently,' admitted Plautius. 'His reputation as a Legatus was impressive enough, his campaigns in Illyricum were textbook operations. But this deeper history... it explains much about his approach to certain matters.'

'What if he doesn't return,' said Vespasian.

'Then we will face that problem when it arises,' replied Plautius. 'For now, we focus on preparing for the Emperor's arrival while Lepidus pursues his own path. Each of us serves Rome in the manner best suited to our abilities.'

Outside, darkness had settled over the fort. Beyond its wooden walls lay territories where Rome's authority ended and ancient powers held sway, territories that would soon see a Roman Senator moving through them with the practiced stealth of a man returning to the shadows he had once called home.

Chapter Twenty-Two

Castra Victrix

Dawn had not yet broken over the fort when the eastern gate creaked open just wide enough to allow a small party to pass through. In the grey half-light, two dozen mounted auxiliaries stood in formation, their faces grim beneath leather helmets, spears held upright in a forest of deadly points. The men sat straight-backed on their mounts, each rider the product of years of disciplined training, each horse carefully selected for strength and steadiness in difficult terrain.

Apart from the main group stood Talorcan, holding the reins of two more horses. The scout's appearance had transformed overnight, gone was any trace of Roman influence in his attire. He now wore the practical garb of a border tribesman: leather breeches, a rough-spun tunic of muted browns, and a cloak of undyed wool fastened with a simple bronze pin. Only the quality of his weapons hinted at his connection to Rome, the sword at his hip and the knife in his boot were of legionary steel, though their sheaths had been carefully disguised with local designs.

The horses he held were similarly prepared, their military saddles replaced with simpler versions typical of border merchants. Attached to each mount was a sarcina, the standard field pack used by Roman scouts, though these too had been modified to appear as the travel bundles of itinerant traders rather than military equipment.

From the direction of the commander's quarters came two figures, Lepidus and Vespasian, deep in conversation. The Senator, like Talorcan, had undergone a transformation. Gone were the finer robes of an officer, replaced by practical clothing similar to the scout's.

'This remains, in my professional assessment, an unnecessary risk,' said Vespasian as they approached the waiting horses. 'We could send a full cohort to sweep the area, establish a proper

147

presence.'

'A cohort would alert every tribal scout within ten miles,' replied Lepidus, 'and whatever is happening would simply move deeper into territory we cannot reach.' He gestured toward the distant hills, barely visible in the pre-dawn gloom. 'These new rituals occurring so close to the route the Emperor will take when he arrives represent a potential threat that must be investigated thoroughly, not merely pushed back temporarily.'

Vespasian did not immediately respond. As a military commander, he understood the tactical logic, yet as a Roman officer responsible for the safety of those under his authority, including, technically, a visiting Senator, the mission offended his sense of proper protocol.

'Without the Occultum, Talorcan and I are the only men with sufficient experience to do this,' continued Lepidus, his tone softening slightly. 'Two men can go where a century cannot, see what others would miss and withdraw without engagement if necessary.'

They reached the horses, where Talorcan acknowledged them with a slight nod, his pale eyes already focused on the territory beyond the gate, mind mapping the journey that lay ahead.

Lepidus accepted the reins of his mount, checking the sarcina's fastenings with practiced hands. The ease with which he performed this simple soldier's task betrayed his unusual background, this was a man who had indeed spent years in field conditions, despite his current Senatorial status.

Vespasian watched with grudging respect as Lepidus mounted without assistance, settling into the saddle with the unconscious comfort of an experienced horseman. The commander's assessment of the Senator had undergone significant revision since learning of his connection to the Occultum.

'The auxiliaries will escort you as far as the site where Talorcan discovered the remains of the Tribune,' Vespasian said, his voice now carrying the formal tone of a commander issuing final orders. 'They will wait there precisely three days for your return.

148

After that, they withdraw to safer territory. From that point forward, you are entirely on your own. No reinforcements, no extraction. May Fortune favour you. With that, he stepped back and watched as Lepidus turned his horse to follow the patrol out of the gate.

The patrol headed west, moving through increasingly wild country. Talorcan rode at the front, his keen eyes constantly scanning the terrain ahead, while Lepidus positioned himself just behind the scout. The mounted auxiliaries followed in tight formation, their discipline evident in their spacing and vigilance.

Unlike their original plan, there was no attempt at disguise or subterfuge, they rode openly under Roman colours, spear points glinting in the morning sun, the unmistakable presence of imperial power projecting into contested territory. The display was intentional, a show of confidence and strength that would serve its purpose for what was to come.

As they rode, Talorcan provided Lepidus with a running commentary on the lands they traversed.

'We're passing through the traditional hunting grounds of the eastern Ordovices,' he explained as they crossed a shallow stream. 'The tribes here practice different burial customs than those to the south. They place their dead in trees, platforms built among the highest branches. They believe it allows the spirits easier passage to the sky realm.'

'And their attitude toward Rome?' asked Lepidus.

'Cautious hostility,' replied Talorcan. 'They've avoided direct confrontation thus far, preferring to retreat deeper into their territories when Roman patrols approach. But that doesn't mean they've accepted Roman presence.' He gestured toward a distant hilltop. 'Their scouts watch us even now.'

Lepidus followed Talorcan's gaze and caught a brief flash of movement, a figure silhouetted momentarily against the sky before disappearing again.

'Will they attack?' Lepidus asked, his hand instinctively

moving closer to his sword.

Talorcan shook his head.

'Not a force this size, not in daylight. They respect strength and calculate odds carefully. But they will track us, note our direction. That information will spread through their network of runners faster than we can travel.'

By midday, they had covered significant ground, moving from open meadowlands into more densely forested terrain. The Centurion called a brief halt to rest the horses and allow the men to take water and a simple meal. Throughout the break, guards remained posted in a defensive perimeter, eyes fixed on the surrounding forest.

As they resumed their journey, the signs of observation grew more frequent, occasional glimpses of tribal scouts on ridgelines, the distant sound of signal horns carrying messages across valleys, once even the deliberate placement of a severed deer's head on their path, its eyes replaced with red berries in what Talorcan explained was a warning symbol.

When dusk approached, the Centurion selected a defensible clearing for their night camp. The site offered good visibility in all directions, with a small stream providing fresh water and natural barriers on two sides. The men established their positions with practiced efficiency, placing the horses at the centre of the camp where they would be both protected and serve as an additional alarm system if startled.

'Half the men will remain on watch at all times,' the Centurion informed Lepidus. 'We'll rotate shifts through the night.'

Lepidus nodded his approval and as darkness fell, the men ate a sparse meal, speaking in hushed tones. Even laughter was muted, aware as they were of unseen eyes monitoring their every movement from the surrounding wilderness.

Talorcan approached Lepidus as he was finishing his meal.

'Tomorrow we'll reach the sacrifice site before nightfall,' he said quietly. 'The terrain grows more difficult from here, narrower paths, denser forest, more places for ambush.'

'And the tribal presence?'

'Will increase,' confirmed Talorcan. 'We're approaching areas they consider sacred. Our previous patrol was eliminated precisely because they ventured too close to ritually important sites.' He paused, considering his next words carefully. 'The Centurion is competent, but he doesn't understand what truly threatens us here.'

Lepidus studied the scout's face in the dim light.

'And what is that?'

'Not all enemies can be seen or fought with conventional weapons,' replied Talorcan cryptically. 'Some threats require... different approaches.'

The night passed without incident, though few men managed much sleep. The darkness surrounding their camp seemed alive with subtle sounds, movements that might have been animals or men, distant chanting carried on the breeze, once even the unmistakable growl of some large predator that silenced all other forest noises for several minutes.

At first light, they broke camp and continued westward. The signs of observation were now obvious and frequent, deliberate markers left on their path, tribal symbols carved freshly into tree trunks, occasional glimpses of painted warriors moving parallel to their route just beyond effective bowshot.

As Talorcan had predicted, they reached the site of the Tribune's death in the late afternoon. The clearing stood empty now, no visible evidence remaining of the ritual slaughter that had occurred there. Yet something in the atmosphere, a heaviness, an unnatural stillness, marked it as different from the surrounding forest.

The Centurion ordered his men to establish a camp, positioning sentries at greater distances than usual to provide early warning of approach. As the auxiliaries busied themselves with their tasks, Lepidus approached him.

'Centurion,' he said, quietly, 'I need to speak with you privately.'

The officer followed Lepidus to a position slightly removed from the main group, where Talorcan joined them. Once certain they could not be overheard, Lepidus outlined his plan.

'When darkness falls, Talorcan and I will depart,' he explained. 'Your men should maintain normal camp activities, talking, movement, routine guard changes.

The Centurion's brow furrowed slightly.

'Will you be taking your horses?'

'No,' replied Lepidus. 'You will take them back with you but make them look like they are carrying packs. This will maintain your apparent strength while allowing us to disappear.'

'What about your return? Vespasian ordered us to wait three days.'

'The plan has changed.' said Lepidus. 'At first light, return to camp and tell Vespasian I gave you a direct order to withdraw. I take full responsibility for any consequences.'

The Centurion nodded, though concern showed clearly on his face.

'It shall be done as you command, Senator.'

Throughout what was left of the day, the men maintained their vigilant watch while Lepidus and Talorcan made subtle preparations, adjusting their sarcinae to contain only the most essential items, ensuring their weapons were readily accessible and studying the surrounding terrain for the best route of departure.

As darkness fell, the camp settled into its nighttime routine. Men sat in small groups, cleaning equipment or engaging in quiet conversation while guards paced their assigned perimeters, occasionally challenging shadows that proved to be nothing more than wind-stirred branches or nocturnal animals until eventually, several hours after full darkness, Lepidus and Talorcan slipped into the deepest shadows at the edge of the clearing.

Chapter Twenty-Three

The Western Coast

The sparse meal of dried meat did little to fill their bellies, but the Occultum had survived on far less in past operations. They ate methodically, preserving every morsel, carefully storing the remainder in their sarcinae.

As darkness settled more completely over the landscape, Seneca gave the signal to move out. Their path would hug the coastline, following the sweeping curve of the bay to the northeast before eventually turning inland toward the mountain range visible in the distance. Beyond those formidable peaks lay Isla Mona, and Raven.

'Sica, take point,' ordered Seneca quietly.

The Syrian scout nodded and melted into the darkness ahead, his slight frame disappearing so completely it seemed the night had simply absorbed him. The others followed at carefully maintained distances, close enough to maintain visual contact, far enough apart that a single ambush couldn't ensnare them all.

They moved with the disciplined stealth that had earned the Occultum its fearsome reputation among those few who knew of its existence. Each man placed his feet with deliberate precision, testing the ground before committing weight, freezing at the slightest unusual sound, communicating with subtle hand signals when necessary. Their progress was slow but steady, gradually eating away at the considerable distance that separated them from their objective.

The coastline provided both guidance and caution, the rhythmic sound of waves against the shore offered navigational certainty in the darkness, yet the open terrain along the water's edge left them more exposed than they preferred. Seneca had chosen a compromise path that kept the sea within sight and earshot while utilizing whatever cover the coastal vegetation offered.

As they rounded a rocky promontory, the bay opened wider

before them. Across its dark expanse, they could make out the distant silhouette of mountains against the star-filled sky, a jagged black line cutting off the horizon. Their objective lay beyond that natural barrier, a fact that weighed on each man's mind as they calculated the challenges ahead.

Near midnight, Sica froze suddenly, raising a closed fist, the signal to halt. The others immediately reacted, melding into whatever cover was nearest. For several heartbeats, the only sound was the soft whispering of the sea against the rocky shore.

Seneca eased forward to join Sica who pointed toward nearby beach. Approximately fifty yards ahead, a small fishing vessel was being pulled onto the shore by several figures moving around a dim lantern.

Seneca nodded and signalled for the men to move inland, away from their planned route but avoiding detection. They retreated silently into deeper vegetation, circling widely around the fishing party and only when they were well past the potential threat did they angle back toward the coastline to resume their northward journey.

It was the first of several such detours. As they progressed, signs of habitation became more frequent, distant flickering lights of small villages perched on hillsides, smoke rising from isolated huts, and once even the distinct shape of a tribal watch post silhouetted against the night sky on a promontory overlooking the bay.

Each obstacle necessitated careful navigation for while their Roman identities were concealed by darkness, any close encounter could prove fatal. The tribes of western Britannia, although not part of Togodumnus' initial resistance, were no allies of Rome and the discovery of armed Romans deep in their territory could bring a swift and merciless response.

Shortly before dawn, Decimus spotted a patrol of tribal warriors following the shoreline from the north. The Occultum immediately took cover in a dense thicket, lying motionless as the group of painted warriors passed within twenty yards of their

154

position.

'Scouts,' whispered Decimus after they had passed, his lips barely moving. 'Looking for something specific.'

Seneca nodded, filing away the information. Increased tribal vigilance suggested either awareness of Roman presence, perhaps related to their own landing, or some other activity that warranted heightened security. Either possibility warranted caution.

As they resumed their journey, the terrain began to change subtly. The relatively flat coastal area gradually gave way to rolling hills, the first indication of the mountain range that loomed before them. Vegetation grew denser, offering better concealment but making silent passage more challenging.

By the time the eastern sky showed the first pale harbinger of dawn, they had covered nearly eight miles along the curving shoreline. Not the pace they might have maintained on open terrain in daylight, but respectable progress given the need for absolute stealth.

Seneca called a halt as the grey predawn light began to seep through the trees. Night travel was their safest option, and daylight hours would be spent in concealment, resting and planning for the next stage of their journey. Sica scouted ahead briefly before returning to guide them to a suitable hiding place, a natural depression ringed by dense shrubs and overshadowed by a rock outcropping that would shield them from casual observation.

As the men settled into the concealment, establishing watch positions and preparing their meagre morning rations, Seneca unfurled the map once more. In the growing light, they could now clearly see their position relative to their objective.

'We've made good progress,' he said softly, pointing to their approximate location. 'Another two nights of similar pace should bring us to the northern edge of the bay. From there, we'll need to turn inland toward the mountains.'

Marcus studied the intervening terrain on the map, his experienced eyes assessing the challenges ahead.

155

'The foothills will slow us. And crossing the range itself...' He shook his head slightly. 'Not a journey to undertake lightly, especially with limited supplies.'

'One challenge at a time,' said Seneca. 'Let's focus on reaching the mountains first. We'll assess our approach to crossing when we're there.'

As full daylight finally bathed the countryside in golden light, the Occultum lay hidden from sight, six shadows among many in the dappled forest floor. Above them, birds resumed their morning songs, small animals rustled through the undergrowth, and a light breeze stirred the canopy of leaves, nature itself providing auditory camouflage
for the intruders in its midst.

In the distance, the mountains that separated them from Isla Mona rose in shadowed majesty, their peaks occasionally visible through gaps in the trees, and as most of the men drifted into the light sleep of experienced soldiers, never fully unconscious, always partly alert, Seneca remained awake, his mind calculating distances, assessing risks, formulating contingencies. The mission had grown more complex since their betrayal on the beach, yet its importance remained unchanged. Somewhere beyond those mountains, Raven awaited, providing intelligence to Rome's enemies that cost Roman lives daily.

With that certainty fixed in his mind, Seneca finally allowed himself to rest, one hand resting on the hilt of his gladius, ears still attuned to any sound that might signal danger. In four hours, they would rotate watches, allowing others to rest while maintaining vigilance and when darkness returned, they would resume their journey northward, drawing ever closer to the mountains... and to Raven.

Evening shadows lengthened across the forest floor and as the last golden rays of sunlight filtered through the canopy above, the Occultum stirred from their concealment, each man rising silently from the undergrowth that had hidden them through the daylight hours.

Decimus stretched carefully, easing the stiffness from limbs that had remained largely motionless for hours. Nearby, Marcus and Cassius checked their weapons with methodical precision, while Sica took stock of their remaining provisions.

'Another two days at most,' murmured Sica, his voice barely audible as he assessed their dwindling supplies of dried meat and hard bread. 'Then we forage or steal.'

Seneca nodded grimly. The unexpected change in their circumstances had left them with limited rations, carefully measured and distributed to stretch as far as possible. But even with strict rationing, they would soon face difficult choices. Hunting risked noise that might attract attention; stealing from settlements risked detection but going hungry risked diminished strength when they would need it most for crossing the mountains.

'We'll address that when necessary,' said Seneca. He gestured toward the water pouches gathered at his feet. 'Falco, let's replenish our water while the others prepare to move out.'

The ex-gladiator nodded, picking up two of the empty waterskins while Seneca took the remainder. Together they moved away from the group's position, following a faint animal trail that led toward the small stream they had seen the previous day. The sound of flowing water grew louder as they approached, a gentle gurgling that promised at least one necessity would be easily acquired.

The stream itself was modest, perhaps three feet across at its widest point, with clear water flowing over a bed of smooth stones. It emerged from between rocks higher up the slope before disappearing into denser vegetation downstream. Ideal for their purpose: clean, accessible, and sheltered from casual observation.

Seneca scanned the surrounding area carefully, noting potential approach routes, listening for any sound that didn't belong to the forest's natural symphony of rustling leaves and small creatures moving through underbrush. Falco did the same, his experienced eyes sweeping the opposite bank with practiced intensity.

After several minutes of silent observation, satisfied they were alone, Seneca nodded toward the water.

'I think it's safe. I'll fill, you watch.'

They moved to the stream's edge, where Seneca crouched and began the methodical process of filling each waterskin. Beside him, Falco maintained his vigilance, one hand resting on the pommel of his gladius, gaze constantly moving across their surroundings.

Seneca had just finished filling the final waterskin when Falco's hand touched his shoulder, the lightest of contacts, yet instantly communicating urgency.

'Seneca,' he whispered, 'look.'

Seneca raised his head slowly, following Falco's gaze across the narrow waterway. There, partially concealed behind a gnarled bush on the opposite bank, stood a small boy, perhaps five or six years old. He was dressed in the rough homespun clothing of the local tribes, a simple tunic belted at the waist, his feet bare despite the cool evening air. His dark eyes stared unblinkingly at the two Romans, his expression a mixture of curiosity and apprehension.

For a moment, no one moved. The tableau held, two hardened Roman operatives frozen in place, a tribal child watching them with the wary stillness of a young deer assessing potential danger.

The implications cascaded through Seneca's mind with lightning speed. A child meant a settlement nearby, closer than they had realized, and if the boy reported what he had seen to the adults, their presence would no longer be secret.

Falco's body tensed subtly, his hand shifting toward his dagger, a movement so slight that only someone intimately familiar with the ex-gladiator's reactions would have noticed. Seneca understood immediately what his companion was considering and made his decision just as quickly.

With deliberate slowness, he rose to his feet, allowing his posture to remain relaxed, non-threatening. His face, typically guarded and severe, softened into what he hoped was a reassuring smile. He raised one hand in a simple greeting, a universal gesture of peaceful intent.

'What are you doing?' Falco hissed, tension evident in his whispered words.

'The only thing we can do,' replied Seneca quietly, maintaining his smile toward the child. 'We can't undo being seen. Our options are limited.'

'We could...' Falco began.

'No,' interrupted Seneca firmly. 'We don't harm children. Not for any reason. And taking him with us would only guarantee a search party. Our best chance is to appear unthreatening, like travellers who have nothing to hide.'

Falco grimaced but nodded almost imperceptibly, acknowledging the logic if not embracing it. With visible effort, he forced his own features into what approximated a friendly expression, raising his hand in a mirroring gesture of the Tribune's greeting.

The effect was not what either man hoped for. Falco's enormous frame, intimidating even to fellow soldiers, combined with his scarred face and the artificial smile that didn't reach his eyes, created an impression more frightening than reassuring and the boy's eyes widened perceptibly, his small body tensing.

For another heartbeat, the child remained frozen, staring at the strange men with their foreign appearance and odd clothing. Then, with the sudden decisiveness of youth, he turned and scurried away, disappearing into the undergrowth with barely a sound.

The two Romans stared at the empty space, the implications of the encounter hanging heavy between them.

'That complicates matters,' said Falco after a moment.

'We need to move immediately,' said Seneca. 'Let's get out of here.

They turned away from the stream, moving quickly back toward where the rest of their unit waited. Their presence was no longer unknown, their passage no longer completely secret. The already difficult journey to Mona had just become significantly more dangerous.

'What is it?' asked Marcus when they returned, seeing the stress on their faces.

'We've been seen,' said Seneca simply. 'A boy at the stream. He ran.'

The impact of the information registered immediately on each man's face.

'How far do you think it is to the nearest settlement?' asked Decimus.

'Not far,' replied Seneca, bending down to adjust his own sarcina. 'The child was too young to be wandering alone. Perhaps a mile, maybe less. We have to move now.'

The men agreed and within minutes, they had obliterated all signs of their presence. Sica once again took point and as darkness settled over the landscape, the Occultum slipped away from their temporary haven, moving deeper into the forested hills. Behind them, somewhere in the gathering night, a small boy was undoubtedly breathlessly describing the strange men he had seen by the stream, men whose appearance marked them clearly as outsiders. The race had begun, and the stakes were their lives.

Chapter Twenty-Four

Isla Mona

Veteranus stood motionless at the centre of the pit, his feet planted firmly on the stone slab when the first unearthly scream shattered the silence and a shape exploded outward from a crate, launching itself into the air toward him.

Veteranus reacted instinctively, hands flying up to protect his face, and as his body twisted sideways to avoid the impact, his right foot slipped off the stone slab, touching the earth beyond its boundary.

The anticipated collision never came as the creature jerked backward violently, yanked by a heavy chain around its neck that Veteranus hadn't noticed until that moment. It crashed to the ground just short of where he stood, thrashing and clawing at the earth in frustrated fury.

Another inhuman scream erupted from behind him and Veteranus spun around, heart thundering in his chest, to see a second creature charging toward him from the opposite crate, its movements a grotesque parody of both animal and human.

Realizing his vulnerable position, Veteranus quickly stepped back onto the stone slab, regaining his centre just as the second attacker lunged forward. Like the first, it was brought up short by a chain anchored deep within its crate and claws that had been aimed at his face slashed through empty air mere inches from his skin.

The noise within the pit rose to a deafening level as the other two crates disgorged their occupants, all four creatures now straining against their restraints, circling the limits of their chains like predators testing the boundaries of a cage. Each one launched repeated attacks toward the stone slab, only to be jerked back at the critical moment.

The stench that filled the pit was overwhelming, a noxious blend of unwashed bodies, rotten meat, and something putrid that defied identification. It caught in Veteranus's throat, making him gag

161

even as he struggled to maintain his footing on the increasingly precious safety of the stone.

As the initial shock of the attack subsided, Veteranus gained his first clear look at his assailants and what he saw froze the blood in his veins.

They were not beasts. Not entirely... they had once been men.

Their bodies were emaciated yet corded with unnaturally defined muscle. Matted hair hung in filthy tangles from misshapen heads and the nails on their grasping hands thickened and curved into claws that left gouges in the hard-packed earth. Their teeth had been filed into points that gleamed yellowed and sharp in the torchlight.

But it was their eyes that struck the deepest horror into Veteranus's heart. Within those twisted, bestial faces, the eyes remained human, aware, intelligent, filled with a hatred and hunger that no animal could possess. These were not mindless creatures; something of the men they had once been remained trapped within corrupted flesh.

Gradually, the attacks became less frequent until one of them ceased its frenzied lunges and crouched at the limit of its chain. It tilted its head, studying Veteranus with an unsettling focus as a sound emerged from its throat, not the feral screams of before, but something that horrifyingly resembled words, distorted and mangled yet recognizably an attempt at human speech.

The other creatures began to pace the boundaries of their restraints, launching occasional half-hearted lunges toward the stone slab but seeming to recognize the futility of their efforts. They stalked in endless circles, always watching Veteranus with those terribly human eyes, waiting for him to make a mistake.

As his immediate fear subsided, a deeper horror took root within Veteranus's mind. These had been men once, but what power could transform them like this? What minds could conceive of such a transformation, let alone execute it?

Above the pit, Mordred stood watching, his ancient eyes revealing nothing of his thoughts as Veteranus confronted the truth of his druidic power. This was no mere ritual, no symbolic representation of ancient beliefs. This was tangible, physical evidence of capabilities that Rome, with all its civilization and learning, had never suspected. They were a demonstration, a warning, a glimpse of the power Veteranus was being invited to serve… or oppose.

The choice that had seemed made when he entered the pit now presented itself anew, with stakes he had not fully comprehended until this moment. The initiation was not merely a test of courage or commitment; it was a revelation of truths that could not be unlearned and, standing on the stone slab, surrounded by the broken remains of humanity transformed into something else, Veteranus understood at last what Mordred had meant when he spoke of powers beyond Rome's understanding. And he recognized with terrible clarity why Rome feared the druids enough to cross an ocean to destroy them.

Eventually, the creatures' frenzy subsided. Their attacks grew less frequent, then ceased altogether as exhaustion or resignation overtook them. One by one, they settled onto the ground, some sitting with knees drawn up to their chests in a disconcertingly human posture, others lying on their sides, chains pooled around them like metallic serpents. All kept their eyes fixed on Veteranus, their gazes never wavering from the man who stood tantalizingly beyond their reach.

The silence that settled over the pit was somehow worse than the previous cacophony of screams and growls and in that quiet, Veteranus could hear the laboured breathing of the creatures, the occasional clink of chains as they shifted position, the distant murmur of the crowd above. His own heartbeat gradually slowed from its panicked rhythm, though adrenaline still coursed through his veins, keeping him rigidly alert.

Movement at the pit's edge drew his attention upward where several men appeared, leaning over the excavation's rim with severed

163

goat legs clutched in their hands. Without warning, they hurled the bloody limbs into the pit, one toward each of the creatures.

The effect was immediate and horrifying. The formerly languid figures exploded into motion, seizing the meat with desperate intensity, tearing into the raw flesh with their filed teeth, and ripping away chunks with savage efficiency.

While the creatures were distracted by their meal, a group of druid warriors climbed down into the pit, each carrying a long spear tipped with iron. Working in pairs, they approached the feeding creatures, using the spears to prod and guide them back toward their respective crates.

The creatures seemed to recognize this routine. Though they snarled and snapped when the spear points touched their flesh, they each retreated into their wooden prisons without serious resistance, carrying what remained of their bloody feast with them. The warriors slammed the sliding doors down with a final, resonant thud that echoed through the pit and only when the last crate was secured did Veteranus realize he'd been holding his breath. He exhaled shakily, his legs suddenly weak beneath him now that the immediate danger had passed. Looking up, he saw that most of the clan had dispersed. The torches that had ringed the pit still burned, but the human circle that had watched his ordeal was gone.

All except for Raven. The former scout remained at the edge, looking down at Veteranus with an expression that mingled respect with something harder to identify, perhaps pity, perhaps warning.

Veteranus walked over to the ladder and climbed out of the pit. Behind him, the crates were dragged out and carried away, the creatures inside now silent, perhaps sated by their feeding, perhaps resigned to returning to whatever darkness held them between these demonstrations.

Soon, only Veteranus and Raven remained. The forest around them had fallen into an unnatural stillness, as if the local wildlife instinctively avoided the place where such horrors had been briefly unleashed.

Veteranus found himself unable to speak for several long moments. He had witnessed countless brutalities during his years of military service, the calculated violence of Roman legions, the frenzied attacks of tribal warriors, the cold efficiency of his own operations with the Occultum. Yet nothing had prepared him for what he had just seen.

'What, ' he began, then paused to clear his throat when the word emerged as little more than a croak. 'What manner of creatures were they?'

Raven's gaze shifted from Veteranus to the distant point where the crates had disappeared among the trees. When he spoke, his voice had a hollow quality, as if the words emerged from somewhere deep within him.

'They are the lost,' he said. 'The creatures of the night.' His eyes
returned to Veteranus, reflecting the torchlight like pools of dark water. 'They feel no pain. They feel no fear. They feel only hatred and hunger.'

Veteranus processed these words, comparing them with what he had witnessed.

'But they must have been men once,' he said.

'No,' said Raven, his voice hollow in the torch-lit darkness. 'None of them were ever men. They were the children of our enemies, taken in battle many years ago and changed by Mordred's own hand. Captured before they could speak, before memory could form… before humanity could take root.'

A chill ran through Veteranus that had nothing to do with the night air.

'How? What process could transform them into... that?'

Raven's eyes reflected the distant flames as he spoke.

'They know no other life. From the moment they were taken as babes, they were kept in perpetual darkness, in pits and caves

165

beneath the sacred groves where no light ever reaches. Our women gave them just enough nurture to keep them alive. Over time, their eyes adapted to see what others cannot and their only memories are of hunger and pain.' He continued, his voice detached as though reciting ancient texts. 'As they grew, they were fed only raw meat, often rotting, to accustom their bodies to corruption. When they cried, they were beaten. When they showed affection to one another, they were separated. When they tried to stand upright as humans do, their legs were bound until they learned to move on all fours as well as any beast.'

Veteranus felt bile rising in his throat but could not stop listening.

'Their teeth were filed into daggers while they were conscious, so they would associate their new weapons with the pain of their creation. Their fingernails were not merely sharpened but treated with mixtures of poisonous herbs and minerals that caused them to thicken and grow curved like talons. Mordred himself would cut their growing bodies and rub potions into the wounds that twisted their muscles, their bones.' Raven traced a pattern in the air, a druidic symbol Veteranus did not recognize. 'They were given special brews that altered their minds and bodies further, hallucinogenic fungi, the blood of sacrifices. His voice dropped lower. 'At first, they were given small animals to kill, mice, rats, foxes, with only those who killed with sufficient savagery allowed to keep the meat. Later, larger animals like dogs and deer until they were even exposed to the beasts that would fight back, and as a group they would face wolves or even a young bear. Eventually, prisoners taken in battle were thrown into the pit where they waited... without the chains that held them at bay earlier. Over time, they grew a taste for human flesh, especially the heart, and slowly learned to hunt as a pack, communicating through sounds no human throat should make.'

Raven's gaze seemed to turn inward, as if seeing something Veteranus could not.

'I have watched them during the sacred hunts. They move

like shadows through the forest, following scents no normal hunter could detect. They can track a man for days without rest, without food. They feel neither exhaustion nor mercy.'

'If I had not seen them with my own eyes,' said veteranus, 'I would never have believed they existed.'

'Oh, they exist,' said Raven. 'They are the hounds of Cerunnos himself, the bridge between our world and the next. They are the Wraith.'

Chapter Twenty-Five

Castra Victrix

The newly constructed Principia stood at the heart of Castra Victrix, its timber frame a testament to Roman efficiency. The wooden structure, while not as grand as the stone Principia of permanent fortresses, nonetheless conveyed a sense of Roman permanence on Britannic soil.

Vespasian surveyed the command room with quiet satisfaction as he awaited the arrival of the other officers. Oil lamps hung from overhead beams, casting a steady light throughout, a marked improvement over the flickering illumination of the field tents that had preceded this structure.

Outside, rain had begun to fall once more, a gentle patter against the wooden roof that served as a constant reminder of the island's challenging climate. The Principia, however, remained dry and secure, another small victory against the elements that had seemed to conspire against the Roman advance since their landing.

Vespasian's contemplation was interrupted as officers began to file into the room. Quintus Leontius, the Primus Pilus of the Second Augusta, entered first. At fifty, his weathered face bore the scars of three decades in service to Rome, and his spine remained parade-ground straight despite years of carrying armour across diverse and difficult terrain. His practical experience would be invaluable in the coming advance, particularly his knowledge of maintaining formation discipline over challenging ground.

Cassius Longinus followed, the intelligence officer's keen eyes immediately drawn to the maps laid out on the table. Unlike many of his military counterparts, Longinus had spent years as a merchant before joining the legions, and his understanding of local customs, trade routes, and regional politics had proven essential to their campaign thus far.

Three cohort commanders entered together, their easy

168

manner with one another testament to the many campaigns shared across the empire. Quintus Severus commanded the First Cohort, Marcus Vitruvius the Third, and Gaius Petronius the Fifth. Each led approximately five hundred men, and their coordination would prove critical in the coming advance.

Titus Livius, Tribune Militum of the Second Augusta, arrived with the confidence that came from both youth and noble birth. At twenty-five, he represented Rome's next generation of military leadership and despite the initial scepticism from some of the older Centurions, he had proven himself capable during the river crossings, showing both courage and sound tactical judgment.

The remaining cohort commanders filed in next: Aulus Severinus of the Second Cohort, Lucius Claudius of the Fourth, Tiberius Nerva of the Sixth, Marcus Sulpicius of the Seventh, Decimus Trebius of the Eighth, and Gnaeus Octavius of the Tenth. Each man brought his own expertise and temperament to the council, but all shared the disciplined bearing that marked them as products of Rome's military system.

The room fell silent as General Plautius entered and the officers straightened almost imperceptibly at his entrance, a reflexive response to the presence of authority.

Plautius moved directly to the head of the table, his gaze sweeping across the assembled commanders before he spoke.

'Gentlemen,' he began, his voice carrying easily in the hushed room. 'Our campaign has reached a critical juncture.' He placed both hands on the table, leaning forward slightly as he continued. 'We have accomplished much in a short time. The Tamesis crossing, while costly, broke the back of organized resistance in this region. We've established this forward position at Castra Victrix, secured our supply lines back to Rutupiae, and consolidated our hold on the territories between.' His eyes moved to the medical officer present. 'We have honoured our dead with proper rites, and the wounded are being well cared for. Many will rejoin our ranks in the coming weeks.' He straightened, gesturing to a section of the map

169

that showed troop deployments. 'The Fourteenth Gemina has now fully deployed to support our operations, providing the reinforcement we require for the next phase.' His finger traced a path northward on the map, stopping at a clearly marked settlement. 'Camulodunum,' he continued, the name hanging in the air between them. 'The tribal capital and our next objective.'

Vespasian stepped forward, assuming the role of tactical briefer as they had arranged beforehand.

'The distance is approximately twenty-five miles from our current position,' he said, indicating the route on the map. 'Under ideal conditions, the journey would take two days of normal marching but given the terrain and the need to maintain defensive formations, we're allocating three days for the advance.' He gestured to specific points along the projected route. 'The land between here and Camulodunum consists mostly of open, rolling countryside with occasional wooded areas. The path follows an established tribal roadway for much of the distance, though the term *road* might be generous by our standards. Our engineers will improve sections as we go for the passage of our heavier equipment.'

Cassius Longinus stepped forward at Plautius's nod.

'Our sources indicate that no major opposition is expected,' he reported. 'We've accepted the formal surrender from many local clans, including substantial elements of both the Trinovantes and Catuvellauni. His expression grew more guarded as he continued. 'However, Caratacus himself remains at large. Our latest intelligence suggests he has fled westward, seeking support among the more distant tribes, the Silures and Ordovices particularly. While he gathers allies, some of his loyal warriors may attempt small-scale ambushes or raids against our column.'

Plautius nodded, then addressed the assembled officers once more.

'While we don't anticipate pitched battle, we will advance as if expecting one. The legion will move as a single entity, in full battle formation.' His gaze swept across the officers, ensuring they understood the significance of this approach. 'This serves two purposes,' he continued, 'first, it ensures we're prepared should Caratacus have planned something we haven't detected; second, the sight of a full Roman legion on the march will further demoralize any who might still consider resistance. We are not merely a military force, we are the visible manifestation of Rome's power.' He turned to Aulus Severinus. 'Your Second Cohort will form the vanguard. Your men will march one-half mile ahead of the main column, with scouts deployed to your front and flanks.'

Severinus nodded sharply.

'As you command, General.'

'The Ninth Legion will follow us by one day,' Plautius continued. 'They'll secure our rear and reinforce positions along our supply line. Once we reach Camulodunum, both legions will establish camps outside the settlement's walls, a show of overwhelming force, but disciplined and controlled.' He paused, allowing the information to settle. 'According to our intelligence, Camulodunum itself will not be defended. The settlement expects our arrival, and the tribal leadership remaining there has indicated their willingness to submit formally to Roman authority.'

Titus Livius, the young Tribune, spoke up.

'And if this proves deception, General? If we find the settlement fortified against us?'

Plautius acknowledged the query with a nod.

'A legitimate concern, Tribune. Our advance elements will conduct thorough reconnaissance before the main force approaches but if the situation differs from our intelligence, we have the siege equipment necessary to reduce their defences, though that would be... unfortunate for all concerned.'

The implied threat hung in the air, unspoken but understood by all present. Rome preferred surrender to destruction but was entirely capable of the latter when the former was refused.

'And once Camulodunum is secured, General?' asked

Quintus Leontius. 'What then?'

'Then we begin the process of establishing a permanent Roman administration,' replied Plautius. 'Camulodunum will become our provincial capital. Governor Plancus and his administrative staff are already preparing to sail from Gaul once we confirm the area is secure. A permanent legionary fortress will be constructed, and the beginnings of a proper Roman city laid out.' His gaze swept the assembled officers once more. 'Make no mistake, gentlemen. What we do here is historic. Julius Caesar touched these shores, claimed victory, and departed. We will not merely touch, we will conquer, and we will remain. We are laying the foundation of what will become the newest province of the empire.'

The weight of this statement settled over the gathered men. They were not merely soldiers fighting another campaign; they were the vanguard of Roman civilization, extending the reach of the empire across previously uncrossed waters.

'Questions?' Plautius asked, opening the floor to the assembled commanders.

Marcus Vitruvius of the Third Cohort raised a hand.

'General, what intelligence do we have on potential guerrilla activity? The forests here could conceal significant forces.'

'A valid concern,' Plautius acknowledged. 'Longinus, address this.'

The intelligence officer stepped forward again.

'We've identified several wooded areas along the route that could serve as ambush points. Each will be thoroughly scouted before the main column approaches, and our flanking elements will sweep through them as we pass. Our auxiliary cavalry will patrol wider circles around our advance, denying the enemy any opportunity to mass forces undetected.'

Gaius Petronius, commander of the Fifth Cohort, spoke next.

'What of our supply train? It presents a vulnerable target.'

'The supply wagons will move at the centre of our

formation,' Vespasian answered. 'Protected on all sides by cohorts in battle readiness. Additionally, the Batavian auxiliary cohort will provide dedicated security for essential supplies and equipment.'

The questions continued for some time, each officer raising concerns specific to their responsibilities. Plautius and his senior staff addressed each thoroughly, demonstrating the careful planning that had gone into the coming operation.

Tiberius Nerva of the Sixth Cohort eventually asked about the defensive situations of any settlements they might encounter along the route.

'Most are unfortified farming communities,' said Longinus. 'Those directly on our path have largely been abandoned, the inhabitants having fled either to Camulodunum or westward with Caratacus. We expect little civilian presence until we near the capital itself.'

When the questions finally wound down, Plautius straightened, drawing himself to his full height.

'If there's nothing else, gentlemen, we march at dawn tomorrow. The advance will proceed in the order outlined in the documents being distributed now.'

An orderly moved among the officers, handing each a sealed packet containing their specific instructions.

'Review these carefully,' Plautius instructed. 'Commit the timetables and formations to memory. I expect flawless execution from each of you.' His stern expression softened slightly. 'You've all performed admirably thus far but Rome is watching. The Emperor himself takes a personal interest in our progress so do not disappoint him, or me.'

The officers stood a little straighter at this reminder of the imperial attention focused on their campaign.

'Return to your units,' Plautius concluded, 'and ensure your men are prepared for tomorrow's advance. We move at first light. Dismissed,'

The commanders saluted and began filing out of the

Principia, many already breaking the seals on their order packets, reviewing the details of the coming operation. Soon, only Plautius, Vespasian, and Longinus remained, the three senior officers contemplating the map between them.

'What troubles you, Longinus?' Plautius asked, noting the intelligence officer's furrowed brow.

Longinus hesitated before speaking.

'It's Caratacus, General. He's proven more resourceful than we anticipated. The ease with which he slipped away after the Tamesis crossing concerns me.'

'You think he might have some surprise waiting for us?' Vespasian asked.

'I think a man who abandons his capital without a final stand does so for a reason,' replied Longinus. 'He's preserving his forces, gathering allies. The question is, for what purpose?'

Plautius studied the map, his finger tracing the western territories where Caratacus was believed to have fled.

'Those tribes, the Silures, the Ordovices, the Deceangli, they're mountain people, fierce fighters on their own terrain. If he's rallying them to his cause...'

'We could face a protracted guerrilla campaign,' finished Vespasian grimly.

'Perhaps,' acknowledged Plautius. 'But that's a concern for after we've secured Camulodunum. One objective at a time, gentlemen. Let's establish our foothold first, then worry about what lurks in those western mountains at a later date.'

The three men fell silent, each contemplating the campaign ahead. Beyond the structure's walls, the sounds of the camp continued unabated, legionaries drilling, the clang of the smithy, the calls of Centurions directing work parties. The machinery of Rome's military might, preparing once more to advance across foreign soil.

Chapter Twenty-Six

Central Britannia

Lepidus and Talorcan remained motionless in their concealment, watching
as the auxiliary cavalry column disappeared into the distance. The thundering hoofbeats gradually faded, replaced by the natural sounds of the forest, birdsong, rustling leaves, the occasional scurrying of small creatures through the undergrowth.

'They've gone,' said Talorcan eventually, his keen eyes still fixed on the point where the Romans had vanished. 'Both the cavalry and the tribal watchers. They followed the column as I expected.'

Lepidus rose from his crouched position, muscles protesting after hours of enforced stillness. Despite his years away from field operations, the old habits returned with surprising ease, the careful movement, the constant awareness, the economical conservation of energy that might mean the difference between life and death behind enemy lines.

'How clear is the trail?' he asked, brushing forest debris from his rough-spun tunic.

Talorcan moved toward the site where they had discovered the mutilated remains of Tribune Atticus days earlier. The clearing itself had been trampled by the Roman patrol during their investigation, but beyond its perimeter, the scout found what he sought, faint impressions in the soil, barely visible to untrained eyes.

'The tracks are weak,' he reported, crouching to examine the signs more closely. 'But still followable. See here, ' he pointed to a barely perceptible depression in the forest floor. 'Roman military boots, the hobnail pattern is distinctive. And here,' his finger moved to another mark nearby. 'Celtic boots, many of them.'

Lepidus joined him, studying the subtle signs that Talorcan read with such expertise.

'That means at least some of them are still alive,' he said, 'but taken into captivity.'

'Yes,' confirmed the scout. 'See how they walk, not in formation, but staggered, irregular. Their stride is shortened. They were likely bound and being led.' He rose, studying the surrounding terrain. 'The tracks lead westward, toward the territories controlled by the Ordovices.'

'And deeper into druid influence,' added Lepidus grimly.

Talorcan nodded, his expression serious.

'The trail is faint. We'll need to move in daylight as much as possible to follow it.'

'That increases our risk of detection,' Lepidus pointed out, the tactician in him automatically calculating the danger.

'We have little choice,' replied Talorcan. 'The signs are too subtle to track in darkness. We'd lose the trail within the first mile.'

Lepidus nodded.

'Very well. But we stay in the shadows where possible, utilize the thickest forest cover available, and drop into concealment at the first sign of others.'

'Agreed,' said Talorcan, moving to retrieve his sarcina from their hiding place. 'We should move now. We've already lost several hours waiting for the patrol to depart.'

Lepidus recovered his own pack, checking the contents briefly before securing it to his back. As a precaution, they had removed anything that might identify them as Roman, military insignia, standardized equipment, even distinctive fastenings on their clothing.

With Talorcan in the lead, they set off westward, following the nearly invisible trail left by those who had taken what remained of the missing patrol. Lepidus matched his pace, staying approximately five paces behind. It was standard procedure for small units operating in hostile territory, tactics he had helped develop during his years with the Exploratores and later refined for the Occultum.

They maintained silence as they travelled, communicating only when necessary and then through hand signals rather than words. Sound carried deceptively far in forests, and tribal hunters possessed hearing honed by lifetimes spent stalking game through these same woods.

The pace was necessarily slow. Talorcan frequently paused to examine the ground, sometimes backtracking when the trail became too faint to follow immediately. Several times, he knelt to brush aside fallen leaves or move branches for a better view of the soil beneath, revealing to Lepidus's eyes the subtle impressions of footprints, broken twigs, or disturbed moss that told the story of those who had passed this way before.

By midday, they had covered perhaps three miles, a fraction of what seasoned legionaries might march on established roads, but respectable progress through dense forest while maintaining both stealth and a difficult trail. When they paused briefly to rest, Lepidus noted with approval that Talorcan selected a position that offered both concealment and clear lines of sight in all directions.

Their meal consisted of dried meat and a handful of parched grain, consumed quickly and efficiently. No fire, no hot food, nothing that might produce smoke or scent that could betray their presence. Water came from their half-filled skins, carefully rationed despite the relative abundance of streams in the region. They would refill at the next suitable water source, but experience had taught both men never to assume resources would be available when needed.

After no more than fifteen minutes, they resumed their westward journey. The terrain gradually changed as they progressed, the relatively flat woodland giving way to increasing undulation. Small hills and shallow valleys created a landscape of natural defensive positions and potential ambush points.

Twice during the afternoon, they detected signs of others nearby, once the distant sound of voices that sent them immediately into concealment among thick ferns, and later the faint but distinctive scent of woodsmoke that prompted a wide detour around what Talorcan suspected was a small hunting camp. The discipline was automatic, ingrained in both men during years of operating in

177

territory where discovery meant death.

As dusk approached, Talorcan led them into a small ravine, its steep sides offering protection from casual observation.

'We should rest here tonight,' he suggested, indicating a small overhang in the ravine wall that would provide minimal shelter. 'The trail continues westward, but we risk losing it in failing light.'

Lepidus nodded his agreement.

'The position is defensible, and the running water will mask any
sound we might make. Good choice.'

They established their simple camp with practiced efficiency but still no fire, despite the deepening chill of the Britannic evening. Their sleeping arrangements were rudimentary, cloaks spread on cleared ground, packs serving as pillows, weapons positioned for immediate access. One man would sleep while the other maintained watch, rotating throughout the night to ensure continuous vigilance.

'I'll take first watch,' offered Lepidus, settling himself against the ravine wall with a clear view of both approaches.

Talorcan nodded, stretching out on his cloak.

'Wake me at midnight.'

Within minutes, the scout had fallen into the light sleep of an experienced campaigner. Lepidus kept his vigil in silence, his mind turning over the implications of what they were tracking. The reported mutilation of Tribune Atticus's body represented something beyond conventional tribal aggression. Throughout his military career, Lepidus had witnessed numerous atrocities committed by both Rome's enemies and Rome itself, yet this suggested something different, ritual purpose, perhaps, or demonstration of some power beyond normal capability.

The night passed without incident, the two men rotating watch as planned and by the time dawn began to lighten the eastern sky, both were awake, consuming a sparse breakfast and preparing for another day of tracking.

'The trail will be clearer today,' said Talorcan as they prepared to depart. 'Rain fell sometime in the night, not enough to wash away signs, but sufficient to settle the soil and make fresh impressions more visible.'

They climbed out of the ravine and resumed their westward journey. As Talorcan had predicted, the trail became somewhat easier to follow, the damp ground preserving footprints more clearly. The scout set a slightly faster pace, though still maintaining the caution necessary in hostile territory.

By midmorning, they had entered terrain that was noticeably different from the previous day's landscape. The relatively mixed forest with its blend of oak, ash, and hazel gave way to ancient pine and yew, trees of considerable age forming a high canopy that limited underbrush. The forest floor became a carpet of needles, and the perpetual twilight beneath the towering trees created an atmosphere of primeval solemnity.

'We've entered one of the sacred groves,' Talorcan explained in a whisper when they paused briefly. 'The druids maintain these spaces, preserve them from clearing or hunting. They're thought to be dwelling places of spirits and gods.'

'Are they used for rituals?' asked Lepidus, eyes constantly scanning their surroundings as they spoke.

'Some,' confirmed the scout. 'Though those involving blood are typically conducted in specifically prepared locations, not the general sacred groves.' He frowned slightly. 'Still, we should proceed with extra caution. Even in times of peace, trespassers in these places risk severe punishment.'

They continued through the ancient forest, their progress now marked by an added layer of tension. The tracks they followed remained consistent, Roman prisoners being led by tribal captors, moving purposefully westward. Occasionally, they found other signs that confirmed their interpretation, a deeper footprint from a Roman boot, a small torn piece of Roman fabric caught on a thorny bush.

When night fell on the second day, they sought shelter

beneath the exposed roots of a fallen pine, its enormous trunk creating a natural windbreak. Again, they maintained their rotation of watch, though both men found sleep elusive in the unsettling atmosphere of the grove. Even the natural sounds of the forest seemed muted here, as if the wildlife itself observed some unwritten protocol of reverence.

Dawn brought heavy mist that clung to the forest floor, reducing visibility but providing additional concealment as they resumed their journey. The trail continued westward, eventually leading them out of the forest and into more varied terrain. The land began to rise more dramatically, suggesting they were approaching the foothills of the western mountains that formed the spine of northern Britannia.

By midday of the third day, they had covered approximately thirty miles from their starting point, a respectable distance given the challenging conditions and need for stealth. The trail they followed had begun to show signs of converging with others, suggesting they were approaching some form of destination or gathering point.

Late in the afternoon, Talorcan suddenly froze, raising a closed fist and Lepidus immediately dropped into a crouch, all senses alert for whatever had triggered the scout's warning.

Talorcan's nostrils flared slightly as he tested the air. Slowly, he turned his head toward Lepidus, mouthing a single word:

'Smoke.'

Now that it had been identified, Lepidus detected it too, the faint but distinctive scent of woodsmoke carried on the light breeze. Not the pleasant aroma of a cooking fire, but something ranker, more acrid, as if materials other than clean wood were being consumed by flame.

With extreme caution, they advanced toward the source of the smoke, moving from cover to cover with practiced stealth. The forest had begun to thin slightly, suggesting they were approaching some form of clearing. They abandoned their sarcinae beneath a dense thicket, taking only essential weapons to improve their mobility for what lay ahead.

As they neared the apparent source of the smoke, both men dropped to their bellies, crawling the final distance through undergrowth that provided concealment while affording limited visibility of what lay beyond. Pushing aside a screen of ferns with excruciating slowness to avoid any sudden movement, they gained their first clear view into a substantial clearing.

At the centre of the open space, a large fire pit still smouldered, wisps of grey smoke rising lazily into the afternoon air. Around it, the ground had been trampled by many feet, the soil compacted and disturbed in patterns that suggested significant activity. Various items lay scattered about, broken pottery, discarded bones, fragments of cloth, evidence of what might have been a substantial gathering. But it was the sight at the far side of the clearing that immediately captured their attention and froze their blood.

Bound to a crude wooden frame stood what remained of one of the missing men. The face had been partially eaten away, with cheeks, lips and one eye missing entirely, exposing the stark white of the skull beneath. The chest cavity had been violently rent open, ribs splintered outward like broken fingers, and the space where the heart should have been now a gaping hollow. Deep gouges marked the surrounding flesh, as if clawed hands had frantically dug to reach the precious organ and blood had dried in thick rivulets down the torso, pooling and congealing at the feet. Most disturbing was the sheer ferocity evident in the attack, not the calculated violence of human enemies but the overwhelming brutality of an unknown predator.

Talorcan's face had gone pale, recognition dawning in his eyes as he took in the gruesome tableau. He had seen this before, at the site where they had found Tribune Atticus, but the horror had not diminished with repetition.

Lepidus studied the scene with clinical detachment yet even his experienced eye was troubled by what lay before them. This was

181

not merely killing, not even merely ritual. This was a demonstration, calculated to inspire terror in those who discovered it.

'The same as Atticus,' whispered Talorcan, his voice barely audible. 'The same pattern of destruction.'

'Not human,' Lepidus agreed, his voice equally low. 'No man possesses the strength to tear apart a body like that.'

'Not merely strength,' replied Talorcan, his gaze fixed on the mutilated remains. 'Look at the bite patterns, the way flesh has been ripped away. This was done with teeth and claws, not weapons.'

They remained frozen at the clearing's edge, cataloguing details that most men would have fled from in terror. The angle of attack, the selective consumption of certain body parts while others were merely destroyed, all spoke to something beyond normal predatory behaviour.

'The others were here,' Talorcan observed after several minutes of silent observation. 'See how the ground is disturbed around the fire pit? Many feet, perhaps thirty or forty individuals. But the gathering dispersed, leaving this lone victim.'

The disturbing scene raised more questions than it answered. What had happened to the remaining prisoners? What manner of creature could inflict such damage to a trained soldier? And most pressingly, what purpose did such ritualized violence serve in the druids' greater plans?

As the afternoon light began to wane, Lepidus signalled their withdrawal. They retreated with the same painstaking care used in their approach, recovering their sarcinae from their hiding place before putting distance between themselves and the clearing. Neither spoke until they had travelled at least half a mile, finding temporary concealment in a dense thicket.

'We need to follow their trail,' said Lepidus. 'Whatever happened in that clearing is connected to what they're planning. We must discover what it is before the Emperor arrives.'

Talorcan nodded gravely.

'The gathering was large but departed recently. Their trail

will be clear.' His expression hardened. 'But understand what we're tracking, Senator. This is not merely tribal resistance or druidic ritual as Rome understands it. This is something older, darker. The creature that killed that soldier, and Atticus before him, is not natural.'

'Natural or not,' replied Lepidus, checking his weapons for the third time, 'it can be tracked. And what can be tracked can be found.' His eyes met Talorcan's, unflinching. 'And what can be found can be killed.'

As night began to fall over the Britannic wilderness, the two men continued westward, following the clear trail left by the departed gathering. Ahead lay answers, though whether they would discover them in time, or survive the discovery, remained uncertain. Behind them, in the now darkened clearing, the mutilated remains of the Batavian bore silent witness to powers beyond imperial understanding, powers being gathered against Rome's advancing eagles.

Chapter Twenty-Seven

The Western Coast

The Occultum moved like shadows through the deepening twilight, abandoning the measured caution that had characterized their journey thus far.

The unexpected encounter with the child had forced their hand. In tribal lands, strangers were not merely unusual, they were threats to be investigated, captured, or eliminated.

'Faster,' Seneca urged as they crossed a small clearing, his voice barely audible above their controlled breathing. 'The boy will have reached his settlement by now.'

The six men maintained a ground-eating pace that balanced speed against noise, sacrificing some stealth for the urgent need to put terrain between themselves and the inevitable pursuers.

The landscape rose steadily as they advanced, the relatively flat coastal plains giving way to increasingly rolling terrain. Low hills emerged from the darkness ahead, their silhouettes black against the star-filled sky. Each incline taxed already tired muscles, each descent offered momentary respite before the next climb began.

They paused only when absolutely necessary, brief moments to verify direction or consult their crude map by starlight. Water was consumed sparingly from their skins, despite the exertion that left tunics damp with sweat. Food was eaten while moving, dried meat chewed methodically, providing sustenance without the luxury of enjoyment.

'The land rises more sharply ahead,' reported Marcus during one such pause. 'We're entering the foothills proper.'

Seneca nodded, studying the terrain visible in the faint moonlight.

'Good. The higher and more broken the ground, the harder we'll be to track.'

They maintained their pace through the night, pushing tired

bodies beyond normal endurance. These were not ordinary men but veterans of countless campaigns, their physical capabilities honed through years of the most demanding operations Rome conducted. Where common legionaries might have faltered, the Occultum pressed forward, converting fear into focused energy, transforming danger into heightened awareness.

As dawn approached, Decimus signalled from his position as rear guard, drawing their attention to the faint glow of burning torch lights far behind them, visible as tiny pinpricks of fire against the receding darkness.

'Warriors,' said Seneca, studying the distant lights. 'Perhaps four miles back. We've gained ground, but not enough.'

'We need cover,' said Cassius. 'Somewhere to hide until darkness returns.'

Marcus pointed toward a rocky outcropping ahead.

'There. The higher slopes have less vegetation. More stone, fewer tracks.'

'Move,' ordered Seneca, and the group immediately resumed their accelerated pace, angling toward the indicated terrain.

The coming dawn revealed a landscape transformed from the previous day's journey. Gone were the dense forests of the coastlands; in their place stretched a rougher, more barren terrain of rocky slopes interspersed with hardy vegetation. Stunted trees clung to crevices where soil had accumulated, their twisted forms testifying to harsh winds and minimal nutrients. The mountains proper loomed ahead, their peaks catching the first golden light while the land below remained veiled in shadow.

They reached the rocky outcropping as full daylight claimed the countryside, selecting a position among tumbled boulders that offered both concealment and a view of the land below.

'Two men on watch at all times,' said Seneca. 'The others sleep while they can.'

The men arranged themselves among the rocks, finding what comfort was possible on the hard ground. Despite exhaustion from

185

their night-long journey, sleep came fitfully to those off watch, their bodies too tense with awareness of pursuit to fully surrender to unconsciousness.

Midday found all six men alert, watching the terrain below with focused intensity. The distant torch lights had vanished with daybreak, but occasional movement amid the landscapes' contours revealed their pursuers hadn't abandoned the hunt. Groups of tribal warriors swept the foothills, working their way upslope in a coordinated search pattern.

'They are good,' observed Marcus with reluctant admiration. 'Not just angry villagers, trained hunters.'

'They're thorough,' added Falco, watching as one search party carefully investigated a small ravine. 'But slow. They've covered less than half the ground between their starting point and our current position.'

'We have until nightfall,' said Seneca. 'Then we move again.'

As the day advanced, the men conserved energy while maintaining vigilance. They consumed minimal rations, acutely aware of their dwindling supplies. Water remained the greater concern, their skins were less than half full, with no immediate prospect of replenishment and the rocky terrain that provided their concealment offered few water sources.

The afternoon brought an unexpected advantage. Dark clouds gathered over the mountains, gradually spreading across the sky to cast the landscape in premature twilight. Thunder rumbled in the distance, and the air grew heavy with imminent rainfall.

'A storm comes,' said Decimus, studying the approaching weather front with a veteran's experienced eye. 'Strong, by the look of it.'

'Good,' replied Seneca. 'It will wash away tracks and limit visibility. We'll use it for cover.'

The first heavy raindrops began to fall as the light faded, quickly intensifying into a downpour that sheeted across the rocky slopes. Lightning flashed across the darkened sky, momentarily illuminating the wild landscape in stark relief before plunging it back into shadow. Thunder crashed overhead, echoing between the mountain peaks.

'Now,' ordered Seneca when the storm reached its full intensity. 'While their search is hampered.'

The men emerged from their shelter, securing their equipment against the elements as best they could. Rain plastered their hair against their skulls and soaked through their clothing within moments, but none complained. The discomfort was a small price for the concealment the storm provided.

They moved to the northwest, scrambling across increasingly steep and broken terrain. The wet rock proved treacherous, forcing a slower pace than Seneca would have preferred, but still they made steady progress toward the nearby mountains.

By midnight, the storm had passed, leaving behind a landscape washed clean and a sky gradually clearing to reveal stars and a waning moon. The temperature dropped noticeably in the storm's wake, adding the discomfort of wet clothing in cold air to their existing challenges. Still, they pushed forward, driving tired bodies through sheer determination.

Dawn of the second day found them high on a rocky slope, the coastal plains now far behind them. Below, a natural mountain pass carved a sinuous path through the formidable range, visible as a winding cleft between towering peaks. They found concealment among a cluster of boulders that provided both cover and an excellent vantage point over the pass below.

As full daylight illuminated the landscape, the strategic significance of the pass became evident. It represented the most viable route through the mountain range for many miles in either direction, a natural corridor connecting the southern lands of the Ordovices to the north where Mona lay.

'Look,' said Sica, pointing toward movement in the pass.

A small caravan of traders made its way through the narrow

valley, carts drawn by sturdy mountain ponies laden with goods bound for coastal markets.

'The pass is well-used,' observed Marcus as they watched the caravan's progress. 'A natural trade route.'

Throughout the day, they observed the pass from their elevated position. More travellers appeared, individual traders with pack animals, a family group with all their possessions, a band of hunters returning with their game. More concerning were the periodic groups of warriors moving through the corridor, some in small patrols of three or four, others in substantial forces of twenty or more.

'Tribal movements,' noted Seneca, studying a particularly large group passing below. 'More than normal patrol activity. They're gathering for something.'

'Or responding to something,' suggested Decimus. 'Perhaps news of our presence has spread farther than we thought.'

This possibility hung heavy in the air as they continued their observation. If knowledge of unknown intruders had spread throughout the tribal territories, their mission faced even greater challenges than anticipated. Six men, however skilled, could not hope to evade the combined hunting parties of multiple tribes determined to find them.

As the day progressed, their immediate tactical situation became increasingly clear. The pass below represented both opportunity and danger, the most direct route toward their objective, but also the most heavily travelled and potentially guarded approach. Attempting to move through it, particularly with any increased tribal vigilance, would expose them to almost certain discovery.

'We could try to slip through at night,' suggested Falco. 'Find a gap between patrols.'

'Too risky,' replied Seneca, shaking his head. 'One encounter, one alarm raised, and we'd be trapped in a natural bottleneck with enemies on both sides.'

'What about going around?' asked Cassius. 'Is there another

pass within reasonable distance?'

Marcus consulted their crude map. 'The next viable passage is at least three days' journey east, and probably as closely watched as this one.'

The six men fell silent, each contemplating the limited options before them. The mission that had already transformed from challenging to desperate now seemed to approach the impossible. Yet none spoke of abandoning their objective, of turning east toward Roman lines and safety.

As the light began to fade on their second day in the mountains, Seneca studied the towering peaks that rose directly above their position. Unlike the relatively hospitable pass below, these heights offered no easy route, only sheer rock faces, treacherous scree slopes, and thin air that would make exertion twice as demanding. No sensible traveller would attempt to cross directly over such terrain when a viable pass lay within reach.

'If we cannot go through,' said Seneca finally, giving voice to the thought that had been forming in his mind, 'and we cannot go around...'

'We go over,' finished Sica, following his commander's gaze toward the forbidding peaks.

The implication hung in the air between them. Crossing directly over the mountains meant challenging not just human enemies but nature itself. The heights were dangerous even for experienced climbers in ideal conditions. For six exhausted men with limited supplies and improper equipment, it approached suicidal.

'It would be unexpected,' acknowledged Marcus after a moment of consideration. 'No one would think to look for us on the high ridges.'

'Because no one would be fool enough to attempt it,' muttered Falco.

'We've survived worse,' said Decimus.

Seneca surveyed his men, reading in their expressions the same grim determination he felt. Impossible odds were nothing new to the Occultum; they had built their reputation on achieving what conventional forces deemed unattainable. This would simply be one more seemingly insurmountable obstacle overcome in service to Rome.

'We move at first light,' decided Seneca. 'Travel light, one tent and essential weapons only, Anything that might slow our ascent stays behind.'

The men nodded their agreement, already mentally cataloguing their limited possessions, deciding what could be abandoned and what must be retained. Their lives would depend on these calculations, on balancing the need for equipment against the demands of swift movement over treacherous terrain.

As night settled over the mountains, each man prepared in his own way for the challenge ahead. Weapons were checked and secured, bootlaces reinforced, and water skins arranged for optimal weight distribution. Some slept briefly, storing energy for the coming exertion, others kept watch, their eyes tracking the movement of tribal patrols through the pass below, confirming again that their chosen route, however dangerous, was their only viable option.

Seneca remained awake longest, his gaze fixed on the dark silhouette of the mountains against the star-filled sky. Tomorrow they would attempt what few would even consider, gambling their lives against the primal forces of nature in a desperate bid to complete their mission. The risk was immense, but the alternative, failure, was unacceptable.

Somewhere beyond those forbidding peaks lay Mona, and Raven. The path between seemed impossible, but the Occultum had made a practice of achieving the impossible. One more time, they would attempt the unthinkable, or possibly die in the attempt. Dawn would tell which outcome awaited them.

Chapter Twenty-Eight

Isla Mona

Veteranus sat motionless on the weather-worn rock overlooking the western shore of Isla Mona, his gaze fixed on the restless sea beyond. The incoming tide crashed against the jagged coastline below, sending plumes of white spray skyward before retreating, only to gather strength and assault the unyielding stone once more. Hours had passed since he had sought this isolated vantage point, yet time held little meaning as his mind wrestled with the weight of choice.

Sleep had eluded him for days now. Each time he closed his eyes, the visions returned, twisted creatures that had once been children, transformed through years of systematic cruelty into something no longer fully human, the creatures they called the Wraith. Most disturbing was not what they had become, but the deliberate process that had created them, their filed teeth, their distorted limbs, their eyes that somehow retained terrible awareness despite the horrors visited upon them.

He pulled his cloak tighter against the pre-dawn chill. In all his years serving Rome, through campaigns across three continents, through the shadow operations with the Occultum where morality was always subordinate to necessity, he had never encountered deliberate cruelty so systematic, so purposeful in its application.

'What manner of mind conceives such a thing?' he whispered to the uncaring sea. '

The question troubled him more than he cared to admit. The druids, with their ancient wisdom and connection to natural forces, had always been presented in Roman accounts as primitive, superstitious, bloodthirsty in their sacrifices yet limited in their understanding. What he had witnessed in the pit, and later learned from both Mordred and Raven, suggested something far different, a culture capable of patience spanning decades, of knowledge beyond

Roman comprehension, of calculated cruelty that rivalled anything the 'civilized' world had produced.

Yet even as he condemned what he had seen, his mind turned inevitably toward uncomfortable comparisons. Had Rome not also inflicted systematic suffering throughout its expansion? Children torn from conquered peoples, raised as slaves, their identities erased, their bodies used for labour, pleasure, or spectacle according to their masters' whims. Entire populations crucified as examples, left to die in prolonged agony along public roads. Gladiatorial games where men were forced to slaughter one another for the entertainment of cheering crowds.

The scale differed, perhaps. The Wraith represented a handful of transformed beings, while Rome's victims numbered in the hundreds of thousands. But did scale matter when evaluating the darkness of the human spirit that conceived such things? Could the minds that created the Wraith be judged more harshly than those who designed the ingenious tortures of Roman interrogation chambers and amphitheatres?

Veteranus ran a hand across his face, feeling the rough stubble that had accumulated during his sleepless vigil. The simple physical sensation offered momentary respite from the circular arguments that had occupied his thoughts through the long night.

He had been a killer for Rome, an instrument of imperial policy whose hands had ended lives deemed threatening to Roman interests. Some of those deaths had been clean, quick, merciful if execution could ever be called such. Others had been slower, more calculated, designed to extract information before delivering final release. He had not questioned those actions at the time, he had compartmentalized them as necessary in service to the greater peace Rome provided.

Yet Rome had abandoned him, had sentenced him to death when his usefulness ended, when the political winds shifted. Colleagues who had shared meals with him, fought beside him, called him brother, had turned their backs when orders came to eliminate him. He owed Rome nothing, not loyalty, not service, certainly not the benefit of moral doubt.

So why did he hesitate? Why did the decision before him, to assist Mordred in his plan against the empire, cause such turmoil within him?

The eastern horizon had begun to lighten, the first pale suggestions of dawn breaking over the island. Soon the village would stir to life, fishermen preparing their boats, craftspeople beginning their daily labours, druids conducting their morning observances in the sacred groves. Normal life continuing despite the extraordinary choices being made within their midst.

Mordred's proposal was elegant in its simplicity yet devastating in its potential impact. It would not stop Rome's conquest, nothing could, not permanently. The empire's resources were too vast, its determination too ingrained, its hunger for new territories too profound to be permanently thwarted by any single action.

But what Mordred proposed would send a message that would echo through the marble halls of Rome's power, would whisper in the ears of Emperors yet unborn: you are not invincible. Your power has limits. Your legions can bleed. And someday, perhaps centuries from now, *you too will fall!*

Was that message worth his participation? Worth allying himself with those who had created the Wraith? Worth turning against the empire of his birth, flawed and cruel though it might be?

The first golden rays of sunlight broke over the eastern hills, illuminating the coastline in warm light that belied the weight of the decision before him. Veteranus watched as a pair of seabirds wheeled above the churning water below, their movements graceful and precise as they searched for morning prey.

In that moment of natural beauty amidst his moral struggle, clarity began to emerge from chaos. The question was not whether Rome or the druids could claim moral superiority, for both had

193

committed atrocities, both had blood on their hands stretching back generations. The question was simpler, more personal: which path could he live with? Which choice could he make and still recognize himself afterward?

Rome had ordered his death when he became inconvenient. His former brothers in the Occultum had accepted that order without question but had been overridden when he had been unexpectedly pardoned. Whatever loyalty he had once felt toward the empire had been severed not by his own choice, but by theirs.

The sound of approaching footsteps on the rocky path behind him broke his reverie. He did not turn, recognizing the deliberate tread of Kendra, the warrior-priestess who had shown particular interest in
him since his arrival.

'Dawn greets you, Veteranus,' she said, coming to stand beside him. Her dark hair was bound in intricate braids that spoke of both rank and heritage, and her face bore the blue ritual markings of her status. 'Did you find answers in the night?'

'Perhaps,' he replied, his gaze still fixed on the horizon. 'Or perhaps merely more questions to replace those already answered.'

'The old ones say wisdom begins with the acceptance that some questions have no answers,' she offered, settling onto a nearby rock. 'Only choices, each with its own consequences.'

'A convenient philosophy for those who wish to avoid moral judgment,' he observed.

'Or a realistic one for those who understand that life rarely offers perfect paths,' she replied. 'What troubles you most? The choice before you, or what you witnessed in the pit?'

Veteranus turned to look at her directly, studying the composed features of a woman born and raised within druidic tradition yet clearly possessing an intellect that questioned and evaluated rather than merely accepted.

'Both,' he admitted. 'The Wraith... they represent a cruelty I struggle to comprehend, even having witnessed atrocities across half the known world.'

Kendra nodded, accepting his assessment without attempting to justify or defend it.

'They are inherited darkness,' she said, 'maintained because they serve a purpose deemed necessary by those who came before us.'

'Does that distance absolve those who maintain them now?' he asked. 'Those who feed them, who use them as weapons?'

'No more than Rome is absolved of the systems of suffering it inherited and maintains,' she replied. 'The auction blocks where children are sold, the estates of the rich where slaves die by the thousands, the arenas where death is entertainment, all existed before living Romans were born. Does that distance absolve those who maintain them now?'

Her question mirrored his own internal struggle so precisely that he could not help but appreciate the parallel. They sat in silence for a time, watching as the day brightened further, the blue of the sea deepening as shadows retreated.

'Mordred believes you will join us,' Kendra said eventually. 'He sees in you not merely a useful ally because of your knowledge, but something more, a recognition of the truth that neither Rome nor Britannia holds moral high ground in this conflict. Only different perspectives on what survival requires.'

'And what do you see?' asked Veteranus.

'I see a man who has lived too long in shadows to be comfortable in either full darkness or full light,' she replied with surprising insight. 'A man accustomed to operating in the space between opposed forces, taking what he needs from each while belonging fully to neither.'

'And if I choose to assist Mordred?' he asked, though he suspected he already knew the answer.

'Then you would not be asked to become something you are not,' she said. 'No oath of eternal loyalty, no surrender of your judgment, no pretence that our ways are perfect or without cost. Only your expertise applied to a specific purpose, with the

195

understanding that all involved recognize the moral complexity of what we do.'

The sun had fully cleared the horizon now, its warmth beginning to dispel the morning chill. Below them, the first fishing boats were being launched from the village harbour, men calling to one another as they prepared for the day's work. Life continuing, as it always did, regardless of the momentous decisions being made in its midst.

Veteranus rose from his rock, his muscles stiff from hours of immobility yet his mind clearer than it had been in days.

'I have sat here through the night,' he said, 'playing each argument over and over in my mind. And I've reached a conclusion. I will assist Mordred, not because I believe in all the druids stand for, not because I have abandoned all that Rome gave me, but because this specific action feels right in this specific moment of history.'

He turned away from the sea, facing inland toward the village where Mordred awaited his decision.

'I've made my choice. Now let us see what consequences follow.'

Together they walked down the rocky path, leaving behind the isolation of the clifftop for the activity of the village below, and as they approached the first dwellings of the settlement, Veteranus knew that whatever happened next, he had made this choice not out of hatred for Rome or love for Britannia, but from the hard-won wisdom of a life spent observing the true nature of power and its effects on those caught within its currents.

Rome would continue its conquest, would likely succeed in subduing much of Britannia as it had subdued countless lands before. But perhaps, through his actions and those of others like him, the empire would learn that conquest had costs it had not anticipated, that some knowledge could not be destroyed by sword and fire, that the seeds of its eventual fall were being sown even as it reached the height of its power. It was enough. It had to be.

Chapter Twenty-Nine

The Road to Camulodunum

Dawn broke over the Roman column, as if even the sun had been conscripted into imperial service. Four thousand men stirred from their temporary camp, Centurions barking orders as legionaries dismantled tents, packed equipment, and formed into their designated units. By first light, the Second Augusta stood ready to march, a machine of war oiled by discipline and driven by the unshakable certainty of Rome's manifest destiny.

The engineers, protected by a cohort of Batavian auxiliaries, had spent weeks clearing and improving the route. Where once a narrow tribal track had wound through the countryside, a proper military road now stretched northward toward Camulodunum. Trees had been felled, rough terrain levelled, and streams bridged with sturdy timber constructions that would eventually be replaced by stone. Rome did not merely pass through territories, it transformed them, imposed its vision of order upon the landscape itself.

'Second Augusta! *Advance!*'

The command echoed down the line, passed from officer to officer until it reached the furthest ranks.

Two centuries of Exploratores had already been deployed, experienced scouts spreading ahead and to the flanks, eyes constantly scanning for any sign of ambush or resistance. These men were Rome's sensory organs in hostile territory, alert to dangers that conventional forces might miss. Behind them came the auxiliary cavalry units and the vanguard cohort, shields aligned in perfect formation, spear points gleaming in the morning light.

Then came the heart of the legion, cohort after cohort of heavy infantry, the legionaries who had conquered half the known world. Each man carried his equipment with practiced ease: gladius at the right hip, pugio dagger at the left, pilum javelin held ready, large scutum shield protecting his left side. Their hobnailed caligae

197

boots struck the ground in unison, creating a rhythmic percussion that announced Rome's advance far beyond visual range.

At the centre of the formation rode the legion's commanding officers. Vespasian sat straight-backed upon his mount, his gaze constantly scanning both his men and the surrounding terrain. Beside him, General Plautius maintained similar vigilance, the weight of overall command evident in his measured assessment of their progress.

Behind them, carried with reverent pride, came the standards. First and foremost, the eagle, symbol of imperial power and legionary pride, its Golden form catching the sunlight as if the gods themselves blessed their advance. Then the Vexillum, the large square flag bearing the legion's designation and honours, followed by the individual signa of each cohort, decorated with the phalerae, torcs, and crowns earned through past victories.

The sight was deliberately impressive, not merely a military advance but a visual statement of Rome's unstoppable might. This was how empires expanded, not furtively or apologetically, but with open declaration of power and intention. The spectacle was designed to inspire courage in Roman hearts and instil despair in those who might consider resistance.

Behind the main infantry force came the legion's artillery units, ballista and scorpion engines disassembled for transport, their components carried on mule-drawn carts. Then the baggage train proper, hundreds of supply wagons bearing food, equipment, medical supplies, and all the material necessities for an army on campaign. Camp followers brought up the rear, the unofficial but essential support network of craftsmen, merchants, servants, and others who orbited the military structure.

Flanking the entire column rode auxiliary cavalry, mainly Batavians and Thracians, men recruited from conquered territories who now served the empire that had subdued their homelands. They maintained a loose screen to either side, ready to respond to threats from any direction or carry messages along the column's considerable length.

'Magnificent, isn't it?' observed Plautius as they crested a small rise, providing a view of their formation stretching behind them. 'The visible manifestation of Rome.'

Vespasian nodded, appreciating both the tactical efficiency and symbolic power of the spectacle.

'The natives watching from those hills will receive the message clearly enough,' he said. 'This is not a raiding party or temporary incursion, this is occupation, administration, transformation.'

They rode in companionable silence for a time, each man occupied with his own thoughts as the legion continued its inexorable progress northward.

'We've lost fewer men than expected,' Vespasian noted eventually, returning to their ongoing assessment of the campaign. 'The crossing of the Tamesis was costly, but since then, casualties have been minimal.'

'The decisive victory had its effects,' replied Plautius. 'Many tribes see the wisdom in accommodation rather than resistance. Why die fighting when surrender brings the benefits of Roman trade, Roman law, Roman protection?'

'Some might question whether those benefits outweigh the loss of independence.'

Plautius shrugged slightly.

'A philosophical question beyond our concern as military men. Rome decides to expand; we implement that decision. The political officers who follow will manage the transition from conquest to governance.'

The conversation shifted to logistics as they continued their march, the mundane yet critical concerns of supplying over four thousand men in foreign territory. Water sources had proven more reliable than initially feared, local grain supplies more extensive, and the weather had remained unseasonably dry, sparing them the infamous Britannic mud that could transform roads into quagmires

199

and simple marches into exhausting ordeals.

By midday, the column paused for a brief rest, legionaries consuming a cold meal of bread and dried meat while standing in formation, ready to resume the advance on short notice.

As they prepared to resume the march, Plautius turned the conversation toward the topic that had occupied much of their private discussions in recent days.

'I've had word from Rome,' he said quietly, ensuring their conversation remained between them. 'The Emperor will arrive within two months, expecting to find a secure province awaiting his formal recognition.'

Vespasian's expression tightened almost imperceptibly.

'A political spectacle that diverts resources from actual pacification.'

'Yet one we must accommodate,' replied Plautius pragmatically. 'Claudius needs this triumph to secure his position. Without it, his support in Rome remains precarious.'

'I understand the political necessity,' said Vespasian. 'I merely question the timing. The western tribes remain unsubdued, Caratacus still rallies resistance, and our intelligence about druidic activities suggests they're planning something significant.'

'All valid concerns,' acknowledged Plautius. 'But there's little to be done. The Emperor has decided, and we must implement his decision.

The second day brought them into more densely settled territory. Fields of grain stretched across the fertile river valley, punctuated by small settlements and isolated farmsteads. Unlike the previous day's abandoned villages, some of these showed signs of continued occupation, thin smoke rising from cooking fires, livestock in pens, occasional glimpses of people observing their passage from doorways before retreating inside.

'They stay,' noted Vespasian with interest. 'These communities closer to Camulodunum don't flee.'

'They've accepted reality,' replied Plautius. 'The tribal elders of both Trinovantes and Catuvellauni have formally surrendered so these people follow their leaders' example.'

The tentative acceptance they encountered did not prompt any reduction in vigilance. The legion maintained full battle readiness throughout their advance, scouts constantly probing ahead and to the flanks, cavalry patrols sweeping wider arcs to ensure no forces gathered undetected. Rome had learned through bitter experience that apparent submission could mask deadly ambition.

That evening, as the legion established its marching camp with practiced efficiency, Plautius summoned his senior officers to review the following day's approach to Camulodunum. Maps were once more spread across a campaign table in the command tent, each showing different aspects of their objective, topographical features, defensive structures, approaches and withdrawals.

'We'll arrive by midday tomorrow,' Plautius informed them, tracing the final stage of their route. 'The legion will deploy in full battle formation before the main gates, not as direct threat but as demonstration of capability.'

'I assume the settlement expects our arrival?' asked the Primus Pilus, practical as always.

'Yes,' replied Plautius. 'Our messengers have been received and returned safely. The tribal leaders remaining within Camulodunum have indicated their readiness to formally submit to Roman authority.'

'And we believe them?' pressed another officer.

'Their actions support their words,' answered Plautius. 'They've made no preparations for siege, gathered no significant fighting force, stockpiled no unusual supplies. All indicators suggest genuine acceptance of their situation.'

The briefing continued, details of formation and procedure outlined with precision, and despite the expectation of peaceful entry, every contingency was addressed, from unexpected resistance to potential treachery to natural disasters. Rome's military success rested not merely on superior equipment and training, but on this relentless anticipation of all possible challenges.

The third day dawned clear and warm, ideal conditions for the final stage of their advance. The legion broke camp with practiced efficiency and resumed its northward march, each man acutely aware that today they would reach the tribal capital that represented their primary objective since landing on Britannic shores.

Near midday, they crested a gentle hill and the column ground to a momentary halt. Before them stretched a broad valley, its fertile bottomlands cross-crossed with small streams and cultivated fields. And there, on the far side, stood Camulodunum.

Plautius reined his mount to a stop at the vanguard's position, Vespasian beside him. The settlement was substantial by Britannic standards, far larger than the villages they had passed in recent days. Hundreds of round houses arranged in roughly organized streets filled the area within a stout wooden palisade. Smoke rose from cooking fires within, and figures could be seen moving along the walls, observing the Roman arrival.

Most structures followed traditional tribal design, but several larger buildings of stone construction stood prominent among them, a temple complex near the centre, what appeared to be a council hall, and several substantial residences likely belonging to tribal leaders or druids. None represented significant military concerns; these were not fortifications but symbols of status and religious importance.

The palisade itself stood approximately twelve feet high, sturdy enough to deter casual raiders but never designed to withstand a determined assault. No defensive earthworks complicated the approach, no ditches or other obstacles to slow attacking forces. This was a population centre, not a fortress, precisely as their intelligence had indicated.

'Sentries on the wall, but no warriors in formation,' observed Vespasian. 'No signs of prepared defences.'

'As expected,' replied Plautius. 'They've chosen submission over resistance.' He studied the settlement for several more moments, mentally comparing what he saw with the reports and maps prepared by his intelligence officers. Satisfied that no surprises awaited them, he turned to his signaller.

'Signal the advance. Standard deployment.'

Trumpets sounded down the length of the column, their clear notes carrying precise instructions to each unit. The legion responded with machine-like precision, cohorts breaking from marching formation into the battle deployment that had proven so effective across countless battlefields.

The advance resumed down the gentle slope toward Camulodunum, not as a column now but as a broad formation designed both for maximum tactical advantage and psychological impact. Shields aligned in overlapping protection, spear points glinting in precise rows, standards held high to proclaim Rome's presence. This was the apex of ancient military science, thousands of men operating as a single organism, power amplified through unity, strength multiplied through order.

As they approached the cleared ground before the settlement's main gates, the full magnificence of the Second Augusta became apparent. Thousands of men and horses in battle formation, their discipline evident in every precisely maintained interval, every synchronized movement. Behind them came the support elements, the artillery, the supply train, all the components that transformed a fighting force into a self-sustaining machine of conquest.

From within Camulodunum's walls, faces appeared along the palisade, more numerous as the Romans drew closer. Not warriors preparing for defence, but ordinary people, men, women, children, watching with expressions that ranged from fear to curiosity to resignation as their world changed irrevocably before their eyes.

The gates remained closed, though no hostile action came from the walls. No arrows arced toward the Roman lines, no stones were hurled, no battle cries raised in defiance. Only watchful silence

203

as the legion completed its deployment, forming a massive crescent before the settlement's main entrance.

Plautius rode forward with a small honour guard, positioning himself where he could be clearly seen from the walls. His armour gleamed in the midday sun, his crimson cloak fluttering slightly in the gentle breeze. The picture of Roman authority, projecting both power and confidence.

For several moments, nothing happened. The tableau held, Roman might arrayed before tribal walls, each side watching the other across a divide that represented far more than mere physical space. Then, with deliberate slowness, the wooden gates began to swing open.

A small party emerged from the settlement, eight figures in total. They wore no armour, carried no weapons, their hands held open at their sides in the universal gesture of peaceful intent. At their head walked an elderly man, his white hair and beard contrasting with the blue woad patterns visible on his face and hands. The golden torc around his neck marked him as a chief of significant standing, likely the senior remaining tribal leader after Caractacus's flight.

They advanced to the midpoint between walls and Roman lines,
then stopped, waiting. The message was clear, they would come this far in peace, but expected Rome to meet them halfway.

Plautius turned to Vespasian, the hint of a satisfied smile touching his weathered features.

'And so, Britannia begins its transformation,' he said quietly.

He gave a brief signal to his honour guard, and together they rode forward to meet the tribal delegation. Behind them, the full legion maintained their perfect formation, a living embodiment of Rome's method, negotiate where possible, overwhelm where necessary and as the sun reached its zenith above Camulodunum, it illuminated the moment when ancient Britannia and imperial Rome finally met in formal recognition.

204

Chapter Thirty

The High Mountains

The mountain loomed before them, its weathered slopes rising toward cloud-shrouded peaks that seemed to scrape the very floor of heaven. What had appeared merely formidable from a distance now revealed itself as truly daunting, a natural barrier that had deterred travellers for centuries, forcing them toward the passes that the Occultum could not risk using.

'We'll ascend here,' said Seneca, indicating a sloped ridge that offered the most gradual approach to the higher elevations. 'The terrain provides some cover, and the angle is manageable.'

They began their ascent at first light, moving in single file with Sica taking point. The initial slopes proved relatively forgiving, rocky but stable, with occasional stands of stunted pine providing both handholds and concealment from potential observers below. The men moved with careful precision, testing each foothold before committing their weight, maintaining awareness of both the terrain and their surroundings.

'Pace yourselves,' advised Decimus. 'Conserve energy for the steeper sections ahead.'

By midday, they had ascended perhaps a third of the mountain's height, reaching a relatively level shelf that offered brief respite. The men paused to catch their breath, drinking sparingly from their dwindling water supplies. Below, the valley they had traversed spread out in panoramic detail, the pass they had observed now visible as a thin line snaking between adjacent peaks.

'No pursuit visible,' reported Falco, scanning the terrain below.

'I'm not surprised,' said Cassius. 'No reasonable men would attempt this route.'

Their rest was necessarily brief. The weather in mountain regions could change with startling rapidity, and spending a night

205

exposed on the higher slopes would test even their considerable endurance. They resumed their ascent, Sica leading them toward what appeared to be a viable route up the next section.

After an hour of steady climbing, they encountered their first major obstacle, a near-vertical rock face approximately thirty feet high, blocking their intended path. Sica studied it carefully, testing handholds and searching for a way up or around.

'Too smooth,' he reported after several attempts. 'We'd need proper climbing equipment.'

'We backtrack,' decided Seneca. 'Find another approach.'

The detour cost them precious time and energy. They descended a hundred yards before locating an alternative route, a steep gully that offered a challenging but possible path upward. The loose stones filling the ravine made for treacherous climbing, each step dislodging material that clattered down behind them, but gradually they made progress upward.

As the afternoon advanced, the temperature dropped noticeably. The winds that had been merely bracing in the valley below became bitter at this elevation, cutting through their clothing with icy persistence. Clouds gathered around the mountain's peak, obscuring their objective and bringing the threat of precipitation that would make their already difficult ascent potentially deadly. What had begun as a challenging hike transformed into a true climb, requiring the use of both hands and feet, testing the strength of arms as well as legs.

A sharp cry of alarm cut through the wind's constant moan as Falco slid backward, gathering momentum, arms clawing at the rock as he sought desperately for a handhold, but before disaster could claim him, a jutting boulder caught his slide, stopping his descent with a bone-jarring impact that drove the breath from his lungs.

The others converged quickly, Decimus reaching him first.

'Anything broken?' he asked, hands already moving to check limbs and ribs with practiced assessment.

Falco grimaced, his face pale beneath weather-darkened skin. 'Just my dignity,' he managed, 'and perhaps a rib or two.'

A more thorough examination confirmed bruising but no fractures or dislocations. The former gladiator had been fortunate, a matter of feet in either direction and his fall would have continued unchecked down several hundred yards of unforgiving slope.

'Can you continue?' asked Seneca, the question direct rather than sympathetic. In their situation, hard choices might be necessary.

Falco struggled to his feet, wincing but stable.

'Of course,' he replied, as if any other answer were inconceivable. 'It would take more than a tumble to stop me seeing Raven's face when we find him.'

They resumed their climb with renewed caution, the near-miss a stark reminder of the mountain's indifference to their mission's importance. Nature recognized neither Rome's authority nor the Occultum's determination; it simply existed, to be respected or to exact harsh penalties for ignorance or arrogance.

As they climbed higher, the temperature continued to drop. The wind acquired a new edge, carrying occasional ice crystals that stung exposed skin like tiny daggers. Their breath formed clouds before their faces, and the sweat generated by exertion cooled rapidly against their skin, creating a dangerous chill that sapped warmth and energy.

By late afternoon, they reached the snowline. White patches appeared first in shaded crevices, then spread to cover larger areas as they ascended. The snow was old and compact, offering deceptively stable footing in some sections while concealing treacherous ice beneath in others. Each step required testing before commitment, progress slowing to a crawl as they navigated the increasingly alien landscape.

Progress came in increments, a few yards gained, a brief pause to recover, another advance and the light began to fade, adding urgency to their efforts. Being caught on the exposed mountainside after dark would dramatically reduce their chances of survival.

'Last push,' urged Seneca as the final section loomed before them.

With muscles burning and lungs straining in the thin air, they drove themselves upward. Hands were bloodied from sharp rock, feet numbed with cold, but suddenly, there was nowhere higher to climb and one by one, they pulled themselves onto the final rocky ridge, collapsing briefly to recover from the final exertion.

The view that greeted them surpassed anything they had imagined. The sun, beginning its westward descent, cast golden light across a panorama of breathtaking scale. Behind them lay the territories they had traversed, mountains, valleys and forests stretching back as far as the eye could see, while before them, in the distance, lay the sight they had come so far to see, Isla Mona, stronghold of the druids, refuge of their target.

'How far?' asked Falco, his breathing still laboured from the climb.

'A couple of days,' replied Marcus after studying the terrain before them. 'Depending on conditions.'

The assessment was sobering. They had overcome the mountain, but their journey was far from complete. Between their current position and Mona lay miles of unknown territory, potentially hostile tribes, and the strait itself, which would require some means of crossing when they eventually reached it.

They had little time to contemplate these challenges. The wind across the ridge blew with shocking force, carrying a cold that penetrated to the bone.

'We need to descend,' said Seneca, 'find some shelter before nightfall.'

The western slope offered a different character than the side they had ascended, less sheer but covered with deeper snow that concealed the nature of the ground beneath and as they lost elevation, the worst of the wind diminished. The snow gradually thinned, exposing more rock and, eventually, signs of vegetation.

The light was failing rapidly when they spotted their salvation, the dark line of the treeline emerging from the mountainside perhaps five hundred yards below their position. The sight gave them renewed energy for the final stage of their descent, the promise of shelter driving tired bodies beyond normal limits, and they reached the treeline just as darkness claimed the mountain.

'We stop here,' announced Seneca, selecting a relatively flat area beneath the largest trees and working with practiced coordination despite their exhaustion, they established a basic camp.

Seneca and Marcus constructed a rudimentary windbreak from fallen branches while Sica prepared a fire pit, carefully selecting a position where the flames would be shielded from view from below. Decimus assisted Falco in gathering suitable firewood, the ex-gladiator moving stiffly but insisting on contributing despite his injuries.

Cassius, meanwhile, prepared what remained of their rations, a meagre collection of dried meat, hard bread, and grain. Combined with melted snow and heated over the fire, it would form a simple but warming soup, desperately needed after their exposure to the mountain's punishing conditions.

They gathered around the fire, bodies aching from the day's exertions, spirits simultaneously buoyed by their achievement and sobered by the challenges still ahead. Steam rose from damp clothing as they thawed, the simple pleasure of returning warmth to frozen extremities momentarily overshadowing larger concerns.

'Soup's ready,' announced Cassius eventually, stirring the improvised meal in their single cooking pot. He distributed portions in wooden bowls, the food simple but transformed into something approaching luxurious by their desperate hunger and the heat it provided.

They ate in silence for several minutes, the only sounds the crackling of the fire and the distant moan of wind still torturing the heights they had left behind. Eventually, Seneca spoke, his voice reflective rather than commanding.

'We've done what few would attempt and fewer would achieve,' he said, gesturing toward the mountain above them. 'We'll rest here for two nights and recover our strength, but after that, we'll follow the tree line until we can safely descend to the valley.'

The plan was simple but sound. The higher elevation would provide better visibility of the terrain ahead while still offering the concealment of the forest. Once they had identified a safe route to the lower ground, they could resume their journey toward Mona.

As the fire settled into glowing embers, the men arranged themselves for rest, establishing the usual watch rotation despite their fatigue. Three would sleep while three maintained vigilance. The going had been harder than they had envisaged, but now, with the mountain range behind them, they were a lot closer to their goal and Raven, whether he sensed it or not, was now within their reach.

Chapter Thirty-One

Central Britannia

The early morning mist clung to the forest floor as Lepidus and Talorcan continued their pursuit, moving silently through the dense undergrowth. They had been following the trail for almost ten days, and the signs indicated they were drawing closer to their quarry with each passing day. The landscape around them had gradually changed; this region of central Britannia was more populous than the wild territories they had traversed earlier, with scattered villages and well-worn paths crisscrossing the valleys.

Talorcan paused to examine fresh footprints in the soft earth beside a small stream.

'They passed here no more than a few hours ago,' he whispered, glancing up at Lepidus. 'But they circled the village rather than pass through it.'

They travelled on until dusk, making good progress despite their caution. As twilight descended, they found themselves on a ridge overlooking a small valley thick with ancient oak and elm. Talorcan suddenly raised his hand, signalling Lepidus to stop.

'There,' he whispered, pointing toward a gap in the trees perhaps half a mile distant.

Lepidus squinted and saw the faint orange glow of campfires flickering between the trunks of massive trees. His heart quickened. After days of following tracks and signs, they had finally caught sight of their quarry.

'We've found them,' he murmured, a mixture of satisfaction and apprehension in his voice. 'Now comes the dangerous part.'

'It's too dangerous to move closer tonight,' said Talorcan. 'But by nightfall tomorrow, we should be able to see what is going on. Let's set up camp in the valley.'

They descended the ridge using every shadow and contour of the land to mask their movement. The forest floor was a treacherous

211

maze of fallen branches and leaf litter, each step requiring careful placement to avoid making noise. Eventually, satisfied with their position, they unwrapped their sleeping rolls and ate some cold food.

'Rest,' said Talorcan. 'I'll wake you if anything changes.'

Lepidus nodded. He hadn't slept properly in days, and the constant vigilance was taking its toll. He wrapped himself in his cloak and settled against the base of a broad oak, his sword within easy reach but despite his exhaustion, sleep came fitfully, his mind racing with questions about their mission and the men they pursued.

The following morning, both men woke before dawn and packed away their kit into their sarcinae.

'Do you think they know they're being followed?' asked Lepidus.

Talorcan shook his head.

'No. If they knew, they would have either confronted us or set an ambush.'

Once set, they headed west again, keen to not let their quarry get too far ahead. The terrain became more challenging as they progressed and as the sun began its descent, Lepidus caught sight of something through a break in the trees ahead: a hilltop cleared of forest, upon which stood a settlement unlike any they had passed thus far. It was fortified, surrounded by a substantial palisade of sharpened logs. Earthen ramparts and ditches formed additional defensive layers, and even from this distance, he could make out the silhouettes of guards patrolling the perimeter.

'Not what I expected,' Lepidus admitted, studying the fortification with growing concern.

They spent the remainder of the day establishing a secure observation point with a clear view of the settlement.

'We watch and wait,' Lepidus decided. 'If they decide to leave again, we'll be ready.'

The first day of observation revealed little beyond the routine activities of a well-organized settlement. People moved around outside the palisade, tending to daily tasks, smoke rose from several fires, and livestock could be heard from pens within the walls. There was nothing outwardly sinister about the place, yet something about it set Lepidus's

nerves on edge.

When darkness fell, the settlement became more active rather than less. More fires were lit, and the sound of voices carried faintly across the distance to their hiding place. Lepidus and Talorcan took turns watching through the night, but the men they had followed did not emerge.

They settled in for a night of vigilance, their unease growing with each passing hour. The night grew darker, the cloud cover blocking the stars and moon, leaving only the reflected glow from the settlement's fires to illuminate the landscape.

Despite his determination to remain alert, Lepidus found his eyelids growing heavy as the quiet hours passed. He was fighting against drowsiness when Talorcan suddenly sat up beside him, fully awake in an instant.

'Listen,' he whispered.

At first, Lepidus heard nothing beyond the normal sounds of the night forest, but then a faint, rhythmic thumping carried on the night air, drums, coming from within the settlement.

'Something is happening,' he said.

The drums increased in tempo, and the chanting grew louder, more fervent.

'What are they doing?' Lepidus whispered, though he knew Talorcan had no more answers than he did.

They watched in tense silence as the noise from the settlement continued to build, the drums and chanting reaching a frenzied pitch, and then, abruptly, everything stopped. The silence that followed was absolute, unnatural in its completeness, as if the entire forest held its breath. The silence stretched for several heartbeats, and then it was shattered by a sound that froze the blood

213

in Lepidus's veins: a terrifying scream echoing through the night, human yet filled with such agony that it scarcely seemed possible. Almost immediately, it was joined by something else, an animalistic roar of such primal ferocity that both men instinctively reached for their weapons.

'By all the gods,' Lepidus breathed, his knuckles white around the hilt of his gladius. 'What was that?'

Talorcan shook his head slowly, his normally impassive face showing genuine alarm.

'It was like nothing I have ever heard before,' he admitted.

The screaming intensified, rising to a pitch that seemed impossible for human lungs to produce. It continued for what felt like an eternity but was likely no more than a few heartbeats before cutting off with terrible suddenness.

In the silence that followed, Lepidus could hear his own heart hammering in his chest, until, a few moments later, a collective roar of approval erupted from within the settlement, followed by the resumption of drums and triumphant chanting.

Gradually, the noise subsided, and the night eventually returned to something resembling normalcy. But for Lepidus and Talorcan, nothing would be normal again. They sat in stunned silence for a long while, neither willing to voice the thoughts racing through their minds.

'What have we stumbled upon?' said Lepidus finally.

'Something old,' replied Talorcan. 'Something that should have remained buried in the darkest corners of these islands.'

Lepidus stared at the now-quiet settlement.

'And the men we followed? What part do they play in this?'

'I fear we will discover that soon enough,' Talorcan said.

A cold wind whispered through the trees around them, carrying with it the faint scent of smoke and something else, something metallic and unpleasant. Lepidus found himself thinking of the reason why they had come on this mission, the careful wording that now seemed deliberately vague.

'We should withdraw,' Talorcan suggested. 'Report what we've found before proceeding further.'

But Lepidus shook his head.

'No. We've come too far to turn back now. We need to find out what is going on. We'll continue our observation tomorrow. Perhaps in daylight, we can make more sense of what we've witnessed.'

As they settled back into their watchful positions, Lepidus couldn't shake the feeling that they had crossed a threshold from which there was no return. Whatever awaited them within that palisade was beyond the scope of his experience as a soldier of Rome.

In the darkness, the distant settlement stood silhouetted against
the night sky. To all appearances, it was simply another fortified hill settlement, one of many scattered across Britannia, but Lepidus knew better. Within those walls lay answers to questions he was no longer certain he wanted to ask.

Chapter Thirty-Two

Camulodunum

The stone building stood as an anomaly amidst the wooden structures of Camulodunum, its weathered walls a testament to the influence that had already begun to seep into Britannia long before Rome's legions arrived. Sunlight filtered through the high windows, casting long beams across the gathered assembly within. At the head of the great hall, seated at an ornate table elevated on a wooden platform, General Aulus Plautius surveyed the gathering with the measured gaze of a man who had conquered nations. Beside him, Vespasian sat with rigid military bearing, his scarred hands resting atop the wooden table, his expression betraying nothing of his thoughts.

Both commanders wore their full military regalia, gleaming breastplates adorned with intricate embossing, crimson cloaks draped over one shoulder and fastened with golden clasps, and the unmistakable insignia of Rome's imperial authority displayed prominently. Behind them stood a row of officers, each bearing the standard of their respective cohorts, their faces impassive as they gazed out over the assembled representatives.

The tribal elders sat on benches arranged before the Roman commanders, each adorned in their own ceremonial dress that marked their rank and tribal affiliation. Intricate torcs of gold encircled their necks, their arms bearing spiral bracelets of silver and bronze. Their clothing, richly dyed and adorned with complex patterns, stood in stark contrast to the uniformity of Roman military dress. Some wore elaborate headdresses featuring antlers or feathers, while others displayed facial tattoos that marked their status among their people.

Despite their finery, there was no mistaking the reality of the situation. These were not allies meeting as equals, but subjugated peoples paying homage to their conquerors. The tribal leaders' expressions ranged from thinly veiled hostility to resigned acceptance, but all bore the weight of their newfound status under Rome's expanding shadow.

'We gather today to formalize what has already been decided by strength of arms,' Plautius began, his voice carrying easily through the hall. A translator at his side rendered his Latin into the Celtic tongue for those who did not speak the language of their conquerors. 'Camulodunum now belongs to Rome and through it, Emperor Claudius extends his protection to those who acknowledge his authority.'

Vespasian watched the faces of the tribal elders as Plautius spoke. Some maintained steady eye contact, a gesture of defiance that impressed him despite himself. Others stared at the floor, their pride visibly wounded. A few nodded slightly, pragmatists who had already calculated that alliance with Rome offered better prospects than continued resistance.

'The Emperor is generous to those who accept his friendship,' Plautius continued. 'Roads will be built, connecting your settlements. Trade will flow. Justice will be administered with fairness to all who live under Roman law. Your children will learn to read and write, and the brightest among them may one day serve in the administration of this province.'

A murmur passed through the assembly at this, not all of it negative, Vespasian noted. The promise of education and advancement for their children held appeal for some, even as others clearly viewed it as cultural erasure.

'In recognition of Rome's authority and protection, tribute will be collected,' Plautius announced, moving to the heart of the gathering's purpose. 'Each clan will contribute according to its means. Those who demonstrate loyalty will find the burden lighter with each passing year.'

One by one, the representatives were called forward. The first to approach was an elder from the Trinovantes, a tribe that had suffered under the dominance of their neighbours, the Catuvellauni,

217

before Rome's arrival. Perhaps for this reason, he seemed less resentful than many of his counterparts as he approached the Roman commanders.

'The Trinovantes offer tribute to Rome,' he announced in accented but intelligible Latin, a choice that Vespasian recognized as deliberate diplomacy.

At the elder's gesture, two men entered bearing a small wooden chest. They set it before the Roman commanders and opened it, revealing hundreds of silver coins, many bearing the images of tribal leaders but some clearly of Roman origin, collected through decades of trade.

Plautius nodded, and scribes at a smaller table to the side made note of the tribute's contents.

'The Emperor acknowledges the Trinovantes' wisdom in choosing peace,' he responded.

The procession continued, with representatives from tribes both large and small approaching to present their tribute. The Iceni, whose lands lay to the north, sent a contingent led by a stern-faced man who approached the table with unconcealed reluctance.

'The Iceni acknowledge Rome's presence in our lands,' he stated carefully, avoiding any language that suggested submission. 'We offer these gifts in the spirit of mutual respect.'

The choice of words was not lost on Vespasian or Plautius, but they allowed the implicit challenge to pass without comment. The Iceni tribute was substantial, several chests of silver, finely worked jewellery, and several exquisite horse trappings adorned with enamel work of exceptional quality.

'The Emperor values the friendship of the Iceni,' Plautius responded diplomatically. 'Your craftsmanship honours your people.'

As the ceremony progressed, both Roman commanders found themselves increasingly surprised by the sophistication of the tributes presented. They had expected raw metals, basic foodstuffs, and perhaps some crude ornaments, the typical spoils one might extract from a conquered barbarian territory. Instead, they were witnessing a display of craftsmanship that rivalled much of what could be found in the markets of Rome itself.

A delegation from a small coastal tribe presented a collection of amber jewellery, each piece containing perfectly preserved insects or plant materials, set in intricate gold filigree. The Dobunni offered delicately worked silver vessels, embossed with hunting scenes of remarkable detail while the Durotriges brought forward several cloaks dyed in a blue so vibrant that Vespasian found himself wondering what process they used to achieve such colour.

Most impressive were the religious artifacts, small statues and ritual objects dedicated to Celtic deities. There were figures of horned gods carved from oak with such skill that they seemed almost alive, bronze representations of animals that captured their essence in stylized form, and stone heads with serene expressions that somehow conveyed both benevolence and terrible power.

Vespasian found himself particularly drawn to a small silver figurine of a goddess with three faces, each gazing in a different direction. The craftsmanship was exquisite, capturing in miniature form a concept of divinity that, while alien to Roman sensibilities, nonetheless conveyed profound spiritual meaning.

'They call her Brigantia,' a soft voice explained in Latin, and Vespasian looked up to see one of the tribal elders, a woman of perhaps fifty years with silver threading through her dark hair, watching him examine the figurine. 'She sees what was, what is, and what will be.'

Vespasian considered the artifact with newfound interest. 'The workmanship is remarkable.'

'We are not the savages your people believe us to be,' she replied with quiet dignity before returning to her place among the tribal representatives.

As the ceremony continued, the accumulated wealth before the Roman commanders grew to surprising proportions. Gold and silver coins by the thousands, jewellery, ceremonial weapons with hilts of bone and amber, drinking vessels adorned with mythological scenes, and textiles dyed in colours so rich they seemed to glow in the slanting afternoon light.

Finally, as the sun began to set, and the last of the tributes was presented and recorded, Plautius rose to his feet and the hall fell silent.

'The Emperor accepts your tributes as symbols of your loyalty,' he announced. 'In return, Rome extends its protection. You may retain your local customs where they do not conflict with Roman law. Trade routes will be established, and your people will benefit from commerce with all parts of the Empire.'

He paused, letting his gaze sweep across the assembly before continuing.

'Those who abide by Rome's authority will prosper. Those who resist will be dealt with swiftly and without mercy. The choice is yours.'

With these words, Plautius signalled that the ceremony was concluded and the tribal elders rose and filed out of the hall, escorted by Roman soldiers.

When the last of them had departed, Plautius turned to Vespasian with a sigh of relief.

'That went more smoothly than I anticipated,' he admitted, rolling his shoulders to release the tension of maintaining a formal posture for so many hours.

'They are pragmatists, if nothing else,' Vespasian replied, gesturing to a slave to bring wine. 'They've calculated the cost of continued resistance and found it too high.'

The two commanders retired to a smaller chamber adjoining the main hall, where a table had been prepared with refreshments. Several other senior officers joined them, including Hosidius Geta and Gnaeus Sentius, both of whom had distinguished themselves during the campaign.

'I confess I'm surprised by the wealth they've accumulated,' Sentius remarked, gesturing toward the main hall where soldiers were now carefully cataloguing and securing the collected tribute. 'The intelligence reports described them as painted savages living in mud huts.'

Plautius nodded, accepting a cup of wine from a servant.

'Our understanding of these people has been... incomplete,' he acknowledged. 'They are not Romans, to be sure, but neither are they the primitive barbarians we were led to expect.'

'Their metalwork is particularly impressive,' Vespasian added. 'Some of those pieces would fetch high prices in Rome's markets but I am under no illusion that this is all there is. I expect these is much more to uncover as we consolidate our position.'

'Undoubtedly so,' said Plautius, 'but we will avoid further demands until Claudius arrives.'

'The question is whether their apparent acquiescence is genuine,' Geta interjected. They smile and bow and present gifts, but I've seen the look in their eyes. Many are simply biding their time.'

'Possibly,' responded Plautius, 'the tribes have never been united, they've spent generations fighting amongst themselves but that
works to our advantage.'

'Until it doesn't,' Vespasian pointed out. 'If they ever found common cause against us...'

'Then we would face a formidable enemy indeed,' Plautius conceded. 'Which is why we must ensure they find more benefit in Rome's peace than in rebellion.'

The officers fell into a discussion of security measures, the positioning of garrisons, the establishment of watchtowers along key routes, the recruitment of local auxiliaries who might provide intelligence on any brewing discontent

As the evening wore on, the officers gradually departed, returning to their respective duties until only Plautius and Vespasian remained. They sat in companionable silence for a time, both men mentally reviewing the events of the day and their implications.

'The tribes seem cowed enough for now,' Vespasian offered.

'For now,' Plautius echoed. 'But their memories are long,

221

and their grievances run deep. We've won battles, Vespasian, but conquering hearts and minds, that's the work of generations.'

'We also have work to do here,' said Vespasian, gesturing out of the window. 'This is hardly a setting worthy of an Imperial visit. Camulodunum is still essentially a tribal settlement with a Roman garrison imposed upon it.'

'Precisely,' Plautius replied, turning back to face him. 'Claudius cannot be received in a muddy frontier outpost. We need transformation, and quickly.'

The implications of this statement hung in the air between them. Transforming a tribal settlement into something resembling a Roman city would require immense resources, manpower, and time, none of which they had in abundance.

'How soon?' Vespasian asked, already mentally calculating what might be achieved in different timeframes.

'Two months or so,' Plautius answered. 'He'll want to arrive before the autumn rains make travel difficult.'

'That's barely enough time to construct proper defences,' said Vespasian, 'let alone the kind of civic buildings that would impress an Emperor.'

'Nevertheless, it must be done,' Plautius insisted. 'Claudius needs this victory to be magnificent, not just in military terms but as a demonstration of Rome's civilizing influence. When he arrives, he must find a city taking shape, not a barbarian stronghold with Roman standards planted in its soil.'

Vespasian nodded slowly, recognizing the political necessity behind the impossible timeline.

'We'll need architects, engineers, skilled craftsmen...'

'Already on their way from Gaul,' said Plautius, 'as are additional resources. In the meantime, we'll employ local labour for the basic construction.'

The two men fell silent again, each contemplating the enormity of the task ahead. Taking Camulodunum had been fairly straightforward, but now they faced the more challenging prospect of transforming it into a city worthy of an Imperial visit, all while maintaining control over newly subjugated tribes whose loyalty remained questionable at best.

'We will start immediately,' Vespasian said finally. 'A forum first, I think, and proper headquarters for Claudius and the legionary command. Then housing for the administration, and only then civic amenities.'

Plautius nodded approval.

'Prioritize a temple as well. Claudius will expect to see visible signs of religious conversion. I want stone walls, not wooden palisades, at least for the administrative areas where Claudius will spend his time.'

Vespasian mentally calculated the huge manpower such a project would require.

'We'll need to pull soldiers from all four legions for construction duties.'

'Do it,' Plautius authorized, standing up. "The show of submission we witnessed today buys us some security so use it. Now get some rest. Tomorrow, we begin transforming Camulodunum from a conquered settlement into the northernmost jewel of Rome's empire.'

Chapter Thirty-Three

Isla Mona

Standing once more at the edge of the cliff overlooking the restless seas surrounding Mona, Veteranus closed his eyes and breathed deeply of the salt-laden air. Behind him lay the path back to Rome, to the life he had known, before him stretched something new, something that both repelled and fascinated him in equal measure.

He had spent three days in solitude after his last meeting with Mordred, wrestling with his conscience and his oath to Rome. In the end, it wasn't ideology or promises of power that swayed him, but simple pragmatism. Rome was far away. Whatever was happening on this island was immediate, visceral, and beyond anything he had encountered in his years of service.

As he walked back, the island itself seemed alive in a way he couldn't quite articulate, as though the very soil pulsed with hidden power. Kendra was waiting for him at the edge of the settlement, her tall figure unmistakable even at a distance. The warrior-priestess had shown particular interest in him since his arrival, and now her presence suggested she had anticipated this outcome all along.

'They're waiting for you,' said Kendra before turning and walking toward the longhouse.

Veteranus fell into step beside her, noting how the locals regarded them as they passed, some with open curiosity, others with carefully veiled hostility, and a few with what appeared to be something close to pity.

They found Mordred and Raven in the council hall, both bent over a table covered with maps and parchments. The druid leader straightened as they entered, his penetrating gaze immediately fixing on Veteranus.

'So,' said Mordred, 'the Roman returns.'

I am ready,' Veteranus confirmed, meeting his gaze steadily.

A smile, genuine yet somehow unsettling, spread across Mordred's face.

'Then we welcome you, Veteranus, to the true heart of Mona.'

He rolled up the parchments on the table with practiced efficiency. 'There is much to do, and your integration must begin immediately.'

'Integration?' asked Veteranus.

'A necessary step for what lies before you,' said Mordred. 'Raven will guide you through the first steps. Listen to him carefully, your life depends on it.'

Before Veteranus could respond, Mordred had swept past them and out of the hall, leaving an expectant silence in his wake. Raven finally straightened from the table and gestured toward the door.

'We begin now,' he said. 'There is no value in delay.'

They traversed the settlement, moving past the common areas Veteranus had become familiar with during his time on the island, into narrower paths that wound between structures built partially into the earth itself. Few people walked these ways, and those they encountered gave them a wide berth, their eyes averted.

'Where are we going?' Veteranus finally asked as they approached a cave entrance set into the base of a hill, its mouth reinforced with timber and stone.

'To understand those you faced in the pit,' Raven answered, 'It is necessary that you become... acquainted.'

A chill ran through Veteranus that had nothing to do with the cool air emanating from the cave. The memory of his trial in the pit remained vivid, the darkness, the stench, the sounds of creatures moving just beyond his reach, and the sudden, terrifying attacks. Raven paused at the entrance, fixing Veteranus with a level gaze.

'You may question the need for what you are about to learn,' he said. 'But wisdom has little to do with necessity. They must know you, and you must know them. This is the way.'

Two guards at the cave entrance nodded respectfully to

Raven but regarded Veteranus with open suspicion.

'We are here by the command of Mordred,' Raven informed them. 'We require passage.'

One of the guards handed Raven a torch while the other unlocked a heavy wooden door set into the cave mouth. The sound of the bar lifting echoed ominously in the confined space behind.

'Keep close,' Raven instructed as they entered. 'The path is treacherous for those unfamiliar with its contours.'

The passage descended steeply, the torch's light revealing rough stone steps cut into the living rock. The air grew thicker as they descended, heavy with moisture and other, less pleasant scents that Veteranus recognized as the same stench of filth and decay that had permeated the pit.

They walked in silence, the only sounds their footfalls on stone and the distant dripping of water and, after a few minutes, the passage widened into a larger chamber. Torch brackets lined the walls, and Raven lit several, illuminating a space perhaps thirty feet across. At the far end stood an iron grill that spanned the entire width of the chamber, from floor to ceiling, a barrier between the chamber they occupied and whatever lay beyond.

'Wait here,' Raven instructed, moving to speak with another guard who had been seated on a stone bench near the grill, previously invisible in the shadows.

Veteranus remained where he was, his eyes drawn to the darkness beyond the iron barrier. At first, he saw nothing, but as his vision adjusted, he detected movement, subtle shifts in the deeper shadows, suggesting the presence of something alive and watchful.

'They sense you,' Raven said, returning to his side. 'They always know when someone new enters their domain.' He gestured toward the grill. 'Approach. They need to become accustomed to your scent, your presence.'

Swallowing his trepidation, Veteranus moved forward until he stood just a few feet from the iron bars. The stench was stronger here, an assault on his senses that nearly made him gag. He fought the urge to retreat, forcing himself to stand his ground as his eyes strained to penetrate the gloom beyond the barrier. The guard approached, bearing a wooden tray that held several chunks of raw meat, dark and glistening in the torchlight. Beside the meat lay a long, slender spear with a pronged tip.

'They fear the light,' Raven explained, coming to stand beside him. 'It hurts their eyes after so long in darkness, but hunger will draw them forward eventually. Take the spear, skewer a piece of meat and offer it through the bars. Do not extend your arm beyond the grill, no
matter how far away they seem to be.'

Veteranus took the spear and speared a chunk of meat before cautiously extending it through the bars.

For long moments, nothing happened, the meat dangling from the spear's end, then
without warning, something lunged from the darkness, a blur of pale, mottled flesh that snatched the meat and retreated so quickly that Veteranus barely had time to register its presence. The spear jerked in his grip, but the meat was gone, taken with unnatural swift movement.

'Good,' Raven murmured. 'Again.'

Veteranus repeated the process, skewering another piece of meat and extending it through the bars. This time, the wait was shorter, though he still couldn't clearly see the creature that claimed the offering.

On the third attempt, however, one of them lingered momentarily in the dim light cast by the torches, seizing the meat with long, clawed fingers before fixing Veteranus with a gaze that contained unmistakable intelligence amid the animal hunger.

'There should be four,' said Veteranus, recalling his ordeal in the pit. 'I've only seen three come forward.'

'One has been taken elsewhere,' replied Raven.

'What do you mean elsewhere?'

'Let's just say he has been taken on a hunt, you will meet him

227

soon enough. You have done well, Veteranus. We will return tomorrow. They must become accustomed to you, and you to them. Come, there is more to your integration than this, but each step must be taken in its proper time.'

They retraced their path through the tunnel, climbing back to the surface in silence. Veteranus found himself oddly relieved when they emerged into the open air, the simple act of breathing becoming pleasurable again after the fetid atmosphere below.

'You have questions,' Raven observed as they walked back toward the settlement.

'Many,' Veteranus admitted. 'But I doubt you'll answer most of them.'

A rare smile flitted across Raven's face.

'Perhaps more than you think, but not all at once. Knowledge, like trust, must be earned incrementally.'

'Then tell me this,' Veteranus pressed. 'What purpose do those creatures serve? Why keep them at all?'

Raven considered the question for several moments before responding.

'They are weapons, after a fashion. But also keys to understanding what came before, and what may come again.'

'That's not an answer.'

'It's all you need for now,' Raven countered. 'Focus on becoming familiar with them. The rest will follow.'

The following days fell into a pattern. Each morning, Veteranus would train with the warriors of Mona, learning their fighting techniques and sharing some of his own. The afternoons were spent in study with an elder named Branwen, who taught him the rudiments of the local language and shared carefully selected information about the island's history and customs. But despite the journey of accumulating knowledge and earning trust, it was the evenings that he looked forward to the most, the time when he descended into the cavern to feed the creatures behind the iron grill.

By the fifth day, they no longer retreated immediately after taking the offered meat and by the tenth day, as he prepared to spear another chunk of meat, the largest creature made a sound, not the animalistic growls he had grown accustomed to, but something that might have been an attempt at speech. The sound was malformed, emerging from a throat not used human language, but the intent seemed clear enough.

'They're trying to communicate with you,' Raven observed from where he stood several paces back. 'It's rare, but not unprecedented.'

'What do you think they want to say?' Veteranus asked, never taking his eyes from the creature at the grill.

'Who can say? Perhaps they simply recognize that you are different from their usual keepers. Or perhaps they sense your purpose.'

As they left the cavern, they passed another tunnel branching off from the main passage, one Veteranus had noticed before but never explored. A warrior emerged from it as they approached, his expression grim and his forearm wrapped in a blood-soaked bandage.

'What's down there?' Veteranus asked, nodding toward the side passage.

'The female,' Raven answered, his tone careful. 'but she is kept separate from the others.'

'Why?'

'She would kill them,' Raven said simply. 'Or they her. The balance is... delicate.'

Veteranus pondered this as they continued their ascent. The creatures, whatever they were, clearly followed some form of social hierarchy, yet it was distorted, unnatural. Like everything on Mona, they seemed to exist in a space between worlds, neither fully one thing nor another. As they emerged into the fading daylight, Veteranus made his decision.

'I'm ready for the pit again,' he stated firmly. 'Whatever

comes next, I need to face it directly.'

Raven regarded him thoughtfully.

'Yes,' he agreed after a moment. 'I believe you are. We'll speak to Mordred tonight.'

They walked in silence back toward the settlement. He had crossed a threshold in these past days, committed himself to a path that led away from everything he had known. There would be no returning to his former life, no reclaiming the man he had once been. And strangely, he found himself at peace with that reality. Whatever awaited him in the pit, whatever purpose Mordred and his followers had in mind for him, he would face it with the same resolve that had carried him through decades of military service.

Chapter Thirty-Four

Isla Mona

The mountain range loomed behind them, ancient and indifferent to the small band of warriors huddled in its shadow. Seneca raised a hand, signalling the others to halt as they reached the crest of a wooded hill overlooking the strait separating them from the Isle of Mona. Below, the waters churned with swift currents, narrower than their intelligence had suggested but no less treacherous.

'There's a bridge,' Marcus murmured, pointing to where a sturdy wooden structure spanned the strait in the distance, its weathered planks supported by stone pillars sunk deep into the churning water.

Seneca nodded, his keen eyes already noting the guards positioned at both ends of the bridge, six men visible on the mainland side, likely more on the island itself. The Occultum spread out along the hillside, establishing a crude observation post screened by dense vegetation. From this vantage point, they could monitor the bridge and the surrounding area without being detected, provided they maintained basic precautions. Each man found his place with practiced efficiency, settling into the positions that would become their home for at least the next day or two while they planned their approach.

Falco crept to Seneca 's side after completing a circuit of their immediate area. 'No signs of patrols on this side of the strait,' he reported. 'They seem to concentrate their forces at the bridge itself.'

'It makes sense,' replied Seneca. 'The currents in the strait would make a crossing elsewhere difficult, if not impossible. Why waste men patrolling when nature provides better security than any guard?'

By midday, they had established a reasonable picture of the bridge's defence patterns. Guards rotated every few hours,

231

maintaining consistent numbers but changing personnel. Occasional boats passed beneath the bridge, fishing vessels and small transport craft carrying supplies from the open sea on either end of the strait. Each was challenged by the bridge guards before being allowed to proceed.

'We could steal a boat,' Cassius suggested, watching a small fishing craft navigate the churning waters.

Seneca shook his head.

'Too visible,' he said. 'They'd spot us before we made it halfway across, and there's nowhere to hide on open water. Our only option seems to be the bridge.'

As the afternoon wore on, the reality of their situation became increasingly apparent. They had exhausted their meagre supplies, and hunger began to gnaw at their concentration. Water, at least, was plentiful from a nearby stream, but they needed food if they were to maintain their vigilance and strength for what lay ahead.

'We need provisions,' said Seneca, looking over to Sica. 'Have a quick look around for anything you can get without drawing attention.'

Sica nodded, already reaching for his cloak.

'I'll come with you,' said Falco, but Seneca shook his head.

'Stay here with the others,' he said. 'You need to recover from that fall. He turned to Marcus. 'You go with Sica. See what you can find.'

A few minutes later, Marcus and Sica headed out into the forest and after walking less than half a mile they detected the first signs of human habitation, a thin wisp of smoke rising above the treeline, the distant sound of an axe striking wood. They adjusted their course, approaching cautiously from downwind to avoid detection by any dogs.

Eventually, the small farmstead appeared at the edge of a cleared area, a crude but sturdy wooden structure with a thatched roof, surrounded by a plot of cultivated land. Behind the main building stood a simple animal pen where several goats milled about, occasionally bleating as they nibbled at the weeds between the fence.

The two men settled into observation, studying the patterns of movement around the farm. An older man, stooped but still vigorous, worked at repairing a section of fencing near the animal enclosure and a woman, his wife, presumably, appeared occasionally from the house, fussing around the livestock. No children were visible, though the sound of a metal implement striking stone suggested another adult might be working behind the structure, out of their line of sight.

'Farmers,' Marcus assessed. 'Not warriors.'

'Still dangerous,' Sica cautioned. 'And we don't know who might be within earshot if they raise an outcry.'

They continued their surveillance as the afternoon waned, noting the couple's routines and the layout of the property. The goats presented the most accessible target, small enough to transport quickly, secluded enough behind the main structure that a swift operation might go undetected until the animal was long gone.

'One goat,' Marcus decided finally. 'After dusk, when they're settling in for the evening meal but before full darkness makes the animals more nervous.'

Sica nodded agreement.

'The pen is poorly constructed. We won't even need to enter it, just lure one close enough to the edge.'

They retreated deeper into the forest to wait, conserving their energy and mentally rehearsing the operation. As the sun began to dip toward the western horizon, casting long shadows across the landscape, they made their final preparations.

'One chance,' Marcus reminded Sica unnecessarily. 'Clean and quiet.'

The light was fading rapidly as they approached the edge of the forest nearest the goat pen. The farmers had retired to their home, though the glow of a hearth fire was visible through the single window, suggesting they remained awake. The goats had settled somewhat but were still alert, several of them raising their heads at the subtle sounds of the men's approach.

Sica reached into his tunic and withdrew a small pouch containing berries they had earlier collected from the forest, hardly appetizing to humans but potentially enticing to a curious goat. He scattered a few morsels just inside the fence line, making a clicking sound with his tongue to attract their attention.

The wait seemed interminable. One goat, younger than the others, with a distinctive white patch on its otherwise brown coat, approached cautiously, stretching its neck to investigate the unfamiliar scent.

'Not yet,' Marcus whispered as Sica tensed beside him. 'Let it commit.'

Slowly the goat walked closer to the fence, its curiosity overcoming caution, and as it finally stretched for the last of the berries in the Syrian's outstretched hand, Sica lunged forward to grasp one of its horns while the blade in his other hand sliced across the goat's throat in a single, precise cut. Blood spurted from the severed arteries and the goat fought to get away, but Sica maintained his grip, controlling the animal's death throes until it went limp in his arms.

Without a word, they dragged the carcass over the fence and deeper into the forest, moving swiftly but carefully to avoid leaving an obvious trail. When they had put sufficient distance between themselves and the farm, they paused to complete the bleeding, suspending the animal from a tree branch by its hind legs.

The butchering was conducted with grim efficiency, both men working together to skin and quarter the animal, placing the meat in their packs before burying the less useful organs and entrails in a shallow pit.

'Let's move,' said Marcus. 'We've been gone too long already.'

They returned to the observation post by a circuitous route, taking extra precautions to ensure they weren't followed.

'Any luck?' asked Seneca as they approached.

234

'Goat,' said Marcus.' But we'll need a fire.'

'Then we'll need to withdraw further into the trees,' said Seneca. 'We'll come back at first light.'

They retreated deeper into the forested hills, finding a small hollow surrounded by dense undergrowth that would contain both light and sound and only when Decimus confirmed they were well-hidden did Marcus authorize the preparation of a meal.

Sica produced their small iron pot and filled it with water from a nearby stream before suspending it over a carefully constructed fire pit, designed to minimize smoke and visible flame.

'Boil it thoroughly,' said Marcus as Sica added chunks of goat meat to the pot. 'We can't risk the smell of roasting, and raw meat might sicken us at a time when we can least afford weakness.'

The resulting meal was far from delicious, tough meat in a bland broth, with no herbs or salt to enhance the flavour, but it filled their bellies and provided the protein their bodies so desperately needed. They ate in silence, each man lost in his own thoughts as strength gradually returned to their limbs and with the edge of hunger blunted, they prepared for the next day by boiling a second batch of meat, this time extracting it early and arranging the pieces on hot stones around the fire's perimeter. The slow heating would dry it sufficiently to prevent spoilage for at least another day or two, portable rations for whatever lay ahead. Eventually they sat around to discuss the following day's plans, weighing risks against probabilities. Eventually, Seneca raised a hand for silence.

'We return to the observation point at first light,' he decided. 'One more full day of surveillance before we make our final plan. We need to understand their patterns completely before we commit.'

The others nodded agreement, recognizing the wisdom in patience and as the fire burned down to embers, they packed the dried meat carefully before distributing it among the remaining packs to ensure no single loss would leave them without rations. Once done, the night watch was divided into shifts, with each man taking his turn to maintain vigilance while the others rested.

When dawn broke, they extinguished all traces of their camp and moved silently back toward their observation point overlooking the strait. Nourished and refreshed, they settled in to continue their surveillance, each man focused on identifying patterns, weaknesses or opportunities that might facilitate their crossing. Somewhere in the continuous flow of activity, they knew there would be a moment of vulnerability, a brief window when vigilance faltered, or attention diverted. All they had to do now was find it.

Chapter Thirty-Five

Central Britannia

Dawn was still hours away when Lepidus and Talorcan retreated deeper into the forest, putting sufficient distance between themselves and the fortified settlement to speak without fear of detection. The night sounds, owls calling, the rustling of nocturnal creatures in the undergrowth, provided a stark contrast to the horrific screams that still echoed in Lepidus's mind.

Lepidus crouched, gathering a handful of leaves and small twigs, arranging them in a shallow depression before thinking better of it.

'No fire,' he muttered, discarding the kindling. 'Too risky.'

Talorcan nodded, settling his back against one of the trees, his eyes never ceasing their methodical scan of the darkness around them.

'We should be moving,' he said after a long silence. 'Every moment wasted gives them time to...' He didn't finish the thought. He didn't need to.

Lepidus ran a hand over his face. His muscles ached from days of travel and tension, but physical discomfort was the least of his concerns now.

'Our orders were explicit,' he said. 'Observe and report. Do not engage unless directly threatened.'

'Orders,' Talorcan repeated, the word carrying a weight of contempt that surprised Lepidus. 'Those men in there, they are your brothers in arms, and they are being slaughtered like animals while we debate the niceties of our instructions.'

'Do you think I don't know that?' Lepidus snapped. 'This isn't a simple situation.'

'Few worth facing ever are,' responded Talorcan.'

They fell silent again, each man lost in his own thoughts. The logical course of action was clear: retreat to Castra Victrix with all

237

possible speed, report what they had witnessed, and return with sufficient force to storm the settlement and rescue any survivors. Standard military procedure, unambiguous and straightforward.

Yet they both knew the reality that procedure failed to address.

By the time they reached the fort, secured an audience with the commander, convinced him of the urgency of the situation, assembled a rescue force, and returned, days would have passed. Perhaps weeks. And the men imprisoned in that nightmarish place would long since have met fates too terrible to contemplate.

'How many do you think are still alive?' Talorcan asked finally.

Lepidus considered the question carefully.

'We know of three who have already died,' said Lepidus. Probably a few more when we were back in the fort. My best guess is between six and ten. Based on what we observed... perhaps ten at most.'

'And how many defenders in the settlement?'

'Thirty warriors that we know of,' Lepidus replied. 'Possibly more we haven't seen. Plus, whatever... *creatures*... they've brought inside.'

The word hung between them: creatures. Not men, not animals, but something that defied easy categorization. The sounds they had heard were not the product of anything natural, of that much Lepidus was certain.

'So,' Talorcan summarized bluntly, 'possibly ten weakened, unarmed prisoners against at least thirty warriors and unknown horrors. And to rescue them, two men with limited weapons who have explicit orders not to intervene.'

Put that way, the situation seemed not merely challenging but absurd. Any rational military assessment would conclude that the prisoners were already lost, and risking two more lives in a futile rescue attempt served no strategic purpose. But Lepidus hadn't spent over half is life in the Exploratores or managing the Occultum because he adhered slavishly to rational military assessments.

'We can't just leave them,' he said quietly.

Talorcan studied him for a long moment before nodding.

'No. We cannot.'

The simple agreement settled something in Lepidus's chest. They were abandoning their orders, potentially sacrificing themselves in what might well be a doomed endeavour, but the alternative was unthinkable.

'Even if we succeed,' said Lepidus 'we'd still need to get the survivors back to Castra Victrix through hostile territory, with limited supplies and pursuing enemies.'

'One problem at a time,' Talorcan replied, 'First, we need to get into a heavily fortified settlement without being detected, locate and free the prisoners, and escape without alerting thirty warriors and whatever unholy things they've captured. After that, a simple cross-country march should hardly present a challenge. I've faced worse odds.'

'Have you?' Lepidus asked, genuinely curious.

'No,' Talorcan admitted after a pause. 'But it seemed like the sort of thing someone should say in these circumstances.'

The moment of levity passed quickly, replaced by the serious business of planning what might well be their final mission. They had observed the settlement for two days, noting guard patterns, identifying potential weaknesses in the defences, mapping the internal layout as best they could from their vantage point. It wasn't enough, not nearly enough for the kind of precision operation they were contemplating, but it was all they had.

'The northern wall,' Lepidus began, sketching a rough diagram in the dirt between them. 'It's their blind spot. The guards focus primarily on the main gate and the approach from the east.'

Neither of them needed to elaborate on the implication. Talorcan had spent his life navigating the rugged terrains of Germania in the service of Rome and Lepidus, though born into wealth, had carried out countless missions over the years, both with

239

the Exploratores and ultimately the Occultum.

'The palisade itself is the greater challenge,' Lepidus continued. 'Fifteen feet of sharpened logs with no obvious handholds.'

'We've got this,' Talorcan replied, patting the coiled rope secured at his waist. 'We have no grappling hook, but it is enough.'

They continued their planning, methodically addressing each phase of the proposed operation: the approach, the infiltration, locating the prisoners, the escape. Each step presented its own challenges, its own potentially fatal complications. And underlying it all was the unknown factor, the nature of the creatures they had heard but not seen.

'We move tonight,' Lepidus decided once they finalized their preparations. 'We'll need whatever advantage darkness can provide. First, let's get some rest.'

Decision made, Talorcan settled himself against the base of a tree, drawing his cloak around his shoulders against the chill, and within moments, his breathing had settled into the rhythm of sleep, a skill developed through years of hunting and scouting in the forests of Germania.

Lepidus envied him that gift. His own mind continued to race, analysing possibilities, calculating risks, imagining scenarios both successful and catastrophic. The odds against them were overwhelming, the likelihood of success minimal at best.

The hours passed swiftly as Lepidus maintained his vigil, scanning the surrounding forest for any sign of danger while his mind continued to wrestle with the challenges ahead. Eventually, when it was time, he gently roused Talorcan, who transitioned from sleep to full alertness with the instantaneous focus that had kept him alive through countless dangerous situations.

'Any disturbances?' he asked, already scanning their surroundings.

'Nothing out of the ordinary,' Lepidus confirmed as

Talorcan took his place. He settled into Talorcan's vacated position, allowing his body to relax while maintaining a state of readiness that years of training had instilled. Sleep would not come easily, perhaps not at all, but even a brief respite would help sharpen his senses for what lay ahead.

As he closed his eyes, the sounds from the previous night echoed in his memory: the rhythmic drumming, the chanting, the sudden terrible screams. What had the prisoners experienced in those moments? What horrors had they witnessed or endured? The questions haunted him, reinforcing his resolve even as they underscored the desperation of their planned rescue.

A few hours later, both men checked their weapons one final time.

'Ready?' Talorcan asked simply.

Lepidus nodded.

'No man left behind,' he responded, invoking one of the oldest traditions of the legions, a principle often honoured more in rhetoric than in practice, but one that still held meaning for men like themselves.

'No man left behind,' Talorcan echoed, and though he was not Roman by birth, the sentiment clearly resonated with his own tribal values.

They moved out, ghosting through the forest with the silent efficiency that years of specialized training had instilled. The settlement lay ahead, its palisade a dark silhouette against the star-filled sky. Within those walls, their comrades awaited either rescue or a fate too terrible to contemplate. The odds were impossible, the danger extreme, the likelihood of success minimal at best, but they were Occultum. They would find a way, or they would die trying… that was how it worked.

Chapter Thirty-Six

Isla Mona

The darkness pressed in around the edges of the pit, held at bay only by the torches mounted along the earthen walls. Their flames flickered and danced in the gentle night breeze, casting long shadows that seemed to move with predatory intent of their own. Unlike Veteranus's previous experience, there were no druids in elaborate ceremonial garb looking down, no rhythmic drumming to heighten the tension, no audience watching his every move.

This time, it was just Veteranus standing alone on the stone slab at the centre of the pit, a wicker basket of freshly butchered meat at his feet. He breathed deeply, trying to calm the hammering of his heart as he glanced up to where Raven stood watching from above. Beside him, several handlers waited silently, their spears held ready.

This time, only three wooden crates had been positioned at equal intervals around the pit's circumference. From within came the familiar sounds of movement, occasional scratches against wood, and low, guttural noises that were neither fully human nor entirely animal.

Veteranus took a deep breath and nodded up at Raven, signalling his readiness.

Without ceremony or preamble, Raven gave a sharp gesture to the handlers, and with practiced efficiency, they pulled on ropes that lifted the sliding doors of all three crates simultaneously.

The creatures burst forth in a frenzy of movement, launching themselves toward Veteranus with a horrible wrongness that sent ice through his veins despite his preparation.

Just as before, they jerked to violent halts as they reached the limits of the chains fastened to their metal collars, thrashing and clawing at the air just beyond the stone slab where Veteranus stood.

Although Veteranus knew they couldn't reach him, it was still terrifying. Their appearance, twisted approximations of humanity, with deformed limbs, filed teeth, and eyes that contained too much awareness for comfort, struck at something deep within him as fundamentally cruel and wrong.

Veteranus forced himself to remain still, to show no fear despite the churning in his stomach. He waited, watching as they gradually exhausted themselves, their initial frenzy giving way to a more calculated aggression. Their movements became less chaotic, more deliberate, as they paced the limits of their chains.

When the largest of them finally stilled, watching him with predatory assessment, Veteranus slowly reached for the basket at his feet. He withdrew a chunk of bloody meat, speared it deliberately on the tip of his knife, and extended it toward the creature.

The wraith tensed, then sprang forward in a blur of movement, snatching the meat from the blade before retreating to the edge of its cage. It tore into the offering with savage efficiency, dark fluid dripping from its chin as it fed.

Veteranus repeated the process with each of the creatures in turn, noting subtle differences in their behaviour. One snatched the meat and immediately backed away to consume it in relative privacy. Another maintained eye contact even as it fed, never turning its back on what it clearly perceived as a potential threat.

When they had finished, the largest wraith approached again, staying at the limit of its chain. It made no attempt to lunge, merely sniffed the air, catching the scent of the remaining meat in the basket. A low snarl rumbled from its throat, but the sound held a different quality now, less attack, more demand.

Veteranus fed each of them again, and with each feeding, the creatures grew noticeably calmer. By the third round, they had settled into an almost orderly pattern, waiting at the ends of their chains for their turn rather than attempting to intimidate him into faster service.

It was unnerving how quickly they adapted, how efficiently they learned the parameters of this new situation. These were not mindless beasts but intelligences that could assess, anticipate, and modify their behaviour accordingly.

As the basket emptied, Veteranus found himself studying their eyes more closely. Behind the feral hunger, the predatory assessment, he occasionally caught glimpses of something else, flickers of recognition, calculation, perhaps even memory. Something that, despite their grotesque appearances and savage behaviours, suggested humanity not entirely extinguished.

When the meat was gone, the handlers moved in with their spears, prodding and forcing the creatures back toward their crates. The wraiths retreated reluctantly, snarling defiance but ultimately complying with the implicit threat of the sharpened points directed at them.

As the sliding doors slammed shut and were secured, Veteranus finally allowed himself to exhale fully, the tension draining from his body. He stepped off the stone slab and climbed the crude ladder that led up to where Raven waited.

'You did well,' Raven observed, genuine approval evident in his typically impassive voice. 'Most men cannot maintain such composure in their presence, even knowing the chains will hold.'

Veteranus wiped his bloody hands on a rag offered by one of the handlers.

'There's something in their eyes,' he said quietly. 'Behind the hunger and the rage. Flashes of... awareness. Recognition.'

Raven's expression revealed nothing, but something shifted in his posture.

'What remains of their humanity is fragmentary at best,' he replied carefully. 'Shards of memory, perhaps, or instincts not fully erased by their transformation. Do not mistake it for true consciousness.'

'And yet they learn,' countered Veteranus. 'They adapt. Those are not traits of mindless beasts.'

'No,' agreed Raven. 'They are not mindless. That is what makes them so valuable... and so dangerous.'

Veteranus looked back at the pit, where handlers were now

244

securing the crates for transport back to their underground chamber.

'I'll do this again tomorrow night,' he said. 'And every night after. They're growing accustomed to me quicker than I expected.'

Raven nodded, seemingly unsurprised by this declaration.

'Mordred will be pleased with your progress. The bonding process is…

He was interrupted by the sudden appearance of a young warrior running towards them, his breathing heavy as if he had sprinted some distance.

'Raven,' the messenger called. 'Mordred summons you to the longhouse immediately. You as well,' he added, with a glance toward Veteranus. 'He has news of great importance.'

The longhouse was alive with activity as Veteranus and Raven entered. Warriors congregated in small groups, their voices raised in animated discussion, an energy permeating the air that hadn't been present in previous gatherings. At the centre of it all stood Mordred, gesturing emphatically as he addressed several of his most trusted lieutenants, his usually measured demeanour replaced by something more intense, more vital.

Veteranus immediately recognized the transformation. Gone was the paternal figure who presided over family meals, the philosophical teacher who spoke of ancient traditions with quiet reverence. In his place stood a different incarnation altogether, Mordred the warlord, the strategist, his eyes alight with a cold fire and murderous intent.

As they approached, Mordred glanced up, his gaze locking immediately onto them. A smile, thin and sharp as a blade's edge, crossed his face.

'Leave us,' he ordered, and the rest of the warriors departed without question. When the last had gone, Mordred beckoned Raven and veteranus closer.

'Everything has changed,' Mordred announced without preamble, his voice vibrating with barely contained excitement. 'The

245

gods have delivered us an opportunity beyond my most ambitious hopes.'

Raven moved closer to the table.

'What news, Mordred?'

'I have received word from Camulodunum,' Mordred replied, looking between them. 'News that will alter the course of our plans entirely.' He paused, his eyes gleaming in the lamplight. 'Up until now, our target was Plautius, the general who leads the invasion force, but that has all changed.'

'Why? asked Veteranus.

'Because,' replied Mordred, 'there is a bigger fish on offer. My spies inform me that Claudius himself is on his way to accept the surrender of Britannia.'

'Claudius is coming here?' gasped Raven.

'He is,' said Mordred. 'And that changes everything.' He turned to stare at Veteranus. 'I suggest you get yourself and the Wraith ready, my friend,' he said, 'for in a few weeks, we are going to kill the Emperor of Rome,'

Chapter Thirty-Seven

Isla Mona

The strait between the mainland and Mona churned with treacherous currents, its swirling waters a natural barrier more formidable than any man-made wall. The Occultum had spent days studying the bridge, mapping every detail of its defences, learning the rhythms of the guards with the patience of hunters tracking elusive prey. Now the wooden structure loomed above them, a dark skeleton against the starlit sky, its support struts disappearing into the churning waters below.

Marcus pointed to the far end of the bridge. Two guards stood near a brazier, its small flame casting flickering shadows. They appeared relaxed, conversation passing between them as they waited to be relieved.

Minutes stretched like hours. The cold bit through their clothing and they pressed themselves against the bridge's massive timber supports, feeling the rough wood slick with moisture and river scum. Voices carried down from the bridge above, punctuated by the occasional laugh, the clank of weapons, the shuffle of feet.

'Let's go,' breathed Seneca.

Sica led, his smaller frame sliding quickly between the massive wooden struts. Marcus followed, then Decimus, and Cassius close behind. Falco's bulk made stealth more challenging, but years of training had taught him movements that belied his size.

They climbed carefully between the bridge's supports, using the massive timber structures as cover, moving with a speed that balanced urgency against the risk of detection.

Seneca brought up the rear, his eyes constantly scanning both the bridge and the shoreline. They had minutes, perhaps less, before the fresh guards were in place. One cough, one slip into the water and they would be discovered.

As they made the final approach, the guards above started to

247

move and one of them peered down over the handrail, scanning the waters below.

Ice formed in Seneca's veins, and he pressed against the last timber, barely daring to breathe. For a few heartbeats, he was sure they had been discovered but as the guard turned away, he launched towards the bank. Sica's hand was there, pulling him up, dragging him into the dense bushes that lined the shore, and they fell into the undergrowth, bodies pressed close, hearts thundering in their ears.

Voices drifted from the bridge. The new guards were descending to the bank, lanterns swinging, checking the area with professional thoroughness. The Occultum didn't move, didn't breathe, they just remained motionless, becoming part of the landscape. Moments stretched like hours until gradually the voices retreated and only when silence returned did Seneca give the signal, a nearly imperceptible hand gesture, and they began to crawl.

Slowly, methodically, inch by painful inch, they moved away from the bridge, putting distance between themselves and potential discovery and it was only when the sounds of the bridge had faded completely did Seneca finally allow them to rise.

'We move inland,' he whispered. 'We need to find cover.'

Several hours later, Seneca awoke to the warm, musty breath of a pig inches from his face. He blinked, momentarily disoriented by the pungent smell that permeated their hiding place. The pigsty was cramped, but it had provided them with a perfect concealment after their dangerous bridge crossing.

Sica sat near the entrance of the small wooden hut, his slight frame barely visible in the morning light.

The pig that had been snuffling near Seneca grunted and shifted, clearly intrigued by the human intruders in its domain while outside, the sounds of a farm beginning its day drifted through the air. They heard the farmer moving about, the distant clang of a metal gate, the shuffle of animals in the nearby field.

A short while later, they watched as the farmer approached

the fence, tossing a collection of rotting vegetables into the paddock. The other pigs ran forward eagerly, quickly joined by their uninvited guest and as the farm sounds gradually quieted, Sica moved closer to the group.

'The coast is clear,' he whispered.

Seneca nodded and retrieved the dried meat they had prepared earlier.

They ate in silence, each man lost in his own thoughts. The reality of their situation was stark. They had successfully crossed to Mona, but finding Raven in this unfamiliar terrain would be no simple task.

'We'll wait here until dark,' said Seneca. 'I know it stinks but nobody is going to come anywhere near. Tonight, we'll follow the main tracks. One of them is bound to lead to the druid encampment. Once there, we'll find somewhere to go to ground until we learn of Raven's whereabouts and when we do, well, that will need to be decided when we find him.'

The plan was simple but their best option. With nothing more to do but wait, they shifted closer together, using each other's body heat to ward off the morning chill.

Sleep would be fitful, interrupted by the sounds of the farm and the constant need to remain alert, but they would rest while they could.

Chapter Thirty-Eight

Central Britannia

The forest floor was a treacherous carpet of fallen leaves and hidden roots as Lepidus and Talorcan moved towards the fort their bodies low, their eyes constantly scanning the terrain around them. Talorcan carried two long saplings lashed together with strips of leather and the coil of rope secured at his belt.

'There,' he whispered staring towards the northern wall.

Lepidus followed his gaze. The palisade rose before them, a stark barrier of sharpened logs standing twelve feet high, each trunk stripped of bark and carved to a wicked point. Between the logs, small gaps allowed glimpses of movement within the settlement, but not enough to provide an easy view of the interior.

They crouched down and Talorcan checked then lashings on the makeshift pole before examining the pre-formed noose at the end of the rope, designed to catch securely over one of the pointed logs.

'Ready?' asked Lepidus.

Talorcan nodded and slipped the noose into a notch at the end of the pole before slowly lifting it up towards the top of the palisade.

One careful movement at a time, he guided the noose over one of the pointed poles before pulling the rope taut, testing its grip.

'Secure,' he whispered.

Lepidus nodded, his pale eyes scanning their surroundings. The forest remained still, save for the occasional rustle of leaves or distant bird call but both men knew stillness could be deceptive. Finally, satisfied they had not been seen, he begun to climb.

Halfway up the wall, he paused. Voices drifted from within the settlement, close enough to hear but not distinguish clearly. He froze, pressing himself against the wooden logs, becoming as motionless as the palisade itself and eventually, as the voices passed, he resumed his climb.

At the top, he used his knife to blunt two of the logs before placing one of their sleeping mats on the top to make the crossing easier. Once done, he peered over, seeing the settlement spread before him. Campfires burned in strategic locations and people moved calmly between buildings, their movements evidence that they felt perfectly safe within the palisade. He signalled down to Talorcan. The way was clear.

Once over the top, Lepidus lowered himself carefully, finding purchase on the interior supports before dropping silently to the ground. He immediately pressed himself into the deepest shadow, every sense alert for any sign of discovery.

Moments later, Talorcan lowered the rope from the top, ready to be used on their escape, before dropping down to join him. They exchanged a brief glance and began to move inward, using the settlement's own structures as cover, always moving from one area of darkness to another. Occasional sounds drifted from nearby huts, muffled conversations, a distant bark of a dog, but no alarm was raised, no indication that their presence had been detected.

As they drew closer to the settlement's centre, the character of the space changed. The haphazard arrangement of living quarters gave way to a more intentional layout, the ground cleared, prepared for some greater purpose.

A pile of timber dominated the central area, unlit, but clearly a giant pyre ready to be ignited.

Talorcan touched Lepidus's arm, drawing his attention to a wooden pole standing near the unlit fire. Empty restraints hung from its upper section, their leather straps swaying slightly in the night breeze. Another ceremony was planned, another sacrifice awaited.

The settlement slumbered around them, and the two men continued their methodical exploration, each shadow a potential sanctuary, each structure a possible hiding place for the prisoners they sought. The night sounds were subtle, a low murmur of conversation from a distant hut, the occasional shift of animals in their pens, the soft crackle of dying embers from scattered fire pits.

251

To less experienced men, these would be mere background noise, but to Lepidus and Talorcan, each sound was a potential signal, a piece of information to be catalogued and understood.

Suddenly, Lepidus raised his fist, dropping to one knee. Talorcan froze instantly, his body becoming part of the surrounding darkness, eyes following the direction of his companion's gaze.

Before them stood a stone roundhouse that immediately distinguished itself from the wooden structures surrounding it. Where other buildings spoke of temporary habitation, this structure was permanent, almost defiant in its solidity. Its stone walls rose squat and sturdy, designed to withstand more than mere weather and a heavy oaken door secured its entrance.

Two guards stood outside and Lepidus and Talorcan withdrew silently, melting back into the shadows between two nearby huts.

'They have to be in there,' said Lepidus, 'but we haven't much time. 'The night is half gone.'

Talorcan nodded,

'We'll have to kill them,' he said, 'There's no other way,'

'Agreed,' said Lepidus. 'But we need to be precise. If either manages to raise an alarm...'

'I'll take the first with my bow,' said Talorcan, already reaching for the weapon secured across his back. 'Can you position yourself behind the second? Once he sees his companion fall, he'll likely draw his weapon rather than immediately call out.'

Lepidus nodded.

'I'll circle around behind the building. Give me time to get into position. When you see I'm ready, take your shot.'

They slipped back deeper into the shadows, circling away from the roundhouse before separating. Talorcan found a position behind a stack of firewood with a clear line of sight to the guards. He nocked an arrow to his bow but didn't draw, conserving his strength as he waited for Lepidus to get into position.

On the far side of the hut, Lepidus moved with painstaking

care, using every available shadow, freezing whenever a sound suggested movement nearby. When he was in position, he looked toward Talorcan's hiding place and raised his hand, knowing the scout's keen eyes would catch the subtle movement even across the distance between them.

Talorcan saw the signal and drew his bow in one fluid motion, the bowstring taut against his cheek as he sighted along the arrow. He controlled his breathing, waiting for the perfect moment, and when both guards were relatively still, he released.

The arrow cut through the night air with deadly accuracy, striking the first guard directly in the throat. The man's eyes widened in shock and pain as his hands instinctively rose to the shaft protruding from his neck. He tried to cry out, but only a wet gurgle emerged as blood filled his airway. He staggered, then collapsed to his knees.

The second guard turned at the sound of his companion falling, confusion giving way to alarm as he registered the arrow. His sword cleared its sheath with a metallic hiss, but before he could raise his voice to alert others, a hand clamped over his mouth while another dragged a razor-sharp knife deep across his throat, severing the vessels that carried blood to his brain. The guard struggled briefly, his sword dropping from suddenly nerveless fingers, before his body eventually went limp in Lepidus's grip.

Lepidus lowered him carefully to the ground, ensuring no sound would alert others nearby. He glanced up to see Talorcan already moving from his position, bow once again secured across his back as he approached with silent steps.

They met at the roundhouse door, standing over the bodies of the two guards. It had been clean, no alarm raised, no witnesses to their approach. But they knew the respite was temporary. Eventually, someone would come to relieve the guards or check on the prisoners.

'We need to move them,' Talorcan whispered, already bending to grasp one of the fallen men under the arms. Together they dragged the bodies into the deepest shadows beside the roundhouse. It wouldn't fool any serious search, but it might buy them precious minutes.

Blood darkened the earth where the men had fallen. Talorcan scattered a handful of dirt over the worst of it, obscuring but not eliminating the evidence of their deaths.

With the immediate area secured, they turned their attention to the iron-strapped door. A heavy wooden bar secured it from the outside, designed to keep those within from escaping rather than to keep rescuers out. Lepidus grasped one end while Talorcan took the other, and together they lifted it clear of its brackets before easing the door open.

Lepidus stepped inside while Talorcan remained at the threshold, watching for any movement that might signal danger. The interior was shrouded in near-complete darkness, save for a single guttering candle in the centre that cast feeble, dancing shadows across the stone walls. The darkness seemed to press in from all sides and his eyes struggled to adjust from even the dim starlight outside to the murky interior. Gradually, he began to make out the shapes of bodies lining the perimeter of the room, slumped or kneeling figures secured to stakes driven into the earthen floor. He counted quickly, nine men in total, all still alive, though their conditions varied.

All were awake, their eyes reflecting the meagre candlelight as they turned toward the opening door. Their expressions showed not hope but dread, men expecting not rescue but selection for whatever horror awaited beyond.

'Romans,' Lepidus whispered, keeping his voice low enough that it wouldn't carry beyond the thick stone walls. 'I'm here to help. We're getting you out.'

Confusion rippled through the prisoners, disbelief warring with desperate hope on their haggard faces.

'Who's in charge here?' Lepidus asked, already moving toward the nearest man, knife in hand.

'I am,' came a hoarse voice from his right. 'Decurion Lucius Faber, Batavian Auxiliary, Second Augusta.'

Lepidus made his way to the decurion, a powerfully built man despite his current condition. His beard had grown wild during captivity, and dried blood matted one side of his face, but his eyes remained clear and focused.

'What's happening here?' Lepidus asked as he began sawing through the thick ropes binding the man to his stake.

'Sacrifice,' Faber replied, his voice tight with remembered horror. 'They take one of us and then they bring it.'

'Bring what?'

'I don't know what it is,' said Faber. 'It's neither man nor beast. Something else entirely.'

The ropes gave way beneath Lepidus's blade, and Faber immediately began massaging his wrists, working feeling back into hands numbed by extended confinement.

'Whatever it is,' Faber continued, keeping his voice low as Lepidus moved to free the next prisoner, 'it doesn't just kill. It... tears men apart.'

'How many have they taken?' Lepidus asked, working quickly on more bindings.

'Five so far,' Faber answered, already helping to free another of his men. 'Atticus was the first. They made us watch that one, to understand what awaited us. The others they've taken at night.'

'And the rest of your men?'

'Dead in the initial ambush or separated from us. I don't know their fate.'

As each man was freed, they immediately set about helping the others.

'We have no weapons,' Faber said, 'but we'll fight with our hands and teeth if necessary. Anything rather than face that... thing.'

'Fighting may not be necessary if we move quickly and quietly,' said Lepidus, evaluating each man with an experienced eye. Most could walk, though two would need assistance. All appeared determined, the near-mindless terror of extended captivity now replaced by the desperate focus of men granted one final chance at survival. 'Listen carefully,' he continued, gathering them close. 'The settlement is asleep, but guards patrol regularly. We need to reach the northern wall without being seen. My comrade has a rope secured there. We need to climb over and once outside, we head east, back toward Roman lines. We move quickly but in complete silence. Anyone who makes noise endangers us all. Understood?'

Nine heads nodded in grim affirmation.

'Good. Follow me and do exactly as I say.'

He led them to the door where Talorcan waited.

'Clear for now,' Talorcan whispered. 'But we need to move. Dawn is no more than a few hours away.'

The freed prisoners filed out into the night air, each man blinking at even the faint starlight after days in near-total darkness. Faber positioned himself at the rear with Talorcan, ensuring none of the men fell behind, while Lepidus led the way, melting into the shadows of the settlement to begin the precarious journey that would lead either to freedom or death for them all.

Chapter Thirty-Nine

Isla Mona

Night had already fallen over the island when the Occultum emerged from their hiding place in the pigsty. Seneca led the way, his senses heightened by the danger that now surrounded them on all sides. The island seemed alive with activity despite the late hour, distant voices, the occasional glow of cooking fires, the movement of people between settlements.

'More populated than expected,' whispered Decimus as they paused in a dense thicket.

Seneca nodded, studying the pattern of settlements spread across the valley below. They had anticipated finding isolated druidic enclaves, instead they discovered a landscape dotted with tribal communities, farmers, fishermen and craftspeople going about their lives under the protection of their spiritual leaders.

'It makes our approach more challenging,' Marcus observed, eyes constantly scanning their surroundings. 'More eyes to spot us.'

Their progress was agonisingly slow. What might have taken a few hours on open ground stretched into a night-long endeavour as they were forced to freeze at every unexpected sound, to detour around areas where tribal hunters had set camps, to backtrack when paths led too close to occupied dwellings.

By the time the first hint of dawn lightened the eastern sky, they had covered less than half the distance they had hoped and sought concealment as daylight once more became their enemy.

The pattern repeated over the following night, and the next, careful movement through darkness, concealment during daylight, always pushing further into the heart of the island. They foraged as opportunity allowed, supplementing their dwindling provisions with berries, roots, and eggs stolen from nearby farms.

Water, at least, was plentiful on the rain-soaked island, with small streams and springs offering regular opportunity to refill their

257

skins. But hunger became a constant companion, their bodies burning energy faster than their limited rations could replace.

'Smoke ahead,' whispered Marcus on the fourth night, gesturing toward a distant glow that illuminated the low clouds above. 'It looks like a substantial settlement.'

They altered their course, drawn toward what might be their objective and as they drew closer, the true scale of the settlement became apparent. This was no mere farming village or fishing community but something far more substantial, a tribal centre that sprawled across a natural basin in the landscape.

Dozens of roundhouses formed concentric rings around a central area dominated by a massive longhouse. The structure rose above its surroundings, its timber frame elaborately decorated with carvings that caught the moonlight. Torches burned at regular intervals throughout the settlement, casting pools of light amid the greater darkness.

'That must be it,' said Seneca with quiet certainty, his experienced eye recognising the unmistakable signs of a seat of power. 'The druids' stronghold.'

They withdrew from the settlement's perimeter, seeking higher ground that would provide both concealment and observation advantage. A densely wooded hill overlooking the village offered an ideal position, its elevation granting them clear sightlines while the thick vegetation ensured they remained hidden from watchers below.

There, deep in the undergrowth, the Occultum established their position. They cleared only the minimal space necessary, ensuring no broken branches or disturbed earth would betray their presence to keen-eyed hunters or patrolling guards. After their gruelling journey across sea and mountain, after the betrayal that had nearly cost them everything, they had finally reached the heart of druidic power and somewhere within that settlement moved the man they had come to kill.

As their second day of observation drew to a close, Seneca

signalled the Occultum to withdraw deeper into the forest. They retreated in pairs to their secondary position, fifty yards back from their observation point, where the dense foliage provided additional concealment for their discussion.

The men gathered in a tight circle, their voices barely above a whisper. The frustration was evident in their postures, the tension of inaction weighing heavily upon warriors trained for decisive movement.

'Two days and nothing,' said Seneca, his weathered face tight with concern. 'No sign of Raven, no unusual activity.' He glanced back in the direction of the settlement, now hidden from view by the intervening trees. 'I'm beginning to question whether we have the right village. We've seen nothing to confirm Mordred's presence, let alone Raven's.'

Marcus shook his head slowly.

'There's something wrong,' he said slowly. 'The village appears normal, but there's a significant omission.'

'No warriors?' said Sica, his dark eyes narrowing in thought.

'Not in the usual numbers,' clarified Marcus. 'In a settlement this size, we should see warriors training, patrolling, eating, resting. There should be a constant back and forth, but I've seen none.'

Seneca's eyes narrowed as he processed this observation.

'If the warriors are elsewhere...'

'Then Mordred and Raven may be with them,' finished Decimus, completing the thought. 'A gathering, perhaps. Or preparations for some larger action.'

'But where?' asked Falco.

'That's what we need to find out,' replied Seneca. 'If they're planning something significant, Raven's knowledge of Roman tactics would be invaluable to the druids.' He looked around at the five men who had followed him across sea and mountain, who had overcome betrayal and hardship to reach this point. Despite their exhaustion and hunger, their eyes remained sharp, their focus unwavering.

259

'We'll maintain our observation through the rest of today,' he said, 'but tonight we move in. We need more information, and we won't find it by watching from a distance.'

'The village is well-populated,' cautioned Decimus. 'Even without warriors, there are many eyes.'

'We've infiltrated busier settlements than this,' replied Seneca. 'And we can't afford to wait any longer. We are starving and growing weaker by the day. Remember, we're here for information only tonight. Even if we spot Raven, we don't engage. Not until we understand the
full situation.'

With the plan agreed, the Occultum separated to their assigned positions and as the afternoon wore on, they rechecked their weapons, preparing themselves mentally for what awaited. When darkness finally fell, Seneca gathered them one last time.

'No unnecessary risks,' he reminded them. 'In and out, swift and silent.

With silent nods of acknowledgment, the Occultum prepared to descend upon the druid settlement, determined to uncover the truths hidden within its apparently peaceful façade.

Chapter Forty

The Settlement

Lepidus led the freed prisoners away from the stone roundhouse, guiding
them through the shadowed paths of the settlement with Talorcan
bringing up the rear. They moved as a tight group, the stronger men
supporting those weakened by captivity, all maintaining the silence
that might mean the difference between life and death.

'This way,' Lepidus whispered, directing them away from the
main gate. The heavy bar securing it would make too much noise to
remove, and the guards they had killed would eventually be
discovered. Their only viable escape route was the rope they had left
at the northern wall.

After a few minutes, one of the prisoners gasped and lurched
backwards, his eyes wide with terror but before he could make
another sound, Faber clamped a hand firmly over his mouth and
dragged him into the shadow of a nearby hut.

Lepidus immediately backtracked, signalling the others to
hold position. He found the younger man trembling violently, still in
the steel grip of Faber as his eyes fixed on something across the
narrow path,

'What happened?' demanded Lepidus in a harsh whisper.

Faber nodded towards a small stone building set apart from
the surrounding wooden structures. Unlike the roundhouse where the
prisoners had been held, this building had no windows, and its door
was reinforced with heavy metal bands.

'They keep it in there,' he said. 'The thing that killed our
comrades.'

Lepidus glanced at the structure. Nothing about its exterior
seemed particularly threatening, yet the man's terror was undeniable.

'Get him moving,' he said. 'Join the others. I'll be right
behind you.'

261

Faber nodded and guided his still-shaking comrade away, rejoining the main group as they continued their careful progress toward the wall. Talorcan shot Lepidus a questioning look, but remained with the prisoners, now taking his place at the front.

As they headed away, Lepidus found himself drawn toward the stone building, circling the structure cautiously, noting its unusual construction. Unlike other buildings in the settlement, this one had been built with clear defensive intent, thick stone walls, no windows, and a single heavily reinforced door secured with multiple iron chains wrapped through massive staples. Whatever was inside, the builders had gone to extraordinary lengths to ensure it stayed there.

A scratching sound emanated from within, followed by a low, guttural noise that was neither growl nor speech but somewhere unsettlingly between. Lepidus froze, every sense suddenly heightened by the unmistakable presence of danger. He knew he should leave, return to the prisoners and continue their escape. Yet something compelled him to investigate further, to understand what manner of threat they might be facing.

Moving with extreme caution, he approached the wall nearest the sounds. A small crack between stones provided a narrow viewing point into the interior and he pressed his face close, one eye against the opening, straining to penetrate the darkness within.

At first, he saw nothing, just impenetrable blackness beyond the crack. He waited, allowing his vision to adjust, sensing rather than seeing movement in the gloom when suddenly, without warning, a single clawed finger stabbed outward through the opening. The movement was so swift, so unexpected, that Lepidus barely had time to react, and the deformed nail slashed across his cheek, missing his eye by the barest margin, but opening a thin, burning line across his skin.

He jerked backward, his hand flying to his face where he felt the warm wetness of blood. He staggered away from the wall, heart hammering in his chest, as a sound that might have been laughter, distorted and inhuman, echoed from within the structure.

For several moments, he stood frozen, blood trickling between his fingers as the reality of what he had just encountered sank in. The young auxiliary's terror no longer seemed excessive but entirely rational. Whatever was contained within that building was not merely dangerous, it was something outside the normal boundaries of his experience, something that activated the most primitive responses in his brain.

He forced himself to take a deep breath, to regain his composure. The wound was minor, a superficial cut that would heal quickly but he realised they needed to get as far away from this place as they could, as quickly as they could move.

Wiping the blood from his cheek, he turned and hurried after the escaping prisoners, every step carrying him away from the stone building and the aberration it contained.

A few minutes later, he reached the palisade where the others were already climbing the rope, but their progress seemed agonisingly slow.

'It's taking too long,' he muttered, glancing over to Talorcan.

'You should get over,' said Talorcan. 'We need at least one man who knows the way back on the other side in case we're caught here.'

Lepidus hesitated, reluctant to leave. His gaze swept one final time across the darkened settlement before acknowledging the wisdom in Talorcan's words. If they were separated, someone needed to guide the survivors back to Roman territory.

'I'll move them to the ridge,' he said.

Talorcan nodded, his attention already returning to the remaining men.

'You go. I'll make sure everyone gets over.'

Without further discussion, Lepidus turned and climbed the rope before dropping to the ground on the other side. The moment his feet touched solid ground, he felt a subtle shift in his awareness, the oppressive tension of the settlement giving way to the more familiar dangers of open territory. They were far from safe, but the

263

immediate threat had diminished.

He organised the men as they landed, directing them in hushed tones toward the ridge about two hundred yards from the palisade. One by one, they departed, moving in a crouched run, using the natural contours of the landscape for concealment.

The procession continued methodically, a man would reach the ground, Lepidus would indicate the direction, and another escaped prisoner would disappear into the darkness. Eventually, the final prisoner descended, a heavyset man whose weakened state made his movements painfully slow.

Lepidus waited for Talorcan to follow, but there was no sign of him.

For a brief, terrible moment, Lepidus considered climbing back up to investigate, but the practicalities immediately became clear. The rope was still on the inner side of the palisade; he would have no way to ascend. Whatever was happening to Talorcan on the other side, he had no means of reaching him. The realisation struck like a physical blow. Something was wrong.

Precious moments passed in which he remained rooted to the spot, staring up at the empty space where Talorcan should have appeared. The settlement beyond the wall remained ominously silent, no shouts of alarm, no sounds of struggle, nothing that might indicate what had occurred.

Finally, with a bitter acceptance of the immediate priorities, Lepidus turned away. The freed prisoners needed guidance, needed his leadership to have any chance of reaching Roman territory. He could do nothing for Talorcan from here, and remaining exposed near the settlement risked everything they had accomplished.

He moved swiftly toward the gathering point, his mind working through contingencies. When he reached the ridge, he found the freed prisoners huddled in its shadow, tense with uncertainty and the disorientation of sudden freedom after days of captivity.

'Where's the scout?' asked Faber.

'He'll be here, said Lepidus. 'We wait.'

264

He ushered them deeper into the undergrowth with clear sightlines back to the palisade, each man scanning the darkness for any sign of Talorcan's approach.

Chapter Forty-One

Isla Mona

Darkness settled over the druid settlement, bringing with it the concealment the Occultum had waited for. Village life had quietened with nightfall. Fires were reduced to glowing embers and most inhabitants had retired to their dwellings with only the occasional torch illuminating the pathways between buildings.

The night was unusually quiet. No dogs barked, no night birds called. The stillness, rather than offering comfort, put the men further on edge. Nothing appeared outwardly threatening, just a settlement slumbering peacefully beneath the star-filled sky. Yet both men sensed the same wrongness Marcus had identified during their observation. Where were the night patrols? A stronghold of this significance should have warriors standing watch, especially given the tensions between the tribes and the advancing Romans. Instead, they encountered only emptiness, as if the settlement had been abandoned.

They converged slowly on the central longhouse, the structure's roof silhouetted against the night sky. The building stood dark and silent, with no movement visible around its perimeter and no sentries posted at its entrances. The absence of guards seemed odd for such an important structure, especially if it housed the druid leadership as they suspected.

Seneca considered their options. The lack of guards might indicate the building was empty, its occupants elsewhere and if Raven and Mordred were indeed absent, entering the longhouse might alert the settlement to their presence for no gain. But having travelled so far, overcome so many obstacles, they couldn't leave without being certain.

The decision crystallized in his mind. They would investigate the longhouse, but with minimal engagement. With his mind made up, he turned to instruct the men but as they watched from the shadows, the longhouse door creaked open.

The Occultum tensed, hands moving instinctively to weapons, but instead of a warrior or druid, a small child emerged, no more than three years old, laughing as he darted down the steps and into the open area before the building.

They withdrew quickly, moving deeper into the darkness to avoid detection. Seneca signalled for absolute stillness as, a few moments later, a young woman followed, her exasperated expression visible even in the dim light as she called out after the escaping child.

The child darted between huts, clearly delighting in the impromptu game, his bare feet pattering on the packed earth. The woman followed, her pace quickening as the boy disappeared around a corner, heading directly toward where Marcus was hiding and before he could retreat further into the shadows, the child rounded the bend at full speed and collided with his legs. The scout instinctively steadied the boy, hands grasping small shoulders to prevent him from falling backward.

For a moment, child and warrior stared at each other, mutual surprise reflected in their faces. Then, with the acceptance of the very young, the boy grinned up at the unfamiliar man, showing no fear of the stranger in the darkness.

Marcus lifted the child into his arms, a reflexive action born from some distant memory of his own family. The boy remained remarkably quiet, seemingly intrigued rather than frightened by the encounter.

The woman appeared seconds later, her hurried steps faltering as she confronted the scene before her, her child in the arms of a stranger. Her breath caught, a small sound of fear escaping her lips as she froze in place. Her eyes darted between Marcus and the child in his arms, calculation and terror mingling in her expression. She took a single step backward, preparing to flee or perhaps to scream, when Seneca emerged from the deeper shadows.

He lifted his finger to his lips, signalling for silence then beckoned her forward with a deliberate motion.

267

Still, she hesitated, maternal instinct warring with self-preservation. She turned to retreat in the other direction, only to find her path blocked by Cassius, who had circled behind her while her attention was fixed on Marcus and the child.

Understanding dawned in her eyes, she was trapped between these silent warriors, her child effectively hostage to her cooperation. Whatever these men wanted, her only hope of protecting the boy lay in compliance, at least until an opportunity for escape presented itself. With visible reluctance, she moved toward Marcus, each step slow and hesitant. Her hands trembled slightly at her sides, but her eyes remained clear, alert for any opening that might allow her to snatch the child and run.

Marcus adjusted his hold on the boy, ensuring he maintained control while appearing unthreatening and as the woman drew near, Seneca moved to intercept her, clamping one hand over her mouth while the other grabbed her arm, preventing any attempt to flee. With the woman secured, they quickly withdrew behind a nearby haystack, dragging their captive into deeper concealment.

'What do we do now?' Falco whispered as he stared at their captives. 'If we let them go, she'll raise the alarm.'

Seneca's mind raced through their limited options. Killing civilians, especially a woman and child, went against everything he believed in, yet releasing them meant certain discovery. Before he could formulate a plan, the woman spoke, her voice muffled against his palm but words distinctly recognizable.

'Please don't hurt him.'

Seneca released his hand from her mouth in shock, maintaining his firm grip on her arm. The words had been Latin, heavily accented and crude, but unmistakably the language of Rome.

'How do you know our words?' he demanded, studying her face with new intensity.

She glanced anxiously between the Occultum members, her eyes lingering on her child who had begun squirming in Marcus's grasp, small arms reaching toward his mother. After a moment's hesitation, Seneca nodded to Marcus, who carefully transferred the boy to the woman's waiting embrace.

She clutched the child protectively against her chest but remained silent, eyes darting between the men who surrounded her.

'I asked you a question,' said Seneca, 'How do you understand our language.'

When she still didn't respond, Seneca exchanged a meaningful glance with Sica, briefly directing his gaze toward the Syrian's belt knife. Sica understood immediately, slowly drawing the blade from its sheath with theatrical deliberation.

The woman gasped, clutching her child tighter as she registered the implied threat.

'We don't want to hurt you,' said Seneca slowly, ensuring she understood each word. 'Just some information. First of all, tell me how you know our language.'

The woman swallowed hard, her voice trembling when she finally spoke.

'Before the armies came,' she said haltingly, struggling with the unfamiliar Latin, 'my father spent much time with the eastern tribes. Many traders there. I watched the bartering, learned some words.' She paused, gathering her thoughts. 'But my mother taught me more. She knew your speech well.'

'And who is your father?' asked Seneca.

The woman hesitated, fear flickering across her features before she answered.

'Mordred.'

The name sent a jolt through Seneca. If they couldn't locate Raven, the druid leader himself would be an alternative target of immense value. Eliminating the spiritual and strategic head of resistance against Rome could cripple the tribal opposition.

'Does Mordred live here? In this settlement?' he asked, careful to keep his tone neutral despite the surge of anticipation he felt.

'Yes,' she replied, adjusting the child in her arms as he began to fuss. 'This is his home. But he has gone east with the warriors.'

Seneca cursed silently. The confirmation of Marcus's observation about the missing warriors now had context, but it also meant their primary targets were elsewhere.

'East,' he repeated. 'Toward the Roman forces?'

She nodded, her eyes downcast.

'And is there a man called Raven with him?' asked Seneca. 'A Roman who now lives among your people?'

At this question, she hesitated noticeably, her gaze flicking toward Sica who continued to handle his blade with casual menace, occasionally glancing toward the child with calculated interest.

The woman's composure broke. Tears welled in her eyes as she clutched her son tighter, turning her body slightly as if to shield him from the Syrian's gaze.

'Please,' she begged, her Latin deteriorating with her growing distress. 'Do not hurt my child. I will tell what you want.'

Seneca's grip on her arm softened slightly, though he remained alert.

'Tell me everything you know about why Mordred has gone east with the warriors,' he said. 'If you tell us the truth, I swear by Rome's gods that you and your child will live.'

'We should kill them anyway,' muttered Sica, but Seneca silenced him with a sharp look.

The woman took a deep breath, her eyes darting between the two men.

'They are going to kill the Roman king,' she whispered.

'We have no king,' replied Seneca.

'The... the man who rules Rome,' she struggled, searching for the right words.

'The Emperor?' asked Seneca, suddenly alert.

She nodded vigorously.

'Yes! The Emperor. My father said he is coming to take tribute from the chieftains.

A stunned silence fell over the Occultum, the implications crashing over them like a wave. They did not know that Claudius had planned to come to Britannia but if true, his life was in danger. Seneca's mind raced. They had to warn Plautius immediately and every moment they delayed could mean disaster for Rome, but they would never make it back in time on foot. He turned back to the woman, a new plan already forming.

'Show us where the horses are,' he said, ' and I will let you and your child go free.'

She hesitated, maternal instinct warring with fear. But the life of Mordred's grandson was too precious to risk. The child was her insurance, her protection.

'Yes,' she whispered nervously. 'This way.'

The woman moved silently through the settlement, leading the Occultum between sleeping huts, avoiding the main paths until eventually, the horse paddock came into view. There were still no guards or additional security, just a simple wooden fence surrounding ten sturdy mounts. The animals stood quietly, barely lifting their heads as the group approached.

'These,' she whispered, indicating the most robust horses.

Marcus and Falco quickly checked the animals, testing their girths, ensuring they could bear the weight of heavily armed men. Once done, Seneca turned to the woman, his expression resolute but not unkind.

'I know you must raise the alarm,' he said quietly. 'So, I can't let you go immediately. However, we have to take you with us for a few miles, it gives us a head start.'

Fear flickered in her eyes, but she nodded. Whatever threat these men represented, the safety of her child was paramount.

'You'll be released soon,' Seneca assured her. 'I swear by the gods.'

A few moments later, the horses were ready, and she clutched the child closer as Seneca lifted her onto one, before climbing up behind her. When all the men were mounted, he turned his horse and led them out of the settlement, moving quietly to avoid drawing unnecessary attention and when they were finally clear, he leaned forward and whispered into the woman's ear.

'Now, show us the way to the bridge.'

After several miles, as promised, Seneca signalled a halt and helped the woman down, setting her onto solid ground with her child.

'You are free,' he said. 'Now go.'

She hesitated, meeting Seneca's gaze before turning and walking back the way they had come, the child nestled against her.

Seneca watched her for a moment, then turned his horse toward the bridge and his waiting men. They had a new mission now, one far more critical than hunting Raven and as they urged their horses further into the night, they knew they were in a deadly race to save the Emperor's life.

Chapter Forty-Two

The Settlement

Talorcan crouched in the shadows at the base of the palisade. The last of the prisoners had gone but as he had been about to climb the rope, the sound of approaching footsteps had made him freeze in place. Now he was pressed into the deepest shadows at the base of the nearest hut, his knife already in his hand.

As he watched, a lone guard appeared out of the darkness, his spear resting casually across one shoulder. Under different circumstances, Talorcan might have waited for him to pass, but he knew the rope hanging from the palisade would immediately betray their escape route.

The guard paused, his attention drawn to the footprints in the soil where the prisoners had gathered before climbing. His

272

posture changed, alertness replacing the previous lethargy as he moved closer to investigate.

Talorcan remained motionless, weighing his rapidly diminishing options, the guard was now following the trail directly toward the rope. Discovery was moments away, and with it, the alarm that would bring warriors swarming through the settlement.

The guard's eyes lifted from the ground, tracking upward until they found the rope dangling against the palisade. His eyes widened with alarm, but as his one hand reached for the horn at his belt Talorcan appeared behind him and drove his knife deep into the man's throat.

Hot blood spilled over his hand as the guard struggled, but within moments, his victim stilled, and he lowered the dying man to the ground. He dragged the body into the shadows before taking the guard's knife and tucking it into his own belt. Quickly he returned to the rope and pulled himself upward with renewed urgency but as his fingers grasped the sharpened point of one log to stabilize himself, he heard another noise and glanced down to see a second guard standing near the body of the first, his face contorted with shock and rage. Their eyes met for a brief moment, a frozen tableau of hunter and hunted, but before Talorcan could react, the guard raised a horn to his lips and blew a piercing blast that shattered the night's silence.

With the alarm raised, stealth no longer mattered and Talorcan hauled himself over the top of the palisade. He hit the ground hard, his body instinctively rolling to distribute the impact, but pain still lanced through his ankle as it twisted beneath him. Ignoring the injury, he scrambled to his feet and sprinted toward the treeline where Lepidus and the others were already disappearing into the trees, away from the settlement and the pursuit that would inevitably follow.

Talorcan pushed himself harder, each stride sending fresh pain through his injured ankle and as he reached the trees, Lepidus grabbed his arm to support him as he stumbled on his injured leg.

273

'What happened?' he demanded.

'Perimeter guards,' said Talorcan. 'I killed one but the other saw me on the wall and raised the alarm. They'll have riders after us as soon as they can open the gate.'

Lepidus nodded, his face tightening with grim determination as he considered their limited options. Ahead, the freed prisoners were already moving as quickly as their weakened condition allowed.

'Can you run?' Lepidus asked, eyeing Talorcan's injured ankle.

'I'll manage,' Talorcan replied, testing his weight on the joint. It held, though pain flared with each step. 'But we can't outrun horses, not with these men in their condition.'

Lepidus scanned the surrounding forest, his experienced eye assessing the terrain for defensive possibilities.

'Then we'll have to outsmart them,' he said. 'This way.'

They plunged deeper into the forest, leaving behind the settlement and its awakened fury, racing against time and the mounted warriors who would soon be on their trail. They had succeeded in liberating the prisoners, but the most dangerous part of their mission still lay before them, getting back to Roman lines with their enemies in hot pursuit.

The forest canopy provided both concealment and challenge as Lepidus led his group eastward through the darkness. Moonlight filtered sporadically through the dense branches overhead, creating a patchwork of dim illumination and absolute shadow that made every step treacherous. Still, they pushed forward, the urgency of their situation overriding all other concerns.

'Keep moving,' Lepidus urged as a prisoner stumbled. 'Every mile between us and them improves our chances.'

The night seemed endless, a gruelling marathon of silent movement punctuated by brief pauses to catch their breath or help someone who had fallen. They avoided the easier paths where mounted pursuers might follow, instead choosing steeper, more difficult terrain that would favour those on foot.

'High ground,' Talorcan whispered during one such pause, gesturing toward a ridge that loomed as a darker shadow against the night sky. 'Better visibility. We'll see them coming.'

Lepidus nodded agreement. The tactical advantage of elevated terrain was undeniable, and by dawn, they would need to make more informed decisions about their route.

The climb was punishing, especially for men already pushed to their physical limits. Several prisoners needed to be supported by their stronger comrades, and even Talorcan's face was drawn with pain as the ascent put greater pressure on his injured ankle. Yet not a single complaint was voiced, each man understood that capture meant a fate much worse than mere exhaustion.

They reached the summit as the first hint of grey light appeared on the eastern horizon. The ridge offered a commanding view of the surrounding territory, including the settlement they had fled hours earlier. The men collapsed into exhausted heaps, gasping for breath in the pre-dawn chill.

'Rest,' said Lepidus, his own fatigue evident in the hoarseness of his voice. 'Talorcan, give them what food we have left. We'll move again soon.'

Talorcan handed out the last of the dried meat before settling beside Lepidus at the ridge's edge.

'There,' he said quietly, pointing to movement in the distance. 'They're gathering.'

Lepidus stared towards the settlement. Figures moved around
the main gate, the distance rendering them as mere specks against the earthen backdrop. Yet even from this distance, certain details were discernible, the glint of morning light on metal, the distinctive silhouettes of mounted warriors.

'Twenty, perhaps more,' Lepidus estimated, counting the mounted figures. 'Twice that on foot.'

They watched in silence as their pursuers prepared to follow but what struck him as odd, was the fact that the alarm had been raised hours ago, yet the warriors seemed in no particular hurry to begin their chase. It was as if they knew something that Lepidus did not, some advantage that allowed them this casual confidence despite the significant head start their quarry had gained.

'Something's wrong,' he murmured. 'They should have been after us immediately. Why wait until now?'

As the gathering light strengthened, more details emerged from the distant scene. The mounted warriors had formed into a rough circle, surrounding something Lepidus couldn't quite make out. Then, as the circle parted, he saw it, a cart emerging from the settlement's gate, pulled by two sturdy horses. On the cart rested a crate secured with chains that glinted in the early morning light.

The air seemed to freeze in Lepidus's lungs as recognition dawned. Not a supply cart. Not reinforcements, something far worse.

'Gods above,' he whispered, the blood draining from his face. 'That's the thing that killed their prisoners. They're not just pursuing us, they're *hunting us.*' He swallowed hard, forcing down the fear that threatened to overwhelm his tactical thinking. He turned away from the sight, already calculating their diminishing options.

'Get ready to move,' he ordered, his voice carrying to the resting men who immediately began to stir. 'We need to get out of here.

As the freed prisoners struggled to their feet, Lepidus cast one final glance toward the settlement. The coming hours would test them beyond anything they had yet endured, but this was no longer merely an escape; it was a desperate race against something he didn't understand, a predator specifically released to hunt them down.

With grim determination, he turned his back on the distant threat and led his exhausted group down the eastern slope of the ridge, pushing deeper into territory that promised both potential refuge and unknown dangers of its own.

Chapter Forty-Three

Isla Mona

Night had settled fully over the land as the Occultum approached the bridge that connected Mona to the mainland. Seneca raised his fist, signalling a halt as they reached the sheltering darkness of a dense copse approximately two hundred yards from the bridge's approach. From this vantage point, they could see the guard fires burning at both ends of the structure, orange flames flickering against the night sky.

'Six men at this end, at least eight visible on the far side,' observed Marcus. 'Alert but they won't be expecting trouble from this direction.'

The others followed his gaze, they could see the Celts had constructed a small barricade across the bridge's exit on the far side, a crude but effective arrangement of logs and interwoven branches. Four guards on this side of it, their weapons gleaming in the firelight.

'Designed to stop outsiders coming in,' noted Seneca, 'but it works just as well against those trying to leave.'

Silence fell as each man contemplated their limited choices. The bridge represented both their only viable route of escape and a formidable obstacle.

'There is only one option,' said Seneca finally. 'We go through them. Speed will be our advantage through the first position as they won't expect a direct charge, but that barricade at the far end...'

'We'll need to dismount to clear it,' Marcus concluded. 'Which means fighting in close quarters.'

Seneca nodded. They would hit the guards at the near end with overwhelming force and speed, break through onto the bridge, and then fight their way past the barricade at the far side.

'Weapons ready,' ordered Seneca quietly, drawing his gladius. 'Follow my lead and don't stop for anything.' With a subtle nod, he turned his horse toward the bridge and after whispering a brief prayer to Mars, dug his heels into his mount's flanks.

The horses burst from their concealment like living projectiles, hooves thundering against the packed earth as they accelerated toward the bridge. The element of surprise worked exactly as intended, the guards at the near end barely having time to register the approaching riders before the Occultum were upon them.

The sentries scrambled to form a defensive line, spears lowering to create a barrier of deadly points, but they were too slow, too disorganized and the riders crashed through them, their gladii sweeping in lethal arcs that caught two guards completely unprepared. The remaining sentries scattered in confusion, their defensive line shattered by the ferocity and suddenness of the attack.

The wooden structure shuddered beneath the combined weight of six galloping horses, the planks booming like war drums with each impact of hooves. Behind them, shouts of alarm and rage erupted from the surviving guards, but the Occultum were already twenty yards down the bridge, their momentum carrying them swiftly toward the mainland.

As they thundered across, the guards at the far end sprang into action. Alerted by the commotion, they turned to face the riders. One man raised a horn to his lips, blasting a warning that would carry to nearby settlements while another notched an arrow to his bow, drawing and releasing in one fluid motion.

The arrow whistled past Seneca's ear, missing by mere inches as the Occultum threw themselves from their saddles, to charge into the defenders.

The shock of the attack and total commitment of the men launching into the attack took the celts by surprise and two quickly fell to sword thrusts from Cassius and Seneca.

Falco, using his massive strength, knocked another aside, smashing his jaw with his elbow before grabbing one of the upright logs on the barricade and wrenching it sideways. Another defender ran to attack him, but Seneca intercepted and drove his blade into the man's unprotected abdomen.

Within moments, five celts lay dead or dying, their bodies sprawled across the bloodied planks of the bridge while others, some previously unseen, ran from the fight into the surrounding bushes.

'Mount up!' Seneca ordered, already swinging back into his saddle, 'we need to get out of here.'

The others complied immediately. Marcus's arm bled freely, and Falco sported a deep gash across his cheek where a desperate defender had managed to land a blow, but none of the injuries were life-threatening.

They thundered off the bridge and onto the mainland path, six riders bent low over their mounts' necks as they pushed for speed. Behind them, more horns sounded, the alarm spreading across the island and to nearby settlements. Pursuit would come, but for now, they had broken free.

They rode hard for several miles, putting distance between themselves and the bridge before finally stopping to address their wounds.

'How far until we reach Roman lines?' asked Marcus to Seneca as Decimus cleaned and bandaged his arm wound.

'I reckon at least five days' hard riding,' replied Seneca, 'and that's if we encounter no further resistance. We pause only when absolutely necessary.'

There were no objections. Their wounds were painful but not debilitating and within minutes, they were mounted again, six riders moving east as fast as their horses allowed them.

Chapter Forty-Four

The Forests of Mid Britannia

Lepidus and Talorcan pushed the pace relentlessly, driving the freed prisoners through dense forest and difficult terrain. The injured and weak struggled to keep up, but none complained. Even the most exhausted among them found reserves of strength they hadn't known they possessed, spurred by the knowledge of what pursued them.

'Keep moving,' Lepidus urged as one man stumbled to his knees, immediately hauled back to his feet by Faber. 'We can't afford to slow down.'

The dense undergrowth made their progress frustratingly slow, but it also offered an unexpected advantage, their pursuers couldn't follow on horseback. The mounted warriors would be forced to dismount or find alternate routes, buying the escapees precious time.

Talorcan led the way, his hunter's instincts guiding them through the wilderness. Despite his injured ankle, he moved with remarkable agility, finding game trails and natural pathways that offered slightly easier passage.

They crisscrossed streams and rivers whenever possible, wading through cold waters to break their scent trail and at strategic points, they deliberately changed direction before doubling back, creating false leads to confuse their trackers. Lepidus even had the men walk backward along certain stretches, leaving footprints pointing in the wrong direction, a simple trick, but one that might buy them valuable minutes.

'It won't fool them for long,' Talorcan noted after watching Lepidus carefully arrange fallen branches to suggest their group had gone north instead of east.

'I know,' Lepidus replied grimly. 'But every delay increases our chances. We just need to reach Roman territory.'

They pushed hardest during daylight hours, knowing that darkness would slow them more than their pursuers. Each night, they took only the briefest rest periods, never building fires despite the biting cold, and eating what little food they could forage while on the move.

On the fourth day, the sound of a nearby hunting horn told Lepidus their pursuers were closing the gap, despite all their efforts to throw them off.

'How much farther?' he asked as they paused briefly to let the most exhausted men catch their breath.

Talorcan studied the surrounding landscape, getting his bearings.

'I think less than a day's march to Castra Victrix,' he replied. 'If we push hard, we might reach the outer patrol routes by nightfall.'

The men, overhearing this, found new energy despite their exhaustion. Safety was within reach, if they could just maintain their pace for a few more hours.

They set out again with renewed determination, their route taking them through increasingly familiar terrain as they neared Roman-controlled territory. Lepidus recognized landmarks from their outward journey, a distinctive rock formation, a stream with an unusual bend, a copse of trees arranged in an almost perfect circle. They were close now, perhaps only hours from safety.

As they crested a final ridge, the one that would finally give them their first view of the road leading to Castra Victrix, Lepidus felt hope rising in his chest. They had done it. Against all odds, they had escaped the settlement, evaded pursuit for days, and were now within sight of...

He froze at the top of the ridge, Talorcan coming to an abrupt halt beside him. The freed prisoners, seeing their leaders stop, did likewise, an instinctive response to the sudden tension in the air.

Below them, spread out along the road that represented their path to safety, were mounted warriors, at least twenty of them, positioned at strategic intervals to intercept anyone approaching from

281

the west. Their distinctive blue woad markings and bronze weapons identified them immediately as men from the same settlement they had escaped.

'How did they get ahead of us?' whispered Lepidus, disbelief evident in his voice. '

'They didn't need to follow our exact path,' replied Talorcan quietly. 'They knew where we were headed so the road to Castra Victrix was the obvious destination. They simply rode the fastest route to intercept us.'

The tactical implications crashed over Lepidus like a cold wave. While he and Talorcan had been carefully laying false trails and making difficult crossings through dense wilderness, a separate group of warriors had simply ridden the established paths to position themselves ahead of the fugitives. It was a basic encirclement strategy, and they had walked directly into it.

As if to confirm their predicament, the unmistakable sounds of pursuit reached them from behind, breaking branches, the occasional voice calling to others, the heavy footfalls of multiple men moving through forest with more concern for speed than stealth. The warriors who had been following their trail were closing in, pushing them toward the waiting ambush below.

'We're trapped,' whispered Faber, who had come up beside them. The decurion's face, already haggard from days of desperate flight, now showed a resignation that was more terrible than fear.

Talorcan suddenly pointed toward a clearing beside the road. 'That's the cart we saw at the gates,' he said. 'Look.'

Lepidus followed his gaze and felt a chill run through him. The crate that had once been loaded on the cart now rested on the ground, guarded by four men who maintained a respectful distance from it. Whatever was contained within was now positioned directly in their path to safety.

Lepidus's heart raced as he considered the implications and the scratch on his cheek, a souvenir from his brief encounter with whatever lay inside that crate, seemed to burn anew with the memory. Faber stared down at the scene, the last of his resolve visibly crumbling.

'We're finished,' he said, his voice hollow with defeat. 'The men are too exhausted to detour any further. Even if we could, that... thing... will find us the moment they release it.' His shoulders slumped, the weeks of captivity and days of desperate flight finally overwhelming him. 'I've seen what it does. There's no escape.'

'Why haven't they already released it?' Talorcan wondered aloud, studying the scene below with analytical detachment despite their dire situation.

'It mainly hunts in darkness,' Faber replied, his voice barely audible. 'At least, that's when they always brought it to kill our men. The druids would say things about it being stronger when the sun sleeps.' He shook his head. 'I don't know if that's true or just their superstition, but they always waited for nightfall.'

The rest of the prisoners had gathered behind them now, each man taking in the scene below with varying degrees of horror and despair. They had come so far, endured so much, only to find themselves trapped between pursuing warriors and the creature that had claimed their comrades one by one.

Talorcan turned to Lepidus.

'We could split the group,' he suggested quietly. 'Send half in one direction, half in another. If the creature attacks one group, the other might reach safety.' His voice remained steady, though the weight of what he was proposing, sacrificing some to save others, was evident in his eyes.

Lepidus considered the suggestion briefly before shaking his head.

'No,' he said firmly. 'We stay together. Divided, we're weaker.' He surveyed the men gathered around him, exhausted, injured, but still alive, and still fighting to remain so.

He studied the landscape once more, his mind working through their dwindling options. They couldn't go forward through

283

the waiting ambush. They couldn't go back into the pursuing warriors, and they couldn't circle around without encountering either group. There was only one choice left.

'If we can't go around, over or back,' said Lepidus quietly, 'we face the threat head-on.'

The men exchanged uncertain glances, fear and exhaustion written clearly on their faces. But in those same faces, Lepidus also saw determination, the stubborn resilience that had kept them alive through captivity and flight.

'What's your plan?' Talorcan asked.

Lepidus's expression hardened as he looked down at the crate and the warriors guarding it. If they were waiting for darkness to release their creature, then perhaps there was still a chance, a desperate, slim chance, but better than resignation to certain death.

'We attack,' he said simply. 'While there's still daylight. We hit them fast and hard, focusing on the men guarding that crate. If we can reach it before they release whatever's inside, we may have a chance to get to the trees on the other side.'

The men around him straightened, drawing on reserves of strength they didn't know they still possessed. Even in their exhausted state, they were still proud Batavians, trained, disciplined fighters who had faced death many times before. If this was to be their last stand, they would make it one worthy of remembrance.

Chapter Forty-Five

The Central Mountains

The small fire burned low between the rocks, its flames carefully contained to prevent any betraying light from reaching beyond their sheltered position. The Occultum had found this natural hollow as dusk approached, a depression that offered protection from both the elements and prying eyes and after days of hard riding, the men welcomed even this brief respite.

Seneca crouched near some heated rocks by the fire, using a stick to turn the several fish they had obtained from a startled fisherman earlier. Across from him, Marcus and Decimus checked their weapons with methodical care, while Falco stretched his massive frame, muscles stiff from long hours in the saddle. Cassius tended to his arrow wound, applying fresh herbs that Sica had gathered during their brief stop by the river.

'Still no sign of pursuit,' Sica reported as he returned from his perimeter check. 'The path behind us remains clear.'

Seneca nodded, unsurprised but still wary. They had seen no indication of Celtic warriors following their trail since crossing the bridge, which seemed odd given the violence of their departure. Logic suggested that riders should have been dispatched immediately to hunt them down.

'The village was practically empty of warriors,' observed Marcus, voicing Seneca's

Seneca distributed the cooked fish among his men, and they ate in companionable silence for a few moments, the only sounds the crackling of the fire and the distant calls of night birds.

Despite their predicament, Seneca found himself smiling slightly as he recalled how they had acquired their dinner. The memory of the fisherman's stunned expression when Falco emerged from the reeds like some massive river god was almost comical in retrospect.

285

'Something amusing?' asked Cassius, noticing Seneca's expression.

'Just thinking about our fisherman friend,' Seneca replied. 'The look on his face when Falco appeared...'

Falco grinned widely, his scarred face transforming with the expression.

'He squawked like a startled hen when I picked him up,' the big man chuckled. 'But he went into that river smooth as you please.'

'He's fortunate you reached him first,' said Sica, his voice carrying its usual deadpan quality. 'Had he fought back, I would have gutted him the same way I gutted his fish.'

The comment, delivered with Sica's characteristic lack of inflection, drew quiet laughter from the group. Even in dire circumstances, perhaps especially in dire circumstances, such moments of levity were precious, sustaining them through the darkness that so often surrounded their work.

As they finished their meal, Seneca unrolled one of their crude maps, spreading it on the ground between them. By the fire's flickering light, he traced their progress and the distance still remaining to their destination.

'I estimate we're about here,' he said, pointing to a bend in a river that they had crossed earlier in the day. 'The Tamesis crossing lies approximately here,' his finger moved eastward across the parchment. 'Based on our pace and the terrain ahead, I think we're about three days away, four at most.'

Marcus leaned forward to study the map, his eyes narrowed in calculation.

'The horses are showing signs of exhaustion,' he said. 'We've pushed them hard since leaving Mona.'

'Too hard,' agreed Decimus. 'If we continue at this pace, we risk losing them altogether. And on foot, our journey time would triple.'

Seneca nodded, acknowledging the reality of their situation.

The horses had been driven beyond their natural endurance by the urgency of the mission.

'We'll need to ease up,' Seneca decided. 'We'll rest here until dawn, then continue at a more sustainable pace. Sica, you'll take first watch, then Falco, then me.'

The men arranged their bedrolls around the fire, positioning themselves to take maximum advantage of its warmth while maintaining defensive postures, and as the others settled down, Seneca remained awake a while longer, staring into the dying flames. Somewhere east of their position, Mordred and his druids were moving quickly towards their target, and Rome, blissfully unaware of the danger, needed Seneca and his men to stop them. It was an almost impossible task, but they would do whatever they could to see it through.

Chapter Forty-Six

The Forests Near Castra Victrix

Lepidus and Talorcan shared all the available weapons between the fugitives, ensuring that each man had at least one each to defend himself before gathering them close.

'We have one chance,' he explained, his eyes scanning each face to ensure they understood the gravity of their situation. 'We hit them hard and fast, before they can react or release whatever is in that crate.' He paused, his expression hardening. 'Those four guards by the cart are our first priority, but once we engage them, the warriors on both sides will be on us immediately. There will be no retreat, no chance to run. We kill or we die. Every man must be prepared to fight to his last breath.'

The freed prisoners exchanged glances. These were not the broken men who had been captives just days ago. Survival, escape, and Lepidus's leadership had transformed them.

'We'll use this ridge,' he continued, pointing out a slight elevation to their left, 'and those bushes to get as close as possible without being seen. When we move, we move together. No hesitation.'

Once done, they crept forward, each man focused on the large crate on the road and Lepidus found a position that offered a clear view. He could see four men, two directly beside the crate, two a short distance away, their horses tethered nearby. The road stretched out before them, a guarded barrier to safety that now represented their only chance of survival.

He looked back at the men alongside him. Talorcan's face was a mask of concentration, his injured ankle forgotten in the immediacy of the coming fight. The freed prisoners gripped their improvised weapons, a mix of the dead guards' swords, Talorcan's hunting knives, and even a woodcutter's axe one man had found near their last hiding place.

Taking a deep breath, Lepidus knew this was their moment. One chance. One charge. Everything depended on absolute surprise and total commitment.

At first, the Celtic guards remained oblivious, engaged in casual conversation but as the prisoners closed in, one guard happened to look up, his eyes widening in alarm, but before he could even draw breath to shout, Talorcan's arrow took him squarely in the face. The man collapsed backward, blood and arrow shaft protruding from where his eye had been moments before.

The remaining guards spun, reaching for weapons, but Lepidus and the men were already among them with a ferocity that shocked even themselves.

Within moments, the four guards lay dead or dying, their bodies sprawled across the road. The prisoners quickly gathered whatever weapons they could, turning to face the new threat that was already thundering towards them.

Four horsemen approached at full gallop, their war cries rising above the sound of hoofbeats and behind them, a larger group of warriors followed. Talorcan's bow sang again, and two riders fell from their mounts, one with an arrow through his throat, another catching a shaft in the chest that sent him tumbling from his horse.

The remaining horsemen charged directly into the group. One prisoner went down immediately, a Celtic spear taking him through the mid-section. Another was trampled beneath a horse's hooves, his scream cut short by the brutal impact. Faber met one of the mounted warriors head-on, catching the horseman's spear on his stolen shield and using the momentum to drag the rider from his mount and as the foot soldiers caught up, the battle became a chaotic whirlwind of violence.

Talorcan moved like a phantom, his bow giving way to a sword as the fight closed in and the bodies began to pile up. Another two of the prisoners fell, one with his throat cut, another with a spear through his chest, but the desperation of the survivors worked in their favour. These were men who had endured captivity, who had survived days of brutal flight, who knew this was their final chance.

Slowly, impossibly, they began to gain the upper hand, and the last horseman fell to Faber's sword, the blade finding a gap in his leather armour. Finally, exhausted and bleeding, the prisoners gathered together, staring at the bloody mess that battle always brought but just as Talorcan slit the last of the wounded warriors' throat, the sound of movement from the tree line shattered their brief respite. The men who had been pursuing them throughout their flight emerged from the forest, over twenty strong, their faces set with grim determination.

Lepidus knew instantly they were finished. There was no way they could fight this many.

His mind raced, desperation driving his thoughts. The prisoners looked to him, exhaustion and fear etched on their faces. They had come so far, survived so much, only to die here on this nameless road. Finally, he came to a decision. It was stupid, a last desperate gamble but it was all he had. He turned to Talorcan and the others.

'Get them out of here,' he said. 'Now.'

Talorcan hesitated, not knowing what Lepidus planned.

'*Move,*' screamed Lepidus, pushing him toward the others, 'that's an order.'

Talorcan turned away and calling out after the others, led them quickly to the top of the slope on the Roman side of the road.

Alone now, Lepidus turned to the crate that had haunted their entire journey. With desperate strength, he pushed it around, positioning its gate toward the oncoming warriors and after climbing on top, took a deep breath before lifting the rope securing the crate's door.

For a few heartbeats nothing moved, then, with a blood-curdling roar that seemed to tear through the very fabric of reality, the creature burst forth on all fours.

Lepidus stared in disbelief as the creature screamed, a sound that was part rage, part hunger, part something beyond human comprehension. The warriors on the hill froze with terror etched on their faces and those who had witnessed its previous attacks, knew exactly what was about to happen.

Some tried to run, but the creature was impossibly fast. Raising itself up onto two feet, it launched itself at the nearest Celtic warrior, moving with a speed that blurred the line between living thing and monstrous weapon. Its filed teeth tore through the man's throat in a single, devastating motion and blood sprayed skyward as the victim collapsed, barely having time to comprehend his own death.

Another warrior turned to flee, but the creature was on him in an instant. Its clawed hands seized him, ripping away his entire face like wet parchment, leaving nothing but a crimson ruin where a human had stood moments before.

Panic consumed the Celtic warriors, their disciplined formation dissolving into chaos. One brave, or foolish, warrior charged forward, his raised sword an act of desperate defiance but the creature knocked him aside with impossible strength, sending him tumbling like a child's discarded toy. Before he could rise, those terrible teeth found his throat, tearing it away in a spray of arterial blood.

The attack was overwhelming, horrific beyond description. The creature moved with a fury that transcended mere animal hunger. It was hunting, but hunting with a cold intelligence that made the slaughter somehow more terrifying.

Lepidus could only stare in horror, his mind unable to process the scene of carnage unfolding before him and as the creature chased down another screaming victim, survival overtook any impulse to watch further, and he ran after Talorcan and the other survivors. Looking back, he saw that those who had pursued them, who had been so confident in their hunt, were now nothing more than scattered, mutilated corpses.

'Keep moving!' Lepidus urged the group as he caught them up. 'Quickly!'

But Talorcan had stopped, his hand moving to the quiver at his side. Only one arrow remained. He looked at Lepidus, a decision forming in his eyes.

'Come on!' Lepidus ordered, but Talorcan shook his head.

'No creature like this should exist in this world,' Talorcan said quietly, and he turned away, walking back down the hill toward the Wraith, watching in cold detachment as it ripped out the heart of its latest victim.

As he walked, he retrieved the single arrow from his quiver, his eyes never leaving the creature. The ground was slick with blood, torn bodies scattered like discarded dolls across the landscape and finally, Talorcan stopped and stared, an unspoken challenge to the monstrosity before him.

The creature looked up, snarling with a sound that was part human scream, part animal rage. Blood and torn flesh hung from its sharpened teeth, a fresh heart still clutched in its clawed hands. A dagger protruded from its shoulder, but it seemed to have no effect, as if the wound were nothing more than a minor irritation.

Talorcan had never seen anything like it before. It looked human, yet was so fundamentally wrong that the very sight of it defied natural understanding. Its skin was pale, almost translucent and scars crisscrossed its body, some surgical, some clearly self-inflicted. Feral, murderous, deformed, the creature was a perversion of humanity that challenged everything Talorcan knew about the world.

Slowly, the creature stood, its spine twisted from years of moving on all fours. Its back remained half-bent, a testament to the unnatural transformation it had undergone. Muscles rippled beneath its skin, coiling with predatory potential and it sniffed the air, nostrils flaring, as it caught Talorcan's scent.

On the hill above, Lepidus and the other survivors watched

in tense silence. Men who had survived days of brutal captivity now held their breath, transfixed by the scene unfolding below.

'Kill it,' whispered Lepidus to himself, staring down at the motionless scout. 'In the name of the gods, what are you waiting for? *Kill it!'*

Down the hill, Talorcan stood solid, the arrow nocked to his bow. His breathing slowed, each exhale measured and controlled. The world seemed to narrow to this single moment, two hunters in opposition, balanced on a knife's edge of survival.

The creature tilted its head, an unnervingly human gesture that contrasted with its monstrous form. Its filed teeth glinted in the sunlight, still wet with the blood of its recent victims. For a moment, it seemed to be studying Talorcan, assessing him as potential prey.

Then it moved, and with terrifying speed, raced across the open ground towards its opponent.

Above on the hill, his comrades held their breath and there were only a few strides between the two combatants when finally, Talorcan sent his arrow straight through the creature's eye, emerging from the back of its skull in a spray of dark blood and brain matter.

Any normal creature would have died instantly. But this was no normal creature. It crashed to the ground but immediately began to push itself up onto all fours, shuffling forward with a determination that defied reason. Blood poured from the catastrophic head wound, one eye destroyed, yet still the Wraith moved. Its remaining eye locked onto Talorcan with a hatred that seemed too intelligent to be animal, too focused to be simply instinctual.

It crawled forward again, despite the mortal wound. Talorcan's knife was already in his hand, but he didn't strike immediately. Instead, he waited, watching the creature's movement, calculating.

As it lunged again, slower and weaker this time, Talorcan stepped smoothly to the side and the monster crashed to the ground. But even now, it tried to rise, pushing its one good arm against the blood-soaked earth, its twisted spine forcing it into that unnatural half-upright, half-crawling position. Its one remaining eye turned toward him, filled with a hatred that seemed to transcend physical pain and Talorcan met that gaze without flinching.

'You shouldn't exist,' he repeated quietly before gripping the creature's matted hair and positioning his knife at its neck.

The creature snarled in defiance and as the knife bit deeper, and it started to choke on its own blood, Talorcan started to saw into its neck. He was not simply killing now; he was ensuring this abomination could never rise again.

On the hill above, Lepidus and the survivors watched in stunned silence as Talorcan began walking back toward them, carrying the creatures head in one hand. Rome had to know what was happening, and more importantly, they had to see. He reached Lepidus and without stopping to talk or making eye contact, he walked past, carrying the evidence into Roman controlled territory.

Chapter Forty-Seven

The Road to Camulodunum

The Occultum rode their horses slowly along the well-worn road, their pace carefully managed to preserve their remaining strength. Seneca knew they were close to Roman-controlled territory, but they still had to remain vigilant.

The road, while not a meticulously engineered Roman highway, was clearly an established trade route and as they drew closer to familiar territories, a subtle relaxation passed through the group as the constant tension of moving through hostile lands began to ease.

Sica and Cassius rode ahead, their keen eyes scanning the route for any potential threats but as dusk approached, the two men returned, their postures signalling they had something significant to report.

'What have you found?' asked Seneca as they reined in their mounts.

'There's a large encampment at the road junction ahead,' said Sica, 'at least a hundred men, with supply carts and significant provisions. I believe they are the warriors from Mona.'

'Let's get off the road,' said Seneca. 'We need to see what's going on.'

They moved swiftly into cover and once far enough into the forest, Falco and Decimus remained with the horses while the others moved forward using the trees as cover.

Within the hour, they could smell the smoke from the fires and crawled forward to gain a clear view of the encampment.

'I don't understand,' whispered Marcus, watching the activity below. 'They are very close to Roman territory so why camp here?'

Seneca stared, equally confused. The road below them forked, one leading southeast, the second directly east. They were clearly on a specific mission so why risk such a large, visible presence

295

so near Roman-controlled lands?

'I think that left fork probably heads towards Camulodunum,' he replied quietly. 'If 'Plautius has already accepted its surrender, it would make sense that Claudius would receive Britannia's tribute there, but even so, I don't understand what a hundred men think they can achieve against four legions.'

As twilight began to fall and they continued their observation, Seneca searched carefully for any sign of Raven or Mordred, but neither was visible among the warriors.

'We need to get closer,' he said finally. 'Perhaps we can get a better understanding of what is going on if we see them close up. Sica, you come with me, Marcus and Cassius, return to the others. If we are not back by dawn, assume the worst and head back to the legions and tell them what we have seen.'

Marcus nodded and as Seneca and Sica turned their attention back onto the camp, he and Cassius retreated back amongst the trees to head back to the horses.

An hour or so later, under the cover of darkness, Seneca and Sica crawled slowly down the slope using the ground as cover. The going was necessarily slow, moving only inches at a time, but eventually they reached the outer ring of carts, crawling through the ruts to hide behind the wheels. It was as safe a place as any and as the night progressed, they settled down to watch. Hours passed without incident but just as Seneca thought it was a wasted effort, a group of warriors lit a circle of torches in the centre of the camp. Other warriors started to gather just beyond the flames, and Sica drew Seneca's attention to the increased activity around three heavily guarded crates towards the centre of the camp.

Seneca narrowed his eyes, trying to make sense of what they were seeing. Whatever those crates contained, it was clearly important.

'We need to get closer,' he murmured.

Sica nodded and the two men crawled from shadow to

296

shadow, freezing in place whenever a sentry looked in their direction. Years of covert operations had taught them to become part of the landscape, to move only when eyes were turned elsewhere, to blend into the background so completely that even someone looking directly at their position would see nothing unusual.

Activity around the crates intensified and as the two men settled into the shadow of one of the tents to watch, they could sense the anticipation building, a palpable tension that rippled through the gathered warriors.

Moments later, four men positioned themselves around the furthest crate, each holding a long rope attached to something within. A fifth man approached with a long pole and as he lifted the crate's lid, something emerged.

Seneca felt his blood run cold as the creature came fully into the torchlight, snarling at its handlers as it moved slowly forward in its half-crouched gait, sometimes on two legs, sometimes dropping to all fours. Each of the guards maintained a careful distance, and as they used their ropes to direct its movements toward the centre of the circle, the assembled warriors fell silent, watching with a mixture of fear and dark fascination.

The smell was overwhelming and after someone called out an order, another warrior approached, dragging a bleating goat tethered to a short length of rope. The animal sensed the danger, its eyes rolling in terror as it struggled against its bonds but with a swift movement, the warrior shoved the goat forward before quickly retreating to the safety of the circle.

The creature's reaction was immediate and horrifying and as it lunged at the goat, a terrifying sound erupted from its throat to echo through the night. The goat had no chance, and the creature seized it with clawed hands, tearing into its throat with its filed teeth before ripping open its belly with a single, devastating strike. Blood sprayed across the packed earth, and the animal's dying bleats were cut sickeningly short. But the creature wasn't satisfied with merely killing its prey, it began to devour it with frenzied intensity, tearing chunks of flesh and swallowing them almost whole, blood running down its chin and chest.

Seneca fought to control his revulsion, to maintain the silent stillness that had kept him alive through countless dangerous situations. Beside him, he sensed rather than saw Sica's reaction, a momentary tensing, then the forced calm of professional assessment overriding the natural horror.

The handlers tightened their ropes, restraining the creature from running amok but allowing it to finish its grisly meal and throughout the camp, the watching Celts maintained an eerie silence, broken only by the wet sounds of the creature's feeding.

Seneca's gaze shifted to the other two crates positioned nearby, each surrounded by a similar contingent of guards and understanding dawned cold and terrible in his mind. Three crates meant three creatures, weapons beyond conventional understanding.

He caught Sica's eye and gave a slight nod. They had seen enough and without a word, they began to withdraw, moving backward with the same careful stealth they had employed in their approach. Only when they had put sufficient distance between themselves and the Celtic camp did they rise again to their feet and quicken their pace, eager to return to their comrades with what they had witnessed.

'What did you see?' Marcus demanded as soon as they entered the small clearing where the others waited.

Seneca gestured for the men to gather close, then described in terse, precise terms what they had observed. He spared no detail in recounting the savagery of the attack on the goat, the unnatural movements of the creature, and the way the Celtic warriors controlled it with ropes and hooks.

'We need to warn Plautius immediately,' he said eventually. Whatever these things are, they cannot be allowed near the Emperor.'

Chapter Forty-Eight

Castra Victrix

The sight of Roman standards flying above the palisade wall was almost enough to bring tears to Lepidus's eyes. So many days of constant fear and vigilance had left him hollow, running on nothing but determination and duty to his comrades.

The small band of survivors, their numbers cruelly reduced from the nine who had escaped the druid settlement, now sat behind mounted scouts, having been found hours earlier on the road.

'Hold!' The sentry's voice rang out from the watchtower. 'Identify yourselves!'

'Patrol returning with rescued prisoners,' the decurion of their escort called back. 'Open the gates!'

The massive wooden doors swung inward, revealing the ordered bustle of a Roman fort in full operation and as they entered, word spread quickly among the garrison. Some of the missing patrol had been rescued by a Roman officer and a Belgic scout.

A grizzled Optio pushed through the gathering onlookers, his expression shifting from curiosity to shock as he took in their condition.

'By all the gods,' he murmured, before quickly regaining his composure. He turned to a nearby orderly. 'Fetch Lucius and his assistants. Tell them we have wounded requiring urgent attention.'

Men moved quickly to help the liberated prisoners, supporting those who could barely stand. Faber waved away assistance, insisting on walking under his own power despite his evident exhaustion. The others were not so proud, or perhaps not so strong, gratefully accepting the offered help.

'These men are in a mess, Domine,' said the Optio, turning to Lepidus. 'What happened out there?'

'Where's Vespasian?' Lepidus cut him off, his voice hoarse from exhaustion.

'The Legate is not here, Domine. He departed for Camulodunum weeks ago. They're preparing for the Emperor's arrival.'

Lepidus and Talorcan exchanged a significant glance. The news that Vespasian had already moved to Camulodunum confirmed their worst fears, the Roman command was proceeding with plans for the imperial visit, unaware of the deadly creatures the Celts had at their disposal.

'We need to speak with whoever is in command here,' said Lepidus. 'Immediately.'

'Of course, Domine,' replied the Optio. Tribune Quintus Severus commands in the Legate's absence, I'll take you to him at once, but perhaps you might wish to refresh yourselves first? The journey appears to have been... difficult.'

'There's no time,' Lepidus replied. 'We carry evidence of a threat that cannot wait for social niceties.'

The Optio nodded and led them across the fort's central parade ground toward the Principia. Inside, the acting commander looked up from a table covered with supply requisitions and duty rosters.

'Senator Lepidus,' he said, rising to his feet with a mixture of surprise and respect. 'Your return is unexpected. We had reports that you were...' He trailed off, clearly uncomfortable with finishing the thought.

'Presumed lost?' Lepidus supplied. 'Nearly so, Tribune. But that's not important now. What matters is that we get to see Vespasian or Plautius. The Emperor is in grave danger, and we need to reach Camulodunum with all possible speed.'

'Of course, Senator. I'll arrange a hot meal, fresh horses and an escort.'

'We have no time to eat,' said Lepidus, 'we need to go now.'

'With respect, Senator,' said Severus, 'it is going to take you two days to get Camulodunum, so one meal will make no difference.'

Lepidus realised the man was making sense and after glancing towards Talorcan nodded his agreement.

'So be it,' he said, 'but arrange a Medicus for my comrade here first. He needs attention.'

Severus nodded, turning to an orderly.

'See to it immediately,' he ordered.

The orderly saluted and departed, leaving Severus to continue his assessment of the two men before him. Both showed signs of extreme exhaustion, their faces gaunt, their eyes haunted by whatever they had witnessed during their ordeal. Yet beneath the physical depletion, the Tribune recognized the steel core of driven men. He pointed to two chairs and minutes later, the orderly returned with a tray of bread, hot meat, and a pitcher of clean water. Behind him came the camp's medicus, an elderly freedman who had served with the legion for decades. His experienced eyes immediately assessed Talorcan's condition.

'Remove your boot,' he commanded, 'let me see that ankle.'

Talorcan complied, wincing as he unstrapped the soft leather boot and as Lepidus helped himself to the first hot food he had had in weeks, the medicus unwrapped the crude bandage, his expression growing grave as he examined the swollen joint beneath.

'You should not be walking on this at all,' he said, 'you need to let it rest.'

'I have no choice,' Talorcan replied simply. 'We will be riding out again as soon as the escort is ready.'

The medicus sighed, recognizing the futility of arguing with such a man.

'I'll bind it properly and give you a tincture for the pain, but you must understand, continuing to stress this injury could result in permanent damage.' The medicus set to work, cleaning the injured area with hot wine before applying a paste of healing herbs and wrapping the ankle in fresh linen bandages. Meanwhile, Lepidus continued to eat, his body desperately absorbing the nourishment it had been denied.

301

'How soon can the escort be ready?' he asked between bites, addressing Severus.

'A detachment of Batavian cavalry can be at your command by dusk,' replied the Tribune. 'Ten men, fully equipped.'

'Good. We'll need light travel rations, full waterskins, and the fastest horses you can provide.'

Severus nodded, issuing the extra orders to another orderly before turning back to Lepidus.

'Is there anything else you require, Senator?'

'A change of clothing, if possible. And a message sent ahead to Camulodunum, warning of our approach and the urgency of our news.'

'I'll see to it personally,' Severus assured him. 'Though I should warn you, the roads are not entirely secure. We've had reports of Celtic war bands moving through territories we thought pacified. Your escort will need to remain vigilant.'

'We're well aware of the dangers,' said Lepidus, his mind already moving ahead to the journey before them. 'But there's no alternative. The message we carry cannot wait.'

As the arrangements were finalized, Lepidus and Talorcan were shown to a small side chamber where they could briefly wash and change into the clean garments provided. The simple act of removing days of grime and sweat, of donning fresh tunics and cloaks, seemed to renew their energy despite their bone-deep exhaustion.

Talorcan ate his fill before drinking the medicinal tincture without complaint, and though its bitter taste brought a grimace to his stoic features, the relief was almost immediate, the sharp pain in his ankle dulling to a more manageable ache. He tested his weight on his foot carefully, finding that the proper bandaging provided much-needed support.

'Better?' asked Lepidus.

'It will serve,' replied Talorcan. 'We should be going.'

They emerged from the chamber to find Tribune Severus

waiting with final instructions.

'The escort is assembled at the east gate,' he said. 'Fresh horses have been prepared, and supplies are being loaded as we speak. The message to Camulodunum has been dispatched via our fastest rider.'

Lepidus nodded. Despite the food, the brief rest and the clean clothing, they remained desperately tired, but the urgency of their mission pushed such considerations aside.

'Let's move,' he said simply.

At the gate, ten Batavian auxiliaries waited, mounted on fresh horses, each man fully armed, with spears, shields, and swords ready for immediate action. Their decurion saluted sharply as Lepidus and Talorcan approached.

'Senator,' he said, his Germanic accent still noticeable despite years in Roman service. 'My men and I are at your disposal. We understand the urgency of your mission.'

'Good,' replied Lepidus, mounting the horse provided for him with a grunt of effort. 'We ride hard for Camulodunum. Can your men maintain the pace?'

The Decurion's expression hardened with pride.

'Batavians were born in the saddle, Senator. We will not fail you,' and as he led his men through the open gates of the fort, Lepidus and Talorcan followed, heading northeast towards Camulodunum.

Chapter Forty-Nine

The Road to Camulodunum

In the protective darkness of the forest, the Occultum gathered in close formation. The fire had been kept deliberately small, casting just enough light for them to see one another's expressions while remaining invisible from the road.

'A hundred warriors, well-armed and organized,' said Marcus, his voice barely above a whisper. 'Plus, those... *things.*'

Seneca nodded as the implications hung heavily in the air. The druids had created something capable of causing havoc among even disciplined Roman troops, and the proximity to Camulodunum suggested a target that was all too clear.

'We could ride around them,' suggested Cassius. 'Push our horses hard, reach Plautius before they can execute whatever they're planning.'

'And then what?' countered Falco. 'Plautius might not believe us and even if he does, and he sends forces, these warriors could simply disappear by the time they get here. They know the terrain better than we ever could.'

Seneca stared into the dying embers, weighing their limited options. The horses were already exhausted, and pushing them much harder might kill them before they reached Roman lines.

The silence stretched between them, each man lost in his own thoughts. They had completed countless missions for Rome, faced overwhelming odds before, but this was different. The stakes weren't merely military victory or intelligence gathering, the Emperor's life might hang in the balance.

'We need to split up,' he said finally. 'Some of us must warn Plautius, while the rest follow this war party.'

'Follow them?' asked Falco, his scarred face illuminated by the dying fire. 'To what end?'

'Knowledge,' replied Seneca firmly. 'We need to understand

what they plan, when they intend to strike. At the very least, we'll know more about these creatures, perhaps even identify a weakness.' His eyes

hardened. 'And if the opportunity presents itself, we eliminate them.'

Marcus nodded slowly.

'It's the only logical approach. Two riders carrying the warning, the rest maintaining surveillance.'

'Exactly,' said Seneca. 'Two of us will take the strongest horses and ride for the legions. The others continue watching this force until we determine they're no immediate threat or until we have an opportunity to act.'

The plan crystallized as they discussed the details. The two messengers would need to circle south to avoid the Celtic camp while those who remained would maintain constant observation, rotating duties to ensure no movement was missed.

'Decimus and Cassius will carry the warning,' Seneca decided. 'Tell them what we found here and do everything in your power to bring a strong force. I reckon we need a cohort at least.'

'And what if you have moved on?'

'With that number of carts and that many men, they should leave an easily followed trail, but we will leave the usual signs anyway.'

The two men nodded, accepting the assignment without protest, and as the first hint of dawn lightened the eastern sky, Decimus and Cassius mounted the two strongest horses. The animals snorted softly, sensing the tension in their riders.

'May fortune favour you,' said Seneca, clasping arms with each man in turn.

'And you,' replied Decimus.

Without further ceremony, the two riders turned south, following a winding deer path that would eventually lead them around the Celtic encampment. The others watched until they disappeared among the trees, then turned their attention back to the task at hand.

305

'We'll need a rotation,' said Seneca. 'Two watching the camp at all times, while the others rest or hunt. Marcus and I will take first watch. Falco, Sica, get some sleep. We'll need you fresh when we rotate.'

As Marcus and Sica moved away to prepare, Falco lingered momentarily.

'This is beyond anything in our experience,' he said quietly, no trace of his usual bravado in his voice. 'Those creatures, they're not
natural.'

'Perhaps not,' agreed Seneca, 'but if they bleed, they can be killed. All we need to do is find out.'

Falco nodded, drawing some comfort from the simple soldier's logic, and moved to find a sheltered spot for rest.

Left alone, Seneca allowed himself a moment of doubt that he would never show before his men. They were pursuing enemies who controlled beasts beyond rational understanding, with no clear plan beyond observation and improvisation. The odds were worse than terrible.

Yet as he gathered his weapons and prepared to join Marcus at their vantage point, Seneca found his resolve hardening once more. The Occultum had never chosen easy paths. Their strength lay not in numbers but in adaptability, in finding weaknesses where others saw only threat. Whatever the druids had planned, whatever those unholy creatures might be, the Occultum would face them.

As dawn broke over the forest, Decimus and Cassius moved through the dense underbrush to the southeast, giving the Celtic encampment a wide berth. The morning dew soaked their boots as they led their mounts by the reins, choosing stealth over speed until they were certain they had avoided detection.

Only when the sun had climbed higher and the terrain gradually opened before them, did they finally mount, urging their horses forward with greater urgency. In peacetime, these lands would have been cultivated, crops growing in neat rows, livestock grazing on the hillsides. Now they stood empty, their owners fled or worse, casualties of the inexorable Roman advance and as the open ground spread before them, both men exchanged a knowing glance. Speed now took precedence over stealth.

The first day passed without incident, the two riders making good progress, stopping only when absolutely necessary, allowing their horses brief periods of rest and water before pushing onward. By nightfall, they had covered impressive distance, finding shelter in a small grove just off the roadway.

'The horses are struggling,' observed Cassius as they unsaddled
the animals. 'We've pushed them hard.'

Decimus nodded, checking his mount's legs with experienced hands.

'We'll need to pace them better tomorrow. A dead horse helps no one.'

They ate sparingly from their limited rations, neither man speaking much. Both understood the weight of responsibility on their shoulders. If they failed to deliver their warning in time, Rome's hold on Britannia might be shattered before it had truly begun.

The second day they set out at first light, maintaining a steady pace that balanced urgency against their mounts' endurance. Occasionally they passed evidence of Celtic patrols, hoofprints in the muddy sections, discarded food fragments, once even a broken spear half-buried in a roadside ditch.

'We need to be careful,' said Decimus as they paused briefly at midday. 'The patrol activity is increasing.'

Cassius pointed to the northeast, where distant smoke rose from what must be cooking fires.

'They are close,' he said. 'We should make another detour.'

Decimus considered briefly before shaking his head.

'We can't risk the delay,' he said. 'Plautius needs to know.'

They pressed on, the sky gradually darkening as rain began

307

to fall. At first, it was merely a drizzle, more annoyance than impediment. But as the afternoon wore on, it intensified, turning the path treacherous with mud and standing water.

The horses struggled, their footing uncertain on the slick ground. What had been a brisk trot slowed to a cautious walk, despite the riders' attempts to maintain their pace. By evening, Decimus's mount was showing obvious signs of distress, favouring its right foreleg and occasionally stumbling.

'We need to stop,' Cassius said finally, as the horse nearly fell after a particularly bad misstep. 'He's going lame.'

Decimus cursed under his breath but couldn't deny the reality before them. They turned off the road, seeking shelter beneath the trees that lined a small stream. The rain had lessened somewhat, but both men were soaked through, their cloaks heavy with moisture.

They made a rudimentary camp, not daring to light a fire that might attract unwanted attention and after unsaddling the horses and securing them to low-hanging branches, Decimus examined his mount more thoroughly.

'The tendon's strained,' he concluded grimly. 'He won't be carrying me further, not at any speed that matters.'

Cassius looked up from where he was arranging their meagre bedding. 'We could take turns on my horse. It would slow us, but…'

'No,' interrupted Decimus. 'The warning must reach Plautius with all possible speed. Tomorrow, you'll continue alone. I'll follow as best I can.'

Before Cassius could argue, both men froze at the unmistakable sound of approaching riders. Multiple horses, moving at speed along the path they had just left.

'Down,' hissed Decimus, drawing his gladius as he dropped into a crouch. Cassius did likewise, both men moving deeper into the shadows of the trees.

The sounds grew louder, hoofbeats, the jingle of harness, the occasional low command in a language that neither man could immediately identify. Not Celtic, certainly, but in the confusion of the moment, not Latin either.

'They're searching,' whispered Cassius. 'I think they know we are here.'

Decimus nodded, his expression grim. Somehow, their flight had been detected. Perhaps Mordred had scouts watching the roads, or maybe they had been spotted during their dash across open ground. Whatever the reason, they were now hunted.

They shifted positions, putting their backs to the largest trees they could find. If they were to die here, they would sell their lives dearly, taking as many enemies with them as possible before the end.

The approaching riders slowed, clearly having spotted the trail leading off the path. A voice called out, words indistinct and moments later, a mounted figure crashed through the underbrush into their small clearing.

Decimus tensed, his gladius half-raised for a killing stroke, then froze in astonishment. The rider before them wore the distinctive helmet and scale armour of a Batavian auxiliary, a Roman ally rather than an enemy.

The Batavian reined in sharply, equally surprised to find armed men in his path. His hand moved to his own weapon before recognition dawned in his eyes.

'Romans?' he called, his Latin heavily accented but clear.

'Romans,' responded Decimus, lowering his blade slightly but not sheathing it. 'Identify yourself.'

The Batavian straightened in his saddle.

'Third Batavian cavalry cohort. We serve under Legate Vespasian.'

Relief washed through Decimus, so profound it made his knees momentarily weak. Not enemies but allies, and powerful ones at that. More riders appeared, each wearing the same distinctive armour, their horses sleek and powerful despite the mud that caked their legs.

309

'We bear urgent news for General Plautius,' said Cassius, stepping forward. 'Can you take us to him?'

'We can,' replied the officer, 'he is at Camulodunum,' 'You can ride behind two of my men. Your own horses will be looked after and brought later.'

Decimus agreed and within the hour, both Occultum members, with Batavian escorts surrounding them, rode at speed toward Camulodunum. Whether their warnings would be enough to avert disaster remained to be seen, but for the first time since leaving Isla Mona, Decimus felt a faint flicker of hope.

Chapter Fifty

Camulodunum

Lepidus and Talorcan reined their horses to a halt on the crest of a low hill overlooking Camulodunum. For several moments, both men sat in silence, taking in the remarkable scene spread before them. The plains outside the city wall had been transformed, and although neither man had seen it before, the Roman influence was obvious.

Many structures had sprung up as far as the eye could see, all made of timber but ornately decorated. Masons, carpenters, painters, and a sea of workers and slaves worked furiously to create an impressive area worthy of accepting an Emperor.

'How long do you think they have been working on this?' asked Talorcan.

'Weeks, at most,' Lepidus replied, his gaze taking in the meticulously ordered construction, 'but Plautius knows the value of appearances. The Emperor must see a conquered territory transformed by Roman efficiency, not a barbarian stronghold with Roman flags planted upon it.'

At the centre of the bustling activity stood a much smaller version of a legionary fortress, still unfinished but impressive in appearance and strength and even from this distance, Lepidus could see the distinctive layout, rectangular walls with rounded corners, watchtowers at regular intervals, and a prominent headquarters building rising at its centre.

'The emperor will reside there,' he said, nodding toward the fortress. 'A compromise between comfort and security.' He stared at the ordered chaos, his mind already calculating the implications. The sprawling building site, with its hundreds of workers, carts, timber piles, and half-completed structures, provided countless potential hiding places. If Mordred and his druids had more of the demon-like creatures, they would find no shortage of concealment.

311

'The message we sent ahead,' said Lepidus, turning to the Decurion in charge of the escort. 'Do you think it reached Vespasian?'

The Batavian shrugged.

'The rider had one of the fastest horses. If he encountered no trouble, he should have arrived yesterday.'

'Yet I see no increased security,' said Lepidus, 'no special measures. If they received our warning, they show little sign of it.' He urged his horse forward, and the small party began descending the gentle slope toward Camulodunum and as they drew closer, the true scale of the transformation became evident. What had once been a simple tribal capital was being systematically remade in Rome's image.

Closer to the fortress, Lepidus spotted a group of officers studying architectural drawings spread across a makeshift table and as they approached, Vespasian looked up, his eyes widening in recognition. He immediately stepped away from the table, dismissing the other officers with a gesture.

'Senator Lepidus! By Jupiter's grace, you've returned!' Vespasian's face broke into a genuine smile. 'And Talorcan as well. When we received no word for so many days, we feared the worst.'

'The journey was... challenging,' Lepidus replied, dismounting.

Vespasian nodded, his expression growing more serious.

'I've been briefed on the success of your mission. While the number of survivors was few, it was a tremendous moral boost for the legion to know their comrades had not been abandoned.'

Lepidus's brow furrowed in confusion. If Vespasian knew they had returned, then he must have received the message sent ahead from Castra Victrix.

'You received our warning, then?' he asked.

'Yesterday afternoon,' Vespasian confirmed. 'A rather dramatic account of your escape and the... shall we say, *beings* you encountered.' A sceptical note had entered his voice, though he

312

maintained a respectful tone.

Lepidus exchanged a glance with Talorcan, whose face had hardened almost imperceptibly.

'If you received our warning, Commander,' he said carefully, 'I'm curious why I see no evidence of increased security. No additional patrols, no special measures to protect against what's coming.'

Vespasian's expression shifted, a flicker of discomfort crossing his features before he regained his composure. He glanced around at the nearby workers, then gestured toward a partially constructed building nearby.

'Perhaps we should continue this discussion in private,' he suggested.

Once inside the timber structure, with its freshly cut beams still smelling of pine resin, Vespasian's demeanour changed. The diplomatic veneer fell away, replaced by the practical scepticism of a military commander.

'With all due respect, Senator, your messenger brought a tale that seemed difficult to credit. Creatures that are neither man nor beast, with supernatural strength and a bloodlust like no other animal known to man. It sounds more like the fevered dreams of exhausted men than a genuine threat.'

'You doubt our account?' Lepidus asked, his voice dangerously quiet.

'I accept that you encountered something,' Vespasian replied, choosing his words carefully. 'Perhaps a diseased or rabid madman, or several of them. The Celts are known to drive certain warriors into battle frenzy with herbs and rituals.' He spread his hands in a placating gesture. 'But demons? Supernatural creatures? Such things do not exist in this world.'

'I assure you they do,' said Lepidus, 'for I have seen them with my own eyes and if Mordred has more of those things, then the Emperor is at risk.'

'Senator,' said Vespasian, 'with the greatest of respect…' but

313

before he could continue, something banged against his feet and he looked down to see the decomposing head of the slain Wraith, on the floor, its filed teeth still bared in a permanent snarl.

Vespasian recoiled, his hand instinctively moving to his sword hilt as he stared at the grotesque trophy and for several heartbeats, he said nothing, his face draining of colour as he processed what lay before him.

'There is your proof,' said Talorcan, still holding the bloody sack that had contained the head, 'now perhaps we can have a real discussion.'

Vespasian stared at the grotesque head, his expression a mixture of horror and disbelief. After a moment, he gestured to one of his officers, who reluctantly stepped forward and picked up the trophy by its matted hair, holding it at arm's length.

'This is...' Vespasian began, then stopped, clearly struggling to find words adequate to describe what he was seeing. He circled the officer slowly, examining the head from all angles, his military mind trying to categorize and understand the threat it represented.

'The filed teeth,' he murmured, 'the malformed skull, the twisted features, they are certainly grotesque, but it is still a human head.' He turned back to Lepidus and Talorcan. 'I appreciate the warning, and I understand why this discovery has affected you both so deeply, but this... *thing*, is, or at least *was*, a man, nothing more, nothing less.'

'You don't understand, Commander,' said Lepidus. 'This is not merely a deformed man, this creature possessed strength and speed beyond natural limits, speed beyond human capability, and a savagery that defies rational explanation.'

'We witnessed one tear through an entire war band,' Talorcan added, his voice steady despite his obvious exhaustion. 'Warriors who would have killed us without hesitation ran in terror from this thing.'

'And yet you killed it,' countered Vespasian. 'Look, I do not discount your experiences, but I must deal with the realities before me. The Emperor arrives in a few weeks and by then, four legions will have been deployed to secure this area. The perimeter will be guarded by our best auxiliaries, the approaches patrolled day and night.' He gestured toward the construction visible through the open doorway. 'All this must be completed before Claudius sets foot on Britannic soil, so I have no time to deal with imaginary threats. Not now.'

'But…' began Lepidus.

'I cannot,' Vespasian interrupted, 'divert significant resources to hunt for creatures that may or may not exist based on a single specimen that, however unnatural in appearance, is fundamentally human.' He straightened his shoulders. 'The area will be fully defended with a secure perimeter. Not even a dog will get through our lines, let alone whatever these things truly are.'

Lepidus and Talorcan exchanged incredulous glances, the realization dawning that their warning, despite the physical evidence they had provided, was being effectively dismissed.

'I extend my gratitude again for your service and sacrifice,' Vespasian continued, his tone shifting to one of formal dismissal, 'and I will arrange suitable quarters for your recovery. But the work here must continue without interruption.' He nodded to a nearby Centurion. 'See that the Senator and his companion are given appropriate accommodation and medical attention.'

With that, he turned away, already calling for his architects and engineers to resume their consultation. The severed head was handed off to another officer with instructions to have it examined by the legion's medicus.

Lepidus stood frozen in disbelief, fatigue and frustration warring on his face as he watched the commander walk away.

'After everything we endured,' Talorcan murmured, 'after everything we saw…'

'Let's get some rest,' said Lepidus finally, his voice heavy with

315

a weariness that went beyond physical exhaustion. 'Tomorrow, perhaps, with clearer minds, we can make him see sense.'

They followed the Centurion out of the building, stepping back into the chaos of construction that would soon welcome an Emperor. As they crossed the crowded grounds toward their assigned quarters, Lepidus felt the weight of responsibility settling across his shoulders once more. This was not the end of the matter, tomorrow would bring another battle, not against creatures with filed teeth and inhuman strength, but against the more familiar human adversaries of scepticism, pride, and bureaucracy. For now, though, their bodies demanded the rest that had been denied them for so long, and they surrendered to that necessity, if not to defeat.

Chapter Fifty-One

The Crossroads

Dawn broke over the Celtic encampment, pale light filtering through the morning mist as Seneca shifted position again, easing muscles grown stiff from hours of immobility. From his vantage point among a cluster of rocks on the ridge overlooking the camp, he had a clear view of the central area where the crates containing the creatures were kept. Three days of constant observation had yielded much information, yet had also presented a perplexing puzzle.

'They're not moving,' Marcus whispered as he crawled into position beside Seneca, replacing Falco who had maintained the night watch. 'No preparations for departure, no scouts ranging ahead to secure a route. Just... waiting.'

Seneca nodded, his eyes never leaving the camp below. The Celtic warriors went about their daily routines with disciplined efficiency, cooking, maintaining weapons, exercising horses, yet showed no signs of continuing their journey toward Camulodunum.

'It makes no sense,' he murmured. 'If their target is the Emperor, they should be advancing, securing positions, establishing hiding places closer to their objective.'

Marcus passed him a waterskin.

'Perhaps they're waiting for someone.'

Seneca drank sparingly, the cool water a momentary respite from the growing heat of the day.

'Perhaps,' he agreed. 'But who?'

That question had haunted their observations for three full days now. The Celtic force remained encamped at the crossroads, maintaining vigilant guards but showing no inclination to move. Each night, one of the crates would be opened, one of the creatures released for feeding in that gruesome ritual they had first witnessed. The pattern was identical each time, a tethered animal, usually a goat or sheep, would be presented, then the handler would withdraw as

317

the creature tore into its meal in a savage feeding frenzy

The feedings appeared to serve multiple purposes: sustenance for the beast, certainly, but also a demonstration of power for the assembled warriors, a reminder of the deadly weapons in their midst. The men would watch in silence, their faces illuminated by torchlight, and Seneca had noted the mixture of fear and reverence in their expressions.

The afternoon stretched on, the monotony broken only by the rotation of their watch and the subtle changes in the camp below. Seneca was considering a brief rest before taking the evening shift when Sica appeared at his side, moving so silently that even Seneca's trained senses hadn't detected his approach.

'Riders approaching from the west,' the Syrian whispered.

Seneca's fatigue vanished instantly. He focused on the approaching figures, initially just dark specks against the landscape but gradually resolving into mounted warriors, perhaps half a dozen in total.

'Get Falco,' he ordered Sica quietly. 'I want everyone observing this.'

Within minutes, all four remaining members of the Occultum lay concealed along the ridgeline, watching intently as the riders drew closer to the camp. The Celtic sentries had spotted them as well, but made no move to intercept or challenge, suggesting these were expected visitors.

The newcomers rode directly into the camp, warriors parting to make way as they approached the central area. Their leader sat tall in the saddle, his bearing commanding instant respect.

'Something's happening,' murmured Falco. 'Look how they're responding.'

Seneca adjusted position slightly, trying to gain a better angle. The leader's cloak billowed in the breeze as he gestured, emphasizing some point in a discussion that seemed to grow increasingly animated.

Then, with a deliberate motion, the man reached up and

threw back his hood, removing the cloak entirely and handing it to an attendant.

Seneca felt his breath catch in his throat. Even at this distance, there was no mistaking the identity of the figure now revealed.

'*Raven,*' he gasped.

The others tensed beside him, each man reaching the same conclusion. After weeks of searching, after crossing a sea, frozen mountains and enduring extreme hunger and exhaustion, here stood their original target, delivered almost as if by divine intervention.

'It's him,' confirmed Marcus, his voice tight with controlled emotion. 'No doubt.'

Raven's distinctive profile was unmistakable, the tall, lean physique, the way he carried himself, the familiar gestures as he spoke. He had grown a beard since they had last seen him, and his clothing was Celtic rather than Roman, but the man himself was unchanged.

'He looks at home among them,' observed Falco with undisguised contempt. 'Like he belongs there.'

Seneca said nothing, his focus absolute as he studied the man who had once been friend, a comrade, a brother-in-arms. Raven moved through the camp with easy familiarity, warriors nodding in deference as he passed. Whatever his position among them, it clearly commanded respect.

Throughout the remainder of the day, the Occultum maintained their vigil, watching as Raven inspected the camp, conferred with various warriors, and most significantly, spent considerable time examining the crates containing the creatures. He circled each one slowly, occasionally pausing to peer through the narrow slats, his expression impossible to discern at this distance but his interest evident in his careful attention.

As evening approached, Raven entered the command tent with the camp's leaders, disappearing from view. Seneca finally allowed himself to withdraw slightly from the observation point, gathering his men in a tight circle just below the ridge.

'This changes everything,' he said. 'We need to get to him while we can.'

'He's surrounded by a hundred warriors and those... things,' cautioned Falco. 'We're four men with limited supplies and no reinforcements.'

'The mission parameters haven't changed,' replied Seneca, 'eliminate the traitor. That was our assignment from the beginning. And we may never get another opportunity. If those creatures are unleashed against Roman forces, against the Emperor himself, the consequences would be devastating.'

The others exchanged glances, each man calculating the near-impossible odds they faced. They were just four men against a hundred well-armed warriors, with no support, no escape route, and those unnatural beasts as additional protection for their target. By any rational military assessment, the mission was suicide.

'If we do this,' said Marcus slowly, 'we need a plan that gives us at least some chance of survival afterward.'

'Agreed, said Seneca. 'We observe one more day to identify patterns and weaknesses. Look for an opportunity that maximizes our advantages.'

'And if no such opportunity presents itself?' asked Falco.

'Then we create one,' said Seneca. 'One way or another, Raven dies. We owe it to every man he betrayed when he turned his back on his oath.'

The conviction in his voice silenced further questions. Each man understood the stakes, understood that their lives were secondary to the mission and as night fell once more over the Celtic camp, Seneca resumed his observation position, watching as torches were lit and the evening routines began. After all this time, after so much sacrifice, Raven was finally within reach and whatever the cost, whatever the odds, one way or another, he would kill him.

Chapter Fifty-Two

Camulodunum

The officers' dining quarters in Camulodunum bustled with activity as men came and went, sharing reports of the day's progress over plates of hot food. The structure, like most in the rapidly developing settlement, was a curious blend of Roman efficiency and hasty construction, solid timber walls supporting a roof that still smelled of fresh pine resin, the floor packed earth covered with rush matting.

Lepidus sat at one of the long tables, mechanically consuming a bowl of stew that he barely tasted. Weariness had settled into his bones, a fatigue that went beyond mere physical exhaustion. In the days since his arrival, he had made little progress in convincing Vespasian of the imminent threat.

The commander had been polite enough, nodding at appropriate intervals during their meetings, making vague promises to 'review security protocols' and 'consider additional patrols.' But it had quickly become obvious that Vespasian's priorities lay elsewhere. Plautius was exerting enormous pressure to complete the preparations for Claudius's arrival, and that pressure flowed downward through the entire command structure. Meetings about security concerns were repeatedly postponed and requests for specialized guards at key approaches were acknowledged but never implemented.

Both Lepidus and Talorcan had grown increasingly frustrated. They had survived a nightmare, witnessed horrors that defied rational explanation, and carried physical evidence back to Roman lines, only to find themselves effectively ignored.

Lepidus pushed his half-eaten stew aside, his appetite deserting him. At the far end of the room, several younger officers were engaged in animated discussion, their voices carrying fragments about building schedules and material requisitions. The entire settlement seemed consumed with construction, with creating the appearance of Roman efficiency and order, while potential threats were dismissed as exaggerations or impossibilities.

He contemplated retiring for the evening when the main door
swung open, admitting a young officer whose uniform bore the dust of recent travel. The man paused in the doorway, scanning the room with obvious urgency until his gaze locked on Lepidus. Without acknowledging the greetings of his fellow officers, he strode directly to Lepidus's table.

'Senator,' he said, as he bent to speak directly into Lepidus's ear. 'You're needed at the eastern gate immediately. Two men have just arrived with information you'll want to hear.'

Lepidus looked up sharply, noting the tension in the young man's face.

'What sort of information?' he asked.

The officer glanced around nervously, ensuring they weren't overheard.

'They mentioned creatures, Senator. Inhuman things being transported by Celtic warriors. I have heard your stories and thought you should know.'

A cold surge of vindication mingled with dread flooded through Lepidus. He rose immediately, abandoning his meal without a second thought.

Outside, the settlement was transforming from a construction site to a military encampment as darkness fell. Torches burned at regular intervals along the main pathways, illuminating work crews still labouring to complete sections of timber buildings. Soldiers moved with practiced efficiency between guard posts, while messengers darted between command structures carrying the day's final orders.

The eastern gate stood partially completed, its massive timber framework rising twenty feet but with sections of the upper walkway still under construction. Torches blazed in iron brackets, casting flickering light over the guards and work crews. As Lepidus approached, he spotted a small disturbance, a knot of soldiers surrounding two seated figures whose exhaustion was evident even from a distance.

'Make way,' commanded the young officer who had fetched Lepidus.

The soldiers parted, revealing two men slumped on makeshift benches, their clothing torn and filthy, their faces etched with fatigue and something deeper, a haunted quality that Lepidus recognized all too well.

'Decimus!' he gasped, quickening his pace, 'Cassius.'

Both men turned sharply, before recognition dawned on their faces.

'Senator Lepidus,' Decimus responded. 'What are you doing here. The last I heard, you were in Rome.'

'I was sent here to re-task you to a different mission,' said Lepidus, 'but alas I arrived too late.' He looked towards the gate. 'Where are the others?'

'They are back out there,' said Decimus with a nod towards the gate. 'Keeping watch on an enemy camp about fifty miles away. We were sent ahead to warn the garrison of a serious threat.'

'Does this threat include a certain type of creature that defies description?' he asked.

Both Occultum members stared at him in shock.

'You know of them?' Cassius asked, speaking for the first time.

'I have seen one,' confirmed Lepidus. 'Talorcan killed it, but only after it slaughtered an entire war band.'

Decimus exchanged a significant glance with Cassius, mutual confirmation passing between them.

'We need to speak privately,' he said. 'What we've witnessed... it changes everything.'

Lepidus nodded and looked towards the officers' quarters.

323

'Come with me,' he said, 'we can talk without interruption there.'

They moved through the settlement, Lepidus nodding briefly to saluting soldiers but maintaining their brisk pace. The implications of the Occultum's arrival, and more critically, their apparent knowledge of the creatures, had set his mind racing. Here at last was the corroboration he needed, testimony from Rome's elite operatives that could not be easily dismissed as the fevered imaginings of exhausted men.

Lepidus led them to a small side room used for private meetings, dismissing the clerk who occupied it with a curt gesture. Once the door was closed behind them, he turned to face the two Occultum members.

'First of all,' he said as the two men dropped into a couple of seats, 'tell me about your mission. Is Raven dead?'

'No,' said Decimus. 'But Raven's betrayal is but one piece of a much larger threat.'

A chill ran through Lepidus at these words, a premonition of what was to come.

'Tell me everything,' he said. 'From the beginning.'

Decimus straightened, gathering his thoughts before speaking.

'Our journey took us first to Mona, where we believed he was based, but by the time we got there, he and a large band of warriors had already left and were headed towards Camulodunum. We followed their trail and caught up with them, nearly a hundred warriors, well-armed and positioned strategically at a crossroads.

He paused, seemingly searching for words adequate to describe what they had witnessed.

'They have creatures,' Cassius interjected, his eyes haunted by the memory. 'Kept in reinforced crates, three of them. Seneca observed one being fed. He said it was…'

'Neither man nor beast,' Lepidus completed for him, knowing exactly what they had seen.

324

Both Occultum members stared at him, grim recognition in their eyes.

'Exactly,' confirmed Decimus. 'Seneca ordered us to bring warning immediately while he and the others maintained observation. If these things were to be unleashed during the Emperor's visit…'

'How do you know about the Emperor's visit?' asked Lepidus suddenly.

'There was a girl in the Celtic camp,' said Decimus. 'She told us the warriors were on their way to kill Claudius in Camulodunum.'

'The druids already knew?' gasped Lepidus.

'Apparently so. I guess Raven still has contacts.'

'If they manage to get one of those things anywhere near the Emperor,' said Lepidus, 'The consequences could be catastrophic. Talorcan and I have been trying to convince Vespasian of this very threat for days, but without success.'

'The others, Seneca, Marcus, Falco and Sica, remained behind to watch the camp,' said Cassius. 'They were considering a direct assault if opportunity presented itself.'

Lepidus nodded, acknowledging the elite unit's formidable capabilities while still recognizing the extreme danger they faced. His mind was already calculating the next steps, how best to use the men's arrival to force action from Vespasian.

'Rest here,' he said, gesturing to the simple benches that lined the room. 'I'll have food and drink brought. Once you've recovered somewhat, we'll approach Vespasian together. Your report, combined with what Talorcan and I have already presented, should finally compel him to take this threat seriously.'

As the door closed behind him, Lepidus quickened his pace. The pieces were finally falling into place, Raven's betrayal, the druidic creatures, the threat to the Emperor, all connected in a conspiracy that could shatter Rome's tenuous hold on Britannia before it had truly begun. But now, at last, he had the evidence needed to force action. The question that remained was whether that action would come in time.

Two hours later, all four men faced Vespasian across the wooden table used to plan the movements of tens of thousands of men.

'Let me understand this clearly,' said Vespasian quietly. 'You expect me to divert significant forces based on the testimony of four men who claim to have seen... what? Monsters? Demons?' All I have seen is a head that could be no more than a battlefield trophy, mutilated after death to inspire fear.'

'With respect, Commander,' said Decimus, 'what we witnessed was no mere battlefield deception. These creatures move with unnatural speed and strength. One tore through a goat like it was parchment, consumed it with a savagery that defies description.'

'And I've seen one in combat,' added Talorcan, his accent thickening with intensity. 'It continued fighting with an arrow through its head and its body broken. Nothing natural behaves this way.'

Vespasian's expression remained sceptical, though Lepidus noted a slight uncertainty beginning to form in his eyes.

'Even if I accept these accounts at face value,' Vespasian continued, 'I have the Emperor's arrival to consider. Four legions are being positioned to secure his route. Construction crews work day and night to prepare suitable accommodation so every man I divert weakens
our overall security posture.'

Lepidus stepped forward, his patience finally exhausted.

'Commander,' he said, 'set aside the creatures for a moment. You have solid intelligence about an enemy position, a hundred warriors gathered at a strategic crossroads with direct access to both Camulodunum and the coastal landing sites.' He placed his finger firmly on the relevant position on the map. 'There is a proven threat against the Emperor with weapons, whether human or otherwise, that your forces have never encountered before. You know their strength, their location, and their likely intention.'

Lepidus leaned forward, his gaze locked with Vespasian's.

'Any one of these factors should prompt immediate action. Combined, they represent an undeniable threat that cannot be ignored.' His voice hardened. 'But beyond all this, four of my men, *your men*, elite operatives of the Occultum, remain in the field, observing this force at tremendous personal risk. They deserve support, not dismissal.'

Vespasian's jaw tightened, his military mind clearly wrestling with the competing priorities before him.

'The Occultum operates independently, Senator. They're trained for exactly these circumstances.'

'They're also outnumbered twenty-five to one,' countered Cassius, speaking for the first time. 'Four against a hundred, facing creatures that...' He shook his head, words failing him. 'If you deny us again,' he continued eventually, 'all four of us will ride out without support and take our chances to rescue our comrades. You, meanwhile, can explain to Plautius, and eventually to the Emperor himself, why you disregarded multiple warnings and abandoned your own men in the field.'

The implied threat hung in the air between them. Vespasian's expression darkened, but Lepidus held his ground. After a moment, the commander's gaze shifted to Decimus and Cassius.

'You would go back out there, even after what you have claimed to have witnessed?'

'Without hesitation,' replied Decimus, his weathered face showing no doubt. 'They are our brothers.'

Vespasian turned away, moving to the map table and studying it
with deliberate attention. The silence stretched for several long moments, broken only by the distant sounds of construction outside the pavilion.

'The timing is problematic,' he said finally, still facing the map. 'If I divert forces now, it will impact our preparation schedule.

Plautius will demand explanations.'

'Better explanations than funerals,' said Talorcan bluntly. 'Especially imperial ones.'

Vespasian's shoulders stiffened at the plainspoken assessment, but he did not reject it outright. Instead, he turned back to face them, his decision apparently made.

'Fifty horsemen,' he said. 'That's all I can spare. Batavian cavalry.' He raised a hand to forestall any objection. 'They're among our best, fast, disciplined, and familiar with the terrain. A full cohort would take too long to mobilize and would be too visible approaching the enemy position.'

Lepidus exchanged glances with the others, reading the shared assessment in their eyes. Fifty horsemen against a hundred warriors were far from ideal, but significantly better than their current situation.

'When can they be ready?' Lepidus asked.

'By dawn,' said Vespasian. 'But I want this handled with discretion, Senator. Strike the camp, rescue your men and have them return with whatever evidence they can gather.'

'Understood,' said Lepidus with a curt nod. He turned to the others. 'We ride at first light. Gather what supplies you need, rest if you can.'

Vespasian stared at Lepidus incredulously as they prepared to leave.

'Why are you going with them?' he asked. 'You are a Senator, leave this to your men.'

Lepidus turned back, his weathered face set with implacable determination.

'I've come this far,' he said, 'and have no intention of abandoning them now.'

Without waiting for a response, the four men turned and exited
the pavilion. Outside, as they crossed the encampment toward the quartermaster's stores, Lepidus allowed himself a brief sigh of relief.

328

'Fifty men,' he murmured. 'It will have to be enough.'

'Fifty-four,' said Talorcan quietly, 'fifty-eight if you include those we left behind. 'With Batavians and the Occultum together, it will be enough.'

As the first stars appeared above Camulodunum, the four men moved with renewed purpose. By dawn, they would ride to the crossroads, bringing either rescue or vengeance to the men who had remained behind. The only uncertainty was what they would find when they arrived.

Chapter Fifty-Three

The Crossroads

The evening shadows lengthened across the Celtic encampment, deepening the natural hollows and creating pools of darkness between tents and cookfires. From his observation post on the ridge, Seneca watched as Raven moved through the gathering with the easy confidence of a man among his own kind. The betrayal still burned like acid in Seneca's gut, the familiar silhouette of his former brother-in-arms now the focus of a killing intent that had only sharpened with each passing day.

Two days had passed since Raven's arrival, yet the camp still showed no signs of breaking. The hundred warriors maintained their position at the crossroads, one path leading to Camulodunum, the other toward the coast where Claudius might land. The strategic significance of their location was unmistakable, they were waiting for something, some signal perhaps, or a specific moment to strike.

Most concerning were the three crates containing the inhuman creatures, guarded day and night by rotating shifts of warriors who maintained a respectful distance even while standing watch.

'He's returning to his tent,' murmured Sica beside Seneca, his dark eyes missing nothing despite the failing light. 'Third night in the same location.'

Seneca nodded. They had mapped the camp meticulously during their observation, identifying the command tent, the warriors' sleeping areas, the positioning of sentries, and most importantly, the smaller tent where Raven retired each night. That knowledge was crucial to what they were now considering.

'It's time,' said Seneca. 'We can't simply observe any longer. Alert the others, we'll gather below the ridge to finalize the plan.'

Minutes later, the four remaining members of the Occultum crouched in a tight circle for the briefing.

'Raven represents a legitimate target,' began Seneca. 'His elimination was our primary objective, but those creatures also pose a significant threat that we cannot ignore. This will be a precision strike, get in, complete the mission, get out before they can organize an effective response.'

Marcus nodded, his tactical mind already working through the possibilities.

'Distraction and division,' he suggested. 'Split their attention, create confusion.'

'Exactly,' agreed Seneca. 'I've been observing their reaction patterns. They're disciplined enough, but they haven't faced a coordinated assault. Their first instinct will be to protect their horses and the command tent.'

He used a stick to sketch a crude outline of the camp in the dirt between them, marking key positions, Raven's tent, the creatures' crates, the horse paddock, sentry positions.

'We'll approach from opposite sides,' he continued, indicating points on his makeshift map. 'Marcus, you and Falco will take the two strongest of our remaining horses and circle around to the eastern perimeter. Your objective is the Celtic horse paddock. Hide your mounts further down the road and then approach on foot. Once you have gained access, I want you to cut the ropes, drive the horses out and generally create chaos. Meanwhile, Sica and I will approach on foot from the west and head directly for Raven's tent.' His finger jabbed at the relevant location on the map. 'He dies first. Then, if circumstances allow, we'll deal with the creatures.'

'How?' asked Falco. 'Those crates looked solid. If you try to open them...'

'We don't open them,' Seneca replied. 'We kill through the crates themselves. Spear thrusts through the gaps between the slats. It won't be clean, but it should be effective.'

The plan took shape as they discussed the specifics, timing, signals, escape routes. Everything would depend on speed and coordination. They would have perhaps a minute, two at most,

331

before the Celtic warriors organized a coherent response to the attack.

'Once the alarm is raised,' Seneca emphasized, 'we withdraw immediately. Falco, you and Marcus will get back to your horses or use two of theirs if you can. Either way, just get out of there and head as fast as you can to Camulodunum.'

'What about you?' asked Marcus.

'We'll escape back into the forest and head for the Tamesis.' said Seneca. 'Hopefully, they will be too busy following you to even realise we were there, but even if they do, in the trees I fancy our chances against any man.'

Each man nodded, acknowledging without words the potential cost of what they were undertaking. It was an audacious plan, perhaps even a desperate one, but they were the Occultum, and audacious plans were what they were good at.

'When?' asked Sica.

'Tonight,' replied Seneca. 'When the moon is at its zenith. The camp will be at its quietest, most warriors asleep save for the sentries.'

They spent the next hour gathering what equipment they would need, checking weapons, securing anything that might create noise during their approach. Weapons were smeared with mud to dull any reflective surface, and faces darkened with ash from their carefully banked fire and as full darkness descended over the landscape, Marcus and Falco departed, leading the two horses eastward to begin their wide circle around the Celtic camp. Seneca and Sica followed soon after, moving in the opposite direction to approach from the west.

The night wrapped around them like a cloak, the familiar embrace of darkness that had sheltered Occultum operations for years. This was their element, the domain in which they had been trained to operate with lethal efficiency. As they moved silently through the forest, Seneca found his mind settling into the calm focus that preceded combat, a state where extraneous thoughts fell away, leaving only the mission.

They reached their designated position well before the appointed time, settling into a natural depression that offered both concealment and a clear view of the western edge of the camp. The Celtic sentries were visible as darker silhouettes against the faint glow of banked fires within the encampment, moving in predictable patterns along established routes.

'They're growing complacent,' whispered Sica, his observation confirming Seneca's own assessment. 'So much time in the same location
with no threat has made them careless.'

Seneca nodded. It was a common pattern in military encampments, one the Occultum had exploited many times before. Initial vigilance inevitably gave way to routine, and routine bred vulnerability.

The hours passed with agonizing slowness, each man lost in his own thoughts as they waited for the appointed time. Seneca found his mind returning to Raven, not as he was now, a traitor in Celtic garb, but as he had been, a trusted comrade who had saved Seneca's life more than once during their years together in the Occultum. What had turned him? What profound betrayal or conversion had transformed a loyal servant of Rome into its dedicated enemy?

These questions would likely remain unanswered for in the world of shadows where the Occultum operated, motives often died with their bearers, leaving only outcomes to be judged by history.

Finally, the appointed hour approached, and Seneca checked his weapons one last time, a gladius secured at his hip, and two daggers positioned for easy access. Beside him, Sica completed similar preparations, his arsenal more extensive and exotic, befitting his background as an assassin before joining the Occultum.

'Remember,' Seneca whispered, 'Raven first. Then the creatures if possible. No unnecessary risks.'

Sica nodded, his dark eyes reflecting the faint starlight and after saying a silent prayer to their respective gods, both men started crawling down to the encampment.

Further to the east, Falco and Marcus left their horses tethered among a dense cluster of gnarled oaks, far enough from the road to avoid casual discovery yet close enough for a swift departure if needed.

The faint glow of the Celtic camp gradually became visible through the thinning trees, cookfires banked for the night but still providing enough illumination to identify the outer perimeter. They dropped to a crouch at the forest's edge, waiting for the optimal moment to advance.

After a few minutes of observation, Marcus tapped Falco's arm. Two sentries were walking the eastern perimeter, their attention focused on each other rather than their surroundings, voices carrying softly in the night air as they conversed.

They waited until the sentries had passed their position, then emerged silently from the shadows. Falco matched Marcus's pace exactly as they closed the distance, feet falling in perfect synchronization to minimize sound. The sentries remained oblivious, one gesturing as he made some point to his companion, neither aware of the death approaching from behind.

Marcus's hand clamped over one guard's mouth while his blade sliced a clean arc across the exposed throat. Blood sprayed forward in a dark fan as the man's struggles weakened almost immediately while beside him, Falco wrapped his massive arms around the second sentry, one hand gripping the chin while the other braced against the back of the skull. A sharp twist produced a sickening crack, and the body went instantly limp in his grasp.

They lowered the corpses silently to the ground, dragging them into the deeper shadows before listening intently for any sign their action had been detected. But the camp remained quiet, the night sounds undisturbed.

Satisfied, they turned their attention to the shallow ditch surrounding the encampment, a basic defensive measure typical of temporary Celtic installations. They crossed it without difficulty, staying low to the ground as they approached the eastern edge of the camp itself.

A third guard appeared unexpectedly around a corner, nearly colliding with them but he had no time to react before Falco's hand closed around his throat, cutting off any attempt to sound the alarm. Marcus's dagger quickly found the man's heart, the blade sliding between ribs to silence him permanently and they eased his body to the ground, concealing it beneath a cart before continuing toward the horse paddock.

The enclosure stood at the northeastern edge of the camp, a simple arrangement of ropes strung between posts to contain the Celtic mounts. Falco counted at least thirty horses, valuable assets that the warriors would be loath to lose.

Working methodically, they moved along the perimeter of the paddock, Marcus using his dagger to slice through the ropes that tethered individual horses to stakes. The animals shifted nervously within the enclosure, sensing the unusual activity but not yet panicked. Falco and Marcus exchanged glances in the darkness, and each selected a mount, and with practiced ease, they mounted their chosen horses, adjusting their positions to ensure proper control before urging their mounts forward, moving toward the paddock entrance.

Chapter Fifty-Four

The Road to Camulodunum

The road stretched endlessly before them, a pale ribbon cutting through the darkening landscape as Lepidus led his mounted force westward. Fifty Batavian horsemen followed in tight formation behind him, their discipline still evident even after more than a day and a half of hard riding. Talorcan rode to his right, while Decimus and Cassius maintained positions at the column's flanks, their eyes constantly scanning the surrounding terrain for potential threats.

They had driven themselves and their mounts mercilessly since departing Camulodunum, stopping only when absolutely necessary to water the horses and allow brief periods of rest. Time was their enemy now, each passing hour increasing the danger to the remaining Occultum operatives at the Celtic camp.

The commander of the Batavian cavalry rode up alongside Lepidus, his weathered face showing concern.

'Senator,' he said in his accented Latin, 'the horses cannot maintain this pace much longer. How much further?

Before Lepidus could respond, Decimus straightened in his saddle, his gaze fixed on a line of hills that had appeared on the horizon ahead.

'The Celtic camp lies just beyond those hills. We are almost there.'

Lepidus studied the distant ridge, mentally calculating distances and timelines. They had made good progress, better than he had dared hope when they set out.

'We'll approach the hills and assess from there,' he decided. 'If the camp remains in the same position, we'll have time to develop a proper assault plan.'

The column continued its steady advance, and as they drew closer to the hills, Lepidus signalled a halt, directing the force off the main road into a sheltered depression where they would be less visible to any watchers on the high ground. The horses were grateful for the respite, heads lowering immediately to crop at the sparse grass while their riders stretched cramped muscles and passed waterskins among themselves.

'I'll take my men on foot to the crest and observe the camp's position,' said Lepidus. The rest of you, remain here with the horses.'

The Batavian commander nodded, and watched as the small group began the climb up the hillside, moving with deliberate caution to avoid outlining themselves against the sky.

They reached the crest as the afternoon sun began its descent toward the western horizon, and dropping to their bellies, crawled to positions that offered clear views while maintaining concealment from observers below.

The Celtic camp spread before them in the valley beyond, precisely where Decimus had described it. Tents clustered around a central area, with horse paddocks visible at the eastern edge. Warriors moved throughout the encampment, their numbers confirming previous estimates of approximately one hundred fighting men. From this distance, individual faces were indistinguishable, but the overall activity level suggested a camp still fully occupied, not one preparing for immediate departure.

'Any signs of our men?' asked Lepidus quietly.

Decimus shook his head.

'Nothing visible from here. If they're still observing, they would be positioned well away from the camp, likely on the opposite ridge.'

They continued their surveillance for nearly an hour, identifying potential approaches, and assessing the overall tactical situation, but what they found was not encouraging.

'The terrain favours them,' said Talorcan as they finally withdrew from the crest to discuss their findings. 'Open ground on all sides, with clear lines of sight from multiple sentry positions. Any approach would be spotted well before we reached striking distance.'

Lepidus nodded grimly. Talorcan had merely confirmed

what he had observed himself. The road provided the only direct approach, cutting straight across open ground with virtually no cover. A frontal assault would be spotted immediately, giving the Celtic warriors ample time to organize a defence, or worse, release the creatures.

'What about circling around?' suggested Cassius. 'Approach from the west instead?'

Talorcan shook his head. 'The western slope is steeper, more exposed. And it would add hours to our approach. By the time we repositioned, we might lose the advantage of surprise entirely.'

They descended back to the main force, the tactical problem weighing heavily on each man's mind. As they reached the sheltered depression where the Batavians waited with the horses, Lepidus called his men together once more.

'Options,' he said simply, looking at each face in turn.

'Wait until nightfall,' suggested Talorcan immediately. 'Darkness will provide some concealment, though not enough for complete surprise.'

'Split our forces,' offered Decimus. 'Send a smaller group to create a diversion while the main body attacks from another direction.'

Lepidus considered each proposal, weighing advantages against risks. Waiting for the Celts to move meant potentially missing their only opportunity if they released the creatures before departing. Splitting their forces risked being defeated in detail if the timing wasn't perfect.

'We attack at nightfall,' he decided finally. 'With the element of surprise on our side, we should cause enough confusion to overwhelm them. Our focus will be to kill as many as we can but more importantly, destroy whatever those things are in the crates.'

'What about Seneca and the others?' asked Cassius.

'When they see us attack, they will probably make themselves known to us,' said Lepidus, 'but if we stay here, we will be seen so let's do what we have to do.'

With their course decided, the hours until darkness became a period of focused preparation. Weapons were checked and rechecked, horses rested and watered, plans refined, and contingencies established. The men ate what rations remained, knowing they would need their strength for what lay ahead. Some slept briefly, the practiced ability of soldiers to rest when opportunity allowed, while others maintained vigilant watch around their temporary camp.

As dusk deepened into true darkness, the men mounted up. Final orders were given in hushed tones, assignments confirmed, signals established for the attack. Lepidus took his position at the head of the group, with Talorcan beside him and the force moved out. At the crest, they paused for one final moment, the Celtic camp now visible only as scattered points of light from cookfires and torches in the valley below.

Lepidus drew his sword, the whisper of steel against leather scabbard lost in the greater silence of the night. Around him, fifty Batavian horsemen did the same, their discipline holding them in check despite the battle-tension that now filled the air.

'For Rome,' Lepidus said quietly, his words carried back through the ranks. 'And for our brothers.'

He nudged his mount forward, and the force began its descent toward the enemy camp, committed now to whatever fate awaited them in the darkness below.

Chapter Fifty-Five

The Crossroads

Seneca and Sica crouched in the darkness at the western edge of the camp, tense and motionless. The night had deepened around them, most of the Celtic encampment now sleeping save for the sentries who maintained their predictable patrols. In the distance, the faint sounds of horses shifting in their paddock carried on the slight breeze, a reminder of the diversion that would soon erupt.

Somewhere across the camp, Marcus and Falco were probably in position, preparing to unleash chaos that would temporarily blind the Celtic warriors to the true threat moving among them.

They moved as one, emerging from their concealment with practiced stealth, keeping low as they advanced toward the first line of supply wagons. The initial moments were the most dangerous, crossing open ground before reaching the camp's perimeter. But fortune favoured them, and they reached the wagons without incident, sliding beneath the nearest one to use its bulk as cover.

They crawled from beneath the wagon, advancing in short, controlled bursts, pressing themselves into the deepest shadows, becoming nearly invisible against the dark fabric. A drunken warrior staggered past, close enough that Seneca could smell the sour odour of sleep sweat still clinging to his skin, but they remained perfectly still until he had moved beyond earshot, before continuing their advance, working methodically toward the camp's centre.

'There,' murmured Seneca, nodding toward a tent slightly larger than those surrounding it. Based on their previous observations, this was where Raven had retired each night since his arrival. The entrance flap hung partially closed, a faint glow visible from within suggesting a lamp or candle remained lit inside. Seneca positioned himself to one side, Sica to the other, both listening intently for any sounds of occupancy.

340

Hearing nothing, Seneca nodded to Sica, who delicately pulled back the entrance flap just enough to peer inside. After a moment's observation, he signalled that the space appeared empty and they slipped
inside, allowing the flap to fall closed behind them.

A small oil lamp burned on the packed earth floor, its flame adjusted to the barest minimum, casting just enough light to navigate the confined space. Seneca immediately scanned the interior, noting the bedroll on the far side, empty, its blankets thrown back as if vacated in haste. Another sleeping space lay on the opposite side, similarly abandoned.

Seneca cursed silently, his mind racing through implications. Had Raven been alerted to their presence or had he simply departed on some routine errand that had taken him elsewhere in the camp?

'We'll move to the secondary objective,' he whispered.

Sica nodded, his dark eyes reflecting the lamplight as he retrieved a spear that leaned against the tent wall, testing its weight and balance with a practised hand. The weapon would serve their purpose better than swords or daggers for what came next.

With a final glance around the empty tent, they moved back to the entrance. Seneca carefully peered through a small gap in the flap, confirming the immediate area remained clear, then, with silent coordination, they slipped back outside into the darkness, darting across the open ground between their hiding place and the crates in a matter of heartbeats.

The smell hit them immediately, a nauseating blend of unwashed flesh, stale blood, and something else, something primal that struck at the deepest recesses of the human mind. It was the scent of predator, of something that fed on men, an odour that triggered instinctive revulsion.

From within the crate came sounds that made Seneca's skin crawl, a soft scraping of elongated fingernails against wood, the occasional low, guttural noise that was neither growl nor speech but somehow contained elements of both. Through the narrow gaps

341

between the wooden slats, he caught glimpses of movement, pale flesh sliding past, and once, the brief reflection of an eye, unnervingly aware, gleaming with unnatural intelligence as it detected the men outside.

Sica positioned himself carefully, placing the tip of his spear against one of the wider gaps in the slats.

'Wait for it to come closer,' whispered Seneca, 'the thrust needs
to kill it instantly so it makes no noise.

Sica nodded once, maintaining his position as he tracked the movement within. His hands adjusted minutely on the spear shaft, finding the perfect grip for what would need to be a devastatingly powerful thrust, delivered with surgical precision. Too shallow, and the creature might survive long enough to alert the camp with its death screams, too wide, and they risked missing vital areas entirely.

The creature inside seemed to sense their presence, its movements becoming more purposeful as it approached the side of the crate where they waited. Through the gap, Seneca could now see more clearly, the malformed face, the filed teeth, the pallid skin stretched over unnaturally developed muscles. The beast pressed its face closer to the slat, nostrils flaring as it scented them.

Sica tensed, the moment approaching. The creature's mouth was now perfectly aligned with the gap, its breath fogging the night air as it exhaled. One clean thrust would drive the spear point through its palate and into the brain stem, a killing blow that would prevent any outcry. His muscles bunched, preparing to drive the spear forward, but before he could complete the motion, a voice spoke calmly from behind them.

'I wouldn't, if I were you.'

They froze, neither man turning immediately. The voice was unmistakable, a voice that had once belonged to a comrade, a brother-in-arms who had shared their dangers and their triumphs.

Slowly, Seneca turned to see Raven standing ten paces away. He looked different to how Seneca remembered him. His hair was longer, beard fuller, his clothing Celtic rather than Roman, but his stance remained the same, the careful balance of a man prepared for sudden violence.

'Hello, Seneca,' he said. 'It's been some time.'

For a moment that seemed to stretch into eternity, Seneca and Raven stared at each other, the years of shared combat and brotherhood colliding with the bitter reality of betrayal. Around them, Celtic warriors emerged from the darkness, materializing like ghosts from between tents and wagons, their spears levelled at the intruders.

Seneca maintained his composure, his mind calculating odds and possibilities even as his heart burned with the rage of seeing his former brother-in-arms standing before him. Beside him, Sica remained perfectly still, only the subtle shift of his weight betraying his readiness to explode into lethal action if Seneca gave the signal.

They were outnumbered, surrounded, caught in the heart of the enemy camp. The rational choice was clear, surrender and seek some opportunity later but Seneca had seen what awaited Roman captives in this camp. The creatures in the crates behind them would feast on their flesh, an end too terrible to contemplate. Better to die fighting, taking as many with them as possible, including the traitor who stood before them.

His hand moved toward his gladius, fingers tightening around the familiar hilt but then something happened that froze Seneca's motion mid-draw. Another figure emerged from the shadows to stand beside Raven. Veteranus.

Seneca's breath caught in his throat, shock temporarily overwhelming his combat instincts. He had believed Veteranus dead, reported killed at the Tamesis crossing months earlier, yet here he stood, alive and apparently allied with Raven and the Celts.

'Surprised, old friend?' asked Raven, noting Seneca's expression with evident satisfaction. 'I believe you know Veteranus, he's been our guest on Mona for some time now.'

343

Seneca's gaze moved between the two men, the terrible truth crystallizing in his mind. Not one traitor, but two. Two men who had once served in the Occultum, who had sworn oaths to Rome, who had fought alongside him in battle after battle. Now both stood with Rome's enemies, complicit in whatever dark purpose the creatures behind him served.

The betrayal cut deeper than any blade. The Occultum was more than a military unit; it was a brotherhood forged in blood and shared danger. Each man trusted the others with his life, depended on their unwavering loyalty when facing impossible odds. For two of their number to betray not just Rome but that sacred bond between warriors...

Raven seemed to read his thoughts, a slight smile touching his lips as he observed Seneca's internal struggle. It wasn't gloating, precisely, but rather the satisfied expression of a man whose actions had been validated by events.

'You always were transparent, Seneca,' he said. 'Your face reveals everything you're thinking. Yes, there are two of us now. Though in fairness to Veteranus, his journey to our side was somewhat more... complicated than mine.'

'Whatever your reasons,' replied Seneca, his voice steady despite the turmoil within, 'you've betrayed everything we stood for. Everything we sacrificed for.'

'Sacrificed for?' echoed Raven, a new edge entering his voice. 'What exactly did we sacrifice for, Seneca? For Rome's glory? For the Emperor's ambition? We were tools, nothing more. Weapons to be used and discarded when we became inconvenient.'

He took a step forward, his face hardening with a conviction that seemed to burn from within.

'Do you know what I discovered on Mona many years ago? Truth, Seneca. Truth that Rome has tried to extinguish for generations. Knowledge that existed long before some shepherd boys decided to build huts on seven hills and call themselves the centre of the world.'

The Celtic warriors had drawn closer during this exchange, their spears forming a lethal barrier that made any attempt at escape suicidal. Yet they made no move to take the Romans captive, seemingly content to let this confrontation play out according to Raven's design.

'Was it truth that created those abominations in the crates?' asked Seneca coldly. 'Was it knowledge that makes you feed Roman soldiers to them for sport?'

For the first time, Raven's composure slipped slightly, a flicker of something, regret perhaps, or doubt, crossing his features before the mask of certainty returned.

'The Wraith are merely one expression of power you cannot comprehend,' he replied. 'A necessary weapon in a war that began long before any of us were born.'

'They're monsters,' countered Seneca. 'And so are you, for using them.'

Raven laughed, the sound devoid of humour.

'Always so certain of your moral standing, Seneca. Always so convinced of Rome's righteousness. Did you ever question the orders you carried out? The men you killed because some Senator decided they were inconvenient, the villages you helped destroy because they happened to stand where Rome wanted a road?'

The accusation struck uncomfortably close to doubts Seneca had harboured in the darkest hours of his service, questions he had pushed aside in the name of duty and loyalty. But he refused to let Raven see the impact of his words.

'At least I never betrayed my brothers,' he said simply.

Raven's expression hardened, and he gestured to the warriors surrounding them.

'Take their weapons,' he ordered. 'Bind them securely. They're far too dangerous to underestimate.'

As the Celts moved to obey, Seneca tensed, preparing for one final, desperate fight. But Raven raised his hand, stopping them momentarily.

345

'Don't make this harder than it needs to be, Seneca,' he said, 'fighting now will only get you killed sooner, and I have questions that need answers.'

Seneca hesitated, torn between the warrior's instinct to die fighting and the possibility that if they remained alive, they still had the slim hope of rescue or escape. Slowly, he made his decision with the cold precision that had kept him alive through countless missions. They were surrounded and outnumbered. To die now would serve no purpose.

He flung his gladius to the ground with controlled force, the blade landing in the dirt with a dull thud.

'Drop your weapons, Sica.'

The Syrian's face remained expressionless, but his dark eyes flashed momentary rebellion before he complied, placing his dagger and spear carefully on the ground. The controlled manner of his surrender was itself a statement, he knew this was strategy, not submission.

Some of the Celtic warriors moved forward immediately, rough hands binding their wrists tightly behind their backs with leather thongs before forcing them to their knees. The bindings cut painfully into Seneca's flesh, but he maintained his stoic demeanour, refusing to give Raven the satisfaction of seeing his discomfort.

With their prisoners secured, Raven and Veteranus approached, standing over the kneeling Romans.

'The mighty Occultum,' said Raven, his voice tinged with mockery. 'Rome's shadow warriors, brought to their knees at last.'

Seneca stared up at his former comrade, his face a mask of controlled fury.

'You won't gloat for long, Raven. Rome doesn't forget its traitors.'

'Rome,' scoffed Raven. 'Rome is a corpse that doesn't know it's dead yet. An empire built on sand, its foundations already washing away.' He crouched down, bringing his face level with Seneca's. 'You still don't understand what's happening here, do you?

What Mordred has set in motion?'

Before Seneca could respond, the night was shattered by the sudden clamour of alarm from the eastern perimeter of the camp. Shouts of warning melded with the thundering of hooves, the chaos of horses being driven from their paddock.

Raven's head snapped up, his eyes widening as understanding dawned. He turned back to Seneca with newfound fury as a grim smile touched Seneca's lips.

'Did you really think we'd come all this way without a plan, Raven? I thought we trained you better than that.'

Raven cursed viciously, turning to the warriors who remained with the prisoners. 'Go!' he ordered. 'Support the others! Kill anyone you find, no exceptions!'

The Celts hesitated momentarily, looking between their commander and the bound prisoners.

'*Go!*' shouted Raven. 'We can handle two bound men!'

The warriors ran to join their comrades, leaving only Raven and Veteranus with the captives. Seneca laughed, the sound deliberately provocative.

'What's the matter, Raven. Things not going to plan?'

Raven's control finally broke, and with a snarl of rage, he drew a long knife from his belt.

'Enough,' he said coldly. 'No more games. No more words. I'll cut your throat myself and be done with it.'

Seneca remained motionless, his eyes fixed on Raven's approach, no fear visible in his steady gaze. Beside him, Sica tensed, though with his hands bound behind his back, he could offer no effective resistance.

Raven raised the knife, its blade catching the torchlight as he prepared to deliver the killing stroke.

'Any last words, Seneca? Any final wisdom from Rome's faithful servant?'

Seneca opened his mouth to respond, but whatever he intended to say died unspoken as Raven's expression suddenly transformed. The hatred gave way to shock, then pain, his features slackening as his forward momentum stalled. He gasped, a wet, choking sound, his eyes widening in disbelief.

Slowly, with the mechanical movement of a man whose body no longer followed his commands, Raven looked down at his chest. A blade protruded from his sternum, its blood-slick length having punched through his back to emerge just below his heart. The knife in his own hand slipped from suddenly nerveless fingers, landing at Seneca's knees. With terrible effort, Raven twisted his head to look behind him, coming face to face with his killer.

Veteranus stood close enough that his breath stirred Raven's hair, his expression coldly resolute as he maintained his grip on the knife buried in Raven's back. Their eyes met in a moment of terrible understanding, betrayer betrayed, the circle complete.

'You...' Raven managed, blood bubbling at the corners of his mouth. 'I thought...'

'You thought wrong,' said Veteranus simply, twisting the blade with surgical precision.

Raven's body convulsed, his knees buckling as life fled. Veteranus supported his weight momentarily before allowing him to crumple to the ground, the once-proud Occultum operative reduced to a heap of bloodied flesh at Seneca's knees.

For a moment, nobody moved, the tableau frozen in the flickering torchlight: Seneca and Sica still on their knees, hands bound; Veteranus standing over Raven's body, bloodied knife in hand.

Chapter Fifty-Six

The Celtic Camp

The thundering of hooves echoed through the night as Falco and Marcus spurred their horses away from the camp. Behind them, chaos erupted as half the Celtic herd scattered into the darkness, whinnying in panic, their powerful bodies crashing through tents and supply carts in their desperate flight.

'*Ride!*' bellowed Marcus, his frame hunched low over his mount's neck. 'Don't look back!'

They burst onto the road, the sudden transition from soft earth to packed dirt allowing their horses to accelerate. For a moment, Marcus dared to hope they might escape cleanly, and that the confusion they'd created would buy enough time for Seneca and Sica to complete their part of the mission, but that hope died as he glanced over his shoulder. In the torchlight, he could see Celtic warriors scrambling to regain control of their camp, but more concerning were the riders already leaping onto bareback mounts, spurring them into immediate pursuit.

'They're coming!' Marcus shouted, urging his horse to greater speed.

Falco didn't waste breath responding, focusing instead on guiding his mount along the darkened road. The beast beneath him was strong but unfamiliar, responding sluggishly to his commands, unused to his weight and riding style.

The road stretched before them, a pale ribbon cutting through the darkness, leading northeast toward Camulodunum. Behind them, the pursuing hoofbeats grew louder, the Celtic riders closing the distance with alarming speed. Marcus risked another backward glance and cursed. At least forty warriors had joined the chase, their riders more skilled on horseback than the Romans.

'It's no use!' he shouted as the gap continued to narrow. 'We need to stop and fight! Look for somewhere we can defend!'

Falco scanned the landscape desperately, searching for any feature that might offer them an advantage, a narrow pass, a defensible rise, anything to offset the overwhelming numbers bearing down on them. But the terrain offered nothing, just the flat, open road flanked by gentle slopes and scattered trees.

'Riders to the front!' Marcus's roared suddenly, his warning cutting through the night. His hand dropped to his gladius, preparing for the desperate, final battle that would see them sell their lives as dearly as possible. Through the darkness, he could make out the silhouettes of horsemen arranged in tight formation, advancing towards them at speed. For a heartbeat, he thought they were doomed, caught between two enemy forces. Then recognition sent his heart racing as the unmistakable voice of Decimus called out from the darkness.

'Clear the road!'

With barely a moment to react, Falco and Marcus pulled their exhausted mounts to the side and the ground shook as the Batavian cavalry thundered past them, driving straight toward the pursuing Celts.

The sudden appearance of fresh Roman cavalry caught the Celtic pursuit completely by surprise and the leading warriors had no time to regroup or form a defensive position before the Batavians crashed into them with devastating force, their disciplined formation slicing through the disorganized pursuit like a spear through flesh. The impact resonated through the night air, steel meeting flesh, horse colliding with horse, battle cries mingling with screams of pain and in the pale moonlight, silhouettes transformed into a chaotic tableau of violence.

The Celtic warriors, having mounted in haste to pursue their fleeing quarry, found themselves catastrophically unprepared, many clutching only the most basic weapons they had managed to grab, knives, light spears, a few swords. Most lacked helmets, their torsos unprotected by the armour they'd left behind in their tents and their pursuit formation, strung out along the road from their eagerness to catch the Romans, now became their undoing.

'*Forward! No mercy!*' the Batavian commander roared, his voice carrying over the cacophony of battle.

A Celtic warrior attempted to wheel his mount around, only to receive a spear thrust that lifted him bodily from his horse. Another tried to engage a Batavian rider with a hunting knife, a desperate gambit that ended with his throat opened by a precise sword stroke. Blood sprayed in dark arcs, and horses screamed in terror and pain, some collapsing beneath their riders, others bolting into the darkness.

At the centre of the attack, Talorcan drove his mount forward relentlessly, his borrowed sword already dark with blood. His tactical eye recognized that the Batavians' momentum was their greatest advantage, and any pause would allow the Celts to regroup.

'Don't slow!' he called to the riders near him. 'Keep moving through them!'

The Batavians responded instinctively to the command, maintaining their forward pressure, refusing to become entangled in individual combats that might stall their advance, and their discipline transformed fifty riders into an unstoppable force that continued to shatter the Celtic pursuit.

For several minutes, the battle hung in perfect, terrible balance, a whirlwind of steel and flesh, blood and courage, then the Celtic resistance began to fragment as individual warriors broke away, the collective will to fight evaporating in the face of such devastating losses.

Lepidus carved his way through to the front of the formation, his unexpected skill in mounted combat evident in every movement. For a Senator, he fought with the proficiency of the career soldier he had once been, his blade finding vulnerabilities with surgical precision. He pulled up momentarily to survey the battlefield, before returning to Marcus and Falco, reining in his mount.

'Where are the others?' he demanded, his face grim in the

351

faint starlight.

'Probably in the camp,' Marcus replied breathlessly. 'Seneca and Sica went after Raven while we created the diversion.'

Without another word, Lepidus turned his horse to rejoin the main battle. His intent was clear even without words, he meant to rescue those left behind, regardless of the danger.
As he raced away, Falco turned to Marcus.

'No rest for the damned,' he muttered.

'It seems not,' replied Marcus, and without further communication, the two men dug their heels in to send their own mounts racing after the Batavians. The Celtic camp loomed before them, its torches and fires now fully ablaze as the alarm spread throughout the position. The element of surprise was long gone, but they pressed on nonetheless, hands tightening on weapon hilts, faces set with grim determination, driven by a bond that transcended mere military duty, the unbreakable loyalty of warriors who refused to abandon their own.

On the other side of the camp, Seneca knelt in stunned silence, his eyes fixed on Veteranus standing over Raven's lifeless body. The blood pooling beneath the corpse appeared black in the torchlight, spreading slowly across the packed earth. Behind him, Sica remained motionless, his expression revealing nothing despite the shocking turn of events.

In the distance, the sounds of battle echoed through the night, shouting, the clash of weapons, the thundering of hooves, but for this moment, this isolated pocket of the camp remained strangely undisturbed, as if existing in its own fragment of time.

Seneca found his voice first.

'Cut us loose,' he said quietly, his tone betraying no gratitude, only wariness.

Veteranus wiped his blade clean on Raven's cloak before moving behind them. The knife made short work of their bindings, the leather thongs falling away as both men immediately reached for their discarded weapons. Seneca rose to his feet, gladius in hand, and turned to face Veteranus.

'Explain yourself,' he demanded, the blade not quite pointed at his former comrade, but positioned where it could strike in an instant if necessary.

'The last I heard, you were dead. Now I find you here, among druids and traitors. What game are you playing?'

Veteranus sheathed his knife, his weathered face revealing little as he met Seneca's suspicious gaze.

'It's complicated,' he said, deliberately vague. 'And this isn't the time for lengthy explanations.'

'Make time,' Seneca insisted, his voice hardening. 'You've been with them for months. Working with Raven, with Mordred.' His sword edged closer to Veteranus's chest. 'Give me one reason I shouldn't consider you a traitor as well.'

Behind them, Sica had retrieved his own weapons, positioning himself to flank Veteranus if needed.

'I just saved your lives,' Veteranus replied calmly. 'That should count for something.'

'Or you're eliminating witnesses to secure your own position,' countered Seneca. 'I need more than that.'

Veteranus sighed, glancing briefly toward the commotion still raging at the camp's eastern edge.

'I will reveal everything later, I swear it. But right now, we have more pressing concerns.'

Seneca's blade didn't waver.

'How do I know you won't turn on us the moment our backs are turned?'

Veteranus met his stare unflinchingly, something in his steady gaze reminiscent of the man Seneca had once known and trusted.

'You don't,' he admitted. 'But ask yourself this. If I meant you harm, why not let Raven finish the job?'

The logic was undeniable, yet Seneca's instincts remained

353

conflicted. The Occultum had been betrayed too many times to accept apparent salvation without question.

'I want answers,' Seneca insisted. 'All of them.'

'And you'll have them,' promised Veteranus. 'But first, we have a job to do. Wait here.' Without waiting for agreement, he turned and strode away, disappearing between the tents.

Seneca exchanged a quick glance with Sica, unspoken communication passing between them. They would remain vigilant, ready to respond if this proved yet another layer of deception but before they could discuss the implications, Veteranus returned, now carrying something in his hands, a clay flask smelling of pine wax and tar.

'What's that?' asked Seneca.

'This,' said Veteranus, unplugging the flask, 'is what is going to make all our problems go away.'

Chapter Fifty-Seven

The Celtic Camp

The Batavian cavalry swept down upon the Celtic camp like an iron tide, their victory over the pursuing riders complete. Those who hadn't fallen to Roman blades had scattered into the darkness, fleeing for their lives across the darkened countryside. Now, with blood still fresh on their weapons, they followed Lepidus toward the heart of the enemy encampment.

The Celtic warriors within the settlement had responded to the alarm, hastily forming defensive lines behind the shoulder-high palisade that ringed their position. Unlike their mounted comrades, these defenders had time to don armour and gather proper weapons, their spear points glinting in the torchlight as they prepared to repel the Roman assault.

Lepidus raised his sword, signalling the final charge and the Batavians responded with a thunderous war cry, spurring their mounts forward. Where lesser cavalry might have hesitated at the sight of the wooden barricade, these elite horsemen saw merely another obstacle to overcome and soared over the defensive wall, their swords already swinging downward as they cleared the barrier, the first rank of Celtic warriors falling before they could even fight back.

Another group of Batavians thundered through the main gateway and crashed into the settlement's interior like a battering ram, trampling anyone unfortunate enough to stand in their path. Within moments, the organized defence collapsed into desperate individual combats throughout the camp. Tents collapsed, cooking fires scattered dangerous embers across the ground, and the air filled with the unmistakable sounds of men fighting for their lives, steel against steel, flesh against flesh, the primal screams of the wounded and dying.

At the heart of the chaos strode Falco, the former gladiator

355

transformed into something more elemental, more terrifying than a mere soldier, each stroke of his gladius ending a life. Blood splattered across his face and chest, turning him into a nightmare figure that seemed to have emerged from the underworld itself.

Three Celtic warriors rushed him simultaneously, attempting to overwhelm him with numbers but Falco met the first with a diagonal slash that opened the man from shoulder to hip, the second with a reverse stroke that separated head from body in a single clean motion. The third managed to score a glancing blow against Falco's arm before a brutal thrust punched through his chest, lifting him momentarily off his feet before he collapsed in a lifeless heap.

'Come on!' Falco roared, his voice cutting through the din of battle as he sought new opponents. 'Is this all you have?'

Friend and foe alike gave him space, the former out of respect, the latter out of fear and he carved a bloody path through the camp, his massive frame at the centre of the most desperate fighting.

Elsewhere, Decimus and Cassius fought alongside each other but where Falco was rage incarnate, they wielded a cold and calculating fight, each stroke economical, each movement thought through.

Talorcan fought differently still, using the quickness and stealth that had served him as a scout. He would appear suddenly from shadows, strike with devastating accuracy, then vanish again before his enemies could respond effectively. Three Celtic warriors fell to his blade before they even realized he was among them and gradually, the Batavians' superior training and equipment, combined with the shock of their unexpected assault, proved too much and the Celtic defenders and warriors began throwing down their weapons, some fleeing into the darkness, others kneeling in surrender, hands raised in supplication.

Through this chaos, a bloodied Marcus led Lepidus deeper into the camp, both men moving with desperate urgency. Their swords dripped red, testimony to the fighting they had endured to reach this point.

'There!' Marcus shouted over the diminishing sounds of battle, pointing toward the central area where the crates had been positioned. 'That's where they were keeping those... things.'

They ran forward, dodging around collapsed tents and fallen bodies, their feet slipping occasionally in the blood-slicked earth. As they approached, a terrible heart-rending scream tore through the night, so primal and inhuman that both men froze momentarily in their tracks. Before they could recover, a second scream joined the first, then a third, the combined sound unlike anything either man had ever heard, a chorus of agony that transcended natural limits.

Marcus broke into a desperate run, fear for his comrades overriding the revulsion triggered by those unnatural sounds. Lepidus followed close behind, his face set with grim determination.

They rounded a final tent and Marcus suddenly stopped in his tracks, his forward momentum arrested by the scene before him. Lepidus nearly collided with him, steadying himself against the younger man's shoulder as both stared at the tableau revealed in the flickering light.

Before them stood Seneca, Sica, and, most surprisingly, Veteranus, their figures silhouetted against a backdrop of roaring flames. At their feet lay a body, unmistakably Raven's, a dark pool of blood spreading from beneath him. Behind them, the source of the terrible screaming became horrifyingly clear: the three wooden crates were engulfed in fire, the pitch-fed flames hungrily consuming both containers and their contents.

Through gaps in the burning slats, they caught grotesque glimpses of the creatures within, thrashing limbs, contorted faces, mouths open in those terrible screams as the fire claimed them. The smell was indescribable, a nauseating blend of burning wood and charred flesh.

Seneca turned toward them, his face streaked with soot and blood, his eyes reflecting the dancing flames. For a moment, he seemed not to recognize them, his gaze distant, as if looking beyond the immediate scene to something only he could perceive. Then awareness returned, his expression settling into something between exhaustion and grim satisfaction.

'It's over,' he said simply, gesturing toward Raven's body and the burning crates. 'We've completed both missions.'

The screams from the crates began to diminish, becoming weaker, more gurgling than vocal and within minutes, they stopped altogether, leaving only the crackling of the fire and the distant sounds of the battle's aftermath. As they watched the flames consume the most terrifying opponents they had ever encountered, Falco, Talorcan and Cassius joined them to stare at the inferno.

The Occultum stood in silence, united in witness to the end of
creatures that should never have existed, and the death of a traitor who had once been their brother. The completion of the mission had pushed each of them beyond the limits of endurance and what they had seen, what they had done, would remain with them forever, a shared burden that only they could truly understand.

Chapter Fifty-Eight

Camulodunum

The interrogation chamber in Camulodunum fort was spartan in its functionality, a wooden table, four chairs, and walls thick enough to ensure privacy.

Lepidus sat staring across the table alongside Seneca, their eyes never leaving the man sat before them. Veteranus was sitting in a chair with his hands bound before him and secured to a metal ring sunk into the table. Alongside him stood two large legionaries, there to ensure the dangerous ex-Occultum member was suitably detained.

'Let us begin again,' said Lepidus, with a sigh. 'You were reported killed at the Battle of Tamesis, yet months later we find you among the druids, apparently trusted by Mordred himself.' He leaned forward slightly. 'I know of no mission that would explain this. So, tell me once more, what truly happened?'

Veteranus exhaled slowly, the frustration evident in his face.

'As I've said repeatedly,' he replied, 'I saw an opportunity at the river and seized it. As you know, there is apparently a high-level officer right here in Britannia that plots against Claudius and apparently Mordred was waiting for a message from him. I found out and pretended to be that messenger. I was brought to Mordred, who claimed to see something in me and claimed I had druidic blood in my veins. He also claimed a tattoo on my shoulder proved it.'

'And you simply went along with this tale?' Seneca interjected, scepticism evident in his voice.

'I played along,' Veteranus replied evenly. 'What would you have done? Fight and die uselessly? Or learn what I could about our enemies?'

Lepidus tapped his fingers thoughtfully on the table.

'You had months amongst them,' he said. 'If you remained loyal to Rome, why not assassinate Mordred when you had the chance or Raven when he appeared? A single knife thrust could have

359

severely disrupted their plans.'

'And accomplished what, exactly?' countered Veteranus. 'A momentary victory at the cost of any chance to understand their true capabilities?' He leaned forward, his bound hands resting on the table. 'I chose to learn about our foe, their strengths, their weaknesses, their plans. Knowledge that would serve Rome far better than a symbolic killing.'

'And when you learned about the Wraith,' said Seneca, 'did that knowledge serve Rome as well?'

'I was horrified, yes,' replied Veteranus, 'but also fascinated. Here was a weapon of potentially devastating power, something that could change the nature of battle. Understanding it became crucial.'

'So, you continued your charade,' Lepidus stated. 'Deeper and deeper into their society.'

'I did what was necessary,' said Veteranus. 'I merged into their culture, learned their language, absorbed their customs. I gained their trust, or enough of it to access information no Roman had ever seen. I also learned things about the druids that generations of Rome's enemies never discovered.'

'And in the process?' Seneca asked quietly. 'Were you ever tempted to forget your purpose? To truly become one of them?'

The question hung in the air between them. Veteranus fell silent, his eyes dropping to his bound hands as he considered his response. When he finally looked up, something had changed in his expression, a vulnerability that hadn't been present before, a crack in the composed facade he'd maintained throughout the interrogation.

'Yes,' he admitted. 'There were moments... days... perhaps when I found myself thinking as they did, seeing the world through their eyes.' He paused, seeming to struggle with the admission. 'Their perspective has a certain... clarity to it. They see Rome not as the bringer of civilization, but as the destroyer of something precious, something ancient.'

The guards behind him shifted uncomfortably at this confession, but Lepidus motioned for them to remain still.

'And yet, in the end, you killed Raven to save Seneca,' Lepidus observed. 'What changed?'

Veteranus's gaze moved to Seneca, something passing between the two men that transcended words.

'Seeing you at the crossroads brought me back to reality,' he said. 'Reminded me of who I truly was, of the oaths I had sworn.' He straightened in his chair. 'Whatever doubts I may have entertained, whatever sympathies I might have developed... they vanished the moment I saw Raven raise his knife against a brother of the Occultum.'

Seneca's expression hardened, scepticism etched in every line of his weathered face.

'Or when you realised the camp was under attack,' he suggested coldly, 'you saw an opportunity to save your own skin when the tide turned against your new allies.'

'If that were true,' said Veteranus, 'I would have done nothing. I would have stood by, watched Raven kill you both, then simply disappeared into the woods during the confusion.' He leaned forward, eyes locked with Seneca's. 'Instead, I drove a knife into Raven's back and cut your bindings. Those are not the actions of a man looking to abandon ship.'

Lepidus raised a hand, redirecting the increasingly heated exchange.

'Let's take a different approach,' he said. 'Tell us about the druids' plans. What were Mordred's intentions with the Wraith?'

Veteranus settled back in his chair, exhaling slowly.

'Initially, they planned to kill Plautius. He was their primary target for months, the symbol of Roman occupation, the military genius behind the invasion.' He paused, gathering his thoughts. 'But everything changed when they learned of the Emperor's planned visit and Mordred saw an opportunity too valuable to ignore.'

'And what exactly was this new plan?' pressed Lepidus.

'They intended to position themselves as close as possible to the Emperor during the surrender ceremony,' Veteranus explained.

361

'Then release the Wraith among the gathered dignitaries.' His expression darkened. 'You've seen what one of those creatures can do, imagine three of them loose among unarmed officials, with the Emperor at the centre.'

'That hardly seems practical, said Seneca. 'Imperial security would never allow unknown Celts close enough to matter.'

'I don't know the specifics,' admitted Veteranus, 'I wasn't privy to every detail. Mordred kept certain aspects of the plan to himself, especially after Raven arrived but he is a very clever man and would have a plan in mind.'

'And the camp at the crossroads?' Seneca asked. 'Why remain there so long? They were days from Camulodunum with plenty of time to reach it before Claudius's arrival.'

Veteranus shrugged as much as his bindings would allow.

'Again, I don't know. Perhaps they were waiting for something, a signal, additional forces, or specific instructions from Mordred. The warriors there answered to Raven directly, not to me.'

Lepidus and Seneca exchanged glances, the same unspoken thought passing between them. For all his apparent cooperation, Veteranus's answers left crucial gaps in their understanding, gaps that could represent either genuine ignorance or calculated deception. Finally, Lepidus pushed back his chair and stood.

'I think we've learned what we can for now,' he said. 'The Emperor is due within days, and there are still preparations to complete.'

Seneca rose as well, his gaze never leaving Veteranus.

'Take him back to his cell,' he instructed the legionaries. 'and double the guards until the Emperor has left.'

'What happens to me now?' Veteranus asked, his voice carefully neutral.

'That remains to be determined,' replied Lepidus. 'For the moment, you'll remain under guard while we verify what parts of your story we can. Once the Emperor has left, we'll decide what to do with you.'

As the guards led Veteranus from the room, Lepidus and Seneca lingered, waiting until the door closed behind them.

'What do you think?' asked Lepidus quietly.

'I'm not certain,' replied Seneca.' Parts of his account ring true, others...' He shook his head.

'And the Wraith?' asked Lepidus. 'Do you think there could there be more of them?'

'I don't believe so,' Seneca assured him. 'We questioned every
prisoner separately, and they all confirmed the same, Mordred had only created four of those abominations, all of which are now dead.'

'Small mercies,' muttered Lepidus.

They exited the interrogation chamber, stepping into the organized chaos of the fort. All around them, preparations for the Emperor's arrival continued at a fevered pace, soldiers drilling, structures being completed, supplies being arranged with meticulous attention to detail.

'Hard to believe we were fighting for our lives just a few weeks ago,' Seneca observed as they walked through the bustling compound.

Lepidus nodded, his gaze sweeping across the activity.

'And now we prepare to welcome the Emperor as if nothing happened,' he said, 'such is the nature of serving Rome.'

Chapter Fifty-Nine

Camulodunum

A golden afternoon sun cast long shadows across the vast plain before Camulodunum's walls, illuminating what had once been empty countryside but now stood transformed into a testament of Roman power and ingenuity. Timber buildings lined meticulously planned streets, their façades adorned with painted plaster mimicking the marble of Rome's grandest structures. Colourful banners snapped in the gentle breeze, their imperial purple and gold catching the sunlight as they proclaimed Claudius's triumph to all who beheld them.

The temporary city had risen from nothing in mere weeks, a feat that left even the most sceptical Britons awestruck. Each structure had been crafted with painstaking attention to detail, decorated to reflect not merely function but the magnificent occasion they served. Columns had been carved, pediments adorned with reliefs depicting Rome's conquest, interiors furnished with items brought across the sea at tremendous expense, all to ensure that when Claudius toured his newest province, he would feel not the deprivation of a frontier outpost but the dignified comfort of imperial Rome.

The Emperor had arrived days earlier with an entourage designed to overwhelm the senses and crush any lingering doubts about Roman superiority. Praetorian Guards in gleaming armour had marched in perfect formation, their disciplined ranks a stark contrast to the tribal warfare the Britons knew. War elephants, creatures never before seen on the island, had plodded solemnly alongside the imperial carriage, their massive forms drawing gasps from onlookers but most impressive to many were the sleek panthers led on silver chains by Nubian handlers, the great cats padding alongside the procession with deadly grace, symbols of Rome's mastery over nature itself.

The entire spectacle had proceeded with clockwork precision, every element carefully orchestrated to maximize both security and symbolic impact. Tribal leaders from across Britannia had gathered to witness this pivotal moment, some making their submission willingly, others with thinly veiled resentment. All, however, understood the unspoken message conveyed by the display: resistance was futile; Rome's supremacy was absolute.

As the final day of ceremonies approached, Lepidus stood at the edge of the reviewing platform, his gaze sweeping methodically across open space where the crowds would gather the following day. His outward appearance showed nothing of the tension that had defined the preceding weeks, and only those who knew him well might notice the subtle alertness in his posture that spoke of a man prepared for unexpected danger.

'It should be quite the spectacle,' observed Seneca, joining him at the platform's edge. 'Worth the effort, wouldn't you say?'

Lepidus allowed himself a thin smile.

'The Emperor believes so, which is all that matters. Though I confess I'll be relieved when it's finished and he's safely aboard his ship back to Gaul. He glanced over toward the imperial pavilion where Claudius sat drinking wine surrounded by his closest advisors. 'Another few days then it's done.'

'Are your men prepared?' asked Lepidus.

'The Occultum will remain discreetly positioned throughout the closing ceremony,' Seneca said quietly. 'Marcus and Falco are near the northern approach, Decimus and Cassius by the eastern. Sica will be... somewhere.' He shrugged slightly. 'He never tells me exactly where he'll be, but I've no doubt he's watching.'

'And our friend?' asked Lepidus, not needing to specify further.

'Still secured. Three legionaries with him at all times. Until the Emperor's ship disappears over the horizon, Veteranus remains exactly where he is.'

Lepidus nodded his agreement. Despite the days of

questioning, neither man felt entirely comfortable with Veteranus's story. It would be weeks, perhaps months, before intelligence networks could verify portions of his account, but until then, caution prevailed.

Up on a hill overlooking Camulodunum, the rest of the Occultum had established a temporary observation post, a position that provided both tactical advantage and a moment of respite from their duties. For days they had patrolled the outskirts, scrutinizing every approach to the imperial ceremonies, watching for any sign of organized resistance or foolhardy individuals who might attempt to breach the security perimeter.

Now, seated in a rough circle on the grassy slope, they allowed themselves a rare moment of relaxation. Falco had produced a flask of surprisingly good wine, 'liberated' from a supply wagon, while Marcus shared bread and cured meat he'd obtained through more legitimate channels.

'Look at that spectacle,' said Falco, gesturing toward the activity below through a mouthful of bread. 'All that effort for one man's vanity.'

'That 'vanity' is what keeps the empire together,' countered Decimus, though without much conviction. 'The tribes need to see Rome's power made flesh.'

'The tribes need to see Rome's boot on their necks, you mean,' Falco corrected, taking a swig from his cup. 'Though I'll grant the builders did impressive work. Those structures look almost permanent.'

Sica, perched slightly apart from the others pointed to a guarded paddock in the distance.

'The elephants were a particularly effective touch. I saw grown warriors trembling at the sight.'

'They should be more afraid of what follows the elephants,' remarked Cassius. 'Tax collectors and administrators will do more damage than those beasts ever could.'

This prompted a round of laughter, the men united in their somewhat cynical assessment of Rome's methods. For all their service to the empire, the Occultum maintained a clear-eyed view of its workings, they were its instruments, not its devotees.

Their conversation halted as they spotted a lone rider ascending the hill toward their position. Even at a distance, they recognized the straight-backed posture and purposeful approach of Senator Lepidus.

'Speak of the wolves,' muttered Falco, 'and they appear with Senatorial insignia.'

They watched as Lepidus made his way up the winding path, his refreshed clothing marking him clearly as a man of authority, not the formal toga of the Senate house, but attire that befitted his rank while allowing the practical movement required on the frontier.

'Senator,' Marcus greeted him, offering the wine flask. 'Care to join us common soldiers in our poor repast?'

Lepidus accepted the flask with a nod of thanks.

'Nothing poor about this vintage,' he observed after taking a sip. 'I suspect I don't want to know how it came into your possession, Falco.'

The big man grinned unapologetically.

'A gift from an admiring Briton, Senator. I swear it on Jupiter's beard.'

'Of course,' Lepidus replied dryly, settling himself on the ground among them. His military background was still evident in every movement, even in the way he automatically selected a position that gave him clear sightlines while protecting his back.

For a few moments, they sat in companionable silence, passing food and drink between them, all of them aware that such moments of peace were rare in their profession and to be savoured accordingly.

'I bring news,' Lepidus said finally, setting down his cup. 'Vespasian was quite impressed with the outcome at the crossroads.'

'As well he should be,' interjected Falco.

'Indeed,' said Lepidus, 'and now he has a further request, or rather, an order.' He paused, his expression growing more serious. 'He wants two of you to remain close to the Emperor during tomorrow's final tribute ceremony.'

The men exchanged glances, their momentary relaxation evaporating as they recognized the implications.

'Claudius will have his Praetorians, of course,' Lepidus continued, 'but Vespasian feels the Occultum would provide an additional layer of protection, men who understand the specific threats this province presents, and who would be willing to sacrifice themselves if necessary to ensure the Emperor's safety.'

Falco let out a bark of laughter.

'So that's our reward for success? The chance to throw ourselves on a Celtic spear meant for Claudius?'

The others joined in his laughter, but it held an edge of recognition. This was, after all, the essence of their service, to protect Rome's interests at whatever personal cost. Lepidus waited for their amusement to subside before speaking again, his tone now carrying the

unmistakable weight of command.

'This isn't up for discussion. The order comes directly from Vespasian himself, with the Emperor's approval.' He surveyed the group of hardened operatives before him. 'I need two volunteers.'

A sudden, conspicuous silence fell over the gathering. Each man suddenly found something fascinating to examine. Falco became intently interested in the remnants of food in his hand, Marcus adjusted his boot with unnecessary thoroughness, Sica stared impassively into the middle distance as if he hadn't heard the question at all, while Decimus seemed to discover an urgent need to clean his dagger.

Lepidus waited, one eyebrow raised, as the silence stretched uncomfortably until finally, Cassius sighed and cleared his throat.

'I'll do it,' he said, with a sigh. 'On one condition.'

'A condition?' Lepidus repeated warily. 'You understand this is a direct order, not a negotiation.'

'Call it a request for compensation,' Cassius replied. 'For the mental anguish of enduring hours of ceremonial tedium.'

'What exactly did you have in mind?' asked Lepidus, his tone suggesting he might already regret the question.

Cassius held up three fingers.

'Three things,' he said. 'Ten flasks of wine, the good Falernian, not that swill they serve the common legionaries. A full leg of lamb, properly roasted with herbs, and...' his smile widened, 'the company of a woman of ill repute for the evening after. A pretty one.'

The group erupted into laughter, tension breaking as they slapped Cassius on the back, clearly appreciating his boldness.

Lepidus's mouth twitched, fighting a smile of his own. When the laughter subsided, he adopted a thoughtful expression, as if seriously considering the request. Then, to everyone's surprise, he nodded.

'Done.'

The laughter died instantly, replaced by stunned silence.

'Wait, truly?' Cassius asked, clearly not having expected success.

'Rome can be generous to those who serve her well,' replied Lepidus.

Falco's eyes widened comically.

'In that case!' he boomed, rising to his full height. 'I volunteer as well! Same terms!'

'So be it,' Lepidus sighed, shaking his head at the immediate shift in enthusiasm. 'Though finding a woman who won't flee at the sight of your face might prove challenging.'

This prompted another round of laughter, growing louder as they saw the look of shocked hurt on Falco's face at the insult.

Lepidus rose to his feet, brushing dust from his clothing.

'Report to the quartermaster at dawn,' he instructed. 'He'll have your uniforms ready.'

Falco turned to face him abruptly.

'Uniforms?' he repeated, his brow creasing in confusion. 'What do you mean, uniforms?'

'Despite your...' Lepidus paused, eyeing Falco's enormous frame, 'unnatural build, we need you to blend in as much as possible. You can't exactly stand next to the Emperor looking like you've just stepped off a battlefield. I'm sure the quartermaster can find something that can be... modified to fit.' Without waiting for further argument, he mounted his horse and headed back down the hill, the issue clearly settled in his mind.

The remaining men watched him go, various expressions of amusement playing across their faces. Decimus rose to his feet as well, gathering his belongings.

'Leaving so soon?' Marcus asked, looking up at the veteran.

'I need a good night's sleep,' Decimus replied, slinging his pack over his shoulder.

'Why's that?' Falco demanded suspiciously.

Decimus's weathered face broke into a rare, full smile.

'Because I don't want to miss a moment of tomorrow. The sight of you two dressed in ceremonial finery, kissing the Emperor's arse...' He shook his head, chuckling. 'That's worth waking early for.'

The others erupted in laughter once more as Falco's face darkened with the realization of what he had volunteered for. Cassius looked equally dismayed, the full implications of their impulsive offers finally sinking in as Falco groaned dramatically, flopping back onto the grass and covering his face with one massive arm.

'The things we do for Rome,' he muttered.

The laughter that followed carried across the hilltop, a rare moment of simple joy among men who had faced death together more times than they could count, who had witnessed horrors beyond description, and who would, despite their complaints, stand ready when duty called again.

Chapter Sixty

Camulodunum

The golden light of morning bathed Camulodunum in a radiance that seemed almost divine, as if the gods themselves had blessed this final day of triumph. The newly constructed forum square gleamed with an artificial splendour that nonetheless impressed all who beheld it. Roman banners snapped in the breeze, while garlands of fresh greenery adorned every column and archway, transforming the hastily built settlement into something approaching magnificence.

At the centre of this carefully orchestrated display stood the imperial dais, elevated six steps above the ground to ensure the Emperor would literally look down upon those who came to submit. A massive throne dominated the platform, its wooden frame gilded and inlaid with precious stones brought from Rome specifically for this occasion. Purple drapes cascaded from the surrounding columns, their rich hue the unmistakable marker of imperial authority, while behind them, partially concealed in the shadows, stood Falco and Cassius.

The transformation of the two Occultum operatives was nothing short of remarkable. Gone was any trace of the hardened warriors who had battled druids and creatures of nightmare weeks before. In their place stood what appeared to be dignified members of the imperial household, their bodies encased in formal tunics of fine linen, bordered with the subtle patterns that denoted their supposed rank. Falco in particular looked profoundly uncomfortable, the refined garments straining against his massive frame, clearly modified by some despairing tailor who had never before confronted such dimensions.

'Stop fidgeting,' Cassius murmured from the corner of his mouth, his eyes fixed forward as befitted his role.

'This tunic is strangling me,' Falco whispered back, running a finger beneath the tight collar. 'And these sandals pinch my toes. How do the fops in Rome wear this garbage every day?'

'They don't typically have feet the size of fishing boats,' Cassius replied dryly. 'Now be silent. The Praetorians are coming.'

Indeed, the distinctive sound of disciplined marching now echoed through the forum as the elite guards of the Imperial household entered in perfect formation. Their armour gleamed impossibly bright, each plate polished to mirror finish, their crimson plumes cutting a vivid line above the sea of lesser soldiers who filled the square. They moved with mechanical precision, shields held at identical angles, spears perfectly vertical, their faces masks of professional detachment.

The crowd, already substantial despite the early hour, parted before them like water around the prow of a ship. Unlike the typical Roman military display, where soldiers moved through formations designed to intimidate enemies, this procession was choreographed as ceremony, a visual representation of power and protection and the Praetorians took their positions, forming a human barrier between the common spectators and the imperial dais.

From his position behind the throne, Falco scanned the crowd with professional scrutiny, his discomfort momentarily forgotten as he assessed potential threats. Roman officials and their families occupied the front rows, their finery marking them as the privileged elite. Behind them stood ordinary legionaries, granted the honour of witnessing history as reward for their service in the conquest while further back still, carefully screened local inhabitants watched with expressions ranging from awe to barely concealed resentment.

'There's Lepidus,' Cassius whispered suddenly. 'Three rows back, speaking with the Tribune.'

Falco's gaze shifted to the indicated position, where indeed Lepidus stood engaged in what appeared to be casual conversation. The Senator's relaxed demeanour betrayed nothing of the weeks of tension that had preceded this day, nor of the vigilance he was undoubtedly maintaining beneath his sociable exterior.

A sudden blast of trumpets cut through the morning air, signalling the arrival of the imperial delegation and the crowd fell into immediate silence, all eyes turning toward the eastern approach where a procession now appeared, led by standard bearers holding aloft the golden eagles of Rome.

Behind the standards walked Vespasian and Plautius, commanders of the conquest, their armour more ceremonial than practical, adorned with decorations commemorating previous victories.

And then, finally, came Claudius himself, Emperor of Rome, ruler of lands stretching from Hispania to Syria, from Africa to the very ground upon which he now walked. Despite the physical ailments that had plagued him since birth, the slight limp, the occasional tremor, he projected an undeniable authority. Draped in imperial purple, a crown of golden laurels upon his head, he advanced with measured steps toward the throne that awaited him.

The silence deepened as he ascended the dais, the collective breath of thousands held in anticipation. With deliberate ceremony, he turned to face the gathering before lowering himself onto the throne.

'Hail Claudius Caesar!' cried the herald, his voice carrying across the forum. 'Emperor of Rome, conqueror of Britannia!'

'Hail Claudius Caesar!' roared the crowd in response, the sound rolling like thunder across the settlement.

From their positions behind the throne, Falco and Cassius maintained their vigilant watch.

'I preferred the Wraith,' Falco muttered under his breath. 'At least that was an honest fight.'

'Quiet,' hissed Cassius. 'The tribes are arriving.'

Beyond the settlement walls, a different procession was forming. Tribal dignitaries, many traveling for days to reach Camulodunum, arranged themselves according to a hierarchy established by Roman officials. Each delegation had been carefully briefed on the ceremony to follow, how to approach, how to kneel, what words to speak in formal submission. Each carried tributes representing the finest their territories could produce, offerings to their new master that would symbolize their acceptance of Roman rule.

Not all the tribal leaders of Britannia were present, of course. Caratacus and his most loyal followers remained defiant in the western mountains, while many northern tribes had yet to encounter Roman forces directly. But those who had chosen to submit knew their future prosperity, indeed, perhaps their very survival, depended on how they conducted themselves in the hours to come.

'Just a few more hours,' Cassius murmured, almost inaudibly.

'Until what?' replied Falco. 'Until we can drink ourselves senseless in celebration of this farce?'

'No,' said Cassius with the barest hint of a smile. 'Until you can get out of that ridiculous outfit before it splits at the seams. I've been taking bets on which stitch will give way first.'

Chapter Sixty-One

Camulodunum

Veteranus stood at the narrow window in his cell, his fingers wrapped around the iron bars as he gazed out at the gathering crowd at the edge of the valley, each waiting their turn to approach the Emperor. The official ceremony a few hundred yards away held little interest for him, he had seen more than enough pageantry in his lifetime, but the sight of so many indigenous tribesmen in one place was fascinating.

Soon it would all be over. The Emperor would depart and Veteranus would face whatever judgment awaited him. Death, perhaps, or exile to some distant corner of the empire where his knowledge could still serve Rome yet pose no threat. His fate held little importance to him now, he had played his part and would accept the consequences, whatever they may be.

With a sigh, he turned away from the window, ready to retreat to his cot and sleep through the ceremony, let them have their triumph without him. He had taken a single step when something caught his eye, a hooded figure furtively moving through the crowd with practiced ease. There was something familiar in that movement, something that tugged at his memory.

Veteranus froze, and his breath caught in his throat as the figure turned slightly, offering a brief glimpse of the face beneath the hood.

'Impossible,' he whispered, his blood turning to ice in his veins.

But there was no mistake. Even in that fleeting moment, he had recognized the distinctive features, the penetrating gaze, the set of the jaw that had haunted him for months.

Mordred.

The druid leader was here, in Camulodunum, mere yards from the Emperor.

Veteranus lunged back to the window, pressing his face against the bars, desperately searching the crowd as the hooded figure disappeared from view. Panic seized him, driving him from the window to the heavy wooden door of his cell.

'Guard!' he shouted, pounding his fist against the thick planks.

'Guard! Open this door immediately!'

The sound of approaching footsteps echoed in the corridor, followed by the rasp of a viewing panel being drawn back. A legionary's weathered face appeared in the small opening, eyes narrowed with suspicion.

'What's all this noise about?' the guard demanded.

'Listen to me,' said Veteranus, fighting to keep his voice steady despite the urgency pounding in his chest. 'I've just seen something, someone. The Emperor is in danger. You need to release me immediately.'

The guard's expression shifted from annoyance to amusement.

'Oh really? And I suppose you're the only one who can save him, eh? Very convenient.'

'This isn't a trick,' Veteranus insisted, gripping the edges of the viewing panel. 'Mordred is here. I just saw him in the crowd. He's planning something against the Emperor, I'm certain of it.'

'Mordred?' The guard scoffed, 'the druid they say is hiding on that island?' He shook his head. 'The only danger to the Emperor around here is you, prisoner. Now step back from the door.'

Frustration surged through Veteranus as he realized his words were having no effect. Of course the guard wouldn't believe him, a captive claiming to have spotted the enemy's elusive leader through a tiny window was convenient timing indeed. He needed to change tactics.

'Fine,' he said, forcing his voice to remain calm. 'If you won't release me, then at least bring Seneca here. He needs to know.'

'The Tribune has more important duties today than listening

376

to your ravings,' the guard replied.

'Tell him I have information about the Emperor's safety,' Veteranus pressed. 'Tell him exactly what I said, that I've seen Mordred. He'll understand the significance.' He leaned closer to the opening, his voice dropping to a deadly serious tone. 'And know this: if the Emperor is harmed in any way because you delayed, I will personally ensure that your negligence is known to every officer in this fort. Your career, possibly your life, will be forfeit.'

The guard hesitated, uncertainty flashing across his features as he weighed the prisoner's words against his orders.

'Please,' Veteranus added, allowing a note of genuine desperation to enter his voice. 'I know you have your suspicions, but I wouldn't lie about this.'

After a moment of visible internal debate, the guard nodded reluctantly.

'I'll send someone to find him,' he said, already closing the viewing panel. 'But if this is some kind of trick...'

'It's not,' Veteranus assured him, relief flooding through him, 'but hurry. There isn't much time.'

As the guard's footsteps receded down the corridor, Veteranus returned to the window, scanning the crowd with renewed intensity. Mordred had vanished, but Veteranus knew he was out there somewhere, his purpose unknown but undoubtedly deadly. And he was powerless to affect it, locked behind a wooden door with iron bars on his window, his only hope that Seneca would come quickly enough to make a difference.

The corridor outside Veteranus's cell remained silent for what seemed an eternity. He paced the confined space, five steps one way, five steps back, his mind racing with possibilities. What was Mordred planning? How had he infiltrated the ceremony so easily? And most pressing of all, would Seneca believe him?

The sound of multiple footsteps finally echoed through the passageway, growing louder with each passing moment. Veteranus pressed himself against the door, listening intently until the viewing panel slid open once more. This time, Seneca's face appeared in the opening, his expression hard, eyes narrowed with obvious irritation.

'This had better be important, said Seneca with barely contained anger. 'The ceremony begins in less than an hour.'

'Thank the gods you've come,' said Veteranus, relief washing over him. 'Listen to me carefully, Mordred is here. I saw him through that window, not fifteen minutes ago. He was moving through the crowd, hooded, but I caught a glimpse of his face. There's no mistake, it was him.'

Seneca's expression didn't change.

'And I'm supposed to believe that you, locked in this cell, just happened to spot the most elusive enemy of Rome through a tiny window?'

'I lived with him for months,' said Veteranus, desperation edging into his voice. 'I know his face better than my own. The way he moves, the set of his shoulders, I'd recognize him anywhere.' He pressed closer to the opening. 'Seneca, I beg you, if you've ever trusted me in the past, trust me now. The Emperor is in danger.'

'Trust you?' Seneca laughed, the sound hard and without humour. 'After finding you living among our enemies?'

'If I were truly your enemy, why would I warn you now?' Veteranus countered. 'I could simply watch the Emperor die, knowing I'd done nothing to prevent it. You have to let me out of here. I can recognize him again, point him out before he gets anywhere near Claudius. You know what's at stake.'

The tension between them stretched, pulled taut by years of shared brotherhood now tainted with suspicion. Veteranus had never been one for emotional displays, his usual demeanour was calculated, controlled, professional, yet now his eyes burned with an intensity that even Seneca couldn't dismiss.

'Even if I believed you,' Seneca said finally, 'I can't simply release a prisoner during an imperial ceremony.'

'Then don't release me,' Veteranus replied quickly. 'Keep me bound. Assign guards. Kill me at the first sign of treachery if you must. But get me out there so I can identify him.'

Seneca fell silent, weighing the implications of both action and inaction. The risk of releasing Veteranus against the potentially catastrophic consequences of ignoring his warning.

'Very well,' he said at last, stepping back from the viewing panel. 'Open it.'

The heavy lock clanked, and the door swung open to reveal Seneca flanked by two grim-faced legionaries, their hands resting on sword hilts.

'Bind his hands,' Seneca ordered, and bring him out.

'Thank you,' said Veteranus, the relief evident in his voice.

'Don't thank me yet,' Seneca replied coldly. 'If this is some kind of trick, your death will be neither quick nor merciful.' He gestured to the guards. 'Secure him to yourselves. If he attempts to escape or makes any sudden moves, kill him immediately.'

The legionaries efficiently looped additional ropes around Veteranus's waist, tying the ends to their own belts, creating a human tether that would make any attempt at flight impossible.

'Move,' Seneca ordered, and the small procession filed out of the cell, through the corridor, and into the bright afternoon sunlight. The contrast between the dim confines of his cell and the vibrant spectacle outside momentarily blinded Veteranus but as his vision adjusted, he took in the transformation that had occurred in Camulodunum even over the past few days, the decorations, the temporary structures, the assembled dignitaries all arranged with Roman precision to showcase imperial power.

Seneca led them to a wooden stand positioned to one side of the main ceremonial area, close enough to observe the proceedings but far enough away to pose no immediate threat to the Emperor or other officials. The platform offered an elevated view of the ceremony grounds, where dozens of tribal representatives had already gathered, awaiting their formal submission to Rome.

'You'll remain here,' Seneca instructed as the guards positioned Veteranus against a wooden post. 'If you see Mordred, point him out. Make no sudden movements, no attempts to communicate with anyone else. If you do...' He left the threat unfinished, but its meaning was clear.

'I understand,' Veteranus replied, already scanning the crowd below with intensity.

'We'll be watching you,' one of the legionaries warned, his hand resting meaningfully on his sword hilt. 'The slightest suspicious move, and you're dead before you hit the ground.'

But Veteranus barely registered the threat, his attention entirely focused on the column of conquered tribal delegations now forming at the far end of the ceremonial area.

His eyes darted from one delegation to the next, searching for that familiar silhouette, that distinctive bearing that had become burned into his memory during his months on Mona. Every hooded figure was a possible vessel for Mordred's deadly plans and somewhere in that sea of former enemies, a true threat moved undetected, and Veteranus might be the only man in all of Britannia who could identify him before it was too late.

Chapter Sixty-Two

Camulodunum

Seneca stood at the side of the arena, his eyes moving between the procession and Veteranus, seeking any signs of identification. The gathering was impressive, thousands of people gathered together in a relatively small area, all eager to see the Emperor of Rome in the flesh.

Various groups approached in turn before stopping before the line of Praetorian guards and paying verbal tribute and presenting their gifts. Some were ornaments made from precious metals, others cloaks of ornate design trimmed with precious stones. Others gave representative carvings of herds that awaited delivery to Rome's legions, desperately needed cattle to feed the soldiers before they established secure supply lines.

The ceremony was impressive, a seemingly endless river of wealth and tribute as each group was announced to the masses. Falco stood nearby, his massive frame barely contained by the ceremonial uniform that had been hastily altered to fit him. His discomfort was evident in his rigid posture and the occasional tug at his collar, but his eyes remained vigilant, scanning the crowd constantly. On the opposite side of the imperial dais, Cassius maintained a similar watch, his hand never straying far from the concealed dagger beneath his formal attire and from the far side of the arena, Veteranus watched on in frustration, but nobody even resembling Mordred appeared in the procession.

The herald turned to the crowd, reading from his scroll as the next representatives arrived.

'Hear now, citizens of Rome and people of Britannia! We welcome the representatives of the ancient and noble Iceni tribe, whose lands stretch from the eastern shores to the central forests, whose warriors are famed for their courage, and whose craftspeople create wonders worthy of the gods themselves!'

The herald's powerful voice carried across the arena, silencing the murmurs of the crowd. A ripple of anticipation spread through the assembled spectators as all eyes turned toward the eastern entrance. The Iceni had maintained a careful distance from Rome's advances, neither openly hostile nor fully submissive so their appearance at the ceremony carried particular significance.

Two men appeared from the far end, carrying an elaborately decorated chest between them, the gold decoration shining in the sun. The chest was a masterwork of Celtic craftsmanship, its surface adorned with spiralling patterns and animal motifs that seemed to move and shift in the changing light. Precious stones were set at intervals along its surface, catching the sunlight and scattering it in brilliant fragments of colour. The weight of the chest was evident in the bearers' careful, measured steps as they advanced toward the imperial dais.

Behind the two men, a woman walked proudly, her head held high and dressed in luxurious ceremonial dress. Her gown was dyed a deep blue that seemed to capture the very essence of the midnight sky, with threads of gold and silver woven throughout in patterns that told stories of her people's history. Around her neck gleamed a torc of twisted gold and electrum, marking her as nobility among her tribe and bracelets of silver and bronze adorned her wrists, each one commemorating a significant event in her lineage. Her face was tattooed in intricate designs, the blue-black patterns accentuated her high cheekbones and fierce eyes, conveying both beauty and power in equal measure.

The crowd fell silent as she approached, her presence drawing all eyes despite the splendour of the tribute chest. Even the Emperor seemed to lean forward slightly on his throne, his interest visibly piqued by this striking representative of the Iceni nobility.

Veteranus glanced over, the flamboyant woman immediately commanding his attention, but his eyes narrowed in surprise. She looked familiar, very familiar.

A few moments later, his eyes widened with shock when he

finally realised who she was, Kendra, the warrior druidess from Isla Mona. Her hair was unbraided, and the clothing was totally different, but there was no mistake... and she was approaching the Emperor.

His mind raced, trying to work out what she was up to. Even if she attacked the Emperor, she would not get past the Praetorians. His eyes turned to the chest, trying to work out what was going on. He thought back to his time on Mona, the warriors, the Wraith, anything that could be a risk. The threat of a Wraith was the obvious risk, but they had all been killed, hadn't they? Three had burned in their crates at the crossroads camp, and Talorcan had beheaded the fourth. His eyes widened and his heart seemed to miss a beat as he finally realised what he had missed. There was a fifth creature, back in the caves, the female Wraith that Raven had called 'unmanageable.'

The pieces suddenly fell into place. The elaborate chest, large enough to hold a human-sized creature. The unexpected appearance of Kendra, disguised as a representative of a different tribe. The missing female Wraith that had been kept apart from the others, the most dangerous of them all.

His eyes widened as he finally realized what was going on, and he turned to face Seneca, his voice roaring over the crowd.

'Seneca! Don't let them open the box!'

The shout cut through the ceremonial atmosphere like a blade. Heads turned, confusion rippling through the crowd as the bound prisoner's voice carried across the arena. The Praetorians nearest to Veteranus moved to silence him, but the urgency in his tone had already caught the attention of those it needed to reach.

Seneca's head snapped toward Veteranus, years of shared experience telling him instantly that this was no desperate plea from a man seeking attention. This was a warning from a brother-in-arms who had recognized a deadly threat.

He turned his attention back to the procession, his eyes immediately fixing on the ornate box. Veteranus had identified something, what, he couldn't be certain, but instinct screamed of imminent danger. His heart raced as he began to move, first walking, then breaking into a desperate run as he barged his way through the crowds.

The procession was nearing the Emperor, each step bringing the box closer to Claudius. He was running now, legs pumping, weaving through the crowd, but he knew, with a sinking certainty, that he would not reach them in time. Desperation clawed at his throat and in a final, primal attempt, he roared out across the gathering.

'Falco!' Don't let them open the box!'

Falco and Cassius turned at the urgent cry and their attention snapped to the ceremony unfolding just yards in front of them. The woman had completed her verbal tribute, her fingers already working to unwrap the delicate golden chain binding the chest but as the lid began to lift, and a sickening, overwhelming stench erupted, they realised that something terrible had been unleashed.

The moment seemed to stretch into eternity as the chest opened fully and as Kendra stepped back, a terrifying clawed hand emerged over the rim.

Falco was first to react, his massive frame surging forward with surprising speed and he shoved aside a startled Praetorian.

'Close the box!' he roared but it was too late and as the Wraith launched itself directly at the men in front of the Emperor, the crowd's collective gasp became screams of terror.

The initial shock meant they the guards were initially frozen in fear and two immediately fell, their throats sliced open by the wraith's lethal claws. Claudius recoiled, eyes wide with shock and fear, and his attendants froze in momentary disbelief at the horror unfolding before them.

The Praetorians finally broke from their stunned immobility and started to form a protective circle around their Emperor, but the

Wraith moved with terrible speed and another guard fell, leaving the route open to the Emperor. Falco was already running towards the beast with his weapon drawn but before he could reach it, Cassius intercepted the Wraith, his body colliding with it in mid-air. Both fell to the ground in a tangle of limbs, the Wraith's filed teeth snapping inches from Cassius's throat, its claws raking across his chest, but within a few heartbeats, Falco also crashed into the fight, his immense strength managing to tear the creature from his comrade, before plunging his knife over and over again into its body.

'Get the Emperor away!' roared Seneca as he finally reached the scene, and drawing his own blade he lunged forward, driving his blade deep into the creature's throat, then sawing sideways with all his strength.

The Wraith's struggles intensified, then gradually weakened as Seneca continued his grim work. Its inhuman screams died to gurgles, then silence, but still Seneca cut, determined to separate the head from its body completely.

When it was done, he stood back, chest heaving, blood-soaked and grim. Falco released his hold on the now-still limbs, and pushed himself onto his knees, gasping for breath. He turned to speak to Cassius, expecting a sardonic comment about their misadventure, but something in the unnatural silence stopped him.

'Cassius?' he called, his massive frame shifting to get a better view.

No response.

Falco stared at his comrade, the breath leaving his lungs in a terrible, broken gasp. Cassius lay motionless, his throat torn open in a grotesque wound that exposed the raw, glistening muscle beneath. Blood pooled around him, dark and viscous, spreading across the carefully constructed marble floor of the imperial pavilion. Cassius, one of the valued members of the Occultum was dead, his throat ripped out by the Wraith.

Seneca appeared at Falco's side, his weathered face etched

with a grief that transcended words. They had lost men before, countless times, but this, this felt different. This felt like a violation of something sacred.

'He died protecting the Emperor,' Seneca said quietly, the meaningless words sounding hollow even as he spoke them.

Falco said nothing. Cassius, who had laughed with them on the hill just hours before, who had volunteered so casually, now lay dead before them. The threat was over, and the Emperor was safe, but the cost suddenly seemed unbearably high.

Falco's massive hands clenched into fists, and for the first time in years, tears threatened to breach his stoic facade. The Wraith might be gone, but the memory of what they had done to their brother in arms would remain with them forever.

Chapter Sixty-Three

Camulodunum.

The funeral pyre burned steadily against the darkening sky, its flames casting long shadows across the rocky hillside. The remains of Cassius lay within, his body slowly being consumed by the fire, his spirit ascending to whatever afterlife awaited men who had served Rome in the shadows.

Seneca sat closest to the flames, his weathered face illuminated by the flickering light. Beside him, Decimus passed the first of many wineskins across to Sica, its contents a far cry from the Falernian wine Cassius had so ardently negotiated for. The liquid burned going down, but not as sharply as the grief that hung between them all. Marcus was the first to break the silence.

'Remember Alexandria?' he said quietly, 'when we couldn't get into that temple?'

The others knew the story. They had heard it a dozen times before, how Cassius had talked his way past three separate guard posts using nothing but a stolen tunic and absolute confidence. Yet they listened again, because that was how memories were kept alive.

Sica followed with a story about their previous mission in Britannia that made even these hardened men shake their heads in disbelief.

'He wasn't with us long,' said Decimus. 'But he had what it takes and was as much part of the Occultum as any one of us.'

Finally, all eyes turned to Falco. The massive ex-gladiator stared into the flames, wrestling with something inside himself. Then, with a suddenness that caught them all off guard, he spoke.

'I should have had his ten flasks of wine,' he announced. 'And the lamb. Definitely the lamb.' He paused, then added almost as an afterthought, 'And the woman, of course. Cassius would have wanted that.'

The statement hung in the air, so inappropriate, so unexpected that for a moment, nobody moved. Falco looked around, suddenly uncertain, beginning to stumble through an explanation.

'I mean, he negotiated for them, and…'

Marcus's laugh stopped him short. It started low, almost a chuckle, then grew until his shoulders shook and tears streamed down his face. Decimus joined next, his normally stoic facade cracking. Seneca's shoulders also began to shake, and even Sica couldn't help the smile that broke through his grief.

Falco looked bewildered, then slowly began to understand. This was exactly what Cassius would have wanted, to be remembered not with sombre tears, but with the raw, unfiltered humour that had defined their brotherhood.

Their laughter echoed across the hillside, a defiant sound that spoke of survival, of the bond that had carried the Occultum through countless impossible missions. Cassius might be gone, but in that moment, he was more alive than ever, and as the pyre continued to burn, it became a testament to a life lived without compromise, a warrior's final journey marked by the men who had been his truest family.

Epilogue

The fire had long since died, nothing remaining but a pale wisp of smoke rising from the cold ashes. Grey light spread across the hillside, muting the vibrant landscape that had witnessed so much blood and sacrifice. Seneca sat alone, a solitary figure hunched near the remnants of Cassius's pyre, his shoulders bearing the weight of yet another loss. The rest of his men lay strewn across the clearing, still suffering the aftereffects of the drunken farewell they had given their brother the night before. He stifled an ironic laugh. If anyone attacked now, not a single finger would be raised in self-defence. They were all still too drunk.

As he stared back into the ashes, alone with his thoughts, he heard footsteps approaching along the path and looked across to see Lepidus approaching.

'Not yet,' said Seneca quietly with a sigh. 'In the name of the gods, Lepidus, can you not allow us just one day to grieve our Brother?'

Lepidus stopped, understanding etched into his weathered features. When he spoke, his tone was softer than usual, stripped of its usual Senatorial precision.

'I'm sorry,' he said simply, 'but duty will not wait for grief.'

Seneca stared at his old friend.

'Did you find anything out about what happened?' he asked.

'I did,' said Lepidus. 'It seems the camp at the crossroads, the three Wraith in the crates, the hundred warriors, it was all a diversion, simply to get your focus while his true plan was to infiltrate the ceremony all along.'

'So, he was willing to sacrifice all those men in order to keep us off the scent,' said Seneca. 'That is some commitment. He must have realised we would be coming after him and wanted to make sure we were focussed elsewhere.'

'Apparently so,' said Lepidus. 'Raven obviously knew everything about us and how we work. He would have undoubtedly reported the danger we presented, and I guess Mordred thought he needed some sort of diversionary plan in case we did appear.'

'So, what's the mission?' asked Seneca.

'It's simple,' said Lepidus. 'Mordred is just too dangerous. He has to be stopped. He managed to get away, but we have intelligence that reports that he headed south to join Caratacus. We want you to find him and kill him.'

'Do you know where he is exactly?' asked Seneca.

'That's the problem,' said Lepidus. 'We believe Caratacus is trying to recruit the Silures to his cause and if Mordred joins forces with him, he might well succeed.'

'You want us to go into Terra Silurum,' said Seneca without blinking, the shock evident in his voice.

'Unfortunately, yes.' said Lepidus, 'but we feel the best time to catch Mordred is now while he is still licking his wounds. This is essential, Seneca. That man is too dangerous and cannot be allowed to live.'

'Hardly anything is known about those territories, Lepidus, we will need local guides.'

'There are none,' said Lepidus. 'The Silures keep themselves to themselves and rarely allow outsiders into their lands, even Britons. 'This will be a classic Occultum mission, just you and your unique skill sets, alone in enemy territory. It is dangerous and I tried to argue against it, but the Emperor is adamant. He wants Mordred dead, no matter what the cost.'

Seneca shrugged and took another swig of wine from the dregs in one of the flasks. He was too tired to argue and too drunk to care. And besides, what the Emperor wanted he usually got. Refusal was not an option.

'When do we go?' he asked eventually.

'One week,' said Lepidus. 'Claudius is still shaken up and wants to be gone before you set out. He fears any reprisals.'

'A week is enough,' said Lepidus, glancing over at his hungover men. 'I will come to see you tomorrow to make the final arrangements.'

'There is one more thing,' said Lepidus. 'I need you to take someone with you.'

'I'm not acting as nursemaid to anyone, Lepidus,' snapped Seneca. 'This will be hard enough as it is.'

'There will be no need to look after anyone,' said Lepidus, this man can look after himself.' He turned to look down the hill. Seneca followed his gaze and there, standing beside two saddled horses, was the man neither Seneca nor Lepidus fully trusted. Yet apparently, he was exactly the person who now represented their only path forward... *Veteranus.*

The End

Order the Next Book in this Stunning New Series

Or go to KMAshman.com to subscribe to our mailing list

Author's Notes

Travel Between Rome and Britannia

Maritime travel between Rome and Britannia was a complex and challenging endeavour during the first century CE. The primary route followed the coastline, typically departing from ports in Gaul such as Gesoriacum (modern Boulogne-sur-Mer) and landing at Rutupiae (Richborough) in Kent. Merchant vessels and military transports used a combination of coastal navigation and open-sea crossings, carefully timing their journeys to avoid the treacherous autumn and winter storms. The journey could take anywhere from three to ten days depending on weather conditions and the type of vessel. Large military transports carried horses, supplies, and troops, requiring significant logistical planning. Sailors relied on a combination of wind power and rowing, with auxiliary vessels often accompanying larger ships for support and protection.

The Invasion of Britannia

The Roman invasion of Britannia in 43 CE represented a carefully planned imperial expansion under Emperor Claudius. Led by Aulus Plautius, the invasion force comprised four legions, approximately 40,000 professional soldiers, supported by auxiliary troops. Unlike Julius Caesar's earlier expeditions, this was a full-scale conquest intended to establish a permanent province. The Romans initially focused on subduing the southeastern tribes, using a combination of military force and strategic alliances. They faced significant challenges, including unfamiliar terrain, resilient local tribes, and harsh weather conditions. The invasion was motivated by multiple factors: political prestige, potential mineral wealth, strategic positioning, and the desire to prevent Britannia from becoming a potential base for continental enemies.

Landing Beaches for the Legions

The Roman legions primarily landed at Rutupiae (modern Richborough in Kent), a naturally sheltered harbour that provided ideal conditions for large-scale military landings. The site offered protected waters, relatively flat approaches, and proximity to tribal territories. Secondary landing points included Dubris (Dover) and other smaller coastal locations along the Kent and Sussex coasts. These beaches were carefully selected for their strategic advantages: good visibility, defendable approaches, and relatively close proximity to potential tribal settlements. The legions developed sophisticated landing techniques, using specially designed flat-bottomed boats that could approach shallow coastal areas. Each landing was meticulously planned, with advance scouts assessing terrain and potential resistance.

The Battle of Medway

The Battle of Medway in 43 CE was a crucial engagement during the Roman invasion of Britannia, occurring near the River Medway in modern Kent. Led by Plautius and involving the future Emperors Vespasian and Claudius himself, the battle represented a decisive confrontation with the united British tribes. The Romans employed sophisticated tactics, using cavalry and infantry in coordinated attacks that broke the tribal resistance. The battle is notable for the Romans' successful river crossing, a complex military manoeuvre that demonstrated their superior discipline and tactical capabilities. The British tribes, led by kings Caratacus and Togodumnus, fought fiercely but were ultimately overwhelmed by Roman military technology and organization.

The Battle of Tamesis

The Battle of Tamesis (Thames) was a pivotal engagement that effectively broke organized British resistance during the Roman invasion. Following the Battle of Medway, the Romans pursued the remaining tribal forces to the River Thames, where a final major confrontation occurred. The battle saw the death of King Togodumnus and the flight of his brother Caratacus, marking a turning point in the invasion. Roman legions demonstrated their superior military doctrine, using combined arms tactics that overwhelmed the tribal warriors. The battle opened the path to Camulodunum, the first major tribal settlement to fall to Roman control. Archaeological evidence suggests significant casualties on both sides, with the Romans ultimately proving decisive in their military strategy and execution.

Camulodunum

Camulodunum (modern Colchester) was the first major Roman settlement in Britannia and served as the capital of the new province. Originally the stronghold of the Trinovantes tribe, it was transformed into a Roman colonia, a settlement of veteran legionaries granted land as a reward for military service. The settlement was strategically important, serving both military and administrative purposes. Extensive archaeological evidence reveals a carefully planned city with Roman-style buildings, including a large temple dedicated to the divine Emperor Claudius. The town featured sophisticated infrastructure, including water management systems, public buildings, and defensive walls. However, its prominence made it a prime target for native resistance, and it would play a crucial role in the rebellion led by Boudicca in 60-61 CE, when it was almost completely destroyed.

Claudius's Visit to Britannia

Emperor Claudius's invasion of Britannia in 43 CE was a pivotal moment in Roman imperial history. Unlike previous expeditions by Julius Caesar, this was a full-scale military conquest aimed at establishing a permanent Roman province. Claudius personally arrived in 43 CE, spending just sixteen days on the island, a brief but politically crucial visit. His arrival was carefully choreographed to maximize political impact in Rome, where his leadership had been previously questioned. The Emperor brought significant military force, including elephants to intimidate local tribes, and personally participated in the surrender of several British kings. This visit was as much a political performance as a military campaign, designed to cement Claudius's reputation and demonstrate Rome's expanding power. The expedition resulted in the establishment of Camulodunum as the first Roman colonial capital in Britannia.

The Druids of Mona

The island of Mona (Anglesey) was the spiritual and cultural heartland of British druidic culture. More than a mere geographical location, it was considered a sacred sanctuary where the most powerful druids maintained their most important religious and educational centres. These priests played crucial roles beyond spiritual leadership, serving as historians, judges, and political advisors to tribal leaders. Their training was extensive, reportedly taking up to twenty years, and involved memorizing vast amounts of oral history, law, and religious knowledge. Roman sources describe them as performing elaborate religious ceremonies, including human sacrifices, though these accounts may be exaggerated. The Romans viewed the druids as a significant threat due to their ability to unite and inspire resistance against Roman occupation.

Seeds of Empire

From the ashes of tragedy to the pinnacle of power, Seeds of Empire is a gripping series that chronicles the extraordinary life of Gaius Julius Caesar, charting his rise, his triumphs, and his ultimate downfall in a world of war, ambition, and betrayal.

Witness his tumultuous early years, his father's untimely death, his exile from Rome, and the relentless ambition that fuelled his return. March alongside him on brutal campaigns that reshaped the ancient world, from his early battles with sea pirates and legendary conquest of Gaul to his audacious crossing of the Rubicon.

Experience the brutal civil war that tore Rome apart, his decisive victories in Greece, North Africa, and Spain, and his dramatic intervention in Egypt, where he cemented his alliance with Cleopatra.

But Caesar's story does not end with his assassination, and as Rome spirals into chaos, a young heir steps forward, Julius Octavius Thurinus, his great nephew and posthumously adopted son. Through political cunning, ruthless ambition, and strategic brilliance, he will seize control and transform Rome from a fractured republic into a formidable empire, reshaping history forever.

Grand in scope, meticulously detailed, and relentless in its momentum, Seeds of Empire vividly captures the ambition, triumph, and bloodshed of Rome's most pivotal era.

A must-read for fans of gripping historical fiction, this is a saga of power, fate, and the men who built an empire from the ashes of a republic.

Available Now!

Subscribe at

KMAshman.com

Printed in Dunstable, United Kingdom

65412715R00228